ANGEL'S MOON

A Novel

PAUL C. GARDNER

Angel's Moon

ALSO BY PAUL C. GARDNER

2014

Paul C. Gardner was diagnosed with interstitial lung disease in the summer of 2010. He succumbed to the disease in April 2011 while preparing this book for publication. It is a measure of how important this work was to him that he knowingly spent the last efforts of his life to complete it.

Angel's Moon

PAUL C. GARDNER

iUniverse, Inc.
Bloomington

Angel's Moon

iUniverse books may be ordered through booksellers or by contacting:

iUniverse
1663 Liberty Drive
Bloomington, IN 47403
www.iuniverse.com
1-800-Authors (1-800-288-4677)

ISBN: 978-1-4620-0917-6 (pbk)
ISBN: 978-1-4620-0918-3 (ebk)

Library of Congress Control Number: 2011904976

Printed in the United States of America

iUniverse rev. date: 07/12/2011

CAST OF MAIN CHARACTERS

REPRESENTING THE UNITED STATES

United States President James Burns

Vice-President William Pitts

National Security Advisor Roger Williams

Homeland Security Director Charles Swanson

Attorney General Roberto Zapata

Secretary of State Evelyn Colosimo

Secretary of the Treasury Emily Rogers

Secretary of Defense Leroy Adams

Chairman of the Joint Chiefs of Staff Robert Coyle

Chief of Staff Parvis Khademi

Director of Special Operations Edward Grass

Special Operations secretary Lauren Shein

President Burn's Press Secretary Myrna Stein

United States Special Operations,

Triple A team leader Albert "Big A" Garcia

Triple A team member Alexandra Mendez

Triple A team member Alfred "Little A" Cruz

Special Operations Officers, Fabio Pineda, Cesar Catalino, Ernesto Sanchez, Stefania Chavez, Antonio Preciado, Paola Calderon, Francisco Valdez, Edwardo Carvalho, Marco Mendes, Zacarias Vega, Maribell Robles, Rey Oropeza

FBI agent in charge at Fort Mason Tom Eagan

Denver Regional FBI supervising agent David Porter

Cochise County Attorney Felix Burgos

Cochise County's Deputy County Attorney Joanna Castro

United States Border Patrol Deputy Chief John Marrone

Cochise County Sheriff Edwardo "Big Ed" Mata-Villa

Assistant Sheriff Rich Farrell

Pueblo's Police Chief Walter Goff

Sonora State Police Jesus Noriega

German Shepherd Dog, a member of the National Explosives Detection Canine Team, Clancy

Certified trainer, Mary Pelton

Fort Huachuca commander, General Eric Ehrich

Phoenix FBI field office chief Phylis Driscoll

Camp Vigilant commander Sergeant Ralph Mulia

Camp Vigilant staff, Corporal John Kitnoya, and Privates Moosey Briggs and Jesse Charles.

REPRESENTING THE ALLIANCE

Alliance's boss of bosses Angel Figueroa, El Jefe

American attorney, represents the Alliance in Washington, D.C., Abe Silverman,

Alliance bagwoman Lisa Strump

Mexican lobbyist Diego Perez

Gulf Group Carlos Martinez,

Central Syndicate Miguel Vargas

Baja Boys Ruben Miranda

Represents Afghani interests Bashir Matyarzai

Represents Alliance membership in China Charlie Yung

Represents Alliance members from Laos Vang Ly

Represents Alliance members in Columbia Luis Bermudez

Drug dealer Juan "Puggy" Puga

Alliance enforcers Hector and Aliberto Castaneda

Alliance hit man Esteban 'Stewie' Nunez, a.k.a. "Bonecrusher Nunez" and "Angel's Stewmaker."

Hermosillo Municipal Police Detective Arturo Ramirez Zambrano

Homeland Security and Governmental Affairs Committee Senator Harvey Dwight of Idaho

Ranking minority member Senator John Babcock of Delaware

House Homeland Security Committee chairman Representative Ezra Higgins of Newark

Ranking minority member on the house committee Representative Vito LaCrocca of Richmond

Muslim terrorists

Imam Dr. Umar al Jamai

Hafifa Laysee a.k.a. Consuela Huerta

Pramudita Nakhai a.k.a. Maria Huerta

Abdul Ikrirma a.k.a. Leon Huerta

Ahmad Ansari a.k.a. Jose Huerta

Abdullah La Haqq a.k.a. Alphonso Huerta

Nasir bin Ghazia a.k.a. Roberto Huerta

Makhdoom Sunnah a.k.a. Filipe Huerta

Mohammad Ukba a.k.a. Vincente Huerta

Hussain Ghazree a.k.a. Manlio Huerta

Aslam al Khaza'ee a.k.a. Diego Huerta

Attorney, represents the Huertas Sidney Korash

Heavenly Sky Spiritual Camp manager Ozviv Rozaki, Ozzie

Chapter One

11:46 a.m. Mountain Time, August 20

THE WATCHER PUSHED OFF THE WALL he had been leaning on. His eyes, hidden behind dark glasses, followed his prey. A moment ago, the young men walked out of the office building on the other side of the street. They turned, laughing, not a care in the world, strolling in his direction. Totally alert, on edge now, his manner all business, a professional. They would be in the kill zone in less than a minute. For the umpteenth time today he checked the bars on his phone. Methodically, he dialed all but the last digit of the number engrained in his memory. He was ready.

On the fifth floor an ecstatic Joanna Castro, Cochise County's Deputy County Attorney thought, *so far so good.*

Just as soon as her morning meeting with the Rynning brothers ended, she hustled into her boss' office and reported in. Castro said, "They're going to be great on the stand sir. All three of them, Larry, Jimmy, and Craig Rynning are willing to testify they saw the whole thing. I have about another hour with them lined up for after lunch. We'll be set. Both Hector and Aliberto Castaneda are going to go down. It sure is gratifying some people in this town are stand-up guys."

County Attorney Felix Burgos said, "That's good news, Joanna. For a while there, I had the impression we would lose everybody."

Castro and Burgos discussed the near collapse of their case against the Castanedas. Hector and Aliberto, cousins, also illegal alien enforcers for the Mexican drug syndicate, a month earlier in Sierra Vista, Arizona, brutally murdered Juan "Puggy" Puga. Puga a known high level drug trafficker worked for the same cartel. On the fourth day of August, Puga, the Rynnings, and twenty-five other people took pleasure in enjoying a late afternoon beverage at Blaine's Tavern, one of Sierra Vista's favorite watering holes. Typical of popular taverns everywhere, no one noticed all the comings and goings, but when somebody or something unusual stood out everyone paid attention. Most of the customers, just regular guys and women, stopped in for one or two cold ones. Some to see friends before heading home after work. People greeted one another with hellos and goodbyes or maybe a nod others were snubbed. Everyone purposely ignored the Castaneda cousins. It seemed nobody but Puggy, a tough but likeable forty-two year old ex-bouncer, knew them.

According to some of the customers gathered in the vicinity of Puggy, he and the Castanedas exchanged friendly hellos. Some heard the cousins tell Puggy they had something for him outside. Puggy signaled the bartender not to take his drink, that he would be right back. He then followed Hector and Aliberto, both twenty-four years old, six foot, two hundred forty pound, heavily tattooed, scary-looking Latinos out the side door to the parking lot.

Within minutes, a commotion transpired. Patrons closest to the exit door opened it and went outside. Yelling and foul language, in both English and Spanish, could be heard. Loud reports ensued. Noises like a dirty rug strung up for cleaning being whacked. Within seconds, everybody went out to the parking lot. Puggy shrieked in pain. Both cousins beat him with three foot long crowbars. They cursed at Puggy who had fallen to the ground and tried to regain his feet. As Puggy struggled to get up, Aliberto Castaneda swung his weapon into Puggy's head, crushing his nose. Everyone heard the impact, bones breaking, cartilage popping. They saw the blood burst from Puggy's broken face. The cousins beat Puga unmercifully all over his head and body as he vainly attempted to ward off the blows. Several people called the police on their cell phones. Hector and Aliberto screamed at Puggy, calling him a stupid thief. They yelled that he couldn't steal from El Jefe. A couple of the men in the crowd hollered for them to stop, but no one attempted to intercede. Sirens could be heard in the distance. Finally the cousins, tired of swinging the heavy steel bars in the intense Arizona heat, stopped the beating and ran. Puga lay motionless on the pavement. He bled profusely from his mouth, nose, ears, and numerous cuts.

When the Sierra Vista police arrived, they immediately called an ambulance for Puggy. The officers put out an all-points bulletin for the Castanedas based on descriptions from the many eyewitnesses. The police obtained names, addresses, and took statements from each of the bar's patrons before allowing them to leave. Cochise County Sheriff's Deputies took the cousins into custody by as they raced down Highway 92 heading for the Naco border crossing to Mexico. The crowbars used in the assault disappeared. However, later that night the police located all of the witnesses and brought them to the police station to identify Hector and Aliberto. Twenty-eight people made positive identifications. A slam-dunk if there ever was one.

But that was then. At 3:12 a.m. the next morning, Juan Puga died in Sierra Vista Regional Hospital. The doctors determined he bled out from massive internal injuries. Puga had slipped into a coma and never regained consciousness. The charges against the Castanedas changed from attempted murder to murder in the first degree. Castro, an ambitious prosecutor looking to establish an impressive track record, begged Burgos for the assignment to litigate the case.

Over the next two weeks, Castro re-interviewed the witnesses. They all previously gave statements and cooperated with the police. After the local newspaper reported whom the Castanedas worked for, twenty-five of the witnesses recanted. Scared shitless they could no longer identify Hector and Aliberto. They had been drinking. Several shared a joint before the incident. Memories faded. They couldn't be sure. All those Mexicans look alike. Sorry but they made a mistake.

All the witnesses had endless excuses except Larry, Jimmy, and Craig Rynning that is. Born and raised in Sierra Vista the brothers all previously played football for Buena High School, defensive backs because of their slight builds. Larry, the oldest at twenty-seven, married his high school sweetheart, and fathered three little girls. Larry worked as a plumber. Jimmy was twenty-five. He and his wife had a two year old son, Jimmy Junior. He worked as an electrician. Craig a carpenter, twenty-three years old, was single. All three brothers worked for union contractors doing prevailing wage jobs inside the Fort Huachuca military base. They all told Joanna Castro, of course they were afraid, but they lived here and somebody had to stand up. Today, they agreed to come back after lunch to go over the individual testimony they would each give before the grand jury that would determine if the case should go to trial.

The Rynnings used the elevator to come down from the fifth floor offices. Castro recommended Kiki's Restaurant, on the same side as the county building, right down the block and across one street. She said her office sent all their visitors there. They had great food and friendly service. As they walked, Larry and Jimmy both called home on their cell phones, telling their wives it looked like they would be home early this afternoon.

Larry recounted the morning's events to his wife, Suzi, and asked to speak with the girls. Suzi reminded him Lori, the oldest at five, had not returned home from kindergarten yet. She put four year old Kimmie on. He said, "Hi baby. How's my pretty little girl doin' today?"

Kimmie replied, "Hello daddy. I made you a picture this morning. It's a drawing of you and mommy, me and Lori and Jill all holding hands."

"Oh honey, thank you so much. I need something for the wall over my desk. I think I'll hang it there. Would that be okay?"

"Yes daddy. Do you want to talk to Jill now?"

"Yes please."

Jill, who was three, said, "Hi daddy. I'm helping mommy vacuum, what are you doing?"

Larry replied, "Hi to you, Jill. Thank you for helping mom. I'm with Uncle Jimmy and Uncle Craig. They both say hi and send kisses. Put mommy back on okay?"

Suzi asked, "What's up hon? How much longer are you going to be? I told the girls you would be home early today."

"They say not too much longer. We're going to have lunch now then go back and finish up. I'll call again when I'm done. Bye now, love you sweetie."

Jimmy Rynning called his wife Jenny. She told him little Jimmy was listening in. Jimmy said, "Hey son, daddy is gonna be home real soon. You take good care of mommy until I get there." He told Jenny, "The DA said we're nearly done. Call me if you need anything. Love you both. Bye."

As Craig walked, he looked around trying to gauge how fast they had to go to beat the lunchtime rush into Kiki's. He didn't think it would be a problem because nobody else appeared to be heading to the restaurant. There wasn't any other foot traffic right now despite the fact downtown Bisbee certainly appeared especially busy with construction. The boys passed by a group of contractors' trucks. They walked next to a flat bed truck loaded with tools and equipment when it happened. A huge explosion erupted right on the truck's platform. The brothers' bodies literally dismembered instantly. Ball bearings flew out from a detonated Claymore anti-personnel mine. The device had been set on the truck's bed, about four feet above the ground, directionally facing the sidewalk. It blew the young men apart. The Claymore is extremely lethal. One and a half pounds of C4, which when exploded, propels approximately seven hundred one eighth inch steel balls in a definite kill area forty yards square. Castro and Burgos ran to the office window, but could hardly see more than billowing smoke. Then it cleared. Body parts covered with blood and guts became visible. Castro's stomach betrayed her. She bent over and retched on the floor. Sobbing, she asked, "Oh my God. God Almighty, how can this happen? Why did it have to happen to them?"

The following week, without any witnesses, the case fell apart. Cochise County Attorney Burgos dropped all charges. The United States Attorney for the District of Arizona took custody of the cousins. Unable to concoct a prosecutable case the United States Attorney got a federal judge to sign a deportation order. The court ordered the cousins' car sold at auction to compensate the towing company and the storage bill. On the first of September, federal agents escorted the deported Castaneda cousins back into Mexico. As soon as they crossed the border, throngs of cheering admirers greeted Hector and Aliberto. United States Border Patrolmen spat on the ground as the Castanedas got into a black Mercedes Benz limo and drove away.

Chapter Two

1:18 a.m. Mountain Time, October 8

TEN MILES WEST OF DOUGLAS, ARIZONA, along the Arizona/Mexico border, in what is called high desert country by locals, Emmett Thompson snuggled comfortably on the ground. Despite it being the middle of the night, he could see clearly without the help of the night vision goggles hanging from his neck. The full moon on the cloudless night radiated brightly, lighting up the green landscape. Low desert vegetation consisting of a few indigenous rosewood and sycamore trees, native brush, and abundant ocotillo, cactus plants that grew in clumps of spindly stalks up to ten feet tall, were everywhere. The ocotillo waving in the wind created spooky movement in the gloomy environment contributing to his concealment. The cool air, slightly above fifty degrees with a light breeze, did not bother him. Warmly encased in a gillie suit he had made himself, he settled into a slight depression, munching on dried fruit and other snacks he carried with him. The gillie suit, designed to break up the wearer's outline and help him merge in with his surroundings, was lined with the same material used to manufacture the emergency fire protection blankets issued to firefighters when they worked in areas where they could become trapped by out of control wildfires. Emmett had fashioned an over-sized suit, that when the hood was up, it enclosed his whole body and all of the gear he carried in the utility pockets of the fatigues he brought back from his tours of duty in Iraq and Afghanistan. The camouflaged gillie suit blended in perfectly with the desert terrain and native vegetation. So well, in fact, he couldn't be seen by someone standing right next to him during the day, never mind at night like now.

Emmett could feel the ground moving before he heard them. He was not surprised. It is what he expected. After all, large groups came this way all the time. Three hours earlier, he came out into the desert. His father had dropped him off with Sam and Ida Comfort. First he set up the Comforts, retired school teachers from Phoenix. Nice people researching a book they wanted to write about illegal immigrants crossing into the United States. As members of the Phoenix branch of the Border Brigade, they requested and got permission from Emmett's father's group, the Cochise County Border Brigade, to accompany a border watch patrol tonight.

On account of October's full moon, the Cochise County group had three patrols of watchers out tonight. One consisting of Emmett and the Comforts, and two others, which were staking out other trails the Cochise County Border Brigade knew illegal border crossers used. Emmett had left the Comforts in a natural indentation about three hundred yards to the north of his position on the west side of the gully he watched over. He had given them strict instructions to remain hidden, that anyone coming along the trail could be dangerous. He told them he would be back before dawn. Emmett had then continued over a rise to the west before turning south then circling back further to the east side of the gully, and eventually had situated himself on a rise about forty yards above a rock outcropping where the trail he was observing in the crevasse narrowed. He was sure the Comforts never saw where he went and had no idea where he was. The rock rose up on both sides of the trail forcing groups using the trail to proceed in single file. Before settling in, he had positioned a camera five and a half feet above the ground in a tree facing the opening in the rocks. The camera would record for twelve hours or until the battery wore down, whichever occurred first.

Emmett was breathing very lightly, intent on the path, when he heard noise, footfalls, cloth rubbing against cloth, and bodies touching the rock sides. A man, carrying a rifle at the ready, stepped through the rocks. The man looked all around as he quickly moved ahead. He was followed by another man with a rifle, then another. After seven men advanced, all carrying firearms, many men carrying backpacks came. After every forty men bearing packs, another armed man appeared. Following two hundred bearers and five more armed men, a group of people appeared. Unarmed, they did not carry anything except small backpacks over their shoulders and fanny packs around their waists. There were ten of them. Subsequently, Emmett counted two more armed men. Then, finally, the procession stopped coming. In fact, the whole group stopped moving. It appeared someone in authority called for a rest break.

Emmett, about six two, one hundred ninety pounds, had wavy brown hair, and brown eyes. He was thirty-five years old, an army veteran who served two tours of duty as a member of an elite Army Special Forces Team in the Middle East. He had joined the Bisbee Fire Department six years ago. In his off time, he spent a lot of hours in the local boonies trying to do his part to stop what he and other border dwellers call the illegal immigration invasion. He brought his night vision binoculars to his eyes and looked over the personnel assembled in front of him. He scanned the armed men first. It was easy to pick out the leaders, two men standing around the front of the group whom everyone appeared to defer. They were both young, in their twenties, Latino, dressed in black fatigues. Using hand signals, they had deployed the other twelve armed men in a loose perimeter around the group.

The armed men appeared to be soldiers or police of some sort. No insignia, maybe a private army. They all wore black uniforms, boots, helmets, and body armor. They carried automatic assault rifles, the type that used thirty round clips loaded with 5.56 X 45 mm NATO bullets. The leaders whispered quietly to each other. The soldiers said nothing. The two hundred bundle bearers sat back-to-back, supporting each other without removing their packs. Dressed in work boots, dungarees, plaid shirts, and ball caps, they sipped from canteens they carried. None of them said a word. The ten who carried nothing sat together drinking water from bottles they had removed from the fanny packs they each had. They appeared to be late twenties or early thirties, two women and eight men. Dressed casually with jeans, stylish sweat shirts, hiking shoes, and baseball caps, their shirts and caps sported American college and ball team logos. They appeared as though they would blend in on any Main Street, USA.

Emmett sorted notes in his mind when a loud sneeze shattered the serenity. He heard it and so did everyone else. They all looked up the hill to the west. One of the women pointed and screeched, "There is someone up there."

One of the Latino leaders put a finger to his lips and pointed at the woman. When she nodded, he held up four fingers on one hand, pointed to four of the armed men and waved his arm up the hill. The soldiers immediately ran toward where the woman had pointed. Two of the soldiers pulled night vision goggles down over their eyes. They swept the hill and pointed. The four advanced, surrounding a hollow in the ground. They motioned with their rifles and Emmett groaned to himself as the Comforts, short, heavy-set, and older, stood up. The leader who had given the hand signals motioned with two fingers for the Comforts to be brought to him.

Ida Comfort whimpered uncontrollably when she and Sam reached the Latino leader. He put his finger to his lips and pointed at her. She started to shake. Sam put his arm around his wife's shoulders and closed his hand over her mouth. He whispered in her ear. Ida appeared to calm down. Then the Latino grabbed Ida's collar. When she started shaking again, he released the collar grasped a handful of her hair and waved a large knife in her face. Ida's eyes widened as the man drew the knife back, its point aimed directly at Ida's throat. Emmett watched all of this through the scope on his rifle. The crosshairs centered between the Latino's eyes. Emmett relaxed, breathing slowly, confident, if he had to, he could put a bullet in the man's head. The Latino pointed his finger at Sam and said something. He pushed Sam in the chest. Sam shook his head no and held up one finger.

The Latino lowered the knife and, using hand signals, directed his soldiers to use their night vision equipment and to conduct a search of the area. Emmett, knowing Sam gave him up, settled in under his gillie suit. He knew they would not detect him. His custom made suit would not emit any heat signature at all. Still, he silently released the flap on his sidearm holster so, if need be, he could quickly access his pistol. The safety on his 30.06 hunting rifle was still off. After a few minutes, Emmett heard movement around his position. Then the sounds headed away. Shortly thereafter, he raised his hood a half an inch and peeked out. He saw all fourteen soldiers intermingled with the whole group like when they first arrived, the bearers rose to their feet, the civilian travelers took their place near the rear of the assembly, and the Comforts, with their mouths taped and hands tied behind their backs, stood in front of the last two soldiers. The whole group started walking north. The only evidence of their presence ten empty water bottles left along the trail.

Emmett gave the group a few minutes head start before easing his cell phone out of his pocket intending to call his father for help. Activating the power nothing happened. No power. He tried again. Shit. No juice and he didn't bring a spare battery. *What a dumbass,* Em thought. He packed his stuff and set out walking parallel to the gully on the east side of the ridge. Every hundred steps or so, he stretched up and gazed over the ridge top checking on the group's progress. He knew they didn't have far to go. Highway 80 was only a mile ahead. As he walked, Emmett mentally kicked himself for not checking his cell phone. Normally he carries a spare battery, but tonight he figured two phones would be enough. The Comforts maintained possession of theirs. But it didn't do one bit of good. Now without his own phone, he couldn't call his dad to alert the Border Patrol and Sheriff's Office, although, deep inside, he realized notifying the authorities wouldn't help. They were never around when you needed them.

Emmett halted shortly before the highest point short of the highway. Creeping forward on his stomach he peeked over the hilltop. He could see the entire group as they approached one truck and two white passenger vans parked off the road on what he knew to be the abandoned Hernandez ranch. A man got out of the truck's cab stepping to the ground while waving the others to come to him. With his binoculars, Em could see an advertizing sign located on the side of the truck. The sign was mounted on the truck's cargo box up close to the cab. The man grasped the sign sliding it back along rails. With the sign moved a hidden door was exposed. The man swung the door open. The opening accessed the front portion of the truck's cargo container. The porters lined up outside the open door. The bundles they carried were unfastened from frames on the porter's backs and passed onto the truck. In less than five minutes total, all of the bearers unloaded their backpacks, placed the bundles on the truck, and turned around, headed back the way they had come.

The truck, now closed back up, pulled onto Highway 80 heading west toward Tombstone. As soon as the truck was safely on its way, the Latino leader spoke briefly on his cell phone, then huddled with the travelers and the one who appeared to be his number two. They all gestured several times at Sam and Ida Comfort. After several minutes of discussion, heads all nodded in agreement. The travelers walked toward the vans. The commander and his assistant spoke briefly. The second-in-command pointed to five gunmen, one of whom had a Pancho Villa type moustache. They all then followed him with the Comforts between them. Emmett watched as they headed east walking across fields about one hundred feet back from the highway. Unsure what to do, Emmett decided to stay where he was. Doors on the side of the two vans were opened by one of the remaining armed men. The ten travelers each shook hands with the Latino leader then proceeded to climb into the vans. As soon as the doors shut, the two vans drove off traveling on Highway 80 toward New Mexico to the east.

Less than fifteen minutes later, the six soldiers who had escorted the Comforts returned. All fourteen of the armed men then shouldered their weapons and started walking south on the path they had come in on. Emmett followed the tracks left in the fields by the group that escorted Sam and Ida Comfort away. The trail of disturbed ground led off the Hernandez ranch and across three other properties to a drainage ditch next to the highway a little less than a mile from where the vehicles had been loaded. Alongside one of the signs placed by the United States government all over roads by the border warning in big all caps lettering, 'TRAVEL CAUTION, SMUGGLING AND ILLEGAL IMMIGRATION MAY BE ENCOUNTERED IN THIS AREA' Emmett found the Comforts. They were lying face down with their hands still secured behind them. Emmett rolled Ida over. As soon as he did, he gagged, turned his head and threw up everything he had eaten earlier. Her stomach was soaked with blood and there were gaping empty holes in her face where her eyes belonged. The remains of her eyes hung from her face in carved up bits and pieces. Her mouth was still taped shut. Emmett went to Sam. When he rolled him over, he found the same conditions. Emmett mumbled, "Oh my God."

Emmett searched Sam's pockets. In a shirt pocket he found a tape recorder. The recorder was moving. He saw the counter indicated a total of four hours thirty-seven minutes already recorded. In Sam's right front pants pocket Emmett found the cell phone.

Emmett stood up and dialed a number he knew by heart. The phone was answered after the first ring. Emmett said, "Dad, it's me. The Comforts are dead. We are about a mile east of the driveway into the old Hernandez place next to one of those stupid government immigration signs. We are right next to the road. Please come right away."

Andrew Thompson replied, "Em, I'll be there in ten to fifteen minutes. Look for me. I'll be in the Escalade. Carl and Philip are with me. I'll bring them too."

Chapter Three

4:09 a.m. Mountain Time, October 8

NINE MILES WEST OF DOUGLAS, ARIZONA, Emmett Thompson saw headlights slowly approaching from further west. Once he recognized the vehicle, he stood so he could be seen. The Escalade pulled off the pavement, stopped on the shoulder, and the engine was turned off. Emmett's father, Andrew, stepped out of the door on the front passenger's side. His younger brother, Carl, got out from behind the wheel, and his youngest brother, Philip, exited from the back seat. Emmett silently pointed to the bodies of the Comforts. Andrew turned on a heavy duty flexible flashlight which he used to illuminate the bodies. He handed the light to Philip to hold while he knelt down and examined the remains. He turned to his sons and said, "Look here. Whoever did this pushed a blade into their stomachs and pulled the knife up tearing the insides apart. They also did a brutal job cutting the eyeballs out of the sockets. This was meant as a message. Make sure you all understand what these animals are saying. You don't want to fuck with them. Emmett, tell us what happened."

Emmett recounted the morning's events, beginning with the hike into the spot where he left the Comforts, and all the events that subsequently transpired up to the Comforts being walked off to where he found them. He told his father the camera he had set up earlier was still back at the original contact point. He handed him the tape recorder explaining he didn't know what was on the tape, that he had not played it back. In a halting voice, he said there was nothing he could do, it was just him against fourteen of them, all with automatic assault rifles and side arms. He never had an opportunity to help the Comforts and he didn't have an operable phone to call for help. He didn't know they had done this to the Comforts until he found the bodies. He said he didn't hear anything. He figured that was because the Comforts probably couldn't even scream because of the tape covering their mouths.

The four Thompson men standing together all resembled each other. All of them about the same size, about six two, they ranged from one hundred eighty to two hundred pounds. All had wavy brown hair and brown eyes. Andrew was fifty-seven, Emmett thirty-five, Carl thirty-three, and Philip thirty. They stood close with their arms around Emmett. They all mumbled condolences and assured Emmett it wasn't his fault, he did all he could. Finally, they separated.

Andrew announced, "Okay, this is what we are going to do. I'm going to call the sheriff and the border patrol and get them out here. I'm going to tell them I dropped the Comforts off alone last night because they wanted to observe broken borders and I got an anonymous call this morning telling me I could find their bodies here. Emmett, you wipe your prints off Sam's cell phone and put it back in his pocket. I'm going to hold on to the recorder. Emmett, put your gillie suit into the car. You and Phil go back and get the camera. Pick up anything else back there that may help identify the people who did this. Carl, you stay with me. Em and Phil, when you come out of the desert, do it up by the Hernandez place. If we aren't there yet, wait for us. Don't come back here. I don't want the sheriff or the border boys to see you, the camera, or anything else you bring out. Nobody knows anything except I got an anonymous phone call. As far as I know, anybody could have made the call, even the killer or killers. The bad guys will know they didn't make the call. They will want to know who did and what else the caller saw. We don't want them to know it was Em. So our story is all of us were all at the ranch when the call came in. Got it? Any of you have questions?"

When there weren't any, Andrew dialed the Cochise County Sheriff's office in Bisbee. When he explained who he was, where he was, and what the problem was, the operator told him to wait, someone would be there as soon as possible. He got the same response from the main switchboard of the United States Border Patrol in Nogales. Andrew got off the phone, threw up his hands and said, "God only knows what time the authorities will get here. You two take off. Remember don't come back here."

Emmett and Philip backtracked to Hernandez' ranch then cut south following the trail back to the rock outcropping. The sun had risen while they walked. There was nothing on the trail recently dropped by anyone.

If it wasn't for the ten water bottles, no one would ever have known anyone had come this way. Emmett took out a plastic garbage bag and told Philip to carefully place the bottles in it. Philip took a pen from his pocket, placed it into the mouth of each bottle, which he then deposited into the bag. He couldn't snag the loose bottle caps with the pen, so he held the open bag next to each cap and flicked the caps into the bag without touching them. When he was done, he tied the bag to his belt at the back of his pants. He then joined Emmett at the mouth of the passage between the rocks. Emmett retrieved and turned off the camera, which he put into a side pouch pocket in his pants. They went up to the depression where the Comforts had hidden, but didn't find anything. After crossing the gully one more time, they went to the ridgeline Emmett had used and followed it back to the high spot overlooking the Hernandez ranch.

From the vantage place, they could see flashing strobe lights to the east. They sat down and took out Emmett's binoculars. They saw the federal 'TRAVEL CAUTION' sign; a Cochise County Coroner's van, a cream-colored Cochise County Sheriff's patrol car, two green and white United States Border Patrol vehicles, a pickup truck and a patrol car, and their father's forest green Cadillac Escalade Hybrid. Workers moved two bodies, wrapped in plastic and strapped onto stretchers, into the van. The sheriff had a camera and took pictures. Andrew talked with a border patrol officer. Andrew shook his head from side to side, over and over. The border cop kept waving his hands like he was repeating, "What do you want from me?" Then the coroner's van left. The sheriff left and the border patrol vehicles drove away. After they were all out of sight, Carl and Andrew pulled out. The Border Patrol vehicles headed east toward Douglas. The coroner and sheriff went west toward Bisbee. Carl drove west. When he came to the Hernandez ranch, Carl pulled into the driveway, stopping about two hundred feet back from the road. Emmett and Philip stood up and walked down to meet their father and brother. At the same time as Emmett and Philip reached the Escalade, the border patrol vehicles that had driven away turned into the driveway and sped up to them. Four border patrolmen got out of the vehicles, two from the truck and two from the car. The border patrolman who had been arguing with Andrew said, "Whoa, hold on there, fellas. Who are you guys? What are you doing here?"

Andrew immediately jumped out the door of the Escalade. He hollered, "Boys, don't answer him. Chief, what do you think you're doing? These men are my sons, Emmett and Philip. They came out here with Carl and me this morning after we got the call I told you all about. I sent them to look around in the desert. They just got done."

United States Border Patrol Deputy Chief John Marrone, about five-ten, two hundred sixty pounds, puffed his chest, pointed his finger at Andrew and cried out, "Shut your mouth. You didn't say anything about these two earlier. You lied and I'm not talking to you now. I'm talking to these boys. You two, do you always walk in the desert with rifles over your shoulders and pistols on your belts? What did you see this morning? What did you find out there?"

Emmett stared right at Marrone and replied, "Yeah, we carry guns when we go into the desert, don't you? And we didn't see anything or find anything."

Marrone walked up to Philip and asked, "What did you find in the desert son?"

Philip replied, "Nothing."

Marrone pointed to the bag tied to Philip's belt and said, "What's in the bag boy?"

Andrew interrupted, "Boys, I told you, don't answer him."

Philip looked at his father and said, "Dad, its only garbage. Whenever I walk in the desert, I bring a bag and pick up any junk I come across. It's nothing."

Andrew replied, "I don't care. Fuck this clown. He won't investigate the brutal murders of Americans, but he thinks he can harass my family and me, Not going to happen, Marrone. You go fuck yourself. We're all law-biding citizens here. You go bother some smugglers, some drug dealer assassins, or illegal aliens, but get out of our face."

Marrone said, "The border patrol does not have to explain itself to you, Thompson. But, I told you already this morning; the investigation of the murder of the Comforts is the sheriff's job, not ours. Furthermore, I and my border patrolmen were concentrated on the east side of Douglas last night. We received a tip and apprehended over forty illegals trying to cross the border five miles east of town. My men and I did exactly what we get paid to do. We did one hell of a job."

Marrone turned to his driver and told him, "Get on the radio. Call the sheriff back here. We'll have him lock this bunch up for obstruction."

Five minutes later, Cochise County Sheriff Edwardo "Big Ed" Mata-Villa pulled up alongside the border patrol vehicles. He got out, hitched his pants around his ample gut, stood his full six foot four, and glared at Marrone. He said, "This better be good. What's the problem John?"

Marrone explained he wanted to see in the bag Philip Thompson had attached to his belt. He turned to Philip poked him in the chest and said, "This asshole."

Philip shot back saying, "Don't touch me."

Marrone laughed and said, "Who's going to stop me?"

Philip struck like a desert sidewinder, grabbing Marrone's finger and bending it backward. The chief fell to his knees, his acne-scarred, pock-marked face turned bright red. With spittle spouting from his mouth he screamed, "Let me go, you little prick."

Philip bent the finger more. Marrone wailed in pain. The other border patrolmen stepped forward. The Thompsons moved up. Sensing pending disaster, Sheriff Mata-Villa yelled, "Everybody back-off. Philip let the chief go."

Philip looked to his father who nodded. Philip released the finger. The border patrolmen helped Marrone to his feet. Everybody stared at each other for what seemed an eternity. Then, when Chief Marrone composed himself enough to speak, he said, "Sheriff I want this man arrested for assaulting a federal officer."

The sheriff responded, "You have some fucking nerve. If anyone needs arresting, it's you. I'm a police witness to this incident and saw you assault him. He asked you to stop and you continued. He simply protected himself. Now shut up and let me handle this."

Mata-Villa looked at Philip and said, "Why can't he see what you have in there Philip?"

Philip said, "He can, sheriff. It's only garbage I picked up. I pick up garbage whenever I walk in the desert. These fuckin' illegals drop shit all over the place when they sneak in on these paths. I merely try to do my part sir."

Mata-Villa said, "I know that Philip. The chief doesn't know your family like I do."

Andrew said, "Not to prolong this problem Ed, but this fat shithead clown won't investigate Americans getting their eyes carved out and stomachs ripped open, but he wants to make a federal case out of a bag of garbage. This isn't right."

Mata-Villa said, "You are aggravating the situation Andy. Please be quiet. Philip, take the bag off your belt please."

Philip nodded, reached behind his back, untied the bag, opened it and placed right below Marrone's face. He said, "Hold your breath chief, sometimes the garbage stinks."

Deputy Chief Marrone pulled the open bag over, looked inside, and saw the empty bottles and caps. He exclaimed, "You're an asshole Thompson. All of you Thompsons are assholes."

With that Marrone turned to his men ordering, "Let's get out of here."

Once the border agents had left, Sheriff Mata-Villa said, "Andy, I'm sorry about what happened to the Comforts, but there isn't anything the border patrol can or will do about it. I'm investigating the murders. I promise you I will do my best, but there's nothing to go on, no witnesses, no nothing. If something comes up, I'll call you. Now go home."

A somber atmosphere prevailed in the Thompsons' Escalade on their trip back to Bisbee. No one spoke until Philip said, "I guess I speak for us all when I say wow, what a jerk Chief Marrone is."

Everyone nodded in agreement but stayed quiet, their thoughts kept to themselves.

Then Em said, "I feel so damn helpless."

Andrew replied, "Yeah, it's tough. We're all suffering the same way emotionally."

Em said, "There must be something we can do?"

Andrew said, "There is. How about, for starters, we act differently than Marrone and don't simply give up. We can begin by getting back to the ranch and figuring out if the camera or the tape recorder picked up anything useful."

Chapter Four

8:19 a.m. Mountain Time, October 8

AFTER STOPPING FOR A DOZEN MIXED bagels at the Holey Roll bagel shop on Arizona Street in downtown Bisbee the Thompsons pulled past the electrically controlled gate across their driveway entrance from Spring Canyon Road. The driveway rose away from the main street through a dense oak forest until it opened into a large flat area cleared of all vegetation. Several structures were situated in the middle of the seventy-five acre, fully fenced property that backed up to thousands of acres of state lands. A sprawling white stucco ranch with a red tile roof sat in the center of the field. Outbuildings, a large barn, corral, and separate guesthouse were located behind and away from the main house, closer to the state lands. None of the structures had trees or bushes within two hundred feet. Most vegetation had been cleared for protection from the occasional raging wildfires that plagued the west. Two ranch style houses, one where Philip and his family lived, the other for Carl and his wife and kids, flanked the main house. Andrew and his wife, the boys' mother, Catherine built the main house thirty years earlier. Now only Andrew and Emmett lived in the older home. The family added the other buildings, which varied in age, whenever the need arose.

The Thompson family lived happily in their own secluded haven for decades. Until a fateful spring day in 2001 when an illegal immigrant from Mexico, driving drunk, slammed his pickup truck head on into Catherine's Saturn coupe. Catherine, on her way home from grocery shopping when the accident occurred, fought for life but died three days later. Authorities deported the drunk driver back to Mexico after convicting him of vehicular homicide, and after he served four years.

Soon after Catherine Thompson's death, Andrew formed the Cochise County Border Brigade. The group grew rapidly. Presently it numbers over one hundred active members. They are highly aggressive politically, hosting candidate forums, and endorsing those candidates who favor secure borders and strict enforcement of America's immigration laws. During the entire trip home, while Carl drove, Andrew, Philip, and Emmett called members of the Cochise County Border Brigade. They inquired about members' hobbies. Did any among them have interest in or access to, audio and video enhancement expertise?

As soon as they arrived at the house, Carl went to the kitchen and put on a large pot of coffee. The others gathered in the family room and compared notes. None of them had spoken to anybody who specialized in audio or video enhancement as of yet. But they agreed they still had a long way to go before they could say they had completed contacting all of the members. It was a work in progress. Carl leaned into the room announcing coffee was ready. They gathered in the kitchen as soon as Andrew said, "Okay, let's have breakfast while the coffee is fresh."

Carl and Philip called their wives and told them they would be in the main house for a while if they needed them.

Emmett set Sam Comfort's recorder/player on the table. He pressed rewind. When it stopped he pressed play.

"This is Sam Comfort speaking. My wife Ida and I are on a field trip tonight, It is shortly after midnight on the morning of October eighth. We are sitting comfortably slightly north of the United States border with Mexico. We are observing a trail that we have been led to believe is used by drug smugglers and illegal immigrants crossing into Arizona. So far we haven't seen anyone. We hope we are not wasting a good night's sleep."

After a long pause the Thompsons heard, "Ida, stop sniffling."

"I'm trying. There is something irritating my nose."

"Here's my handkerchief. Use it. Then be quiet."

"I'll try."

Later, "It's about twenty past one in the morning. We have just heard some new sounds. We have become accustomed to the noise made by small desert creatures and wind moving vegetation. This is different."

Sam, now whispering, "Someone is near. We can hear movement down on the trail. I can see movement. Be back later."

"They're here. Lots of them. More than a hundred. Some have guns."

"Oh darn. They've stopped right in front of our position."

"Sniff."

"Ida, stop."

"Ah choo!"

"Cover your mouth. Oh poop, they heard you."

Then, "Oh no, they're pointing up here."

Then inaudible sounds combined with voices none of them could understand.

Sam softly whispered, "Get down. Be quiet. Maybe they won't find us."

After a slight pause Sam can be heard again, "We give up. Ida put your hands up. We mean no harm. Amigos, we amigos."

Another voice cuts Sam off, menacingly hissing, "Not another word. Stand up. Quietly now, go down the hill."

Ida can then be heard saying, "We don't want any trouble. Please leave us alone."

"Quiet or I'll cut your throat."

The talk stopped but you could hear Ida whimpering, sniffling, and crying softly. You could hear the sound of the footfalls as they slipped down to the path.

Sam whispered, "Ida stop crying. Be quiet, please."

Another voice said, "Be quiet. Don't speak unless you are answering me. Who else is here?"

"No one else is here. One man brought us here. He went away, left us alone, and said he would be back for us before dawn. Please don't hurt us."

After a prolonged pause, about five minutes with only sounds of shuffling while the area was searched, someone said, "*Vamanos*. Let's go."

Emmett stopped the recorder and said, "I want to clarify, Sam Comfort didn't simply give me up like it sounds. I watched the whole thing. Their leader, he had Ida's throat exposed with a big knife aimed at it. He would have stabbed her for sure if Sam didn't talk."

Emmett turned the recorder back on. Following repeated low sounds of people walking, feet scraping, and cloth rubbing new sounds could be heard, doors opening, things being put in contact with metal, people walking around. Then some murmuring could be heard, several clearly different voices. At times they seemed to be arguing. Then you could hear sounds of agreement. A voice said, "*Ven comigo.* Come with me."

After many more minutes of sounds of movement, walking, they heard the distinct grunting, thumping, and bumping of a struggle.

Then the words, "*Terminado.* It's done. *Vamanos.*"

Following another long pause Emmett could be heard saying, "Oh my God."

Then silence. The recorder turned off.

Emmett asked, "Does anybody want to hear it again?"

Andrew replied, "No. The recording needs cleaning up. We need to know what's said in the background. We have to find somebody who can do that."

Philip said, "Why can't Sheriff Mata-Villa do it? He must have access to a lab."

Andrew replied, "No. We are not going to Ed with this. The Rynning boys trusted the local authorities. I don't."

Philip said, "You can't believe the sheriff is dirty. You've known him forever."

"That's right son, I've known Ed forever. And I trust him, but, not with our lives. We need to go somewhere else. To someone who has no idea what this is about or where this recording comes from."

Philip said, "All right dad. We didn't speak with all the group members this morning. If it's all right with you I want to e-mail everybody inquiring about their hobbies. We have to finish finding out whom among them, if anybody, are interested in, or have access to audio or video enhancement equipment or expertise."

"Okay Philip you go ahead. But remember no details. Tell anyone who asks we want some family recordings and videos enhanced."

"Gotcha."

"Emmett set the video up please."

"It's ready to roll. I already fast forwarded through the first few hours where there was no action." Emmett pressed play. Face after face appeared on the screen. Everyone coming through the rocks paused; they unknowingly posed for the camera, before proceeding along the trail. Every image clear, a little dark, but pretty good. First armed men, then porters mixed with more armed men, then people not armed or carrying anything, then armed men bringing up the rear. Emmett stopped the film twice. First, he pointed out one of the armed men saying, "That one with the Pancho Villa moustache, he was with the group who murdered the

Comforts." Later Emmett pointed to one of the men in the rear saying, "Him too. He's one of the murderers. I think he's second in command of the whole bunch. He led the group who went off with Sam and Ida."

They counted fourteen armed men, two hundred bearers, and ten others coming in. Emmett fast forwarded again. On the way out they counted only two hundred fourteen. Ten people stayed in the United States.

When the video finished Andrew said, "I'm not an expert but I think those images may be all we need. Other than the lighting each person's face should be able to be compared to the criminal mug shot database easily. The shape of the head, the width and length of the face, the placement of the ears, nose, and eyes are obvious. The shape and uniqueness of each jaw, the cheekbones, eye separation, and nose width are explicit. How much more could the FBI need?"

Emmett replied, "Maybe we shouldn't screw with this stuff at all. Why not give it to the authorities?"

Andrew, who sat in a recliner, staring up at the ceiling said, "No. We only put ourselves in danger if the drug dealers find out we have this stuff. Or if they find out we turned the stuff in. A better idea is let's just hold on to everything for a couple of days. We'll figure out what we can safely do."

Carl called from the kitchen, "Lunch is served."

Andrew stood up, looked at the clock hanging on the wall and remarked, "Twelve thirty. Oh boy, on some occasions time flies."

All of the Thompsons gathered in the kitchen table. Carl set out a platter of sliced ham, bologna, Swiss, and white American cheese accompanied by paper plates, lettuce, sliced tomatoes, pickles, mustard, mayonnaise, rye, and sourdough bread. Carl said, "Help yourselves to drinks. Cold beer, soda, and iced tea are in the fridge."

Philip, Emmett, and Andrew all acknowledged Carl, thanking him profusely.

Once they all settled in with sandwiches and something to drink, Andrew asked, "Philip how goes the e-mailing?"

"Fine."

After a few minutes passed Andrew said, "Philip any responses?"

"Only Helen Galindo."

"Damn it Philip, stop making me drag everything out of you. What did Helen say?"

"She said she personally doesn't have any experience with enhancing recordings, but her sister-in-law had it done in Tucson. She included the name, address and phone number of the guy who did her sister-in-law's work."

"Okay, that's a start. If nothing else comes in maybe we can use the same guy. Send a thank you to Helen please, Philip."

"I already did."

After lunch, Philip and Carl excused themselves, explaining they wanted to go home to visit with their wives and kids for a while. Like Emmett, they both worked as firefighters. Their schedules called for them both to work forty-eight hour shifts starting today. They had to report to work at the main Bisbee Fire Station by four this afternoon.

Chapter Five

3:29 p.m. Mountain Time, October 8

A BLAST OF HOT, STIFLING, HUMID air greeted Abe Silverman as soon as he stepped off the small six-passenger prop plane. He had flown into San Jose on the morning's first flight out of Washington's Dulles Airport. After landing at the Juan Santamaria International Airport, right outside of the capital San Jose in Costa Rica's Central Valley, he boarded a local flight to his present destination, Tortuguero Domestic Airport. He knew from travel brochures he received with his confirmed reservations this tiny airport was in actuality a glorified landing strip on a remote island. It was pretty enough; swaying palm trees, sandy beaches, the blue waters of the Caribbean Sea on one side and a densely overgrown canal on the other. The landing strip was located two miles from his destination, the Pachira Lodge, in Tortuguero National Park. Silverman, a good-looking thirty-seven year old sporting a mixed grayish black ponytail, perspired profusely. Sweat from his forehead ran down his face, dripping off his hawkish nose. His shirt, soaked with perspiration, stuck to his chest.

A golf cart drove up and stopped next to the plane. The driver, a young Hispanic man, got out and inquired, "Mister Abe Silverman?"

"Yes."

"I'm here to take you to the resort sir. My name is Jose. Can I get your bags sir?"

"Yes, the pilot put my bags on the plane, in the cargo hold.

Walking toward the plane Jose said, "I'll get them sir. Please get in the cart. Make yourself comfortable. If you like, help yourself to the bottled water in the cooler behind the front seats."

Abe sat down, retrieved a water bottle and rolled the cool container over his face. He removed the cap and put the spout to his mouth. He poured, sloshed the liquid around, swallowed, and exclaimed loudly, "So refreshing Jose, thank you."

After placing Silverman's bags in the back of the cart Jose got behind the wheel and said, "It's a short pleasant ride to the resort sir. Very scenic. If you have any questions along the way, ask me."

"I have a question, Jose. What is this place?"

Jose replied, "Sir this is Tortuguero National Park. It means land of turtles. It is an island, only reachable by air or boat. Extremely private, highly secluded. The beaches are protected areas, for endangered sea turtles. The turtles nest and reproduce here. The island is a conservation area, incredibly bio-diverse; much of the island is protected wetland. The weather is tropical. I can see you are feeling the high humidity. That is because the island receives so much rainfall, over two hundred inches each year. There are rainforest, canals, beaches, and lagoons. There is one road, the one we are on. It goes between the airstrip and the resort. The little village of Tortuguero, where the hired help live, is across the river from the resort. Those people, the help, they travel to and from work by boat. Off the road, other than the resort walkways, the island is a muddy swamp. Everybody gets around by foot or one of the few golf carts. Moreover, that doesn't include many people because not very many people have any business being on the road at all. Everybody, all the guests, and most of the help, stay in the resort complex and park and travel everywhere by foot, boat, or canoe."

"Jose is this what your job is, picking people up from the airport?"

"No, sir. I'm head of security for the resort. I've been asked to verify who flies in while your meetings are going on. The boat dock is at the resort. So anybody arriving there is seen immediately."

"I see. How many are here now Jose?"

Well sir, two boatloads one with sixteen passengers another with seventeen passengers and twelve flights with a total of seventeen people. So fifty guests, total."

"I'm the last one then."

"I believe so sir. I was told fifty altogether."

No more than a few minutes away from the airstrip the road became completely encompassed by vegetation. Abe said, "This looks like Tarzan and Jane live here. It's like a damn jungle."

"Oh it is most definitely a jungle, sir. The island has several hundred species of trees and thousands of different plants, flowers, and shrubs. But you are wrong about Tarzan and Jane. The only ones who live on the island are my wife and me and the manager and his wife."

"Only the four of you and the guests are here at night?"

"Oh no sir, there is always someone in the kitchen, maintenance, housekeeping departments, and several security people are always patrolling. They just don't live on the island."

"I understand. How many security staff members are on duty at night?"

"I can't reveal numbers sir. But I can tell you, you are extremely safe. Armed security personnel are on the beaches, in boats on the waterways, and on foot throughout the resort."

Silverman stopped talking for a minute, looked at the jungle, and saw a lush exotic paradise. He asked, "Jose what kind of trees are those?"

"The tallest ones are rainforest almond trees. Those lining the road with the pretty white flowers are mimosas."

Pointing out some trees with large leaves Jose said, "They are native fig trees, sir."

As they rounded a turn close to the river Jose said, "The palms you see are called raffia palms. The large stumps are what are left from old almond trees that fell over."

Silverman reached for a flower on a branch hanging over the road. Jose quickly said, "Stop sir. Don't reach like that in the jungle. Anything could be on those branches. Even next to the road. People are bitten by snakes, bats, insects, and other wild things all the time."

"I didn't realize. Don't worry, I won't do it again. I'll just look."

"The jungle is breathtakingly beautiful sir, but you must be aware of the dangers. The creatures living here can be dangerous."

"I can appreciate that Jose. What kinds of wildlife are on the island?'

"Not simply on the island, Mister Silverman, in the waters too. On the sea side there are the turtles on the beach, and sharks in the salt water. On the river and canal side you will see a large number of manatees and many varieties of fish who come to the top to feed on insects falling from branches or landing on the surface. You will also come across caiman crocodiles. They are about nine feet in length, very quick. Also, you will see Central American crocodiles. They are much bigger, up to fifteen feet long. You even have to be careful around the frogs. Most green ones are okay, but the brown ones and the red ones can be poisonous. There are many snakes that blend in with the vegetation. The fer-de-lance grows up to eight feet.

Its venom is deadly. Boa constrictors are huge, many fifteen to twenty feet long. They are brown or grayish. They will wrap around and crush their victims. There are little vipers, thirty inches or less, very colorful, green, orange, red, yellow or brown. Then you have the coral snake, so pretty, so deadly. Lizards are all over."

"Are there any regular animals?"

"Yes sir, a lot of deer, monkeys, weasel, possum, skunks, squirrel, anteaters, and raccoons. There are both two and three toed sloths, but they hang in the trees. Rarely do the sloths come to the ground. The island is home to coyotes, and lots of different cats. Small spotted ocelots, about four or five feet in length. Then there are the jaguars, big, eight feet long, and uncommonly fast. Jaguars are spotted or all black, undeniably lethal."

Jose slowed the cart down, turned off the road, which abruptly ended, and mounted a wooden ramp, which took them onto a raised boardwalk. Supported by piers as big around as telephone poles, the boardwalk appeared to be about four feet above the swamp. The walkway was about fifteen feet wide with railings on both sides. A large colorful sign appeared at the top of the ramp. It said 'Welcome to Pachira Lodge Tortuguero Costa Rica.' They had arrived at their destination.

The first thing Abe saw was a covered dock with a dozen or more boats of various sizes tied up. Behind the dock, a large building with a wrap-around covered deck tied into the boardwalk. He could see one huge room entirely screened in. Jose saw where Abe was looking and said, "The dining hall sir. All meals are served there. The resort's office is located inside the door on the far end."

As they drove past the dining complex Jose pointed to another large roofed over area with tables, chairs, what looked to be a bar, and a stage. Jose said, "That covered arena is where groups like yours hold their meetings, Mister Silverman."

Continuing along the boardwalk, Jose made a right then a quick left, before stopping in front of one of the identical cabins. Jose said, "All out sir. This one is yours. Number thirty four."

Abe Silverman stepped out of the cart and gazed around, surrounded by blooming flowers of every size and color imaginable. He recognized red lantana, blue lantana, yellow sunflowers, pink verbena, lavender fuchsia, and orange and white hibiscus. He saw plants with green, reddish, and purple leaves. Vibrantly-colored butterflies were everywhere. Energetic hummingbirds hovered in place for long periods of time and flew in all directions, up, down, and backwards. Silverman said to no one in particular, "This place is amazing."

To get to cabin thirty four Abe walked across a side boardwalk about five feet wide and ten feet long. The walk led to a covered deck the width of the cabin, about twenty feet, at least eight feet deep. Two wooden rockers with a small table set between them sat on the deck. An umbrella stand with two colorful umbrellas inside it stood next to the entryway. Jose brought the luggage, unlocked the door, and motioned Abe to go first. Silverman stepped into a huge room. The solid outside walls of the cabin ended five feet off the floor. Mesh screening completed the uppermost five feet. Heavy cloth curtains hung bunched in each corner. Jose explained the curtains could be drawn over the screens for additional privacy but most guests didn't feel the need. Jose pointed out the long roof overhang saying, "Don't worry sir, no rain will come in."

The room contained two queen beds, a ceiling fan, several chairs and tables, a phone, and an alarm clock. In the rear a walk-in closet and luxurious bathroom with a shower big enough for several people completed the space. Jose handed Abe the key and asked, "Is there anything else sir?"

Silverman replied, "Jose, I want to thank you so very much for picking me up and the guided tour on the way in. You were fantastic. And yes there is something I still need to know. What time do we eat?"

"Dinner is at six in the evening, breakfast at seven in the morning, and lunch is at noon sir. You can also dial up room service anytime. A server brings coffee to the door at or before dawn. He will knock and you can tell him yes or no then."

"Thank you Jose. Is there anything else you think I should know about?"

"Yes sir. You still have time before dinner to take a boat ride. Go to the dock we passed on the way in. A guide will be there. Merely tell him you want to see the birds and you have to be back before dinner. The guide will take care of everything. It's something you shouldn't miss."

Abe handed Jose a twenty-dollar bill saying, "Thanks for all your help. I appreciate everything you did."

Jose replied, "Thank you sir. If you think of anything else I can do for you stop by or call the office. They can always reach me. Good afternoon Mister Silverman. Enjoy your stay."

Silverman sat on a chair inside his cabin mulling what he should do next. One thing was for sure, he wanted to avoid the other attendees as much as possible. He knew many of them would be the same people, or the same type of people, he had contact with during previous yearly meetings. He didn't feel comfortable with any of them. You could say he was afraid of them. He knew who they were and what they did. Silverman stood, looked through the screens in all directions. He didn't see a soul. He decided to take a boat ride like Jose suggested.

After retrieving a wide-brimmed Tilley hat from his luggage and putting it on along with dark sunglasses Silverman went outside. He quickly walked back toward the main building complex. Less than six minutes later he stepped onto the dock they passed on the way in. A short middle aged Latino man with a mustache appeared out of nowhere. He asked, "May I help you?"

"Yes, Jose told me I could get a boat tour of the park if I came to this dock."

"Si sir, that is right. My name is Francisco. I can take you now if you like."

"I can go now. Now is good. How much is the tour?"

Francisco handed Silverman a life vest and said, "There is no charge for guests of Pachira Lodge sir. However, everyone must wear life jacket. Please sir, put this on and follow me."

Francisco led the way to a ten foot long flat bottomed aluminum boat with a small electric outboard motor. He stepped in and held his hand out to help balance Silverman as he got in. Francisco directed Silverman to sit on a seat in the middle of the boat. He started the engine and steered the boat away from the dock. He asked, "What is your name sir?"

"Abe Silverman. Please call me Abe. Everybody does"

"Si, Mister Abe. And you call me Cisco. Everyone they call me Cisco."

Cisco put on a rain poncho. He reached over and handed one to Silverman saying, "Mister Abe, rain is starting. It looks like a short one but sometimes it rains terribly heavy. This will keep you dry."

Silverman laughed and said, "Cisco I'm soaked already from the humidity. But thank you, I'll wear the poncho."

As soon as Silverman had his rain gear on the skies opened up. The rain came down in a driving downpour. He asked Cisco, "Should we go back? Is it safe?"

"No problem, Mister Abe. We safe. Do this every day. It rains here all time. No problem."

Silverman studied his surroundings. The rain didn't appear to slow anything down. There were several other boats on the water. Across the river he could see kids running and playing in the village. In a few minutes the rain slowed then it stopped completely. Cisco directed the boat down a waterway going into the jungle. Soon there was no human activity except for them. Cisco steered closer to the edge and pointed to some small bumps protruding from the water. He said, "Mister Abe big crocs."

Silverman stared at the bumps, examining them closer until he saw the eyes. Next he made out the bodies, huge crocodiles. He said, "I see them."

Cisco steered back out to the center of the channel. Abe spotted two brightly colored birds. One red with blue and yellow wings, the other a luminous green body, blue wings and a long red tail. He asked Cisco, "What are they?"

"Macaws Mister Abe, a great green one and a scarlet macaw. Beautiful aren't they?"

Cisco nodded at the trees and whispered, "A toucan. There, half way up on that branch."

Silverman saw a black and yellow bird with a huge green and red beak. Cisco directed Abe's attention to a pink and white bird with a funny bill flattened at the tip. He said, "A rose spoonbill Mister Abe."

For the next two hours Cisco trolled around pointing out and naming or simply naming different birds Abe saw first and pointed to. They came across pelicans, storks, herons, egrets, peacocks, kingfishers, quetzals, hawks, osprey, woodpeckers, and others. With the sun going down they returned to the boat dock. Silverman thanked Cisco profusely, tipped him twenty dollars, and headed for dinner. It was shortly after six, the dining room was crowded. He entered through double screen doors that led from the covered porch. Abe was greeted by a woman in a white dress who told him, take a dish and follow the buffet table. Point to what he wanted he she told him. Servers would help him. She said, "It's open seating. Sit with whomever you want. Anyplace you can find room."

Abe held his plate out, accepting chicken breast, rice, beans, nachos, cheese, salsa, and banana pie. He took a glass of iced tea and surveyed the tables. He had hoped they would all be full so he could start a new one but as luck had it there were several tables with one or more open places. He sat down at one with all Asians. Nodding to everyone he said, "Good evening, my name is Abe Silverman."

His tablemates smiled and nodded. The man on his left offered his hand saying, "I am Charlie, very pleased to meet you, Abe."

Everyone at Abe's table conversed in a language he didn't understand which was fine with him. He concentrated on eating. Because he arrived late many people soon finished their dinners, stood, said good night, and left. Charlie was one of them. Soon Abe was the only person left at his table. He looked around and noticed Angel Figueroa staring at him. Abe raised his hand and waved. Angel continued staring. The situation unnerved Silverman, who had sought out Figueroa as soon as he entered the dining room. He saw where he was sitting immediately and avoided that table completely. Twice when he looked Figueroa's way during dinner, Angel Figueroa appeared to be brooding, his black eyes glaring at Abe. Silverman felt his stomach turning. Why was he staring at him? Why didn't he acknowledge his wave? He couldn't know. There was no way.

Silverman left his pie on the plate, got up, and walked out the door as quickly as he could. Out on the boardwalk he saw the bar in the other gathering place was open and serving customers. He went over, placed a twenty on the bar, ordered a double scotch on the rocks, and a bottle of water. When served he thanked the bartender, left the change on the bar, took his drink and water and went back to his cabin. Seeing no one on the boardwalk or on any of the cabin decks at all, he decided to sit in a rocker on his porch and pass the time thinking of other people and places.

Chapter Six

5:50 a.m. Mountain Time, October 9

ABE SILVERMAN WAS FORCED DOWN ON his knees, being held firmly by two of Angel Figueroa's thugs. Abe heard the wild screams of the others. He wondered, *what did they do, why is he doing this to them, how does he know about me?* Silverman could feel the cold blade of the knife against his throat. He knew his head was going to be cut off. They are going to cut his limbs off, exactly like the traitors before him were having done to them now. The horrible screams over and over. *How could Figueroa have learned about him, he was always so careful? Now it's clear to him, it's why he was brought here. They're going to cut him up and feed him to the animals.* Someone grabbed his hair and pulled his head back. He screamed. He tried to throw them off. He fought back. He heard noise. Someone was coming. There was a tapping. He opened his eyes. He looked around. He was in a bed. The screaming was louder. Someone was at the door. He heard, "Sir, sir, coffee, sir."

Silverman got up. He moved the curtain aside and gazed outside. He saw a young man with a tray with cups and a pot. He heard the screams. Nothing looked amiss. Cautiously he unlocked and opened the door. The young man inquired, "Coffee, sir?"

Silverman asked, "Who's screaming?"

"Monkeys, sir."

"Monkeys, is someone killing monkeys?"

"Oh no sir. Those are howler monkeys. They live in the trees. Coffee, sir?"

"Nobody is killing them?"

"No sir. Every morning they scream. A troop of howler monkeys live in these trees. Maybe twelve, big and little, boy and girl. Brown ones, black ones, gold ones, you look, you see. Nothing to fear, sir. Coffee, sir?"

Silverman was sweating, shaking uncontrollably. He said, "No, no coffee."

He closed and locked the door. Silverman sat on the bed, his mind racing. *A nightmare, it was only a nightmare. Does he know? He can't know. I'm the only one who knows.* He got up, walked to the bathroom, turned the shower on, stepped in, and promptly slipped and fell. He wound up sitting on his ass on the floor of the shower. He looked at the floor and immediately knew what happened. *Dumb spics, they used eighteen inch wall tiles on the floor. Big slippery wall tiles, no grout lines. How stupid, an accident waiting to happen.* Slowly he got to his feet, reached outside for a hand towel, put the towel on the floor and stood on it. He rubbed his ass, felt around, nothing was broken. He quickly finished his shower, and got out. He brushed his teeth, shaved, got dressed, went outside, re-read the presentation he was going to make, tucked it under his arm, and got up.

It had started raining so Abe took one of the large umbrellas from the stand. Popping it open he put it over his head and walked down for breakfast. He mumbled to himself all the way. No way Figueroa knew, they all loved him, and they always say he's doing a great job. No one is going to kill him. He simply had to be careful not to reach up into the trees and get bitten by a poisonous snake or fall and crack his head in the shower. Abe was smiling, brimming with self confidence when he reached the dining hall. He closed his umbrella he had used, placed it into one of the many stands on the porch, and went through the doors.

Angel Figueroa was standing right there, in front of Silverman. He stood slightly over six feet tall, had closely-cropped black hair and piercing black eyes. He was powerfully built, appearing to be in excellent physical condition. An extremely attractive man, Angel smiled widely. He held out his hand which Abe readily grasped. Angel said, "Buenos dias, good morning Abe."

"Angel, buenos dias to you. How have you been, my friend?"

"Always well Abe. Are you ready for your presentation?"

"Yes I am. Things have never looked better in Washington. I'm hopeful everyone will be pleased with what I have to report."

"Great Abe, enjoy your breakfast. Wish we could talk longer but you understand I have to greet the others as they come in. I'll catch you later."

Paul C. Gardner

Silverman took a plate, got some scrambled eggs, sliced mangos, sliced papaya, orange juice, warm banana bread, and coffee. He saw Charlie sitting at a table by himself and joined him. He said, "Good morning Charlie. Sleep well last night?"

"Hey, good morning Abe. Yes I slept well. How about you?"

"Like a baby. Until this morning. Those crazy monkeys are freaking loud. Couldn't sleep at all once that racket started."

"I know what you mean. They woke me up too. Probably everybody here, no one could sleep through that."

Charlie and Abe were joined by several others. They all complained about the monkeys. Abe repeated what the coffee boy told him, a group of howler monkeys lived in the trees and the screaming was a normal morning ritual. Talk then went to subjects like the flowers, the birds, the heat, and the rain. Abe told them what he had learned the previous day. He highly recommended the boat tour.

Conversation around the table and in the room came to halt when Angel Figueroa rose to his feet and began tapping his spoon on a glass. Angel said, "I want to remind everyone our business meeting begins at nine in the large covered arena across the way. If you want coffee or bottled water please bring it with you from here. There will be no service help at the arena. No outsiders will be allowed. No phones, recorders or cameras either. If you have any of those items with you please bring them back to your cabins. Thanks, that's all. Go back to what you were doing. Enjoy your breakfast."

When Abe arrived at the meeting arena he was one of the first. He took an outside seat at one of the outer tables. From his vantage point he could observe the entire goings on without being obvious. Abe felt he learned a lot by watching at meetings such as this one. A few minutes before nine o'clock, it started raining hard. Some of Angel's men walked through the entire area holding sensor devices. One by one as they completed their area they nodded to Angel. Then they put on ponchos and went outside apparently to patrol the grounds.

Promptly at nine Angel got up from a table in the front and strode to a podium. He smiled directly at the one female in attendance and said, "Good morning my friends. Good morning lady and gentlemen. Welcome to the fourth annual meeting of the Alliance. I hope you are all enjoying yourselves at this beautiful resort. Pachira Lodge on Tortuguero Island here in Costa Rica was chosen not only for its beauty but for its isolation. Our privacy is guaranteed. All of the hired help is in the dining room being watched over by my men. Soft music is being played in there, which

- 34 -

drowns out any sounds that may come from our meeting. My men are walking security in the immediate vicinity. No one who does not belong will be allowed within earshot. All of the resort security personnel are patrolling the island far from the resort. This venue has been swept for any listening devices. We can speak freely. Today's discussion will be in English. It is my understanding you are all fluent. That said I first want to report the total Alliance income has increased to another high; to fifty-four billion dollars for this past year. That is two billion dollars above our previous best. To put it in perspective, that is more than the gross national product of one hundred and seventeen individual countries. More than many of the countries represented here today. Ever since we stopped warring with each other five years ago all of our individual profits have risen. It proves as long as we remain unified we will remain successful, wildly so. Everyone benefits."

As on cue everyone rose began clapping and cheering. Then the chant started, "Jefe, Jefe, Jefe."

Angel Figueroa, whose nickname was El Jefe, meaning he was the Alliance's boss of bosses, raised his hands, requesting calm. He motioned everyone to sit. When they were all seated he said, "To prove we are not male chauvinist pigs as some say, not to our faces of course, I want to ask the beautiful Lisa Strump to come to the podium and brief us on her activities on our behalf. Lisa please come on up. Before Lisa starts let me state the ground rules. You will at some point be invited to ask questions. Anyone electing to do so will please state their name and say which organization it is they represent before posing inquiries. You all may very well be eminent personalities within your own circles but not everybody here knows who you are."

Abe watched as one of the most beautiful women he had ever seen pushed her chair back, stood, then moved toward the podium. In her late twenties, about five-six, long flaming red hair tied back in a ponytail, sparkling blue eyes, wearing tight white short shorts, and a green halter top, Lisa Strump captivated the audience. With all eyes in the arena riveted on her Strump said, "Gentlemen, my friends, please excuse my attire. For business meeting such as these I normally dress much more modestly. But considering the heat, rain, and humidity I hope you don't mind that I dressed comfortably."

To a chorus of no, no we don't mind at all, she continued, "My friends, for those of you who are unaware, my job, the job of my firm, is to pave the way for the unimpeded import into the United States of your products.

Mister Figueroa, when he deems it necessary, informs me when, where, and how a shipment is arriving. I have the contacts to ensure there is no interference. It is my job to get to the border patrol officer, the customs person, whether a lowly clerk with responsibility for only what they have contact with or the higher-up, the person giving the orders, directing the lower echelon. We influence whoever is needed. Sometimes we use sex or drugs. Sometimes we use money. We find what works best one time. That's all it takes, one time and they are ours forever. Whatever action we do we record. One time and we have documentary evidence to use again and again. In most cases we use money, even if it takes sex the first time it always evolves into cash later. After the first time they are put on a monthly retainer. Your money, your cash, so it is all accounted for. In my opinion, and I believe yours, the money has been well spent. In the last five years a shipment has never been lost when one or more of my contacts have been utilized. The Alliance recently purchased World Express Air Freight to expedite air shipments of product. I am pleased to inform you the Customs inspectors stationed at World's main import terminal in Kansas City are all my contacts, people hand-picked by the chief customs agent at World because they previously worked for us in other locations. Rest assured your cargo, regardless of method of shipment or destination, is protected. I look forward to another successful year. Are there any questions?"

A man stood and said, "I am Vang Ly, representing Alliance members from Laos. My question is how much do we pay these people, your contacts? In my country we simply kill any public servant who interferes with our operations. It's cheaper."

Angel Figueroa rose to his feet signaled Lisa Strump not to answer. *Another foreign asshole*, he thought. Angel responded, "Mister Ly, Vang, killing government employees, and each other, is something we have avoided doing since the Alliance was originated. What you do in your country is up to you but collectively we have found paying a fair bribe and having evidence of that payment to hold over public servants is the much better approach in the United States. We reserve the option of physical harm but prefer spending the money. Now Lisa please answer the part of Vang's question related to payments."

Strump smiled brightly and began, "My friends, the payments vary in size. For example, a solitary guard, border or customs, who looks the other way, normally will receive twenty thousand dollars per month. Some of the higher-ups, and we have some lofty contacts, are on retainer. They receive as much as one hundred thousand dollars per month. They schedule and assign our people where they need to be to expedite our operations. On the nights when visibility is highest, when there are full moons, large cross-border shipments are scheduled to be hand-carried across at points away from the check stations. These are referred to as Angel's moon nights. Just the other night one of our supervisory contacts cleared a large area of the border and left a highway checkpoint unmanned while we ran a successful operation of major proportions. Because the Alliance ships through that particular sector at least once every month that person receives a one hundred thousand dollar monthly payment for his help."

Vang Ly said, "That sounds like a lot of money."

Angel rose up again, this time his annoyance plainly visible. He said, "The shipment just referenced comprised of two hundred sixty pound bundles, twelve thousand pounds with a wholesale value of five hundred dollars per pound, a six million dollar shipment. The dollars spent on protection are minuscule in comparison. Please let's move on. If there are no more questions for Lisa I'd like to hear from Abe Silverman, our man in Washington."

While all eyes followed Lisa Strump returning to her seat Silverman went to the podium. The rain had stopped. A pleasant breeze caressed his face. He was comfortable and relaxed. With everyone focused on him Abe was expressionless as he said, "Good morning everyone. Let me start with something I'm sure we can all agree on. Oh boy, Lisa Strump is one hard act to follow."

With everyone nodding their head vigorously in agreement Abe continued, "But I'll try. My name is Abe Silverman. I am an attorney. My firm has represented the Alliance in Washington, D.C. for the last five years. We are what are called lobbyists. For a fee, money well spent, we represent special interests like yours in the halls of congress. Sometimes we operate outside the halls too. We have been profoundly successful at what we do. Over the past five years the majorities in both the Senate and the House of Representatives have changed hands. What it means is, the chairmen of various committees controlling legislation and funding of interest to you men, change. You pay us to maintain influence regardless of who is in power. We do that. We have done that. We will continue to do that. I've got to tell you, keeping track of the players is a tough job but we have been up to the task. But I've also got to warn you, things may not be so easy going forward. There is a new sheriff in town in Washington. The new president, James Burns, wants a secure border now. Up until the present time we have been able to use all kinds of reasons to prevent or slow the border fence construction. In the past the committee chairmen have had hearing after hearing, delayed committee action, slowed the process endlessly, then when finally allowing a vote approving portions of the fence they have allowed funding to expire, which resulted in the whole process having to be restarted, more hearings, more investigations, more delays, and so on. Construction of the fence has been held up time and again by various so-called problems. Environmental concerns have been a favorite of mine. For example, hearings have been held numerous times to determine if the fence will obstruct the flow of drainage courses, rain, rivers, animals, insects, families, friends, students, or if a proposed section of fence interfered with views, farm and ranch feed, and/or water sources. Land ownership disputes, grading for access roads, damage to native plants. Congressmen you control say, 'No you can't put a fence there.' When someone asks why, your congressmen respond, 'Because we have an endangered plant living there.' When that problem gets mediated a special gnat is encountered, then a field mouse, turtle, or a rare cactus ... it's never ending. You name it, the committees you bought and pay for, held and continue to hold hearings on all kinds of dilemmas. You have certainly gotten your money's worth. My friends, I've got to tell you, eventually the border fence, most likely a double or triple fence will be built all along the southern border and a virtual fence will be put in place along the northern border. But that is not going to stop the import of your product."

Abe paused, took a sip of water, and continued, "I'm sure you all want to know what happens after a secure fence. Well you are in good hands. For the future I'm working with the committee chairmen and ranking members to expedite certain trucking across both borders. El Jefe has provided me with a list which I in turn have given to the chairmen. They have told me they foresee no problems at all with the list. They will approve certification of selected Mexican trucking firms to pass through border checkpoints after cursory, speedy, in most cases non-existent inspection. Our people have convinced everyone streamlining inspections in this way will advance traffic management, relieving congestion, minimizing traffic idling, reducing pollution of the environment. Americans bureaucrats love that shit. In return, to alleviate American concerns about the safety of Mexican trucks and drivers, Alliance owned trucking firms will purchase a fleet of new American brand tractor trailers and all of its drivers will be fluent in English. All Alliance drivers will speak and read English effortlessly. Testing and accreditation will be mandatory. The chairmen have suggested the Alliance firms allow their drivers who cross into the United States to become members of, and pay dues to, American teamster unions. Have I mentioned Americans bureaucrats love that shit? I believe that brings you all up to date on the happenings in Washington, D.C. Does anyone have any questions?"

One man rose to his feet. Abe recognized the Asian man Charlie. He said, "Mister Silverman, Charlie Yung representing Alliance membership in China. I know I speak for everyone here when I say thank you for a job well done. We fully expected and honestly didn't quite understand why the United States didn't build a fence along at least its southern border. Now we all know. My question is the American politicians want to provide free passage across the southern and I assume the northern borders to the trucks belonging to firms providing above average equipment which meet your governments safety requirements and are operated by competent personnel. Is that true?"

"Yes, Charlie, that's what the committee leaders want. They feel that they can make the case the United States is bound to do this by its free trade agreements with Canada and Mexico. As long as the United States has assurance every participating truck and driver meets certain standards related to quality control and safety they do not anticipate a problem. Is that clear for you?"

"Yes, thank you again, Mister Silverman."

"Anyone else?"

A man in the back of the room stood. He introduced himself as Carlos representing the Gulf Group. He said, "I'd like to know, who the politicians who are getting paid are? And how much of our money are you giving to these greedy American crooks?"

Angel rose up and said, "Mister Martinez, Carlos, you know naming those names in such an open forum is not wise. There is such a policy 'as need to know' and no one besides Mister Silverman and I need to know who these American politicians are. For security reasons, that is the way it is going to stay. That is the way it has to be. Abe tell everyone how much is paid for the services we are provided."

Abe checked a paper on the podium in front of him and said, "Each of four members of congress receives eighty thousand dollars per month in cash. Several other members of congress and employees of other government agencies, from time to time, get paid various amounts for one-time services rendered. There have been occasions in the past, and I expect similar situations will occur in the future, when a local politician, a state governor or a city mayor can be useful. So far this calendar year I have made seventy-two additional payments ranging from twenty to eighty thousand dollars to other individuals. Eight were for twenty thousand dollars, six for twenty-five thousand dollars, seventeen fifty thousand dollar payments, and forty-one eighty thousand dollar payments. My firm receives one million dollars per year for its services. I believe miscellaneous expenses for travel, entertainment and the like has amounted to about four hundred thousand dollars this year."

Abe wrote a few notes and announced, "The total funds dispensed to and by me for Alliance representation in Washington for the past year is approximately nine million six hundred eighty thousand dollars. I trust that answers your question."

Another man jumped up and said, "I am Bashir Matyarzai representing Afghani interests. Why are we, producers, paying for what amounts to bribes to American hustlers that benefit Mexican handlers? Need I remind you all that we, Afghanis, grow ninety percent of the world's poppy plants? We are tired of getting ripped off by Americans."

Abe looked at Angel who again rose. *Ignorant fucking foreigners*, Angel thought. With his eyes narrowing, he said, "Enough of this bullshit. Without the bribes nothing you produce would be worth anything. Ask yourself, if it wasn't for the Americans, who would be your market? Get with the program. Bribes are the name of the game. We need to pay and all of us need to get along. We have a common interest here." Angel looked at Abe and continued, "Abe, so we are all on the same page, you make damn sure those cocksuckers who've been feeding at our trough to the tune of tens of millions of dollars are aware we don't want no stinkin' fence. Any interference with our cross border passage will piss us off. They don't want that. You make sure they know. And Abe, remember too, you will be held responsible. You took our money too. Now let's move on."

Matyarzai did not sit down immediately. He stared at Angel appearing like he wanted to say more. But then he sat. The Afghani, like everyone else, knew Angel's reputation and was scared stiff of offending him.

Abe scanned the audience and seeing no further questioners returned to his seat. Angel Figueroa went to the podium and said, "I want to clarify, in relation to the southern and northern United States borders, at this time we are not concerned with the Canadian border. The Alliance has no present plans to operate in Canada. Some of the product we sell to distributors in the United States is then brought across from the United States over the northern border into Canada by them. We do not supply Canada. We do not import or export into or out of Canada. To bring product into the

United States via Canada is foolish, doubling our exposure. With that said I would like Diego Perez, our Mexican lobbyist, to come up."

A young man, about thirty, with long black hair and a big grin stood and made his way to the podium. The broad smile, exposing sparkling bright white teeth, never faded. He gazed seemingly at everyone in the room and said, "Thank you Angel. Good morning all. I'm delighted to be here. First let me say you have nothing to worry about where the Mexican authorities are concerned. They are your friends and want nothing more than to see to it the Alliance's operations are trouble-free. I can assure you of that because my access goes right to the top. Your imports, by land, sea, and air, are guaranteed not to be questioned in any way, by anyone of authority in Mexico. The same goes for your exports. It costs plenty of money, but unlike Lisa Strump and Abe Silverman, I only pay one person from the ruling party. We don't concern ourselves with how the pie is split on their end. That is not our concern, so long as no one interferes with us. In return for the single payment, we get safe passage throughout Mexico. All incoming cargo has free, unfettered use of official weigh stations. National troops are responsible for guarding all cargo at air, sea, and rail terminals. I realize none of you use them, but the Mexican government wants me to remind you armed escorts are available anywhere in the country if you need them. I hope you all agree with me this is a great improvement over the violent clashes some of you had with army and police factions in the old days. I will be available for the remainder of the day if any of you want to discuss anything privately. While standing here I'm open for any questions you might have now."

One man rose. He said, "I am Ruben Miranda. I am the representative of the Baja Boys. How much is this one person you interact with paid?"

"Ten million dollars each month."

"That is outrageous. One hundred twenty million each year. Perhaps a twenty cent bullet in his brain would be a better use of our monies."

Angel Figueroa got up, walked to the podium, patted Perez on the shoulder, and said, "Thank you very much Diego. You can sit down, I'll respond to Ruben."

Figueroa shook his head slowly as Perez returned to his place. Once he was seated he said, "Ruben, nobody here wants to go back to the old days. A hundred and twenty million dollars a year is peanuts for what we get. Please remember we are all still alive, out of jail, and living well. The last five years have been the very best any of us have ever had. I also want to remind all of you Mexican members, the government is and has been your friend, your biggest ally. We have a monopoly because of the protection we receive for our payments. For the past five years all of our competition has been taken out by the government. Somebody tries to move in on any of us and I simply notify the government people and the upstarts are wiped out. We sit back and laugh as the government takes out our competition. They get paid by us and the stupid Americans. Don't forget for one minute the anti-drug money the United States sends to Mexico City could be used against you instead of your competition. Enjoy the prosperity. We have never had it so good. Another thing, all of you are producing methamphetamine. It's a big money maker for everyone. You can thank the Mexican government for not banning the chemicals we need for meth production. The American government has. Other countries in the world have. Be thankful for what you have, stop the complaining."

Angel waited for someone to say something more. When no one did he continued, "Now as long as I'm up here and have your attention, I want to bring everyone up to date on some new alternate methods we are utilizing. First the small submarines we attempted to use are being discontinued. The United States Coast Guard is on high alert in regard to the subs. They also do not carry enough product. Another negative is two of them had to surface in the past month, within United States waters, due to mechanical malfunctions. Those subs, their crews, and product were taken into custody and lost. We still have twenty-eight subs but they are being put into dry dock storage for the foreseeable future. Instead, we have developed a sealable plastic thirty by six by six foot container that slides into standard forty by eight by eight foot shipping containers we truck across the border. Drug sniffing dogs are useless against them. Once they are packed and sealed, no odors are emitted at all. When fully set inside the containers, with bags or boxes of innocent materials that are shown on the bills of lading, one foot on top, bottom, and both sides and five foot on either end, the containers can be opened by authorities and all they will see is the innocent material. The new plastic container is an excellent innovation we are using on a pilot basis on the Arizona/Mexico border now. Also, for use when the border fence is completed, we are drilling secret underground tunnels across the border. One of the construction companies under Alliance control has purchased new earth boring equipment. Machinery capable of boring hundreds of feet of tunnel a day under the right conditions. The resulting tunnel is large enough to drive a truck through. We are presently drilling tunnels from land, ranches owned by us, several miles inside Mexico under the border to properties owned by us several miles inside the United States in California, Arizona, and New Mexico. The excavated materials are being spread on our land. To the casual observer this appears to be a typical construction site operation. Buildings are being built, concealing the entrances and exits of the tunnels, so all of our operations can proceed without attracting attention. This is the same boring machine used building hydropower tunnels and mass transit tunnels throughout the world. Are there any questions?"

A man rose from his seat and said, "I am Luis Bermudez representing Alliance members in Columbia. Angel, are there any plans for utilizing fast boats and ocean going container ships?"

Angel responded, "I know some of you use fast boats and sea-going shipping containers for delivery of some of your own shipments independent of Alliance protection. Both of those methods have too high of an intercept ratio for the Alliance to bother with them. Unless our current, abundantly successful, cross-border arrangements are stopped we, the Alliance, will not be challenging the United States Coast Guard with fast boats nor will we risk container shipments into American ports. Remember container ships and airliners leave a foreign port hours, days, even weeks before their eventual arrival in the United States. What we are doing is much safer since the personnel we deal with work set hours, which are scheduled days, sometimes weeks, in advance. We can cancel a border crossing right up to minutes before it's made utilizing our methods. There is no comparison when risk/reward is factored in. The American border security is a joke. Nighttime land border crossings west of El Paso can be made virtually at will. They are my personal favorite as long as a main highway and easy loading area is within easy walking distance from the border. East of El Paso and all along the border most of the American land ports of entry have a system in place where a frequent traveler, someone who crosses the border every day for his job, can get a free pass from inspection, which they call a Portpass card. If you don't have a criminal record and pay a small fee you can qualify for the pass. After someone gets approval for a pass of course, we make the holder of the pass an offer they can't refuse. Then we alter their vehicle to make some hiding places for our product, and just like that we have our stuff driven across the border. The Americans have lanes set aside for pass holders and we have assets in place working as the guards on these lanes. While on this subject let me explain further, the contacts in the American federal government paid by our lobbyist Abe Silverman passed the legislation enabling these passes. They held hearings and convinced their colleagues what a great idea the passes are. One of the many things these guys do on your behalf. Are there any other questions?"

Luis Bermudez asked, "I would like to tour a tunnel and inspect a plastic inner container. Is that possible?"

"I'm afraid that is not possible Luis. First, the Alliance members you represent are producers. I know the people you represent grow seventy-five percent of the world's coco leaves, and that makes you a major player. But, you have no need to know the locations of the tunnels nor do you need to see them. Second, the containers will be used between Mexico and the United States. Again, as producers your people have no need for plastic containers. You and the other producers do not have to smuggle anything into Mexico. Diego just finished briefing us all on the cooperation the Mexican government provides. It is the Mexican members, the wholesalers, who will utilize the containers and the tunnels, which I repeat are on a need-to-know basis. Is there anything else?"

When no one stood or indicated they had a question, Angel said, "Now appears to be a good time to take lunch. After lunch, at one o'clock sharp we will continue here. We will be splitting up at that time. The Mexican members, Baja Boys, Cortez Cartel, Gulf Group, and Central Syndicate will discuss wholesale operations. Diego Perez will attend that meeting to answer any inquiries requiring his expertise. The members from production countries will split into two groups. Those from South America, Bolivia, Brazil, Columbia, Ecuador, Paraguay, Peru, and Venezuela will be in one group. Members from Afghanistan, Burma, China, India, Laos, Nigeria, Pakistan, and Vietnam will form the other. Both groups, if you participate with open minds, can learn by cooperatively sharing and discussing planting, cultivating, harvesting, packing, and shipping tips which are unique to your product and geographical areas. I'm sure you will all agree these frank discussions have proven beneficial when included as part of the agendas during past annual meetings. Any questions on this afternoon's program?"

Silverman asked, "Will I be needed?"

"No Abe, it won't be necessary for you or Lisa to attend this afternoon. I suggest you enjoy the resort. That goes for everyone. Pachira Lodge offers many optional tours. When we're done with business this afternoon, simply go to the office next to the dining room to make arrangements for any activity you may want to go on. At the office you can arrange a tour of banana plantations or the turtles nesting areas, a guided boat ride through the canals, deep sea fishing, or you can walk on the beach or lounge at the pool. Please enjoy yourselves."

Chapter Seven

1:15 p.m. Mountain Time, October 9

AFTER LUNCH ABE RETURNED TO HIS cabin. Following a short power nap he decided to go lie around the pool. He changed into swim trunks, tank-top, sandals, and his Tilley wide-brimmed hat. Abe put on his sunglasses, picked up the novel he was reading during the flight yesterday, and headed out.

The pool, according to the room's visitors' guide was remotely situated at the north end of the resort. Pachira Lodge consisted of an interconnecting maze of boardwalks that wound through the resort. Abe decided to take the long way around to avoid the area where the Alliance meeting was still going on. Following the signs brought Abe to the end of the boardwalk about one hundred feet past the last cabins. Stopping to get his bearings he saw he was close to the canal. It was lonely. He felt apprehension until he remembered everyone else was at the meeting or staying out of the way avoiding it. Cautiously he stepped off the wood planking onto a gravel walkway. He followed a stone path twisting around trees and dense bushes. He walked through an opening in the dense landscaping leading to the pool complex. It appeared deserted.

Then he saw her. Lisa Strump sat on a lounge chair at the far side of the hot tub. Abe stopped and stared. It looked to him like she was naked. He didn't move, not knowing what to do. She was gorgeous. She looked up and gazed back at him. It was then he saw she had a tiny skin-colored bikini on. He waved calling out, "Hi Lisa. I guess we both had the same idea."

To his surprise she replied, "Hey Abe, come on over. There's an empty chair right here."

Abe walked over, saw there were chairs on both sides of Lisa, one in the shade of a palm tree the other in full sun. He sat in the one in the shade.

Lisa smiled at Abe and said, "I'm so glad you came, Abe. There isn't anyone else around and my front is about to get cooked even with sunscreen. I wanted to roll over but I can't spread lotion on my own back. She held out a bottle of sunscreen and asked, "Could you help me out, Abe?"

Abe who couldn't believe his good fortune took the container, smiled his friendliest smile, and said, "Sure Lisa, anything to help. Roll over."

Lisa reached behind the lounge chair, manipulated the props, and lowered the lounge flat. She lay down on her stomach, rested her head on her folded arms looking away from Abe, and told him, "Ready."

As Abe peered at Lisa's back his eyes widened, his breathing paused, the top consisted of only a skinny string, but the bottom was string too, one string across and another down the crack of her ass. Abe asked, "Where do you want me to start?"

"On my shoulders please."

He spread some lotion on her back, poured some more onto the palm of his empty hand, put the bottle down, and rubbed his hands together than started working the liquid around her shoulders. He worked his way down to the string top, lifted the string with one hand and applied lotion with the other. When he had that area covered he moved lower. He put more sunscreen on her lower back and spread it back and forth down to the top of the string across her hips. When he thought he was finished he asked, "How's that?"

Lisa replied, "The back of my legs too, please."

Abe applied lotion to first the left leg then the right leg, all the time examining Lisa's beautiful rear end. He worked his hands right up to the bottom of each cheek and stopped. "How's that?" Abe wanted to know.

Lisa turned her head looked right into Abe's eyes, smiled, and said, "If you stop now my butt will get burned. Do you mind doing my butt too please, Abe?"

"Heck no, I don't mind at all. Please don't be alarmed at the vibration. The trembling you feel is not an earthquake, it's my hands."

Abe poured a generous amount of liquid on each cheek and started spreading with both hands. Some lotion ran toward the crack of Lisa's ass and Abe slid his little fingers along each side catching it before it ran in. To think, he thought, this morning I was having my head cut off, now I'm alive, doing well, and in heaven. After lingering as long as he dared, Abe asked, "How's that?"

Lisa replied, "Fantastic Abe. I don't know what I would have done without you. Thank you so much."

"You're welcome. Glad I could be of service."

Abe propped his chair up so he could read his book in the shade. But he didn't get much reading done at all. He and Lisa hit it off well and went on and on with small talk for more than two hours. Lisa told him she met Angel six years earlier. She attended college in San Diego then. To earn extra money she worked as a hostess in a gentlemen's club. Angel came on to her one night, asked her out, she accepted. A year later when she graduated Angel asked her to come to work for the Alliance doing public relations. He started her at ten thousand dollars a month plus expenses. Now she earned five hundred sixty-four thousand dollars a year plus expenses. She owned a multi-million dollar home on the beach in Carlsbad, California. No one in her graduating class has done anywhere near as well. Abe asked if Lisa still dated Angel. She said no the relationship was purely business.

Abe didn't tell Lisa much about himself. Merely that he was single and lived in the Virginia suburbs. He also worked for the Alliance for five years. He told her he had noticed her at every yearly meeting but had been embarrassed to approach her. He was very pleased they finally met, got along so well, and were becoming friends. When he told her about his boat trip the previous evening and his regret he didn't have a camera along on the trip so he could have taken photos of all the birds and other wildlife, Lisa was enthralled. She had a camera along. She'd love to take pictures. She would e-mail him copies. She asked would he go with her before they ate dinner.

At 3:20 p.m. a young Latino man approached Abe and Lisa and said, "Meeting is over. Everyone back to work. I'm Pedro, pool boy, bartender, you want drink?"

Lisa looked at Abe who shook his head, and said, "No thanks Pedro. We're leaving."

Pedro replied, "Maybe later, this bar at pool open 'til all guests go to bed. I be here."

They gathered their belongings. Lisa put on flip-flops and a cover-up tunic over her tiny bathing suit. Abe pulled his shirt back on and slipped into his sandals. They left the pool as some Alliance members arrived.

Abe left Lisa at her cabin which was off the boardwalk on the way back to his own.

They met at the dock after they changed. Abe wore North Face khaki cargo shorts, a multi-colored Tommy Bahama Hawaii shirt, and his Tilley wide-brimmed hat. Lisa had on blue dungaree shorts, a bright orange tank top, and an orange sunhat. After Abe introduced Cisco to Lisa, they donned life vests, and took off up the river to tour the canals. Following what appeared to be the same route as yesterday Cisco headed down a tributary that went into the jungle. Cisco again steered the boat close to the edge of the waterway and pointed to some bumps protruding from the water. He said, "Miss Lisa, you see the big crocs?"

"Where?"

Abe leaned over and pointed, "Right there Lisa, see the eyes on those bumps in the water? Follow the outline right below the surface."

"Oh wow, I see them now. They're big."

Cisco then pointed to some lizards crawling on a tree trunk saying, "Miss Lisa, you see the lizards?"

She nodded yes.

"They called green iguana."

He pointed to a black and white monkey on a branch about twenty feet up the same tree saying, "Miss Lisa, that monkey called white-faced capuchin."

"Oh goodness Abe, see him? He's so cute."

Cisco steered the boat across to the other side of the channel and idled so they could look at a large black bird with a yellow chest and a lime green beak. He said, "That a Toucan."

Abe spotted several brightly colored butterflies had landed on Lisa's shirt and said, "Look Lisa, butterflies like you too. Give me the camera. You have to have a picture of this."

She reached over and handed him the camera saying, "They're so pretty. What are they Cisco?"

Cisco replied, "The grey, orange, and yellow ones with the circles with black dots in them that look like eyes, they called owl butterflies. Blue ones called morphos. Black and yellow one is swallowtail. Big black with yellow stripes, that zebra longwing."

"Why are they only on me?"

"They go to bright color hat and shirt."

Cisco guided the boat back to the middle of the river saying, "We see more birds out here."

He pointed ahead to a family of pelicans who swam out of the way. Before the afternoon was finished Lisa had pictures of crocs, monkeys, deer, a porcupine, anteater, frogs, and turtles.

Cisco slowly navigated the boat around until dark. He pointed out numerous colorful birds. He knew them all by name. There were swallows, terns, sandpipers, gulls, ducks, egrets, storks, herons, parrots, parakeets, orioles, cuckoos, hawks, and falcons.

Upon arriving back at the dock, Abe and Lisa thanked Cisco profusely. Lisa showed Cisco how to use her camera and asked him to take a picture of her and Abe. She snuggled close to Abe wrapping her arm around his waist. He put his arm over her shoulders. They smiled widely. Cisco clicked away. After Lisa reviewed the pictures Cisco had taken she kissed Cisco on the cheek, thanking him again.

Abe tipped Cisco generously and they went for dinner. It was late. Nearly everyone was gone. They filled their plates and sat alone. Abe found it easy to converse with Lisa. All he did was nod every once in a while. She went on and on about how she was so happy to have been lucky enough to meet up with Abe, and what a great day she had. All the wildlife, she never imagined this trip would be so wonderful.

After dinner Lisa reminded Abe that Pedro said the pool bar would be open. She asked if he would like to join her for a drink. Abe readily agreed. Lisa took Abe by the hand and led him off in the direction of the pool. When they walked up to the bar Pedro greeted them with a huge smile, "I knew you be back. What you want to drink?"

Lisa asked, "What do you make best Pedro? What's your specialty?"

"I recommend Cuba Libre. Absolutely my best, local rum, lime, and cola over ice in a tall glass. So tasty. Everybody like. You want to try?"

Lisa said,"Si. I want a Cuba Libre."

Abe said, "I'll have one too please Pedro."

Pedro pointed to some tables and chairs overlooking the river and said, "You go sit down. I bring drinks over."

Lisa went to a table pulled two chairs together sat in one, patted the other, and motioned Abe to join her. When Pedro brought the drinks they toasted an enjoyable day. Pedro brought several refills and Lisa carried the conversation well into the night. A little past ten Lisa announced she was getting tired and thought she should turn in. Abe, ever the gentleman took the hint. He signaled Pedro for their bill, paid it, and left a generous tip. Lisa and Abe thanked Pedro telling him he was right the Cuba Libre was absolutely the best drink. Abe then got up, reached out, and helped

Lisa to her feet. She leaned into him put her arm around him. He put his arm around her too. They said good night and started slowly out onto the dark boardwalk. Lisa told Abe she was so happy, so comfortable with him. She told him she found a friend. She said all the other men at the meeting scared her. At the first turn in the boardwalk Lisa stopped, she looked around. Abe asked, "Did we forget something?"

Lisa replied, "No, I thought I sensed someone watching. But I don't see anybody."

With that said Lisa grasped Abe's head and pulled it toward her. She kissed him hard, pushing her tongue into his mouth as far as she could. Abe wrapped his arms around her pulling her close, thinking he had no right to believe he was going to be this lucky. He closed his eyes and kissed her back. After a few minutes they continued walking. When they reached Lisa's cabin she stood facing him, took both of his hands in hers, and smiled. Abe was expecting a thank you so much for a wonderful time and a goodnight kiss. But Lisa surprised him, she said, "Abe, I hate to impose but I still have sunscreen on my back. I still can't reach back there so would you mind joining me in the shower and doing my back again?"

Abe turned, took a step away, then broke out grinning and said, "Race you to the shower."

Lisa laughed, led him to the door, unlocked it, looked again all around, then went inside pulling him behind. Lisa locked the door and dropped the curtains on all the screens. She said, "Ready?"

Abe surprised her by taking out his cell phone. He said, "Go turn the water on. Put a mat or towel on the shower floor before you step in. Those shower floors are slippery as hell. You go ahead, I'll be right there."

As he fiddled with his phone Lisa said, "Abe what the hell are you doing?"

"I'm setting my alarm for 5 a.m. There is no way I want to be asleep when those howler monkeys go off in the morning."

Lisa chuckled, "Silly boy, you think I'm going to let you sleep?"

Angel stood alone in the dark, watching. He had watched them for the last two hours, holding hands, laughing, kissing. He brooded over the day's events—those asshole Alliance members who nickel and dimed necessary expenditures, wanted names and details that were none of their business revealed; paranoid thoughts went through his mind—smiling on the outside, raging on the inside.

Double crossing skimmer.

Screw him.
Screw his girlfriend.
Fucking slut.
Bastard. Hope you like sloppy seconds.

Angel mumbled to himself, "Enjoy your night you cocksucker. As soon as I don't need your connections anymore I'm gonna cut your fuckin' head off."

Chapter Eight

10:20 a.m. Mountain Time, October 10

THE GREEN ESCALADE DROVE SLOWLY IN an easterly direction along Speedway Boulevard in downtown Tucson. They were in an older, seedy looking section of the city. Andrew Thompson extended his hand with one finger out saying, "Vern's Audio, there it is. Make the next right and park. We'll walk back. There is no sense in letting anybody from the store see our car."

Emmett turned onto Herbert Avenue and pulled over. They got out, locked up, set the alarm, and walked back to Vern's. When they opened the door and stepped inside a buzzer went off. The buzzing stopped when they stepped off the mat on the floor immediately inside the entry. As they approached a glass counter a man with a flowing mane of pale white hair came through a curtain across an opening to the back. He said, "Hello, what can I do for you?"

Andrew asked, "Are you Vern?"

"Yes."

Andrew said, "I'm Bobby Brown. This is Joe Woych. I called. We have a ten-thirty appointment."

Vern replied, "You're the cops from Yuma with the capture the flag game problem. You have a recording you need enhanced. Do you have it with you?"

Andrew held the recorder in his hand and said, "Its right here."

"Oh, nice, a Sony Pro model, a great machine. That puppy shouldn't be any problem. Let's go into the back."

Andrew and Emmett followed Vern into a well-lit workshop. The centerpiece was a workbench in front of a large array of electronic equipment. Vern sat down in a comfortable padded swivel rocker chair on rollers. He pointed to a couple of regular office chairs saying, "Sit down. As I understand it Mister Brown you guys want to wait. Correct?"

Andrew said, "Call me Bobby. And yes we want to wait. It shouldn't take long, right?"

"Let me see what you have."

Andrew handed the recorder to Vern saying, "It's a long recording, over three hours, but…"

Vern interrupted, "Over three hours is going to take a long time. I have to listen to the whole thing, determine what conversation is easily heard, what portions are impaired, and which impaired audio can be enhanced. Then clean it up. This could take all day."

"No that's not what we want. Let me finish explaining, please. The recorder continuously runs for over three hours but there is very little dialog. A few minutes of talk on the whole tape. Some of those few minutes are not understandable. That's where you come in. That's what we want enhanced."

"Okay. Do you know where those spots are on the recorder, or do I have to find them myself?"

Andrew turned to Emmett and asked, "Joe where's the list of times you wrote down?"

Emmett put a sheet of paper on the workbench in front of Vern. Knowing they did not want Vern to hear Sam Comfort's introduction Em said, "There is nothing for the first seventy-nine minutes. Some talk starts at the eighty minute mark, then some whispering at eighty-eight minutes. You can hear something in the distance at ninety minutes, then there is a low but understandable conversation at ninety-eight minutes. Then you have to fast forward to the one hundred forty-four minute mark. There are several minutes of muffled conversation at that point. That is the portion we need enhanced so it is understandable. At one hundred fifty minutes there are a few more understandable words. It's all written down on this sheet of paper."

Vern asked, "All right Joe, I've got all that. Now let me ask you, does anybody speak at a normal tone on the recording at all? A couple of words even. It will make my job a lot easier if there is."

Emmett responded, "Yes at the one hundred fifty minute mark someone says '*Ven comigo.* Come with me.' in as normal tones as you are going to get."

"Okay Joe so from the eighty minute mark to the ninety-eight minute mark, and from one hundred forty-four minutes to one hundred fifty-one minutes that's what we're working on, correct?"

"Yes that's about it."

"Okay. Bobby you agree, correct?"

"Yes, whatever Joe said. He wrote down the time frame."

Vern pointed to a coffee machine and refrigerator saying, "You fellers help yourselves to coffee. There's cream, soda pop, and water in the fridge if you want any. There's cups and sugar in the tray. I'm going to get busy."

Vern flipped some switches on the equipment in front of him, turned on Sam Comfort's recorder, fast forwarded to seventy-nine minutes, and plugged a wire into a port in the recorder bottom. He put on headphones, turned some dials, and leaned back. He had a notepad and jotted down numbers until the counter read one hundred minutes. Then he fast forwarded to one hundred forty-four minutes and pressed play. He continued writing down notes. At one hundred fifty-two minutes he stopped the recorder. He rewound to one hundred fifty minutes and replayed the last two minutes again. He said, "All right, we have a really nice audio waveform display. You can plainly see the highs and the lows. We have an excellent variation from the normal range, lower voices, whispers, stationary sounds, and inaudible conversations. The multi-channel hearing aid enables me to average the compression ranges, increasing some of the hearing thresholds in order to achieve a higher gain of the low level sounds."

Vern twisted a couple of dials, pressed a few buttons, made some contorted faces, then sat back with his eyes closed. An hour and ten minutes after he started, Vern announced, "I think I have it."

Andrew and Emmett sat down. Vern asked, "Ready?"

Both Andrew and Emmett nodded they were. Vern said, "Okay I'm starting."

Sam Comfort could be heard, "It's about twenty past one in the morning. We have just heard some new sounds. We have become accustomed to the sounds made by small desert creatures and wind moving vegetation. This is different."

Sam, now whispering, "Someone is near. We can hear movement down on the trail. I can see movement. Be back later."

"They're here. Lots of them. More than a hundred. Some have guns."

"Oh darn. They've stopped right in front of our position."

"Sniff."

"Ida, stop."

"Ah choo!"

"Cover your mouth. Oh poop, they heard you."

"Damn, they're pointing up here."

What had been an inaudible sound now was understood as, "There is someone up there."

Then Sam said, "Get down. Be quiet. Maybe they won't find us."

After a slight pause Sam can be heard again, "We give up. Ida put your hands up. We mean no harm. Friends, Amigos, we amigos."

Another voice, gruffly, "Not another word. Stand up. Quietly now, go down the hill."

Ida can then be heard saying, "We mean no harm. Please leave us alone."

"Quiet or I'll cut your throat, bitch."

Sam whispered, "Ida stop crying. Be quiet, please."

Another voice said, "Be quiet. Don't speak unless you are answering me. Who else is here?"

"No one else is here. One man brought us here. He went away, left us alone, and said he would be back for us before dawn. Please don't hurt us."

After a period, about five minutes, with only sounds of shuffling, someone said, "*Vamanos.* Let's go."

Vern stopped the player and said, "That's the first part. It all sounds pretty awful. Who's going to cut whose throat?"

Andrew said, "Nobody. Those people are newspaper reporters doing a story on the Yuma cops versus Yuma firefighters annual paintball game. Those shitheads sounding bad are firemen trying to scare the civilians. They did scare them too. Fact is, they roughed them up, pushed them around a little bit before releasing them later. You'll hear it. When we spoke to the civilians afterward they said they were never so scared in their lives. But move on, it's the next part we really want to hear. I think I told you the border patrol referees the paintball competition. Our "Capture the Flag" game is a highly realistic contest between the departments. Officially, as it stands right now we lost. But we think the firemen got to the border guys. They illegally influenced the referees. That's why we want to hear the rest of what we couldn't understand. Come on, Move on."

Vern said, "I'm ready as soon as you stop talking Bobby."

Andrew replied, "Sorry. Please understand, I hate to lose, even if it's only a game. Go ahead."

What sounded like the other voice from earlier said, "Sorry to bother you Jefe, but there is a situation. No. No big deal. We took two prisoners who we found hiding off the trail, watching us. Two people, a man and a woman. They claim to be reporters researching a story. What should I do with them?"

After a pause, "As you say Jefe. I'll take care of them Jefe. Good night."

Then different voices, a woman saying, "You can't leave them. They've seen us."

"Be quiet Maria."

"Don't tell her that."

"You too Connie."

"Who made you boss Leon?"

Then the earlier voice came back, "It will be taken care of."

One of the women again, "They can't be allowed to say they saw us."

"Relax; we'll take care of it."

The guy, Leon, "Come on, I don't like standing around here. Cops or border patrol could come by anytime."

"Don't worry about that either. The cops are all sleeping or someplace else, and the border patrol are bought and paid for. There is no chance of us or you getting caught tonight."

Another different voice broke in saying, "Yeah the big border guy does what we tell him. He's got all his men twenty miles away. "

"What are you going to do about the couple you caught spying?"

"That's none of your business. I already told you it will be taken care of. Get in the vans and get out of here. An example will be made. You have nothing to fear from anybody here. Now take your people, get in the vans, and get out of here. You have a long trip."

After a pause of several minutes, the voice resumes, "Ali, El Jefe wants you to take a few men and walk those spies down a mile or so. Do them so when they're found others will get the message and nobody will want to interfere with us ever again."

"Si. I'll do it now."

Then a voice said, "*Ven comigo.* Come with me."

After many more minutes of sounds of movement, walking, they heard the distinct grunting, thumping, and bumping of a struggle.

Then the words, "*Terminado.* It's done. *Vamanos.*"

Another pause, then, "Oh my God."

Vern stopped the player and said, "I think that is as clear as you're going to get it. Sounds to me like the border patrol refs are on the firemen's side. Is that it? You guys happy?"

Andrew said, "Oh yeah. We have the goods on those cheating firefighters now. Arguing amongst themselves like children. They say right on the tape the border guys, the referees, are miles away. The capture the flag trophy will go back to police headquarters now, for sure. Thank you Vern great job. We're going to need three copies of the enhanced tape and two copies of the original, okay?"

"All right, I'll print three enhanced chips and two originals. You're paying cash for this right?"

"Yes, what's the damage, Vern?"

"Let's see, a hundred for the use of the equipment and eighty-five per hour for two hours, plus fifty bucks for five chips. Is that okay Bobby, three hundred twenty dollars?"

Andrew put three hundreds and a twenty on the workbench and said, "Three twenty is fine Vern. Thank you Vern, the prompt excellent service is appreciated. In fact, the Yuma Police Department paint ball team is in your eternal debt."

As they approached the front door Andrew turned. He asked, "Vern do you have a local yellow pages I can use?'

Vern reached behind the counter came out with a book saying, "Got one right here. What else do you need?"

"We have a movie chip we want duplicated. Know anyone local you can recommend?"

"A straight dup, nothing elaborate?"

"Yeah, a couple copies of a home video."

Vern opened the yellow pages and pointed to an ad. He said, "This is the place where I take my stuff. Go east on Speedway, you'll pass the University of Arizona campus, make a right on Country Club Road, Mel's Video is the second door on the right. Can't miss it, number four fifty-five"

Chapter Nine

2:10 p.m. Mountain Time, October 10

As ANDREW AND EMMETT STEPPED OUT of the Bisbee Community Bank after depositing the originals and all the copies of both the audio and video chips into the Thompson safety deposit box, Andrew's cell phone went off. He answered, "This is Andy."

After listening quietly he said, "Sure Ed I'm with Emmett now. We'll come right over. We're in town. About ten minutes, okay."

"Bye."

Turning his phone off Andrew told Emmett, "Ed says there have been developments in the Comfort case he wants to discuss with us. He said he doesn't talk over the phone about ongoing cases and he asked that we come in. I told him we could be at his office in ten minutes."

Emmett asked, "He didn't ask for Phil or Carl, just us?"

"Yeah, only us."

"Well let's go see what he wants."

During the short ride to the sheriff's station Andrew could sense Emmett was nervous and asked about it. Emmett said, "I hate not knowing. Could he possibly have found out we have the recording and video?"

"No Em, I'm sure Vern bought our bullshit and Mel's simply copied the chips. I can't conceive how Ed could know about any of that. Let's see what he wants. If either of us feels uncomfortable we'll lawyer up, okay."

"Yeah, I sure don't want to say much."

They parked in one of the spaces set aside for visitors, walked up some steps, entered the low white building's front door, and approached a receptionist. They introduced themselves and were told to take a seat she would let the sheriff know they were there. Shortly after the receptionist spoke softly into her phone Ed Mata-Villa came through a door with another man. Assistant Sheriff Rich Farrell was slightly taller than the sheriff but much thinner. Andrew and Emmett stood, shook hands with the sheriff and Farrell. Mata-Villa said, "Glad you guys could come in so quickly. Follow me. We'll go someplace more private. Em you go with Rich, Andy you come with me."

Emmett and Andy stopped dead in their tracks. Andrew said, "Hold up Ed we're not separating. You want to speak with us we go together."

Farrell responded, "Is there a problem talking to us alone?"

"Damn right there is. It isn't gonna happen. You want us alone, we want lawyers."

"Lawyers, you do something you need a lawyer for?"

"Ed, who the fuck does this guy think he's talking to? We want to help in any way we can. But we stay together or we're out of here. What's it going to be?"

Mata-Villa smiled and said, "It's typical when we question two witnesses we do it separately. Sometimes people remember things differently and if a discrepancy comes up we stay at it until it gets cleared up. That's all, no problem, if you don't want to be separated, stay together. Let me ask you though, do you mind if Rich sits in? The reason I want him there is in case I forget to cover a detail, he can remind me."

"He can sit in."

That settled they all went back through the door and walked down the hall to Mata-Villa's office. Once inside Farrell closed the door and sat in a chair against the wall next to the door. Andy and Emmett sat in front of the big desk that dominated the room. Mata-Villa took his seat behind his desk. Through a wall of glass behind the sheriff was the beautiful view of Arizona mountains, sunshine, and clouds. He asked, "Anybody want anything, soda, coffee, water?"

Everyone declined so he started, "Let's go over what happened the other morning shall we. Stop me if I don't have it right. Andrew you dropped the Comforts off by themselves in the evening and the following morning you received an anonymous phone call telling you where you could find the bodies. You didn't call the report into this office when you received it but instead drove out with Emmett, Philip, and Carl. When you located the bodies you used your phone to call me and the border patrol. When we arrived at the scene Emmett and Philip had gone off picking up trash. You didn't mention they had driven out with you and were wandering around. After everyone left the scene you and Carl met up with Em and Philip at the Hernandez place. The border guys came upon you four, a disagreement occurred, I received a call to go back, and had to separate the border patrol and Thompson factions. That's it right? Do you want to add anything?"

"That pretty much sums it up but I didn't try to mislead anyone about Em and Phil I simply forgot to mention them. I was concerned with the Comforts. It slipped my mind. Now you said on the phone there were new developments. What's new?"

"What's new is Sam Comfort's cell phone was in his pocket. We were able to confirm the last call made on it was to you at three fifty-one in the morning on October eighth."

"You figure the killer called me?"

"We figure it was either the killer or a witness."

"You have a witness?"

"No, not yet."

"So whose prints did you find on the phone?"

"Nobody's, the phone was wiped clean."

"So you are no further ahead solving this?"

Mata-Villa crossed his beefy forearms, leaned back, opened a file, perused some photos and papers and said, "I didn't say that. We retrieved fingerprints off the clothes on the bodies. The fact is the Comforts dressed with layers. They wore matching exterior outermost garments; dark rain gear jackets made out of a smooth lightweight waterproof rubbery material. Although not an ideal surface, we found identifiable latent fingerprints."

"Whose?"

"We recovered the prints of the cousins who beat Puggy Puga to death. Their prints were on the clothes"

"Well lock them the fuck up, Ed. Tell me they are in jail."

"No, we don't have them. And their fingerprints don't prove anything. We need more."

"Why do you need more? Lock them up."

"It isn't that simple, Andy."

"Why not, you have their prints on the bodies. They're killers, cartel enforcers."

"Andy, there were more fingerprints found."

"Whose?"

"Sam and Ida's but they're expected. Four sets of unknowns. We're still trying to identify those. And then there's yours and Emmett's. That is one of the reasons we wanted to talk to you both."

"What do you mean that's why you wanted to talk to us. You prick, I thought I could trust you. You suck. This is why you wanted to separate us. You wanted to try to trick us."

"I'm not trying to trick you. I want you to understand that I'm not going to lock you up because your prints were found on the Comforts' clothing. Same holds for the Castanedas. Simply because their prints were on the bodies, that doesn't prove jack shit."

"Ed you know God damn well that we found the bodies. Of course we touched them. Em rolled them over so we could identify them. But he threw up. He couldn't continue so I inspected the bodies to see how they died. You see, easily explained. All you had to do was ask."

"Andy stop bullshitting me. Emmett didn't simply roll the bodies over. He rolled Ida over. On the other hand he searched Sam. His prints are all over Sam's clothes, especially the pockets, like he was looking for something. Em, why did you search Sam? What were you looking for?"

Emmett spoke for the first time. He responded, "I was looking for Sam's wallet. I tried to figure out if they robbed him or not. His wallet and cash were both in his pockets. It wasn't robbery."

Andrew broke in saying, "Enough Em. Don't say anymore. You answered the question."

Ed said to Farrell, "Did I miss anything Rich?"

"Well I'd like to know if either of you took anything from either body?"

Andy replied, "No."

Farrell asked, "How about you Emmett?"

"No."

Farrell said, "That's all I've got."

Andy asked, "Ed you said earlier the fingerprints were one of the things you wanted to talk to us about. What else is there?"

"I wanted to let you know about Hector and Aliberto Castaneda. If the Castanedas were involved, and it certainly appears they may have been, your family has to be extremely careful."

"Why would they want to bother us? We don't know anything and we didn't see anything. We certainly don't want to attract any attention. Let me ask you, what are you going to do next, any leads?"

Farrell responded, "First, while you may not want to attract attention, the fact your fingerprints were found on the bodies has to go into the report. To answer your question, we are launching an investigation into the backgrounds of the Comforts. There had to be a reason for the cousins to come after them. We know they went after Puggy because he was caught skimming by El Jefe, and we know the Rynnings were eliminated because they witnessed the Puggy murder and agreed to make identifications and testify."

Andrew raged, "Are you nuts? Don't you think it is much more logical to assume Sam and Ida were in the wrong place at the wrong time and observed something that got them killed? Shouldn't you be looking at that possibility?"

"Yeah sure, we're looking at that aspect too, but like we have said all along, no witness pretty much curtails progress on that theory. You are positive neither of you can tell us any more, right?"

Andy and Emmett both shook their heads, Andrew said, "No nothing more."

Mata-Villa stood up and said, "Thank you both for coming in. Say hello to Philip and Carl please."

Andy asked, "One more thing Ed, what is Border Patrol Deputy Chief John Marrone doing about this case?"

"Nothing, this department is doing the investigation. They're busy with the border and highway checkpoints. We will copy him with our report and we will get a copy of his. But I can tell you without seeing it, his report is simply going to confirm he visited the crime scene and determined the case belonged to this office."

"Actually I have one more question. Who was patrolling that area for the sheriff's office that night?"

"Nobody."

"What do you mean nobody? You had to have somebody on patrol."

"No Andy, we don't have deputies on patrol at night. The Sierra Vista substation is the only station manned twenty-four hours a day with live people. The Douglas substation goes on on-call status from midnight until six in the morning. Douglas, like the other four unmanned substations, has a local deputy subject to on-call status. Deputies are required to reside within a thirty minute drive of their station of assignment. Everybody knows that."

"Not everybody Ed. I didn't know your deputies are all home snuggled in bed at night. Who protects the citizens?"

"Usually the local city police cover first. We get called only on a need basis. Which doesn't happen often. Fact is I can't remember the last time we had to get an on-call deputy out of bed to handle an emergency. I don't want to rush you but if that's it I have work to do. Thanks again for coming right in. You men remember anything else call please. Bye now."

After the meeting Emmett had Andrew drop him off at the main fire station. He had a forty-eight hour shift starting at four that afternoon and didn't have time to drive home and back. During the drive to the firehouse, Andy told Emmett he was scared stiff about leveling with Eddie. Nobody local could be trusted, not even Ed. He asked Emmett if he thought his friend in Washington would help. Emmett agreed to make the call. He said he would step outside the firehouse to make the call early tomorrow morning. He knew his friend always arrived at the office early and east coast time was two hours later than theirs. He would let his dad know how things went.

Chapter Ten

5:41 a.m. Mountain Time, October 11

THE SHINY NEW FORD MUSTANG RACED east on Highway 96, past the Elmwood Golf Course and the Pueblo Community College. There was hardly any traffic so early, but the driver slowed on occasion anyway. Wet spots could be icy this time of year. The bright red car turned into a diner parking lot on the corner of Santa Fe Avenue and came to a stop in a space near the well lit entrance. Looking around, not observing many vehicles he recognized, Leon Huerta realized he was early again. That was his reputation, earned over many years, always prompt or ahead of time. He had been out of town and missed several meetings, which he would be fined ten dollars each for. He certainly didn't want to be fined another ten bucks for being late. While waiting for others to show up, Leon reminisced about his successes. It has been pretty hectic since imam's visit, he thought. After coming back across the border he and his cousins had stayed at the Postada Hotel in Las Cruces, New Mexico, taking a Greyhound bus overnight back to Pueblo, Colorado, yesterday. This morning hopefully everything would be back to normal. At ten minutes before six Leon decided to make his entrance. He hurried through the parking lot door into Henny's Diner. A handsome well built young man with fashionably styled pitch black short hair and flashing black eyes wearing a uniform consisting of creased blue pants and a white button down shirt emblazoned on one pocket with the name Huerta's Auto Body Shop and the name Leon on the other stepped inside. Leon took the stairs two at a time smiling widely as he approached the sergeant-at-arms table right inside the private upstairs banquet room. Dave Attig greeted him saying, "Leon buddy, we've missed you. How have you been pal?"

Leon replied, "I'm doin' fine Dave. I missed you guys too. How are you doin'?"

Dave Attig tapped the large bowl on the table saying, "I'm doing okay, but you missed the last four meetings Leon. That's forty bucks you owe the fine jar."

Leon dropped two twenties into the jar and remarked, "All for a good cause. See you later Dave."

All the members knew the fines were used to finance different charitable events. No one complained. It was all in fun.

Leon then strode over to a round table set for eight. Before taking his seat he said, "Good morning everyone. How are you all doing this fine day?"

One by one the occupants of the other chairs at the table reached to shake Leon's hand. Walter Goff, wearing a uniform declaring he was Pueblo's police chief, said, "Hey Leon, we missed you. Glad to have you back."

Bobby Westbrook, Pueblo's mayor, elegantly dressed in suit and tie, somberly asked, "Leon did the family business go well?"

Leon replied, "Oh yeah, everything is good. Thanks for asking Bob."

Kyle Olinda, also wearing a workman's uniform similar to Leon's, was president of the area's largest plumbing contractors, Olinda Mechanical Contracting. He said, "Morning Leon. Good to see you."

Herb Nunez, a young reporter about thirty years old who worked for the Pueblo Times, told him, "Good morning Leon. Just want you to know how concerned we all are for you and yours. Glad you're back."

Sidney Korash, the Huerta's business attorney said, "Give me a call if you need anything."

Jeremy Boss, the Westside High School football coach, six foot five inches tall, trim and fit, clothed in a grey team sweat suit, walked around the table. He greeted Leon with a big hug saying, "Missed you Leon. Hope to see you Friday night. Big game, for the city title, we need all the fans we can get."

Leon said, "I know I'll be there, Jer. Wouldn't miss it."

James Joseph Katella, the dentist Leon and all of his cousins went to, came forward last. He said, "What a beautiful smile. Glad to have your smiling face back Leon. It has been tough the last few weeks only having these mugs to look at so early."

Everyone laughed as Leon took his seat. The waitress brought him coffee and orange juice, his normal. He ordered eggs over easy, bacon, home fries, and rye toast. Harvey Taitz, owner of Belmont Ford located on Bonforte Boulevard and president of the club, presided over the meeting this morning. Dressed in jeans and a loud multi-colored sweater Harvey sat at the center of the head table. He rapped a gavel on the table and announced, "Okay everybody quiet down, grab a seat. This morning's meeting of the Pueblo Central Sunrise Rotary Club is now in order."

He motioned to the sergeant-at-arms saying, "David come sit up here. Bring the fine jar with you. I have some news that is going to cost me some money."

Once the movement stopped Taitz continued, "Before we start the regular meeting I have some good news and some bad news. The bad news is Leon has been missing for the past several weeks. I don't think he minds me saying he and his siblings had family problems they had to attend to. You all know their shop closed down while they took care of their personal business. That doesn't cost me any money but the good news will. Leon is back. The shop will be re-opened today. That is a business plug and costs me ten bucks."

The crowd howled, "Feed the jar."

Taitz dropped ten dollars in the jar and said, "That's not all folks. I also have to tell you about the goodness in the hearts of the Huertas as I'm sure Leon never will."

Everyone in the room now paid strict attention. Taitz went on, "Yesterday started as another dismal day for Belmont Ford. Times have been extremely tough for us the last few months as I'm sure it has been for everybody. But after lunch things began looking up. That's because Leon and his nine relatives walked into the showroom. They had been in Las Cruces for their family problems, a funeral of one of the family's senior members I understand. A funeral we are all aware of or at least should be. What you all don't know is the extended Huerta family members are not nearly as successful as the locals. They are poor and needy. Your friends, our neighbors, the local Huertas gave their cars to the neediest of the relatives who had gathered in Las Cruces. They were left without a ride back here. They took a bus back to Pueblo. When they arrived led by Leon all ten of the Huertas walked from the Greyhound stop on Chinook Lane down Hunter Drive to my place. They came in and leased ten new Fords. Leon gave me a check for north of thirty thousand dollars. That my friends, is the type of people the Huertas are. I am proud to know them as I'm sure you are. In conclusion I am dropping another hundred into the fine jar. Ten bucks for each of the ten car leases."

Again the group called, "Feed the jar. Feed the jar."

With the jar fed and the wait staff bringing out the food Taitz announced, "Before we eat, one more thing is in order. Everybody please join me in a chorus of 'For He's a Jolly Good Fellow.'"

Following Taitz' lead everyone stood and sang a rousing tribute to Leon Huerta.

Leon enjoyed the atmosphere immensely although he had a hard time maintaining a straight face because much of the small talk during breakfast touched on the recently failed Latino secession and the nuclear explosions that occurred in the southwest. Leon went along with whomever he conversed with, lamenting the state of the country, wondering how such events could happen. For sure all the early riser Rotarians loved everyone else. Before leaving after the meeting was over Leon exchanged pleasantries and shook hands all around. He tried to make sure he didn't overlook anyone.

Once outside in the now bright sunlight, Leon sped off in his flashy bright red Mustang. Leaving the diner he made a right, continued driving east on Highway 96 until it merged with Highway 50 where he turned right then a quick left at the Frontage Road exit. Huerta's Auto Body Shop was situated in an industrial park accessed from Frontage Road directly across from Pueblo Memorial Airport. He was still early. None of his cousins had arrived yet. He opened up, immediately removed the closed sign from the window, went to the rear office, brewed a fresh pot of coffee, turned on the TV news, and sat with his feet up reading the newspaper he got out of the machine at Henny's.

When the others arrived he reported everyone at the Rotary bought their story. They all laughed at the stupidity of the song. How gullible these dumb Americans are. Maria was told to expect the same experiences at her Kiwanis luncheon the following day. Roberto said he anticipated similar at his Lions Club dinner meeting the evening after Maria's lunch. They agreed their story should fly. After all, the Huertas had long been associated with service clubs, the Chamber of Commerce, and various charities around town. They were known as real nice people. Respected by everyone.

Chapter Eleven

6:23 p.m. Eastern Time, October 16

Shortly after his and Andrew's meeting with Sheriff Ed Mata-Villa and Assistant Sheriff Rich Farrell, Em reported to work. Early the next morning, while the other firefighters on duty slept, Em went outside the firehouse and called his friend Ed Grass.

It was seven in the morning in Washington. Em explained the situation in Arizona and asked for help. Grass readily agreed taking a commercial flight could be traced to Emmett, needlessly exposing him and his family members to violence. Bringing a trash bag with ten empty water bottles through airport security would definitely arouse suspicion, resulting in questions being asked, unwanted attention by security and onlookers. Checked baggage could also be inspected, resulting in the same problems. Either method could result in security personnel handling the evidence. A better idea was a private plane—no security check, no record of who flew—and Grass had such a plane at his disposal.

Three days later, during the late morning lull at Tucson International, Andrew Thompson dropped Emmett, wearing a sunhat shading his face and sunglasses over his eyes, at the entrance to the terminal for private flights in Tucson. Ed Grass, as promised, had a private business plane waiting. Within minutes Em was ushered onto a luxury jet. The cabin crew got him comfortably settled. They took off immediately. Once cruising altitude was reached the seat belt light was turned off Emmett rose up and looked around. The cabin steward, Jeff, advised they provided the ultimate in cabin comfort for up to nineteen passengers. The main compartment was outfitted with huge recliners, big screen televisions, work tables, and computer stations. Jeff offered lunch, which Em accepted. He was served a roast beef sandwich, chips, and diet cola.

After he finished lunch Em reminisced about his friend. Emmett had served two tours of duty as a member of an elite Army Special Forces Team in the Middle East. One of the men he spent many lonely nights in the desert with was Ed Grass. He knew his friend better than most. Grass was a six five, two hundred sixty-five pound, athletically built, former Pennsylvania high school all-state linebacker. He had been awarded a full scholarship to play football at Holy Cross in Massachusetts where he became the first sophomore elected by his peers to be the defensive captain of the team. Upon graduation from Holy Cross, Grass told Emmett he had turned down a lucrative contract to play professional football with the Philadelphia Eagles, deciding instead to attend Georgetown Law School in Washington, D.C. Two years later when Grass completed the requisite coursework and passed the American Bar Association exams he again turned down huge money offers this time to enter corporate law practice in the Capital. Instead he enlisted in the United States Army Officer Training School. After being assigned as a second lieutenant to the army's Judge Advocate General (JAG) headquarters for twenty-four months and after learning the nuances of military law, Grass had been promoted to first lieutenant and attached to an Army Special Forces Team about to be deployed into the Afghanistan, Pakistan, Iran, Iraq theatre primarily to hunt down terrorists.

For the next two years Grass served alongside Thompson. Em knew Ed Grass had distinguished himself exhibiting countless acts of bravery under fire. Em and Grass separated after Grass was promoted in the field to captain and assigned his own command. His team excelled in bombing investigations and suspect interrogation. Under his command, his team also ran countless successful hostage rescue operations in the field, tracking kidnap victims, freeing most after negotiations or sniper work. His expertise became well known, leading to his advancement to major and bringing him to assignments world-wide. On the few occasions where his group failed and hostages were lost, the hostage takers were always eventually taken, dead or alive. Em knew from reading various news reports over the years that on many occasions, foreign governments disbelieved the after-action reports filed by Grass' teams regarding the extremely poor apprehension rate of live bad guys. He also knew despite the doubts raised, no accusations of wrongdoing or mishandling of prisoners were ever proven against Grass or his men.

Emmett knew after Grass finished his tour, he returned to Washington, D.C. He had been promoted to colonel and assigned as a military attaché, working in conjunction with the Department of Homeland Security, the FBI and CIA pursuing domestic threats. Emmett remembered sending a congratulatory note to his friend at the time.

Two years later, the president had figured out he needed to be able to call upon and direct a group of men and women with special training and field experience when the need for people with their specific expertise arose. The Congress agreed to form a Special Operations group for this purpose. Only thirty-three at the time, Ed Grass was appointed to lead that group. Again Em sent a note.

Today, at forty-one years of age, Grass has held the position of Director of Special Operations since its inception and is to this day the youngest member of the president's cabinet. He's the one person Emmett knew he could trust with the knowledge he possessed about the drug smugglers and their possible connections in the Border Patrol.

After watching a full circuit of headline news and enjoying a brief nap, a cold bottle of water and a warm damp face towel were provided by Jeff. Jeff also suggested Em take a left side window seat where he could get the best view of Washington. After a fasten seat belts announcement and prepare for landing Em noticed a drop in speed and loss in altitude.

Emmett looked out the window as the plane passed over the Washington, D.C. area. The pilot had announced he was flying as close to the city as regulations allowed. He said wind conditions determined their final approach for landing and today air traffic controllers working their plane had instructed them to come in from the west. This pattern brought them over the Potomac River on the south side of the city. Although the sun was setting rapidly and lights were coming on, the view of the nation's capital always stirred patriotic feelings in most Americans. Emmett included.

As the plane touched down Emmett observed numerous military aircraft parked and taxiing about. After landing the pilot taxied up to and into one of the many hangers. As soon as the engines shut down, Jeff directed Em to exit through the door where he had boarded. Em retrieved his luggage, thanked Jeff, and went down the staircase that ground attendants rolled up to the plane. Waiting for him at the base of the stairs was a large man, his face grinning from ear to ear, with his arms outstretched. Ed Grass said, "Welcome Emmett. It is so good to see you. How are you? How was your flight?"

Emmett Thompson replied, "Ed it is so good of you to see me. It has been way too long. The flight was fantastic. How are you?"

"I'm fine Em, especially since you're here now. Did everything go off okay? Any problems? Anyone see you?

"Everything went well. No problems and I don't think anybody saw or took notice of me at all. Where are we? Which airport is this?"

"We're in D.C., or to be specific, close to it. This is Andrews Air Force Base. Andrews is in Maryland, eight miles from Washington. It's totally secure. It's where the president flies in and out of. I figured if it was secure enough for him you'd be safe."

"I'll be safe as long as no one knows I have what I have. Do you want everything now?"

Grass said, "Let's get you settled first. You have only those two bags?"

"Yes, just the two. The bottles and caps are in one bag. I have the video and audio chips in my pocket."

Grass led the way to a black Lincoln Town Car limousine. A huge man, about thirty years old, six four, two hundred fifty pounds, whom Grass introduced as Al Garcia, opened the trunk and reached for the bags. He placed them in the trunk, closed it and opened the rear door of the Lincoln, motioning Emmett inside. Grass entered into the back through the other door. Al settled into the driver's seat and started the car. Grass said, "Al, you know where Em is staying. Drive us over there would you please."

As the car pulled out of the hanger Grass explained, "We're going to put you up in a private room with a bath in the unmarried officer's housing on base. That is about as private and secure lodging you will get here in D.C. Once we get you into your room we'll go to the Andrew's Officer's Club for dinner. We'll pick you up here in the morning, take you into the office, review everything you have, and plan a course of action. We have underground parking at the office. This car, besides being bullet-proof, has tinted glass you can't see into. Nobody but my most trusted people will catch even a glimpse of you. That okay?"

"That's great, Ed."

Garcia exited the hanger complex onto East Perimeter Road turned south, continued through Andrews Air Force Base Golf Course on South Perimeter road turning left onto Virginia Avenue, a quiet residential street. Another left into a parking lot brought them to the base housing for visiting officers. The three men climbed out of the Lincoln. Garcia retrieved Em's luggage from the trunk and led the way into number 27 Virginia Avenue, an attached townhouse, surrounded by well-kept shrubbery. After opening the door Garcia handed the key to Emmett, walked through the living room and placed the bags on the king-size bed in the bedroom. Acting like the bellman in an exclusive hotel Garcia opened the drapes exposing French doors which led to a private patio overlooking the eighteenth fairway of the East Course, one of three courses in the complex. Garcia pointed to the bathroom and led Thompson and Grass back into the living room and to the fully-equipped kitchen the east wall of which also had French doors leading to a table and chairs on the patio adjoining the golf course. He said, "Everything is here for you to use if you want to prepare your own meals, but if you prefer, the Andrews Golf Clubhouse is directly across the street. It's open from six in the morning until midnight. The restaurant in the clubhouse is excellent. Or you can call room service 24/7 if you would rather do that."

Grass interrupted, "Al that's enough. Em's not going to be here that long. In fact Em would you give Al the bottles, caps, and chips please?"

"Give them to Al?'

"Yes, Al can take them into the lab while we have dinner. We will then have the results in the morning when we get to the office."

Emmett retrieved the trash bag and handed it to Garcia. He took the chips out of his pocket and handed them over saying, "Al, the bottles and caps have prints on them and hopefully, DNA on the bottle mouths of people we hope to identify. The original video chip has numerous facial frames the lab needs to enhance and hopefully then be able to identify the people. The original audio tape is labeled, as is the already enhanced copy. Your lab should enhance the original in case our guy missed anything."

Garcia looked to Grass who nodded, "Call me when you are coming back in the front gate, Al. I'll let you know then if we are here or still at the clubhouse. Em and I have a lot of catching up to do."

Garcia waved as he walked out the door. He said, "I'll call later."

Once Garcia left Grass asked, "What do you want to do Em. You want to call for food to be delivered here or go to the clubhouse?"

"I'm all for the fancy restaurant Ed. We don't have too many opportunities like this in Bisbee."

Chapter Twelve

6:53 a.m. Eastern Time, October 17

EMMETT THOMPSON ANSWERED THE KNOCK ON the door ready to go. He looked good, dressed in his Macy's gray wool suit, white dress shirt, red and blue striped tie, black Gold Toe socks, and black Johnson and Murphy lace-ups. Even an Arizona outdoorsman who worked as a fireman needed proper attire for somber occasions and business meetings. He said, "Good morning, Mister Garcia."

Al Garcia said, "You ready to go?"

"Yep."

"Okay then, let's go. And Emmett, we were introduced last night. No more Mister Garcia. My friends call me Al, Big A, or Albert. Ed told me a lot about you and I hope you'll consider me a friend."

"All right Al, and please call me Em."

"I will. No problem."

Once they arrived at the Lincoln Garcia opened the rear door and said, "You can get in the front if you like but Director Grass is concerned about your security. No one will see you in the back and we can still talk. I'll point out anything interesting along the way."

Em settled into the back. From Virginia Avenue Garcia turned left onto South Perimeter Road, which turned into West Perimeter Road as they headed north toward the base main gate. Outside the gate, Garcia took the Capital Beltway west across the Potomac River then north on Jefferson Davis Highway to the Pentagon parking area. Garcia pulled up to a driveway manned by uniformed guards. The guards saluted and waved the director's Lincoln through. They proceeded to an underground parking facility. Garcia parked in a space marked reserved. Out of the car Garcia moved off telling Thompson, "Follow me."

Garcia started walking toward a set of swinging doors. As he went he told Emmett, "Stay close. You won't believe how easy it is to get lost in this place. If we get separated Director Grass is in 5E105. That is the fifth floor of E wing, room 105. The director has reserved parking, one of the closest to the elevators."

They went through the doors, walked about fifty paces and turned into a short dead-end hall with elevator doors on both sides. Garcia ran a card through an identifier on the wall, elevator doors opened and he led the way inside. He pressed the button for 5. Em leaned his back against the rear wall of the elevator car and watched the lights over the door go on and off as they went from B, to M, to 1, 2, 3, 4, and 5. When the elevator car stopped Em followed Garcia out and to the right down an interior corridor. They continued in a clockwise direction passing escalating room numbers until reaching number 105. A sign above the doorway read Edward Grass, Director of Special Operations. Garcia opened the door and proceeded inside. Em followed. They entered a reception area. A gorgeous young blue-eyed blonde woman wearing a light blue sweater and a black skirt looked up and told Garcia, "Go on in Al. They're waiting for you."

"Good morning Lauren. Lauren this is Emmett. Emmett this is Lauren Shein. Emmett served with the director in the Middle East, back in the day."

Emmett smiled shyly and said, "Hi Lauren. Glad to meet you."

Lauren smiled back, "Likewise Emmett. You can go right in also. They're expecting you too."

Garcia knocked and opened the door walking in. Emmett followed him and closed the door. It was a huge office. The outside wall consisted entirely of glass. The Washington Monument dominated the view of the D.C. skyline across the river. Ed Grass rose from his chair behind his desk saying, "Good morning Al, Emmett."

Garcia and Emmett replied in unison, "Good morning sir."

There were two more people in the room, a man and woman sat on a couch. Grass pointed to them saying, "Emmett this is Alexandra Mendez and Alfred "Little A" Cruz. You met Garcia. You have been calling him Al but he is also known as Big A. Al and Alex this is my friend Emmett Thompson. Please everyone sit."

Em looked at Mendez. She appeared to be in her late twenties, close to six feet tall, with curves in all the right places, and pretty. Cruz was about thirty, five seven, a compact one hundred sixty pounds. Emmett smiled and said, "Glad to meet you both."

Grass continued, "Okay everybody has met. Emmett, I want you to know these guys are my absolute best. In government circles, they are known as the Triple A team. They have operated primarily in Florida, California, Arizona, New Mexico, and Texas investigating drug cartels and illegal immigrant smugglers. They have worked cases involving hostage rescue, sniper work, bombing investigations and interrogations. Their assignments have also taken them into the Latin American countries of Mexico, Venezuela, Columbia, Bolivia, Peru, and Panama. They are all perfectly comfortable working both within the United States and in the neighboring countries to the south. They fit in anywhere. Team leader, Big A, is a third generation Spanish-American, whose grandparents came to the United States from Spain in 1940. Team member Mendez, is a second generation Nicaraguan-American. Her parents fled political persecution in Nicaragua in 1983 during the Sandinista revolution. Team member, Little A, is an American of Puerto Rican descent. Cruz was born and raised in Long Island City, New York. The three of them are bi-lingual, fluent in English and Spanish. They can and will operate in Arizona or across the border wherever the investigation takes them. They will do whatever it takes. The Triple A team are all sworn FBI agents on special assignment to Special Operations. I'm confident they will get to the bottom of who murdered your friends, the Comforts, and justice will be served."

"Thank you Ed, I appreciate that."

"All right, everybody from Triple A is up to speed on everything you told me over the phone. Mendez and Cruz picked up the lab report on what they found out overnight on their way in this morning. Alf, you want to update us all."

Al Cruz opened a folder and said, "This is all preliminary. Using the latest image enhancement software the lab transformed all of the dull, dark, ordinary facial images into precise, detailed, professional looking mug shots. No longer do we have nighttime exposures. The under exposure, unwanted shadows, and dark images are now perfect for comparison with the mug shots contained in the federal database. All of the images were run. The lab analyzed the relative size, shape, and position of the jaw, cheekbones, eyes, and nose of the people on the video. They compared them with criminal file records for other images with matching features. When they finished that phase, the only thing confirmed was the presence of the Castaneda cousins, Hector and Aliberto, had been video recorded. The lab is continuing to run the rest of the images through comparisons with other video surveillance tapes, composite drawings, and like files. They'll keep us informed on that front. Fingerprints from the bottles and caps have been put through the Integrated Automated Fingerprint Identification System, the Federal Bureau of Investigation's database containing over fifty million subjects. Nothing came up and that database includes the fingerprint data from all local, state, and federal law enforcement agencies. The DNA obtained from the bottles was recorded. That information was run without success through the criminal biometric database. So all we can positively say so far is the photographic evidence affirms the fingerprint results the sheriff recovered from the Comfort's clothing."

Emmett said, "Is that it? That's not much. We knew all that already."

Cruz responded, "This is merely the beginning not the end. The fingerprints and DNA are being sent to Interpol. We'll hear back from them shortly. My bet is Mexico will have something. Anybody working with or for the Castanedas certainly won't be choirboys. The lab will continue now searching all other state records like Department of Motor Vehicle photos and fingerprint records. All non-criminal federal agencies will also have their records checked. Oh, the lab also did an enhancement of the audio chip. They didn't come up with anything your guy Vern had not already found."

Emmett looked toward Ed Grass and asked, "What next Ed?"

Grass pressed the button on the intercom and asked, "Lauren would you please get Charlie Swanson over at Homeland Security for me?"

"Yes sir."

"Alex, would you tee up the part of the audio where they talk about the Border Patrol please?"

Alexandra Mendez turned on the audio player, fast forwarded, stopped the recording and pressed play. They all heard, "You can't leave them. They've seen us." Mendez pressed rewind briefly and announced, "All set Director."

Then the office intercom came alive. Lauren said, "Sir I have the Homeland Security Director on one."

Grass pressed speaker saying, "Charlie how are you this morning?"

Swanson replied, "Fine Ed, how about you. Lauren said you want to talk to me. What's up?"

"Charlie, I have you on speaker in my office. Triple A is with me. I have a disturbing recording here I want to play for you. It is audio recorded at the site of a huge drug smuggling operation in Arizona. It was taken right before those people, the Comforts, were murdered a week or so ago. Listen up."

Alex pressed play. They all listened to the conversation, "You can't leave them. They've seen us—Be quiet Maria.—Don't tell her that.—You too Connie.—Who made you boss Leon?—It will be taken care of.—They can't be allowed to say they saw us.—Relax, we'll take care of it.—Come on, I don't like standing around here. Cops or border patrol could come by anytime.—Don't worry about that either. The cops are all sleeping or someplace else, and the border patrol are bought and paid for. There is no chance of us or you getting caught tonight.—Yeah the big border guy does what we tell him. He's got all his men twenty miles away.—What are you going to do about the couple you caught spying?—That's none of your business. I already told you it will be taken care of. Get in the vans and get out of here. An example will be made. You have nothing to fear from these people. Now take your group, get in the vans, and get out of here. You have a long trip." Alex stopped the audio.

Grass said, "Charlie, I'm going to send Triple A to Arizona to look into the murder of the Comforts. We believe the people, two of the voices heard on the audio, are the Castaneda cousins, Hector and Aliberto. You know they're the ones who back in August beat that other dirt bag Juan Puga to death in Sierra Vista then had the Rynning brothers, the only witnesses willing to testify, blown up before the authorities eventually deported them back to Mexico. I spoke to the president about the Castanedas and he agreed I should go after them. We can't have killers coming back and forth across the border murdering Americans at will. What specifically I'm calling about is the reference to the 'big border guy' on the audio. One of your people down there may come to the attention of my guys. I wanted to inform you of that possibility."

"Okay Ed, I understand. Can I do anything?"

"A few things, Charlie. First, don't let on to anyone a big border guy may be working with these smugglers. Two, you know Triple A are all FBI agents on assignment to me. I'd like your cooperation for them to use their FBI identifications during the investigation. And please make a courtesy call to your Phoenix field office chief letting him know we may have something for their lab to look at. That's it."

"Fine Ed. Your guys can use their bureau credentials. But Ed, you have to keep up with the program. The Phoenix field office chief is no longer a man. If Triple A has to contact the Phoenix office they need to be aware Phylis Driscoll is in charge. She has been for nearly a year now. I'm sure she'll be happy to help however she can, but remember, the Phoenix office is totally bogged down investigating September's Sky Harbor Airport bombing."

"Thanks Charlie. Hold on one minute please. Looks like Al Garcia has a question. Go ahead Al."

"Good morning sir, this is Garcia. I would like to inquire if you have heard anything suggesting a dirty Border Patrol employee in the Nogales/Douglas sector."

"No Al, just the opposite. The apprehension rate is pretty consistent down there. Not big numbers but a few dozen illegals and a couple of drug busts every month."

"This is Ed again Charlie. I guess that's it. I'll keep you informed. Take care now."

"Good hunting guys. I'll talk to you later Ed. Bye for now."

Ed Grass spun his chair around and looked out the window at the skyline of Washington, D.C. for a few moments. When he turned back his jaw was clenched. He said, "I spoke to President Burns at length yesterday about the situation along the border. He is as incensed as I am and I'm sure all of you are about the lawlessness going on down there. I told him you're the people to find out what is happening. He agreed. Tomorrow morning all of you will fly to Tucson. Triple A will set up in Bisbee, nose around, and get to the bottom of what happened to the Rynnings and the Comforts. The president said 'break eggs if you have to, I've got your back.' Emmett, you and your family stay out of the way."

Chapter Thirteen

1:12 p.m. Mountain Time, October 18

EMMETT THOMPSON, THE BRIM OF HIS sunhat shading his face and his dark glasses obscuring his eyes, walked out of the Tucson International's private flight annex. As he stepped toward the curb a green Cadillac Escalade rolled up. He opened the rear door put his luggage inside, slid into the front passenger seat buckling his safety belt as the car pulled away. In less than sixty seconds the car exited the airport loop road. In a few more minutes the entrance to Interstate 10 came up. They merged with the traffic heading east. Em looked over at his father and said, "That all went well."

Andrew responded, "What do we do now Em?"

"Not a thing, Dad. We go back to the house and leave everything to Triple A."

"Who or what is that?"

"Three of Ed's people, two men and a woman. Ed says they are the best he has. You'll meet them. They told me they will interview us. We have to act like we don't have any idea who they are. Forget I went to Washington. Forget I went to see Ed. We have to be as surprised as everyone else the FBI is taking an interest in Sam and Ida. Oh another thing dad, Ed is having them look into the Rynnings too."

Thirty minutes later three people walked down the steps of a private jet parked at the Tucson annex. The two men and a woman were each dressed casually. Each of them pulled a rolling piece of luggage and carried duffle-like bags on their shoulders. The shorter man had a computer style tote bag attached to the handle of his roll-on. They walked next door to a car rental counter, gave their reservation number, signed some papers, and were given the keys and directions to their vehicle. The woman handling the transaction said, "Your Mercury Grand Marquis is the white one. It is the first car parked in row one across the service road. Can I give you any directions?"

Alex Mendez took the keys and the paperwork. She took an Arizona road map from a pile stacked on the counter. Mendez said, "Thank you very much but we know where we are headed."

Outside on the way to the car Mendez asked, "Where are we going, boss?"

Garcia answered, "Let's get settled into our hotel then look around the area. Lauren made reservations for us at the best place she could find. It's a new hotel, a convention center, called the Copper Mine Inn. It's midway between Sierra Vista and Bisbee on Highway 80. Follow the signs to Interstate 10, go east to the Highway 90 exit, then stay on 90 right through Sierra Vista. Highway 90 intersects with and turns into Highway 80. The Copper Mine is off 80 right past the point where we get on it. Lauren described it as a real big place on the south side of the road."

When they got to the car they loaded the duffle bags and other luggage into the trunk. Whenever Triple A traveled they tried to rent a Crown Victoria, Grand Marquis, or Town Car. They found those models had plenty of room for the team, their bags, and their equipment. Cruz settled into the back seat with his laptop. Mendez drove. Garcia rode shotgun.

Shortly before four o'clock in the afternoon Mendez parked in a space marked reserved for guest check-in. Garcia told them to sit tight while he registered. About five minutes later he returned to the car and told Mendez to drive around the back of the main building and park. They entered through a door providing access to an interior corridor and an elevator. Four doors past the elevator Garcia announced, "We have these three adjoining rooms."

He handed key cards to the others and said, "I'll take one twenty, Alex you have one twenty-two, and Al you're in one twenty-four. Freshen up, unpack, and be back in my room at half past four."

At twenty minutes before five they were back in the car. Mendez asked, "Where to, boss?"

Garcia replied, "Before we meet with anyone tomorrow, I'd like to see where the Rynnings were blown up and where the Comforts were cut up, so head toward Bisbee. Al, can you use your computer to get directions to the Rynning scene?"

"No problem boss. I figured we would go there sooner or later, so I've already bookmarked both sites. Alex, you stay on Highway 80 until I tell you to turn."

Twelve minutes later Cruz said, "The big building ahead on the left is where the County Attorney Burgos' office is. Kiki's, the restaurant the young men were headed to, is right ahead, across the intersection. See it?"

Cruz pointed to an open parking space saying, "Park there Alex. The open space between those two buildings is where the claymore blew the Rynning boys to pieces. That's where it happened."

There was very little traffic, which allowed Mendez to pull to the curb and park directly across the street from the spot Cruz indicated. All three of them got out of the car but then they each went in a separate direction. Mendez crossed the street and stood on the sidewalk in front of the area where the boys had died. She spent several minutes examining her surroundings writing several notes in a small pad. She then returned to the side of the street where she had parked the car. Cruz had walked toward Kiki's and returned. He too wrote down a few notes. Garcia came back from the direction of the county attorney's office building. Garcia announced, "Whoever detonated the explosive had to be in the general area we are standing in. Standing here he or she would best be able to determine exactly when the Rynnings passed in front of the charge. Too far up or down the sidewalk could result in a false sense of proportion. There are no windows in the building behind me where he could've observed from. He stood right here. Anybody disagree?"

Cruz said, "That's the way I see it boss. The building without windows is a bank. The entry is around the corner. There are some cameras in front. There is also a traffic light camera right in front of Kiki's. Any of those cameras could have snapped a picture of the doer."

Mendez nodded in agreement saying, "You're both right and there are also cameras on the county attorney's building."

Garcia said, "Okay as long as we all agree here let's go see if we can find the Comfort crime scene while it's still light."

Back in the car Mendez asked, "Which way, boss?"

Garcia replied, "Take Highway 80 east toward Douglas. Cruz, bring the Hernandez Ranch up on your laptop. The 'TRAVEL CAUTION' sign where the bodies were found is a little ways past the ranch. We'll see it."

Shortly after five in the afternoon the Mercury stopped on the highway apron in front of the sign. Again all three got out. But this time they stayed together. There wasn't much to see; the sign, some brush, and a shallow roadside ditch. Cars going by slowed so the occupants could look at them but none stopped. Cruz finally said, "There's nothing to see even standing here, boss. I can't tell anything happened here. And it's still daylight out. It's not likely anybody would have been driving by at that time of the morning could see anything. Even if a driver went by, they killed them back a ways from the pavement, the shrubs would have concealed all the action going on. On top of that there have probably been dozens of morbid looky-loos who have trampled all over this area. Let's go back and take a peek at the Hernandez Ranch."

Garcia replied, "Of course you're right. This crime scene is a waste of time."

They drove back and turned left onto the driveway to the ranch. They drove past a mailbox on a post and a small sign with 'Hernandez' printed on it. Mendez continued two hundred feet or so and came to a large clearing. She drove in a big circle, stopping facing the direction she had come. Trees fronting on the road, the boarded-up ranch house, and overgrown brush, hid them from view. They exited the car and walked around a bit. Nobody went far. The sun was already going down. In the twilight cars going by on Highway 80 could be seen only because they had their headlights on. Mendez remarked, "Cozy. A tractor trailer, a couple of vans, and a small army of people could be in here and no one would be the wiser."

Chapter Fourteen

9:01 a.m. Mountain Time, October 19

TWO MEN IN BUSINESS SUITS, ONE tall and large the other short and wiry, strode into the Cochise County Attorney Burgos' office. A gorgeous woman, dressed in business attire, dark slacks, jacket, and white blouse accompanied them. They displayed FBI identification and announced, "Agents Garcia, Cruz, and Mendez. We'd like to speak with Felix Burgos and Joanna Castro please."

The surprised receptionist whose desk nameplate identified as Carol Satele, asked, "Do you have an appointment?"

The large man replied, "No."

Satele, questioned, "Can I ask what this is about?"

Garcia replied, "No. You need to tell them we are here and want to talk to them now."

Satele asked, "Take a seat please. I'll tell them you're here."

Garcia said, "We'll stand."

Several minutes later Satele returned with a man in his late fifties. Despite a stooped posture, he stood an inch or two over six feet tall. He had long hippie-like disheveled gray hair. He held out his hand and introduced himself. He said, "I'm Felix Burgos. How can I help you?"

Garcia shook Burgos' hand replying, "We are with the FBI. I'm Agent Al Garcia. This is Agent Al Cruz and Agent Alex Mendez. We would like to speak with you and Assistant County Attorney Castro please."

"Can I ask what this is about?"

"Yes sir, of course, in your office, please."

Burgos told Satele, "Carol please ask Joanna to come to my office now."

He then motioned to the agents, "Come this way please."

Burgos led the way into a large office with large windows overlooking downtown Bisbee. Shortly thereafter, Joanna Castro, a pretty woman about thirty years old with piercing dark eyes and short black hair came in. Once introductions were made Burgos again asked, "Would one of you please tell us what this is about?"

Garcia walked over to the window and said, "Mister Burgos we're here to look into the murders of the Rynning brothers and Ida and Sam Comfort. We understand the boys, Craig, Larry, and Jimmy were going over what they witnessed concerning the Puga murder with you the day they were blown up."

Castro answered, "That's partially right. It was my case. The young men were going over their testimony with me that day. They were on their way to lunch when it happened. I was here discussing what had transpired so far that morning with Mister Burgos when there was an explosion. We rushed to the window and looked out. It was horrible. All we could see from here was smoke, fire, body parts."

Mendez addressed Castro. She said, "We understand the Rynnings were the only witnesses you had. Is that true?"

"Yes. They were the only ones left, not scared off. Once all the other witnesses found out the suspects were drug cartel enforcers they all developed sudden cases of amnesia. The Rynnings were the only ones brave enough to continue the process."

Cruz asked, "Who knew that besides you two?"

Castro replied, "If you mean outside of this office, I didn't tell anyone."

Cruz looked at Burgos and asked, "How about you, sir?"

"I didn't tell anybody out of the ordinary. Law enforcement inquired. I discussed the case with law enforcement, that's all."

Garcia asked, "Who specifically?"

"Where are you going with this?"

"Wherever it leads, wherever it goes. Wouldn't you agree someone told the cartel the Rynnings would be here? Was it you? Was it someone else? Who? Who else knew? That's where I'm going with this."

"All right, it wasn't me and I'm sure neither Joanna nor Carol would tell anyone. We all understand the need for confidentiality. Sheriff Mata-Villa and Deputy Chief Marrone from the border patrol were in the loop.

You would have to ask them if they discussed the case and the Rynnings interview appointment with anybody else."

"Thank you, we'll ask them. Let's talk about what you saw when you went to the window after you heard the explosion, shall we."

Castro said, "I knew right away it was them. One look and I knew. I tried to help. I ran to the desk and called 911. I told the person who answered there was an explosion, people were hurt. The operator who took the call asked if the explosion was in our office. I said no, in the street between here and Kiki's. This office must have come up on caller ID. She told me help was on the way."

"Okay. Did you go back to the window after placing the call?"

"Briefly. There was pandemonium. People running everywhere. I heard sirens. I left the office and went outside. There was nothing I could do. There was nothing anybody could do. When I saw the bodies, the carnage, I threw up. I was sick. I cried. I never want to see something like that again."

Garcia then turned to Burgos. He asked him,"How about you, you stayed at the window, correct?"

"Yes I did for a few minutes. I went outside when Joanna did. There was nothing we could do."

"What do you remember seeing when you first looked outside?"

"I saw smoke, a little fire, the torn up bodies."

"Did you see anybody in the vicinity? Any cars in the street?"

"Yes I saw a couple of cars in the street. They stopped. But no one got out of them right away."

"How about other people in the area?"

"I saw a man across the street on his phone. After a minute several people came out of Kiki's. Millie, Kiki's waitress was on her phone. I figured they were calling 911, the same as Joanna did. Some people came running around the corner. Everybody hesitated. It appeared to me nobody wanted to get too close."

"Okay that's good, anything else you can remember? Anybody act suspicious?"

"No, nobody stood out. Everybody looked like they wanted to help but they didn't want to get too close. It was only a couple of minutes until we went downstairs. Police came right away, so did the firefighters and the ambulance. There was nothing anybody could do."

"Then what happened?"

"Nothing. The police asked if anyone saw what happened. I don't believe anyone came forward. We told them who the boys were and why they were here. They wrote it all down. As soon as the bodies were taken away I closed the office for the day. Joanna, Carol, and I went home."

"When were the charges dropped against the Castaneda cousins?"

"About a week later. I would have to look it up to give you the exact date. We tried. We went back to all of the original witnesses. They told us we were nuts. Nobody saw anything. We had no choice. We turned the Castanedas over to the United States Attorney for the local district. He had them deported. "

Garcia motioned to Cruz and Mendez saying, "Either of you have anything else?"

Cruz shook his head. Mendez said, "Nothing more for these guys but we need to talk to Carol."

Burgos keyed the intercom and asked, "Carol, come in here please."

Carol Satele, a middle aged heavyset woman wearing glasses, came into the office. Burgos said, "Carol, these FBI agents have some questions for you."

Satele appeared to be taken aback. She said, "For me?"

Mendez smiled and tried to put the woman at ease. She said, "We have to cover all of our bases Carol. We need to know what you remember about the morning the Rynning brothers were killed."

"I don't know anything about that."

Mendez gently asked, "You knew the boys were coming in that day didn't you?"

"Of course I did. I made all the arrangements. I called them and set a date acceptable to Ms. Castro and the Rynnings."

Mendez asked, "Did you tell anyone else?"

"No."

"How about Mister Burgos? He was told wasn't he?"

"Not by me."

Burgos interrupted, "Carol didn't tell me, Joanna did. I asked Joanna when John asked me."

Mendez then asked Burgos, "John who?"

"I told you I told John Marrone. I told Ed too."

"You didn't say Marrone asked, you said law enforcement was in the loop, you told Marrone and Mata-Villa."

"Does it make a difference?"

"Maybe. When did Marrone ask?"

"Several days before. Three I believe."

"When did you tell Mata-Villa?"

"Around the same time. I'm not exactly sure."

"What were the circumstances around your telling the sheriff? Did he ask you?"

"I believe I informed the sheriff as part of a regular progress report. He didn't ask, I simply reported to him how the case was proceeding."

Satele broke in and clarified, "It wasn't more than three days because the meeting was confirmed three days prior to the explosion."

Mendez asked, "You're sure?"

"Yes."

Mendez said, "Thank you Carol. Now what do you remember about the explosion? What did you see that day?"

"I was in the bathroom when I heard the explosion. The building shook. I hurried and finished as fast as I could. When I came out of the bathroom at the same time Mister Burgos and Miss Castro came out of Mister Burgos' office. They told me to come with them. I asked what happened. They said there had been an explosion outside. They were going down, I joined them. I didn't see much of anything. Joanna was up front. She threw up and just the smell made me sick too."

Garcia wrapped up the conversation by thanking everyone for their participation. He asked that they keep the meeting confidential, handed out business cards and asked them to call his cell number if they remembered anything else. He wrote down each of their cell phone numbers in case he needed to reach them again.

Outside the Cochise County office building the Arizona sun was shining brightly. No one paid much attention to the well-dressed FBI agents as they huddled on the sidewalk. Mendez nodded her head toward Kiki's restaurant asking, "Where to boss? Are we going to talk to Millie the waitress?"

"No, she can wait. Get in the car. Drive us over to the sheriff's office. There is a Mickey D's out on the highway. Let's stop there for lunch on the way. Al, you get on your computer, send in the cell numbers they gave us. Tell Lauren to have the phone mikes activated and to start recording everything. Tell her to use the normal alert words for drug trafficking and smuggling. Have them add Rynning, Comfort, and Castaneda to the words they are listening for."

The president's Director of Special Operations office was linked to federal intelligence agencies that routinely employ the remote activation of cell phone microphones. The method used enabled the listening facility to activate individual cell phones, which then become undetectable listening devices. Conversations in the vicinity of the phone were transmitted and recorded whether or not the cell was turned on or off. Both sides of all conversations made over the subject cell phone were also recorded. Utilizing the latest software the bug was set and activated remotely without physical possession of the phone or the permission of the phone's owner. The agency's recorder was activated by sound. The operator monitoring the recorders was automatically alerted when a word in a key directory was uttered. If the tap was abandoned later it was done without the phone's owner ever knowing it had happened. Cruz e-mailed the instructions. Minutes later his laptop was alerted the voice recorders were in place and activated. Cruz said, "The bugs are up."

Chapter Fifteen

1:03 p.m. Mountain Time, October 19

Mendez announced, "This is it coming up."

She turned into a parking lot serving a single story white stucco and glass building. Mendez parked in the area right in front of the building entrance marked for visitors. When they got out they followed a walkway up several steps past a water feature consisting of two pools, one flowing into the other. They then proceeded between two flagpoles. The same two flags flying atop the county office building were flown here. One was the stars and stripes of the United States. The other flag was of equal size. It had two halves, a top and a bottom with a five pointed star in the middle. Mendez said, "I guess that is the Arizona state flag. It's the same type that flew over the county attorney's office building. I don't have any idea what the water thingy represents"

Cruz shrugged, "Who cares?"

Garcia walked inside, the others followed. They approached a woman sitting behind what appeared to be a bulletproof glass partition surrounding a waiting area. All three of them flashed credentials, Garcia said, "FBI. We'd like to speak with the sheriff."

The receptionist asked, "Do you have an appointment?"

Garcia responded, "No, would you please inform him we're here?"

"I can't. He isn't in. Would you like to make an appointment?"

"Where is he? Can you get him on the radio? This is important."

"He's in the field. If you sit down a minute I'll try to reach him."

Without waiting for a reply, the receptionist left her seat and walked to the far wall of the room she was in. She picked up what appeared to be a radio microphone and spoke into it. She apparently reached the sheriff because after several animated gestures she returned to her desk and sat down. She said, "The sheriff says make yourselves comfortable. He will be back in about twenty."

Garcia nodded, "Thank you very much ma'am."

Cruz, who had his laptop with him, pointed to the screen, and said to Mendez, "You're always so smart Alex. That is the Arizona state flag. The design has a lot of meaning."

Mendez asked, "Such as?"

"Well, the star in the middle is copper color signifying Arizona is the largest copper producing state in the union. The thirteen alternating red and yellow ray shaped sections in the top half depicts the thirteen original colonies of the United States and the setting sun. The bottom half is blue. The bottom half blue and the yellow setting sun rays are the Arizona state colors. The state of Arizona requires the state flag be displayed alongside the United States flag in front of or over all state buildings the governor directs and all county buildings the various local governments determine."

"Very interesting Al. Now educate me about the water display."

"Sorry, can't find it."

The receptionist, who was listening to the discussion, spoke up. She said, "The architect included the pools. He said they depict how precious water is in Arizona. He designed them as a reminder for everyone to conserve."

Cruz smirked, "Yeah, typical, flaunt a precious commodity to remind others to save it. The architect must be related to Al Gore."

After thumbing through a stack of magazines left for visitors for what appeared to be an eternity the team members all looked up when a door opened. A large man in uniform appeared. He said, "Good afternoon. I'm Sheriff Eduardo Mata-Villa. Are you people the FBI agents who want to speak to me?"

They nodded in the affirmative, standing in unison, and displaying their credentials. Garcia said, "Sheriff, glad to meet you. I'm Al Garcia, this is Al Cruz, and this is Alexandra Mendez. Can we speak in private please?"

The sheriff shook hands all around and responded, "Of course. Follow me."

Once inside his office with the door closed Mata-Villa asked, "What's this about?"

Garcia said, "Sheriff we are here from Washington to look into the murders of the Rynning brothers and the Comforts. We need you to bring us up to date on your investigations."

"There isn't much to tell as far as I know. One of my men handles all of our homicide cases. He would be the person to talk to. Do you want me to call him in here?"

"If he is the man with the answers, yes, please do so."

Mata-Villa excused himself, left the office, returned shortly thereafter with a tall thin man who he introduced as Assistant Sheriff Rich Farrell. Farrell carried two folders he explained contained his case files. He said, "The sheriff explained what you want. Shall we go over the Rynning case first?"

Garcia responded, "Yes that will be fine. Do you have any suspects?"

"No agent, no suspects. Apparently no one saw anything. We have come to a dead end, no leads, no suspects, all we have is motive. The Rynnings were the only witnesses willing to testify against the Castaneda cousins in the Puga murder. But I'm sure you are aware of that."

"Have you figured out how it was done?"

"Yes, a claymore anti-personnel mine set on a truck bed was used. The detonation was triggered by a cell phone. The explosion was fatal; it was about waist high, tore the boys apart. Someone called the number as the Rynnings walked by. Obviously that someone was working for the cartel."

"Who knew the Rynnings would be there that day?"

"We found ten people who knew. The County Attorney, the assistant handling the case, their secretary, Ed here, the border patrol guy John Marrone, Suzi Rynning, Jenny Rynning, and the three employers of the boys. All three Rynning brothers told their employers why they would not be in to work. None of the people who we know admits to telling anyone else."

"You didn't know?"

"Me personally, no, that was not something I needed to know and Ed didn't tell me anyway."

Garcia asked, "Sheriff when did you receive the information about the meeting?"

"I'm not exactly sure, agent. Whenever the county attorney told me, a day or two before the incident if memory serves. I could probably dig up the date if you want."

"No, that's fine. That's what the attorney said too."

He then asked Farrell, "Anybody see anything when the claymore went off?"

"No witnesses came forward. We checked cameras mounted on buildings in the area. We also checked the traffic camera from the intersection nearby. The brothers walked together on one side of the street, one man standing across the street from them, a couple of cars moving on the street. We identified the owners of the cars from film in the cameras. They didn't know or see anything meaningful. We never identified the single man. We had his picture from one of the cameras, showed it around, no one knew him. We sent his photo to the FBI Phoenix office. They weren't able to match it for us."

"Do you have three copies of the picture we can show around?"

"Sure, take this one and I'll have two more printed up before you leave."

They passed the photo between them. It was a head shot of a Latino looking man with a Pancho Villa moustache. Cruz asked, "Can you e-mail that photo to me please? I'll keep it on my laptop."

"Sure, I'll do that."

Cruz continued, "And maybe you can e-mail the camera videos of the street scene from a few minutes before until a few minutes after the explosion? Just so the file we take back to Washington is complete."

"Sure, anything else?"

Cruz said, "Yes, copies of the 911 calls that came in reporting the explosion. I'd like to hear them."

"I can get those for you. There were two calls. We determined Joanna Castro made one and Kiki's waitress Millie Caldwell made the other one. Neither one of them witnessed the explosion. They both simply acted quickly to summons help. Anything else?"

"No other callers, no male callers?"

"No and no. Anything else?"

"Yes, who owned the truck the explosives were set-up on?"

"A contractor from Sierra Vista. He had called at seven-twelve in the morning, long before the incident occurred, and reported the flatbed stolen. We had an all-points bulletin out on the truck. A patrol car officer reported afterward he had driven by, saw that flatbed, but he checked the license plate and it was a different number than the one reported stolen. Anything else?"

"No, not for now."

Mendez chimed in saying, "We could use copies of all the witness interviews."

"Okay."

Garcia asked, "Let's review the Comforts' case."

Farrell opened the other file. He shuffled some papers, took out some pictures, and said,

"These are some crime scene photos, pretty gruesome. You can see the bodies had been cut up something awful. The coroner's report is here. I'll give you copies. It says here they had both been stabbed deeply into the lower abdomen area; the blades were pulled up to the base of the ribcage, slicing through the internal organs. He said in all likelihood their eyes were carved out before they expired. We have no suspects. We have no witnesses. Apparently no one saw anything or at least no one will admit to knowing or seeing anything. Again, we have come to a dead end, no leads, and no suspects. We don't even have a motive."

Garcia asked, "Who found the bodies?"

"The head of the Bisbee Border Brigade, guy named Andrew Thompson, called it in. His story is the Comforts were writers researching a book on illegal immigration. He admitted he dropped them off the evening before. He says he received an anonymous call describing where to find the bodies. He and his three sons, Philip, Carl, and Emmett, went out looking, found the bodies and called us. It all sounds fishy but after what happened to the Rynnings you can't blame anybody for being afraid to come forward. I'll give you copies of our interviews with them, their phone numbers, and directions to the family compound, in case you want to speak with them directly. I'm convinced they know something more than they are saying. Maybe you'll do better with them then we have."

"Thanks that will be good. We'll follow-up on that. If we get anything more from the Thompsons we'll let you know. Did you trace the incoming phone records? What phone made the call to Thompson?'

"We checked that. The call came in as he said. The funny part is the phone used to make the call belonged to Sam Comfort. It was found in his pocket when we searched the remains. It was clean, no prints on it. We theorize the killer must have re-dialed the last outgoing number to tell somebody where to find them."

"That makes sense. Anything unusual reported by your patrols that night?

"We don't run late night patrols all over the county. We don't have the budget for it. The only active substation overnight is Sierra Vista. All other substations have deputies who live in the sector on call. If they are needed headquarters calls them out of bed. So to answer your question none of our people saw anything unusual. Border patrolmen were out and about, but we asked and none of them saw anything that could be tied to the case."

Cruz asked, "What did you find at the crime scene, any shoeprints, fingerprints, DNA?"

"Shoe prints found at the scene were not identifiable. A lot of trampling had taken place, a lot of disturbed vegetation, nothing conclusive on shoes. In addition to the victims prints we found eight sets of fingerprints on the Comfort's clothing. Four sets are unknown; two sets we identified as belonging to the Castaneda cousins, the guys we had to release in the Juan Puga murder, and two locals. Andrew and Emmett Thompson both touched the bodies when they found them. No DNA evidence, other than DNA belonging to the Comforts, was recovered."

Mendez said, "So let me get this straight. Hector and Aliberto Castaneda can be linked to involvement in the Puga, Rynning, and Comfort murders?"

"Appears that way, agent. As far as we can determine they are somewhere in Mexico. They were deported."

Mendez said, "Our records indicate Hector and Aliberto Castaneda have been arrested for violent crimes in the United States twenty-two times, eleven times each, and all that ever happens is they get deported. These fucking clowns are known cartel enforcers, career killers. How do these scumbags keep getting slapped on the wrist, released back to Mexico, only to return to kill again whenever they damn well please?"

Farrell responded sharply, "Don't question us lady. We apprehended them for the Puga murder. The federal government, who you people work for, deported them, what did you say, twenty-two times."

Sheriff Mata-Villa interrupted, "Calm down everybody. We are all on the same side. Agents I recommend you go to see Deputy Chief John Marrone. Ask him your questions about the deportations."

Garcia said, "I agree. We're finished here I think. Here are our cards with our cell numbers. Please call anyone of us if anything comes up we should know about."

"We'll do that."

Garcia then said, "Can we get your cell numbers? Just in case we have to talk again. I'd rather go directly to you both than through your receptionist."

With the cell numbers, case files, photos, tapes, and videos they had asked for the Triple A team left the sheriff's headquarters. Garcia told Cruz to add Mata-Villa's and Farrell's cell phone mics to the ones already being monitored. He also instructed him to send Lauren the photo of the witness so she could forward it to the lab for comparison with Emmett's video images.

Chapter Sixteen

5:17 p.m. Mountain Time, October 19

TRIPLE A GATHERED IN ROOM 120. Garcia propped up the pillows on the bed and lay down. Mendez sat on the edge of the desk studying the printed versions of interviews Rich Farrell had provided them with. Cruz moved the one chair in the room, sat in it, and hooked his laptop to the television. Cruz played through the red light camera images showing two vehicles entering and proceeding through the intersection in front of Kiki's restaurant at the same time as the claymore exploded. The reflection of the flash was easily identified. The camera angle did not include the Rynnings or the witness with the moustache on the opposite side of the street. Cruz then played the surveillance video from the front of the bank. That video didn't have any footage with a view of the explosion either. It did however have a great facial of moustache man coming around the corner as he left the scene. Cruz said, "That is where Farrell got the file ID photo of the mystery man."

One of the cameras outside the county office building had the best view of the Rynnings passing the flatbed and being blown apart. It continued after the explosion showing Kiki's patrons and waitress come out of the restaurant. Cruz said, "That's it. There isn't any video of the moustache man showing him at the time of the detonation."

Cruz' phone rang. It was Lauren. The lab positively matched moustache man's photo with Pancho Villa from Emmett Thompson's video. Cruz informed Garcia and Mendez. Garcia instructed, "Al run all the videos again please. Do it frame by frame this time."

Mendez suggested dinner. She said, "I'm getting tired. Let's go to the hotel restaurant, have dinner, then come back to this refreshed. What do you say?"

Garcia relented. He wanted to continue but realized Alex was right. They went past the lobby on the way. Mendez told them to get a table; she'd be right behind them. She wanted to check something with the front desk. Garcia and Cruz continued on. They were perusing the menu when Alex came up sporting an ear to ear smirk. She said, "Guess what?"

Cruz replied, "Never mind the games, what's up Alex?"

"This is a convention center. They have business meeting rooms. The front desk says we can use a room equipped with a giant display screen and comfortable chairs for twenty-five dollars an hour. You can hook your laptop to the big screen Cruz. It will be easier for us to see more of what is on those surveillance tapes. What do you think boss?"

Garcia replied, "I think you're absolutely right. Your suggestion sounds much more comfortable and practical then trying to see everything on the small screen in my room. We'll do it...right after we eat."

They all ordered the special. It was Chinese—white rice, brown rice, a medley of vegetables and chicken stir fry, egg roll, fortune cookie, almond cookie, vanilla ice cream, and tea. After paying the bill Garcia and Mendez went to the front desk and made arrangements for a meeting room rental. Cruz went to Garcia's room and returned with his laptop. Once settled in they began reviewing the now bigger than life-size videos frame by frame. The red light camera images still depicted the same two vehicles, only slower. The surveillance video from the front of the bank was more revealing. That enlarged video clearly displayed Pancho Villa cracking a smile when he turned the corner and spoke into his phone right before closing it. The prick was undoubtedly content, satisfied. It wasn't until the second time they reexamined the video from the county building that Mendez exclaimed, "Stop it right there. Go back."

Cruz asked, "What? What did you see?"

Mendez replied, "Go back to the beginning, before the claymore was triggered. See Kiki's storefront. See the reflection in the large storefront window. That's moustache man. You can see him leaning against the bank wall looking at the Rynnings. He's dialing his phone, at the last second; just before the blast he hits the last digit. That's when he commanded the ignition. Now look he's dialing again. The fuck is talking and smiling. He's reporting to someone the job is done. See now he walks away around the corner where the bank video picks him up again. The son of a bitch positioned himself right where we thought, right across the street from the flatbed. He watched and waited until they passed directly in front of the mine and touched it off at the optimal time."

Cruz said, "Yeah I see it now. Alex is right boss. How do we handle this?"

Garcia sat quietly for a while. Then he abruptly stood and said, "Let's call it a night. We'll sleep on this development and talk about it after a good night's sleep. Wrap everything up. I'll go tell them we're done with this facility. Meet you both in my room at seven-fifteen for breakfast. Great job, Alex. Good night."

At precisely 7 a.m. Eastern Time, October 20, Ed Grass dialed the phone in his office. Garcia picked up after the second ring. Grass said, "I have news Al. We've identified the travelers. We received both fingerprint and photo identifications from The United States Citizenship and Immigration Services. They had them in their files. All ten of them are naturalized citizens. They are brothers, sisters, and cousins from one family."

Garcia said, "Hold on a minute, Director. You woke me up and I need to piss. Be right back."

After reliving himself Garcia came back, "Okay sir, I'm here. Go ahead; tell me the rest of it."

"They are the Huertas, eight men and two women. They are an extended family of brothers, sisters, and cousins from South America. They range in age from twenty-six to thirty. They're Uruguayans. They admitted to sneaking across the border in the early 2000s. They went to Pueblo, Colorado where they still live and work. The records show they provided copies of Uruguayan police reports detailing the extermination of all of their relatives by a drug cartel who members of the Huerta family had reported to police. They had a letter from the Montevideo police chief attesting to the fact their lives would be in danger if they returned to Uruguay. Once the Huertas arrived in Pueblo, they applied for and then had temporary asylum in the United States granted based on those documents. Less than two months later, after the consular unit of the United States Embassy in Montevideo confirmed the plight of the Huertas with the local police chief, the temporary asylum they had all been granted was changed to permanent asylum. The Huertas obtained a tax ID number and incorporated Huerta's Auto Body Shop in Colorado. In 2008, the Huertas all applied for and were granted green cards. After years of continuous residency and physical presence in Pueblo the Huertas applied for United States citizenship. It says here over all of the time they have been in the USA they all displayed good moral character; none of them had ever been arrested, or charged with a crime, and they all paid their taxes. They all had the ability to read, write, and speak English. They demonstrated knowledge of the United States Constitution, had favorable dispositions towards the United States, and they all passed the citizenship test with flying colors. On the first of April this year, Consuela, Maria, Leon, Jose, Alphonso, Roberto, Filipe, Vincente, Manlio, and Diego Huerta, those are their names, were sworn in as naturalized United States citizens. I'm e-mailing the files to Cruz."

"Any idea what made them come across the border with drug smugglers?"

"You'll have to ask them. Find out."

"We will sir. It would help if we had their last known addresses."

"They're in the file. Is there anything else Al?"

"Yes sir, I have news too. The guy with the Pancho Villa moustache in Emmett's video, we uncovered another picture of him. He is standing across the street at the exact time of the explosion that blew the Rynning boys up. We think he triggered the detonation. Cruz e-mailed the picture to the lab and they positively identified him as the same guy."

"That's great work Al. Now find him."

"Yes sir, we will."

Over breakfast Garcia repeated his conversation with Ed Grass. They each looked at the file compiled on the Huertas. Mendez asked, "When are we goin' to visit these guys, boss?"

"In a couple of days, we still have things to do here. I've been thinking about the guy with the moustache. Giving what we know to the Bisbee cops isn't gonna help. They could not find him before; they are not goin' to find him now. If he pops up anywhere it will be in Washington or from Interpol, and that search is ongoing. I think we should reach out to someone in Mexico."

Cruz said, "I still talk to Jesus Noriega from the Sonora State Police. You guys remember him from when the drug cartel in Nogales assassinated the Sonora State Police Chief, Manuel Pavon, back in oh nine. Jesus is one of the few honest cops in Mexico. Maybe I can reach out to him, boss."

Garcia replied, "Yeah, I remember him, appeared to be a good guy. What would you tell him?"

"Nothing much. How about we have a picture of a Mexican looking guy who is a witness to the Rynning thing and we need help finding him. He's not in any trouble. We naturally want to ask if he may have seen something. He's not in our system, maybe Jesus could do us a favor, look through theirs. Maybe he'll get lucky. Mendez, your input?"

"I concur, call Jesus. It can't hurt."

"Okay we agree. Cruz you call Jesus. E-mail him the photo if he agrees to look. But do it in the car. We need to get on the road. I made an appointment for us with John Marrone at eleven in his office in Nogales. His secretary said it is gonna take about two hours or more to drive there from here. She suggested we go the roundabout way. She said take 80 to 90 north to 82 then 82 west through Sonoita and south through Patagonia into Nogales."

Mendez said, "Boss, I looked on the map. There's a road paralleling along the border in a pretty much straight line. I'd rather take that route. You know get a look at the border first hand. Do you mind if we go that way?"

Garcia threw his hands up, "You're driving Mendez, go however you like."

Once settled in the car Cruz contacted Jesus Noriega to tell him what they wanted. After ten minutes of small talk Jesus gave Cruz his e-mail address and told him to send the photo, he would run it through their system and get back to him. Cruz thanked his friend and hung up. Mendez drove south on Highway 80, went past Bisbee, made a right on Highway 92 and headed west. Soon they went by a sign informing drivers to go to Naco, Arizona if they want to cross into Mexico. Since they weren't going to Mexico Mendez went past the Naco turn-off. Further along the road they observed another sign reading, 'Miracle Valley Straight Ahead,' Mendez said, "That sounds nice. So far it's been real scenic. I like the open country feel."

When no one responded she continued, "Not much traffic."

No one answered. Cruz' cell phone rang. He answered, "Hey Jesus, the picture come through okay?"

He listened then continued, "Oh, no shit! That's great, you know who he is. Yeah Al and Alex are with me. We're in the car, on our way to Nogales for a meeting. Hold on let me ask Al."

Cruz took the phone away from his mouth and said, "Boss, Jesus wants to meet after our eleven o'clock. He'll come across the border. He says, on this the less done by him in his office or in Mexico the better."

"Okay, we should be free by one. Can Jesus meet us for lunch or dinner?"

Cruz went back to his phone, "Anytime after one, lunch or dinner, you tell me."

After a pause Cruz said, "Okay great see you at one. Bye."

Cruz told them Jesus had recognized the guy in the photo, he will tell us all about him this afternoon over a late lunch at a place called Hernando's Hideaway. He says Hernando's is a quiet, private place located in Tubac, a small town twenty miles north of Nogales, right off Interstate 19. You ask me, he sounded kind of spooked."

Mendez took the next left following a sign for Nogales. They had made good time so far. Mendez beamed as she said, "See, I told you, Nogales is right down this road. According to the map we're half way there already."

Then the pavement ended. The road turned into a mix of gravel and dirt. They were leaving a big cloud of dust. Mendez remarked, "I'm glad I'm not driving behind us."

The road got rough. The car vibrated like it was moving on a washboard. Garcia hollered, "Slow the fuck down Alex. My back is going to get thrown out of whack if this keeps up."

Mendez slowed down but the car continued to reverberate as they went along the bumpy road. She pointed to an old abandoned shack as they started into a wide turn. She remarked, "Hey you guys, how old do you think that place is?"

Cruz replied, "Who cares. Turn the air up Alex its hot back here."

Mendez reached for the controls and Garcia called out, "Cows, cows in the road. Look out Alex. Jesus Christ where have you taken us?"

Mendez avoided the cows and said, "Look up there, boss. There's another sign. I bet we're nearly there. Civilization is straight ahead."

As they got closer Garcia said, "Mother of God, Alex that sign says 'Lochiel, Ghost Town, ahead.' There's another sign, it says 'Trespassers Will Be Shot.'"

Cruz interrupted, "I hate to ruin the sightseeing tour but in the dust cloud we're leaving behind there are flashing lights."

Mendez rolled down her window and waved them around. Over a loudspeaker they received orders to pull over, turn off the engine. Mendez complied. A truck with flashing lights and Border Patrol insignia stopped behind them. Two men in uniforms stepped out of the truck, one on either side. They were armed, their hands at the ready on top of their weapons. The one from the passenger side stayed behind the Grand Marquis. The driver walked up and asked Mendez for her license and registration. Instead

Alex pushed the door open and started to step out. The uniforms drew their side arms. The one next to Alex's door hollered, "Stop right there. Put your hands where I can see them. You others put your hands where we can see them, and they better be empty. You, driver, get out of the car. Put your hands on the roof. You other two, get out of the car, keep your hands where they can be seen. Once out, put your hands on the roof."

When the Triple A team was standing with their hands on the roof of the Mercury, Garcia announced, "Gentlemen, we're federal agents, FBI. We have credentials. We can show them to you."

"First tell us what you're doing here."

Garcia replied, "We're on our way to the Border Patrol's Nogales Station to meet with Deputy Chief Marrone. We have an eleven o'clock appointment. If we are delayed here too long we're going to be late."

The Border Patrolman next to Mendez said, "Okay let's see the credentials, one at a time, ladies first."

Alex presented her ID and the man appeared satisfied. He said, "Check the others Mel. This one is all right."

After Mel gave Cruz and Garcia the thumbs up, he asked, "You mind if I ask what you all are doin' out here."

Garcia quickly relied, "Takin' a short cut. We wanted to see the border up close."

Mel laughed, "This ain't no short cut. Fact is fast as you can go on this ole road you won't be in Nogales until after eleven. But you can see the border up close."

Cruz asked, "Where exactly is the border?"

"Right here, you're looking at it. Those pipes in the ground every three or four feet"

Cruz said, "What do you mean. Where's the fence?"

"No fence out here. The fence is only where the public goes. Congress, Homeland Security, all the other fakers in Washington, they call those pipes a fence. It's really only a bad vehicle barrier they label a fence to fool the public. Sometimes there is a fence, sometimes a vehicle barrier, sometimes a lookout tower, sometimes a sensor that works at times, doesn't work at other times, but most times not a damn thing. And the vehicle barrier, it doesn't even stop the smugglers' vehicles. Those guys have portable bridges they lay on the tops of the pipes and drive right over. It's a joke. But the public doesn't know. The politicians don't care, they lie, and reporters believe the lies. Reporters don't come out here. They don't look. Nobody comes out here but illegals, smugglers, and cattle herders. The cattle you saw back there wander back and forth across the border all the time, right between those pipes. Of course aliens and smugglers do too. We pulled you over because you obviously weren't tending the cows, so we figured, you all might be one of the bad guys."

Mendez pouted, "Are you sure we can't make Nogales by eleven?"

Mel responded, "No way."

"Oh oh, I'm in big trouble now."

Mel laughed and instructed his partner, "Joey, call headquarters. Tell them we're explaining the border to the agents who are meeting Marrone. We're all in Lochiel and they will be a few minutes late."

Joey went to use the radio and Mel told the agents, "Drive safe. You'll get there close enough to eleven. Stay to the right shoulder of the road, its smoother. You'll be through Duquesne, an abandoned mining camp, in no time. Then the paving starts again. Make a left when you get to Highway 82. That will take you right into town. You can't miss headquarters. It's the only two story building without boards on the upstairs windows."

Alex beamed, "Thank you so much Mel and Joey. Thank you both for the tutorial on the border fence and the lack of one. You take care now."

Back on the move again Garcia said, "From now on Alex let's follow directions."

Alex sheepishly replied, "I will."

Chapter Seventeen

10:54 a.m. Mountain Time, October 20

It was a beautiful morning in Denver. A slight breeze was blowing. Billowy cumulus clouds sometimes allowed the bright sun to shine through warming the air. Clancy and Mary had completed inspecting one parking facility already and hurried up Blake Street. They turned into the Valet Parking Garage and walked right past the attendant's window. Mary, who resembled the movie star Sigourney Weaver, kept walking, flashed a beautiful smile, held up her badge and said, "Homeland Security. We're going to go through the building checking cars. We'll stay out of your way."

Mary's badge, good looks, and pearly teeth didn't impress the attendant. He stepped out of the booth's door saying, "Hold on. Where do you think you're going? You can't just barge in here."

When they didn't stop he ran after them shouting, "Stop, stop." He got in front, putting his hands up.

Clancy and Mary stopped. Mary stepped forward reading the attendant's nametag. Easily two inches shorter than her, she leaned into his face and said, "Juan, get out of our way." She waved her badge again and told him, "This is official Homeland Security business. If you persist in interfering I'm going to lock you up for obstruction. Get back in your booth now. My partner and I will let you know when we're finished which should be late this afternoon. Move."

Juan replied, "Hell no. This is my job. I watch these cars. Customers see me letting you wander around, it could affect my tips. I want you out of here. Make an appointment. Another attendant can be brought in to accompany you."

Mary repeated, "I'm warning you. This is official business and you're beginning to annoy the shit out of me. Go back to your cage or I'll see to it you get locked up in a real cell for the night."

Juan stepped backwards but didn't get out of their path. It appeared he was going to continue to resist. He started to open his mouth as a car pulled in from the street and stopped. He looked at the car, then at Mary and Clancy. Juan jumped as the car horn beeped. He quickly said, "Lucky for you. I have to take care of this customer. When I'm done with them I'll be back. Later."

Juan trotted to the vehicle, a white Ford two door sedan. He asked, "How can I help you?"

The car's driver, a middle aged man, climbed out saying, "I'm flying out. I won't be back for eight days. I need a spot for my car and a shuttle to Denver International."

Juan said, "Yes sir. Leave the car right there. Let me get your claim ticket. I just spoke to the shuttle driver. She'll be back in three minutes. Pop the trunk I'll get your bags. You make yourself comfortable on the bench out front. I'll take care of everything."

Clancy and Mary ignored Juan and his client. They started up the right side of the parking garage ramp. From past experience they knew the best way for them to inspect was to follow the ramp all the way to the top on one side then return down the other side scrutinizing each vehicle as they came to it. The Valet Parking Garage was an eight story structure. They had a lot of work to do yet today. Without further delay they started, they walked from the back to the front of each vehicle. Clancy inspected under the sides, the engine compartments, and the rear or trunk space of each car. Mary waved a handheld device at each vehicle as she also observed inside whenever she could.

As they emerged from the space between the fourth and fifth cars Juan raced up blasting the horn of the Ford he was parking as he passed alongside. Mary could see him laughing as he went. She heard the tires squealing around the curves as he drove up and up before finally the engine noise stopped and a car door slammed. Mary stood stationary for a few minutes thinking the asshole would have to walk back down past her to get back to his cubbyhole and she would give him a piece of her mind. She could be louder than any car horn when she wanted to be. Then she heard another motor sound. It took a few seconds then she realized the chickenshit was taking an elevator down. The motor stopped, followed by footsteps. She knew she shouldn't but couldn't control herself. She yelled, "Asshole." She heard Juan laughing.

Slightly after one p.m. Mary decided to take a lunch break. They had recently rounded the fourth level and from this vantage point could see the Denver Broncos' Stadium, INVESCO Field at Mile High off to the west. Juan hadn't brought another car up or down. They were alone. Mary took off her fanny pack and sat on the floor with her back against the low outside wall. She unwrapped an egg salad sandwich she had prepared for herself earlier that morning, poured a cup of coffee from a small thermos, and motioned to Clancy. He came over, sat next to her, and rested his head on her right leg. Mary tickled Clancy behind his ears. He was content. Mary was tired. She finished her sandwich and coffee and closed her eyes to rest and to think.

She and Clancy had worked every day since the thirtieth of September. 9/30 is now as infamous as 9/11 in the minds of Americans. September thirtieth, was the day five separate nuclear devices detonated in four cities. Two of the blasts went off in Los Angeles, one each in Phoenix, Albuquerque, and Houston. The epicenters of the blasts had been determined to be the parking facilities at Los Angeles International, John Wayne, Sky Harbor, Sun Port, and Hobby Airports. Blame had been placed on al-Qaeda mainly because they issued a statement claiming responsibility for the attack immediately after the blasts occurred. The al-Qaeda claim was considered reliable because of its timeliness and because they mentioned suitcase nukes left in cars in airport parking facilities. Explosives experts agreed all of the devices appeared to be suitcase type bombs, approximately explosive charges of one kiloton. That means each one had the explosive power of one thousand tons of TNT. The experts said the placement of the bombs was well planned to inflict maximum damage to the targets. They agreed prevention was all but impossible. Los Angeles, Phoenix, Albuquerque, and Houston are the most populous cities in their respective states. LAX, Sky Harbor, and Sunport are the largest and busiest airports in their states. John Wayne Airport and Hobby Airport are also located in extremely populous areas. They had explained a car parked for a period of time in an airport parking facility would not be suspicious or attract attention. That's why Mary and Clancy were here doing what they were doing. Immediately after 9/30 they had been assigned to inspect all vehicles parked in all of Denver International Airport's short and long term parking lots. They worked around the clock for two days with no sleep until all of DIA's parking lots were checked. They were then allowed to rest for twelve hours out of every twenty-four traveling to and inspecting all airport parking lots within ten miles of population centers in Colorado. When they finished that assignment some brainiac sitting behind a desk someplace determined all long term parking facilities near major cities needed to be checked too. Both Clancy's and Mary's expertise were deemed essential to that task.

It was then Clancy decided lunch break was over. He took his head off Mary's leg, stood up, and walked toward the next car. Mary got roused from her nap when she felt the tug on her wrist. Clancy was pulling on the leash. He wanted to go back to work.

Clancy was a specially trained three year old black and tan German Shepherd Dog, a member of the National Explosives Detection Canine Team. In addition to common explosives Clancy was also trained to detect trace radiation emitted by Uranium, and/or Plutonium.

Mary Pelton was a certified trainer, an officer who was provided with canine handler skills, and the basics in indoor and outdoor search practices searching luggage and all types of vehicles. Mary carried a portable sensor produced especially for use to detect the presence of a dirty bomb or a so-called suitcase bomb. Her hand-held detection device effectively sensed gamma and neutron radiation. The use of the dog in conjunction with the mechanical detector lessened the chance of either a false negative or a false positive alarm. They worked well together.

They were partners.

At thirty-three minutes after three in the afternoon Clancy barked. He jumped up and rested his front paws on the rear bumper of a black Chevrolet Astro cargo van. As Mary got closer, her portable sensor emitted a low hum. Mary went to the front of the van and peered into the windows. A curtain stretched across behind two bucket seats. She went to the rear but found solid panel doors with no windows allowing her to see inside the cargo area. Mary wrote down the Colorado license plate number, unhooked her cell phone and dialed headquarters. She reported the make, model, color, and plate number of the van. She gave them the location, the third level, downhill side, left side, of the Valet Parking Garage on Blake Street. Mary and Clancy hurried down the ramps to the entrance. Juan and a woman came out of the booth. The woman had a uniform shirt with the name Maria emblazoned on the front. Mary asked, "Are you the shuttle driver?"

Maria responded, "Yes, my name is Maria. Can I help you?"

Juan interrupted, "Shut up Maria. This is the bitch that's been nosing around with the dog. Why don't you go cruise the airport. We have a couple of customers scheduled to come back in this afternoon. You might as well be over there waiting." Looking at Mary he said, "You're done I hope."

Mary laughed and said, "No Juan you're done. No one comes in or out of this facility until I say so. Maria, same goes for you. Don't bring any customers back here until I say it is okay."

Juan became irate blurting, "Fuck you, the returning clients are the bigger tippers. We have customers to pick up. They have to claim their cars. They depend on us."

Mary shook her head and said, "Not until I say so. This facility is closed until further notice."

Sirens could be heard. The sound got louder, then two National Explosives Detection Canine Team vehicles pulled into the garage. Mary told them, "Third level, left side, black Chevrolet Astro van." They left rubber as they sped up the ramp. Four Denver police cars pulled up in the street outside the entrance. A sergeant stepped out of one of the cars. Mary raised her badge and announced, "Mary Pelton, Homeland Security. Sergeant, we have a potential threat here. Would you please have your men close the streets around this building to vehicles and pedestrians. We may have a nuclear bomb on site."

The sergeant directed his men to block the area and asked, "Do we need to evacuate the area, the city?"

"Not immediately, not yet, we don't want to create a panic unnecessarily. We need to check some more. I'll let you know."

Juan said, "Fuck, a bomb, I'm getting out of here."

Mary said, "Sergeant, stop him. I need that man. I want to know when the black van on level three was left here."

The Denver sergeant took Juan by the arm. He said, "Go in your booth and get the lady the information she wants."

Maria pleaded, "Can I go? I have kids. They need me."

Mary said, "Give the officer your name, address, and phone number and you can go."

Juan came out of the booth and announced, "That van came in on the thirteenth of September at six forty-two in the afternoon. The shuttle took the driver to Denver International, terminal three. The driver said he'd be back on the first of October. He's late. Can I go now?"

Mary said, "Give the officer your information in case we need to talk to you again."

Clancy and Pelton turned and took off at a quick walk back up to the third level. They arrived as one of the explosive detection officers slid a slim jim, a thin strip of flat metal with a hook used by locksmiths and first responders to open vehicles without a key, alongside the driver's side window of the van. He snagged the control rod for the door lock and pulled up. The sound of the door unlocking ensued. The officer carefully opened the driver's door, inspected for booby traps, and finding none, pressed the control unlocking all the vehicles doors. Another officer opened the passenger door, accessed the glove compartment, and removed a stack of papers. He said, "I have the registration and insurance card. The vehicle is a 1997 black Chevrolet Astro cargo van. This thing belongs to the American Charities for Madrassas. Dr. Umar al Jamai signed the registration."

Two other officers went to the rear doors. One of them, an officer named Kurt, swung one door open. He cautiously peered using a flashlight to illuminate the interior. He turned to Mary with a dejected look on his face. He said, "It's empty."

Clancy jumped up on the rear bumper, put his snout inside the van, and barked incessantly. Mary nudged Clancy aside, reached out with her portable sensor which produced a hum emitting louder the further into the vehicle she reached. Mary said, "I don't give a shit it's empty. I'm definitely detecting the presence of gamma and neutron radiation. Everybody close the doors, back away. Don't get too close. Here's what we're going to do. Call a tow truck. Have this thing taken to Buckley Air National Guard Base. Have the tow truck drop the van at the south end of the base. Put it by the dog kennel, but not too close. Put a guard on it until the lab techs can examine it in the morning. I'll notify the charity we impounded their van. I'll also write the report. You guys only have to safeguard the vehicle and escort the tow truck to Bradley. You can handle that right?"

Kurt spoke up, "Yeah what are you going to be doing while we do all the grunt work Mary?"

"First I'm going to say a short prayer thanking God the van was in fact empty, thank him we didn't have to call a code red, and evacuate the city. Then Clancy and I are going to finish the inspection of the other vehicles in this building. That is, if it's okay with you, Kurt." Mary then abruptly pulled on Clancy's leash and started down the ramp toward the other cars.

As Mary and Clancy walked around the next few vehicles she could hear Kurt and the other three officers murmuring amongst themselves. She kept working until she heard footsteps and looked up. Two of the officers, Jerry and Clay, came up to her. Mary asked, "What's up guys?"

They fidgeted, looked back and forth at each other, then Jerry said, "Mary this is a parking garage. It has an unusually low ceiling. No tow truck is going to get in here. Those things have a high boom or a tilt bed. How do you expect us to get the van out of here?"

Mary snickered, "You want a wheel lift tow truck. They're very low. They fit in a pick-up truck. They slide on the floor and a yoke locks around the tires. It lifts one end up slightly off the floor and pulls the vehicle right out. If you tow from the back wheels lock the steering wheel in place. Or better yet once outside the building switch the wheel lift to the front wheels. The rear end will then just follow along. For safety's sake, use your flashing lights and escort the tow truck."

Jerry said, "Thanks Mary we told Kurt you would know what to do."

When Mary finished with all the remaining cars, the van was gone, so she told the Denver sergeant it was okay for them to leave. She assured him there were no explosives in the van everything was all clear. She reminded him to call Juan and tell him it was safe for him and Maria to come back to work.

Mary and Clancy then walked the five blocks to where they had left their car in the morning.

Chapter Eighteen

11:16 a.m. Mountain Time, October 20

A RECEPTIONIST LED THE TRIPLE A team into a large office, actually a suite of rooms. They could see a full kitchen, outfitted with stainless steel appliances, a dining table with six captain's chairs arranged around it. French doors opened from the kitchen to a landscaped patio. An arch led to a short hallway ending in a closed door providing access to another room. The walls were covered with pictures and citations. A heavyset man with close-cropped hair and a face pockmarked with acne scars sat in a huge chair behind a large oak desk. He didn't stand or offer his hand. Instead he waved his arm and said, "Find a seat. Make yourselves comfortable. Can I have my girl get you anything? Coffee, soft drink, bottled water?"

They all shook their heads no. Al Garcia said, "No thank you, sir. We only have a couple of questions, then we'll be out of your way. This is a nice set-up you have here. It's huge. All of our desks plus those of even a couple more agents could fit into this office back in Washington."

John Marrone smirked and said, "What brings you out here, agents? How can I help? I don't have much time and you did arrive late."

Mendez who flashed a big smile replied, "Sir please accept my sincere apologies. Being late is all my fault. I drove and got us lost down by the border. Thankfully a couple of your border patrolmen saved our bacon, such nice men. I thought they called ahead and explained we would be a little late."

"Yeah they called but I don't have more time, so let's get on with your questions. What do you want?"

Garcia said, "Well sir we are here at the direction of President Burns.

Paul C. Gardner

He is awfully upset at the murders of the Rynning brothers in Bisbee and the Comforts outside of Douglas. He sent us out here to try to help you and Sheriff Mata-Villa figure out a solution to these murders."

"I don't know how I can help, agent. You should be taking this up with the sheriff. It is his jurisdiction. The border patrol concerns itself with the border."

"Yes sir, I understand. We already spoke to the sheriff, his assistant sheriff, the county attorney, his assistant, and their secretary. We're trying to narrow down who knew when the Rynnings were going to be interviewed by the assistant county attorney."

"How does that involve me?"

Cruz said, "Sir, the county attorney said you asked him when the interviews would be held."

"I don't remember asking."

"Well he said he distinctly remembered because at the time he didn't know and had to inquire himself. Why did you want to know sir, and who did you tell?"

"I told you I don't remember even asking. If I was told, I didn't tell anybody."

Garcia said, "Okay, you didn't know. That's fine. Let's move on. What did your investigation of the Comfort's murder turn up?"

"I didn't investigate the Comfort's murder. I told you that's the sheriff's job."

Garcia asked, "You were on the scene the morning of the Comfort's murder correct?"

"Yeah that's right. I was called out by some civilian militia guy. Thompson his name is. You ask me, him and his sons had something to do with this."

"Why do you say that?"

"Well their actions were exceptionally suspicious to me. Two of the sons wandering aimlessly around in the hills out there, I didn't at the time and still don't believe it. Bullshit. They became very uncooperative when I questioned them. They found bodies with the bellies ripped open and the eyes cut out and the boys go off to pick up garbage. Bullshit. They claim they received anonymous notification by phone where to find the bodies. Bullshit."

"The sheriff said you arrived at the scene about the same time as him. How did you manage that sir? It took us hours to get here from Bisbee and Douglas is even further away."

- 112 -

"I didn't go there from here. I was in the Douglas area all night. We apprehended a whole load of illegals coming across the border east of Douglas. The whole midnight to eight shift was ten miles east of Douglas. I diverted all of the men on duty during those hours. We had some haul. One of those awards on the wall was given for our performance in the darkness from midnight to before dawn that night."

Cruz said, "No shit. I'm impressed. You have awards from four feet off the floor to seven feet high all around the office. Are they all for apprehensions?"

"Yeah they are. My district is one of the highest apprehension districts on the southern border. I'm obviously proud of our record."

Garcia asked, "How did you stumble on all those illegals? Was it dumb luck?"

"No, of course not, a tip came in. We have confidential sources who us informed about when mass crossings are going to take place. We put as many resources on it as we can. It's worked great for years."

Mendez stood up and went to the wall making sure Marrone got a good look at her ass. She flashed another big smile and said, "I am so impressed sir. It appears you get at least an award a month. Dozens of them."

Garcia said, "Sit down Alex. You're embarrassing the chief."

Marrone nodded and said, "Alex, that's your name? It's all my men, Alex. They do a heck of a job. I'm very proud of them."

Garcia said, "As you should be sir. Now getting back to your investigation, did you uncover anything?"

"If you mean with the Comforts, I already told you, I didn't investigate that incident."

Cruz said, "Sir, the sheriff said he received a call to go back to the area where the Comforts were found after he had left. He said the Thompsons would not cooperate with your investigation. Did the sheriff get that wrong?"

"No, he didn't get that wrong. Three of my men and I came across the Thompson family sneaking around out there. I questioned them and they became irate, abusive, and uncooperative. My men called the sheriff, he came and resolved everything. But I wouldn't refer to the incident as an investigation. If you want to investigate, start with those Thompsons. They're hiding something. I can feel it. And on that note, we're going to have to end this. I have a luncheon appointment. Is there anything else?"

Mendez said, "Our records indicate Hector and Aliberto Castaneda have been arrested for violent crimes in the United States twenty-two times, eleven times each, and all that ever happens is they get deported. These guys are known cartel enforcers, career killers. The sheriff said to ask you how these scumbags keep getting released back to Mexico, only to return to kill again whenever they damn well please?"

"I have no idea. My men apprehend them, lock them up, and turn them over to the federal prison system or release them back across the border depending how we are instructed by the courts or the United States Attorney for the District of Arizona. If I remember correctly the United States Attorney had a federal judge sign a deportation order pertaining to the Castanedas. Ask him. Anything else?"

Garcia replied, "No, nothing else."

As they prepared to leave, Mendez smacked her hand to her head, saying, "Oh, one thing would help sir. Is it possible to get your cell number? Just in case we need to speak with you. I'd hate to make that drive again."

Marrone nodded and gave Mendez his card after he wrote a number on it. He said, "That's my cell number. Can I have yours in case I think of something important?"

Mendez gave him her card and said, "My cell number is on there. Call me anytime. Bye now." Mendez made sure to smile and wiggle her ass as she walked away. As they left the building Cruz called Lauren with Marrone's cell number, adding it to the watch list.

At twenty-five minutes before one Alex Mendez exited Interstate 19 north. The sign at the end of the ramp indicated traffic for Tubac should go to the right. The narrow tree lined two-lane road they took entered a small town. All of the buildings were either re-constructed or built new to match an early Arizona settlement. Failing to see any sign of a restaurant called Hernando's Hideaway, after they came to the end of the main street, Mendez made a u-turn. She proceeded all the way back slower but still didn't find their destination. She pulled into a gas station and said, "I'm going to fill up. Cruz, why don't you go inside and get directions."

Cruz returned when Alex finished gassing up. He said, "It's a hideaway all right. Go back through town, continue one mile and there will be a sign on the right."

Mendez did as directed. When she saw the sign she turned into a gravel driveway meandering back to a single story building completely hidden from anyone passing by. She parked in the shade under a huge cottonwood tree. For such an out of the way place there were a lot of other cars in the lot, about ten. Cruz led the way inside remarking, "Busy place. We're early. Let's get a table."

Cruz told the hostess they were meeting a friend and needed a table for four. She asked if they were Jesus' friends. When they nodded she motioned them to follow her. They did, through the dimly lit bar and the main dining room where couples sat together, past the restrooms, down a corridor, into a private room looking out over a water fountain and the rear parking lot. Jesus Noriega from the Sonora State Police sat at the table. He was dressed in creased jeans, tennis shoes, a button down sport shirt, and a blue blazer. Out the window, they could see a white car with Policia Sonora emblazoned on the side in red parked behind some shrubs in the back parking lot. Noriega stood, held out his hand, and said, "How the hell are you guys? What kind of shit are you stepping in this time?" A clean-cut good-looking Latino in his thirties, he didn't look like a typical Mexican policeman.

The Triple A team all shook Noriega's outstretched hand. Mendez gave him a hug and a peck on the cheek. Cruz said, "We're all good, how are you Jesus? What's all the secrecy about? You wouldn't believe the problems we had finding this place."

"It's hidden away intentionally. Most of the customers are cheaters. You know husbands and wives meeting up with someone other than their spouse. I come here occasionally when I'm looking for privacy." Jesus suggested, "Let's order lunch then talk. I brought some files I know you'll be interested in."

Garcia asked, "What's good here Jesus? I think I speak for all of us when I ask what your recommendation is."

Jesus said, "Rosa, please bring us a pitcher of margaritas, a pitcher of iced tea, nachos, salsa, guacamole to start, then four orders of seafood tostadas for lunch. Is that okay with everyone?"

Seeing no objection Rosa said "Got it. Be right back with the drinks and nachos. Do you want the door shut, Jesus?"

"Yes please, Rosa. Leave the door shut whenever you're not coming or going."

With Rosa gone and the door closed, Garcia asked, "Why all the cloak and dagger stuff Jesus, we would have been glad to go to your office."

"That would have been extremely dangerous for me and possibly you guys also Al."

"How so?"

"The guy whose picture you asked about is a scary, well-connected person."

"So what?"

"Mexico is not the United States. The drug cartels have owned the government and in turn the police and armed forces for years now. You remember when the Sonoma State Police Chief, Manuel Pavon, was assassinated in Nogales, what, five years ago now?"

"Yes, that's when we met you."

"Well the particular group who did the Pavon assassination was the Cortez Cartel. Their leader was and still is a guy named Angel Figueroa. Except now the Cortez Cartel is part of a much larger more organized group called the Alliance. To top it all Angel Figueroa is the leader, head honcho, of both the Cortez Cartel and The Alliance."

"We know who Figueroa is and what the Alliance does. What does all that have to do with the man in the picture?"

Before Jesus could answer they heard a knock on the door. Rosa entered carrying two pitchers. She was followed by a young man with a tray. He had four frosted margarita glasses, a dish with granulated salt that the rims of the glasses could be rubbed in, and four glasses for the iced tea. Rosa asked, "Who wants what?" They all opted for margaritas in salted glasses.

Once the drinks were prepared and Rosa and her helper left Jesus pointed to the picture Cruz had sent to him and continued, "I know him. That's Esteban 'Stewie' Nunez. They also call him 'Bonecrusher Nunez' and 'Angel's Stewmaker.' He lives on Figueroa's ranch. He does a lot of killing, but mainly he gets rid of the bodies. His victims are melted in acid according to informants. He uses a barn set aside for repairing mechanical equipment and cars and trucks on the ranch as his 'body shop,' according to others who turned State's evidence. It's said at first he used acid to dispose of Angel's victims—dissolving their bodies in concentrated sulfuric acid. He put bodies into a forty gallon drum and tipped concentrated sulfuric acid in to fill the barrel. Two days later he would return to find the body had become a pile of bones. He didn't want to be caught with bones and teeth so he asked Angel to buy him an industrial heavy-duty meat and bone sausage stuffer grinder. He didn't need it for meat but it certainly made it easy to pulverize the skeletons. The story goes whenever he had enough smashed bones to fill one or two five gallon pails he would take a small boat out on the Sea of Cortez and throw the pails over the side. He's paid a generous wage for his gruesome duties. It's all in the file. You can keep that if you want."

"If you know who he is can we send a warrant and have him extradited?"

"No. That will never happen. The government will not allow us to do our jobs anymore. The government works for the Alliance. My department works for the government."

"That sucks."

"Yeah, tell me about it. Any policeman who interferes with the Alliance is summarily fired. It used to be some officers resisted but when a few of them disappeared, probably into Stewie's body shop, everybody gave up."

"How about Stewie's fingerprints, are they in the file?"

"No but I may be able to get a set. Is it important?"

"Yeah it could be. We have some unidentified prints that forensic techs recovered from the bodies of the Comforts."

"I'll check around. If I can get a set without arousing suspicion I'll call you."

Rosa knocked on the door again, entered and served the tostadas.

After a pause in conversation as they all ate, Mendez raved about the taste. She wanted to know what the ingredients were. Jesus said, "As far as I know, the tostadas are large deep fried flour tortillas shaped into a bowl shape. For some reason the back of the bowl is shaped higher than the front. Just like these. There's a layer of refried black beans on the bottom, then shrimp, scallops, lobster and crab meat are added. Shredded iceberg lettuce, grated jack cheese, chopped tomatoes, and salsa with onion follow the seafood. That's all mixed together. Then sour cream, guacamole, a hint of fresh squeezed lime juice and diced cilantro goes on top."

After they all finished their tostadas and shared a second pitcher of margaritas, Garcia asked, "Jesus can you get us the particulars on Figueroa's ranch? The roads, buildings, topography, and where Nunez lives? Maybe our boss will let us go in and snatch him some night. Once he's on our side of the border we can always say we found him here."

"I can get some details but so you know, it's a huge place. I've heard nine thousand acres. I'll send the address and coordinates. It is a working ranch with horses, a stable, a winery, grape vines, cattle, and lots of crops. There is also at least a platoon of soldiers and several more hired killers besides Nunez in residence at the ranch. It won't be easy."

"Do you know who Hector and Aliberto Castaneda are?"

"Yes, of course. They are two more of Angel's enforcers. They live on the Figueroa ranch too. Angel Figueroa is surrounded by people like these guys. He has to be. He has a powerful place in the hierarchy of the Alliance. Given the opportunity any number of his rivals would kill him so they could take over. These guys are his protection from his partners. There are always rumors of internal unrest."

Garcia thanked Noriega for all his help and asked if they could do for him.

Jesus said, "Yes there is something one of you can do for me."

He explained what he needed. In case anyone followed him or watched, Alex walked out with Jesus, hand in hand, obvious lovers to any casual bystander. They paused at the fountain, whispering in each other's ears. Alex gave him a passionate kiss goodbye. Jesus drove away, Alex returned inside. Twenty minutes later, after she downed several glasses of iced tea, to dilute the margaritas she had consumed Alex announced, "I'm ready to go."

After paying their bill and leaving a generous tip Alex drove back through Tubac, drove on Interstate 19 south toward Nogales, exited north of the city, took North River Road east to Highway 82, where she followed the sign to Patagonia, stayed on 82 through Sonoita, took the 90 to 80 back to their motel.

When they parked and got out of the car Cruz teased, "Thanks for not taking your short cut back."

Alex laughed and replied, "Screw you, Cruz."

Chapter Nineteen

5:02 p.m. Mountain Time, October 22

THE SPEEDING COCHISE COUNTY SHERIFF'S CAR signaled and made a sharp turn from Route 80 into the parking lot of The Copper Mine Convention Center. Alexandra Mendez pointed to building one hundred and directed Assistant Sheriff Rich Farrell to pull up to the exterior door closest to the corridor leading to her room. When Farrell stopped and put the car in park Mendez opened her door, stepped out of the vehicle, then turned, leaned back inside and said, "Rich I want you to know under different circumstances this would have been a very enjoyable day. Being with you made my job a whole lot easier. I appreciate everything you did today. If I ever make it back to southeastern Arizona I look forward to getting in touch. Give my best to Sheriff Mata-Villa I'll miss him too. It was a pleasure working with you guys."

Farrell smiled a big toothy grin replying, "I don't know how I missed that reflection. It goes to prove you can learn something new every day."

"Don't beat yourself up about it Rich. Look at the bright side. If any of those dirt bags come across the border again we can nail them. The fact is if you get them, one or all, I'm sure Garcia will want us to come back out to help with the interrogation. See you big guy."

Mendez waved and walked away. Farrell watched her all the way inside before he drove away.

After freshening up Mendez noticed the hotel phone blinking. She listened to a message requesting she join Garcia and Cruz in Garcia's room. As soon as she came through the door Cruz wanted to go to the restaurant for dinner. Garcia said no he wanted everyone brought up to date including

Director Grass and thought it best to get Grass on the speaker phone so they only had to discuss the events of the day one time. He dialed and after a few seconds said, "Hello Director. Al here, Cruz and Mendez are with me. I'm going to put you on speaker."

With that he pressed the control and continued, "Sir, I think we had a fruitful day here. We started with a meeting with Sheriff Mata-Villa and Assistant Sheriff Farrell. They were flabbergasted when we showed them the reflection in Kiki's window and compared the image with the mug shot of Esteban Nunez that Jesus Noriega gave to us. We didn't let on about Jesus. They surmised Nunez' photo came from bureau files. We didn't correct their assumption. Based on the Nunez identification and the presence of Hector and Aliberto Castaneda's fingerprints on the clothing of the Comfort's corpses the sheriff agreed to put out a 'detain and notify' order on Nunez and the Castanedas. He sent out mug shots of all three and fingerprint cards for the Castanedas. All law enforcement and border patrol officers have been notified we want those guys. If any contact is made with any of them they are to be detained and Sheriff Mata-Villa is to be informed. The sheriff called the Border Patrol while we stood by, they confirmed they received and understood the order. Alex, who has established a rapport with Deputy Chief John Marrone, spoke with him directly informing him of the links we had established. I called the Cochise County Attorney's office and thanked Felix Burgos the county attorney and Joanna Castro his deputy for their help. They, after all, are the ones who originally spotted Nunez and informed us about a man standing across the street when the Rynnings ambush occurred. I made sure they knew their observations led to the identification of Nunez as the chief suspect. After all of those notifications were done I asked the sheriff if it would be possible for Assistant Sheriff Farrell to accompany Alex to interviews with the Rynning family members and their employers. He agreed it was a good idea for Farrell to bring Alex around since he had already spoken with all parties, knew where to find them, and could generally expedite Alex's visits. She can bring us all up to date on how things went when I'm finished. Al and I went to Kiki's for lunch, got a feel for that location, and spoke with Millie the waitress. Millie went on and on but didn't add anything useful. Nobody present inside Kiki's saw anything before the explosion and afterward everything was in turmoil. Millie called 911, which given the situation was all she could do. We showed the picture of Nunez around but nobody recognized him at all. Not the day of the explosion or at any time before or after. After lunch we went to the Thompson's. We did that mainly for appearances. In case anyone paid attention to our movements we wanted them to think we felt it necessary to interview the Thompsons in order to complete our investigation. Sir, your friend Emmett has a great family. We met with him, his father, his brothers and their wives and children. We did tell Emmett about our progress. But we also told him the most we could do was have the sheriff issue the 'detain and notify' request. That wraps it up for Al and me. If you don't have any questions Alex can report on her day."

Grass said, "Please go ahead, Alex."

Mendez took out her notebook, reviewed some entries and said, "After the meeting at police headquarters I accompanied Assistant Sheriff Farrell in his patrol car. Positively one of the shittiest days of my life. I interviewed Larry Rynning's wife Suzi, and met their kids. Three beautiful little girls, five year old Lori, Kimmie who is four, and two year old Jill. Suzi said as far as she knew only the immediate family and the Rynning's employers knew when and where the meeting with the county attorney was to take place. Farrell and I then went to Jenny Rynnings house. Jenny is Jimmy's widow. They have a young son, two year old Jimmy Junior. She said the same thing as Suzi Rynning. Only the family and employers knew about them meeting with the Burgos' people. The third brother, Craig, was single. Farrell drove me to the offices of Aaron Plumbing, Larry's employer. I spoke to Richard Mantello, the boss. Larry had told him he needed the day off to talk with the attorney. Mantello didn't tell anybody else. We then went to Gateway Electric's office; spoke to a guy named Rudy Salamon, Jimmy's boss. He acknowledged he had been told but adamant he didn't tell anyone else. Then we went inside the Fort Huachuca base to a jobsite where new housing for non-commissioned officers was being built. Bill O'Neil, Craig's foreman confirmed he was told by Craig he would not be into work for the day. He put Craig down as absent on the timesheet. Nobody else was informed. Nobody needed to be. The contractor, Level Framing, is based in Phoenix and relies on O'Neil to call in the correct hours for payroll. Sir, we have to nail this Nunez guy, even if we have to go into Mexico to get him. Today was horrible sir, a lot of emotion, crying, despair, I feel so bad for the families. Suzi Rynning is pregnant with a son. Neither she nor Jenny know how they are going to raise their kids. They both received some small life insurance settlements but not enough to live on. The boys all belonged to trade unions so they received small death benefits, enough to bury them. Some private donations came in but they have dried up. They don't know what they are going to do. Probably welfare. The kids are all so young. They're trying but may lose their houses. They all made good money, Larry and Jimmy both owned their own homes with their wives, but the girls say they don't know how they will continue to pay the mortgages. They are burning through their savings. It's a tough situation. Suzi, Jenny, and the kids may be eligible for some Social Security survivor's benefits. Try to be a good citizen and look what happens."

Garcia interrupted asking, "Is that it Alex?"

"Yeah that's it. I just want to cut Nunez' balls off."

Garcia asked, "You have anything to add Cruz?"

Cruz said, "Yes sir. As you and the director already know, and Alex now knows, Jesus Noriega e-mailed Nunez' fingerprints to me this afternoon. I forwarded them to Lauren. They are being processed through our database as we speak. He also sent Angel Figueroa's address and property coordinates to me. I have them if we need them."

Grass interjected, "Which reminds me. Lauren has gone home for the day but before she left she sent those prints to the lab, they returned a hit already. They confirmed Nunez' prints as among the unidentified prints recovered from the Comforts. He was there."

Mendez said, "Another reason to cut his balls off."

Grass asked, "So I assume everything is wrapped up there?"

Garcia replied, "Yes sir, for now at least. We plan to check out of the hotel tomorrow. As far as everyone around here is concerned we're going back to Washington. But first we want to cover all our bases by speaking with the Huertas. If the company plane is available we can return the car rental, fly to Denver, rent another car, drive down to Pueblo, and interview the Huertas. If the plane is not available we can still checkout and drive to Colorado. We can drop the rental car at Denver International, fly back to Washington or better yet maybe by then Jesus will come back with some ideas about going into Mexico to nab Nunez and the Castanedas. We sure as heck would love to go in and bring them out."

Grass asked, "How long will it take to drive to Pueblo?"

"Fifteen or sixteen hours. We have three drivers. It's not a problem."

"Do that then. The plane is needed elsewhere. Drive up. Check into a motel in Pueblo. Get a good night's sleep then walk in on the Huertas late morning the day after tomorrow. Surprise them. We'll talk again after you have spoken to the Huertas."

"Okay boss, good night. We'll call if anything comes up."

As soon as Garcia hung up Cruz said, "Dinner anyone?"

At 5:40 p.m. Mountain Time. October 23, it began to get dark in northern Mexico. Jesus had been on the move all day long walking the perimeter of the ranch fence. The property was, in his estimation, impenetrable. Entirely fenced, electrically charged with razor wire coiled all along the top. No way over the top, no trees that could be climbed with branches overhanging the fence we could utilize to gain access. No way underneath, the chain link was buried at least three feet deep. Constant armed patrols passing on the interior perimeter road in jeeps equipped with machine guns. The only interruption in the fence was at the one road in and out of the ranch. There was an electrically controlled gate across the road manned twenty-four hours a day by armed guards stationed in a gate house. He tried but couldn't see any way in. He was starting to get tired. It had been a long day.

He had driven by the front of the property, where it paralleled Highway 15, several times yesterday so he only had to cover the top, back, and bottom of the ranch today. The problem—he had to walk one end to the other then retrace his steps in order to keep from being seen from the highway. When he arrived before dawn this morning, he drove down a dirt off-road trail that did not appear to have had any traffic in months. The trail ran in about a quarter of a mile north of the northeast corner of the ranch. He left his Harley far enough in from the highway so it couldn't be seen. He carried a backpack containing food and water, binoculars, a compass, and a topographic map of the entire area. Of course he carried his sidearm. He was never without a gun.

As the sun came up this morning he attached a pedometer to his belt and headed west paralleling the northern fence line. A pedometer senses your body motion and counts your footsteps. This count is converted into distance by knowing the length of your usual stride. It didn't do much good. Given the uneven terrain and the resulting short and long steps, the device did count steps, but could not calculate distance. It did however keep time. He recorded the distance he already knew from corner to corner, noted his pace and the total time. It was something. It could help later.

He saw the lights before he saw or heard the men. They approached from the direction of the highway, right in the way of where he had to go. He dropped to the ground and scurried to cover behind a tree as soon as he saw the first flash of light. Now as he peeked around the tree he counted eight flashlights slightly spread out all coming toward him. He decided to creep further north away from the fence line. He stopped crawling when he thought he was about fifty feet further north than the man with the light who was furthest away from the fence. He could hear them talking amongst themselves. They were looking for a person reportedly seen sneaking around near the fence line a couple of times today. He had been so careful. He didn't think anybody had seen him. Every time he heard one of the jeeps coming he hid. He never saw anyone on foot. No planes flew over. He didn't see any cameras or motion detectors. He never touched the fence. But obviously he screwed up somehow. He had been seen not once but several times. He heard someone order the others to spread out, widen the sweep. Minutes later footsteps approached his hidey hole. Beams of light splayed around him. He tried to squeeze himself smaller. His heart raced. He was scared. *Oh shit, they are going to hear my heartbeat. It's so damn loud.*

Then they past by him. He could breathe again. For over eleven hours he'd been exploring, looking for a weak spot. Exhausted, his pedometer said he had covered over eighteen miles. Shit, with all the breaks, stopping and hiding, checking out possibilities he averaged less than two miles per hour, closer to one and a half miles per hour. He waited until the men carrying the lights were out of sight then he got to his feet and moved quietly through the brush until he came to the trail where he had hidden his motorcycle. He turned east.

Within minutes he found his Harley. He packed up, started it, and drove slowly with his lights off toward the highway. He heard vehicles then saw headlights of cars going by. He started to relax, thinking *I'm gonna make it home tonight.* Ten feet from the trailhead he was blinded. Bright headlights and flashing strobe light bars came on. Sirens wailed. Then there was silence. A loudspeaker commanded, "Stop. This is the policía. Put your hands over your head."

He did as he was told. *Thank God* he thought. He identified himself saying, "I'm a cop too. My ID is in my pocket."

For an answer a rifle butt smashed into the side of his head. Everything went black.

Jesus woke up in pain. His head ached. His right ear throbbed where he was hit. That was the last thing he remembered until now. His hands were cuffed behind his back. He opened his eyes. Everything was dark, very dark. His senses started coming back. He felt motion, movement like he was bouncing along in the trunk of a speeding car. The car slowed, his head roared from intense distress. As his body rocked with the sway of the car he found the physical suffering barely tolerable. He realized he fucked up, bad, really bad. *Why did he come out here? How fucking stupid.* The mental anguish felt as painful as the aching in his head.

The car came to a stop but then moved forward again. It stopped and turned, accelerated then slowed. Every new motion sent more pain through his body. More than that though was the realization he was caught. He shook with fear.

Finally the car stopped and the engine turned off. The trunk lid opened. He was dragged out of the trunk and stood up. He looked around and immediately recognized his surroundings. He faced the Hermosillo indoor market. Closed for the day now but before dawn tomorrow it would be bustling as farmers and vendors stocked the tables in the booths lined up and down inside. Fresh produce, fish, and meat in one section, clothing in another. Home furnishings, decorations, appliances, anything that could be bought or sold would be found tomorrow in the market. Rough hands spun him around. He saw lights from the cantina on one side and the blinking sign for the taco shop on the other. They stood directly in front of the Hermosillo Police Station. No one was in the street. There were no witnesses as he was pushed and pulled inside the front doors of the stationhouse.

He was dragged past the front desk, down a corridor, in full view of men in police uniforms. He thought he knew some of them. He tried to make eye contact but everyone he thought he recognized diverted their eyes. He pleaded, 'Help me. I'm a cop."

The man walking behind him slapped his right ear with an open hand. The pain stabbed through his head. He screamed. Everyone ignored him.

A solid door in the hall opened. He knew that was where the cells were located. Quickly he prayed no one here heard him cry out he was a cop. If he was thrown in with other prisoners who knew he was a cop he would be dead by morning.

His worst fears subsided when his escorts led him to an isolation cellblock. A door opened. He was roughly shoved inside a cell. He was uncuffed and pushed down to sit on a single bunk bed. The man who was walking behind told the two other guards to wait outside in the corridor. He stood in front of the bunk and said, "I am Detective Arturo Ramirez Zambrano of the Hermosillo Municipal Police. You are under arrest for trespassing. Do you have anything to say for yourself?"

"Yes detective, I am Jesus Noriega. I am a detective also. I am with the Sonora State Police. I work out of the Nogales State Police Headquarters.

There has been a big mistake here. I was simply hiking. I took some personal time to get away. Please call my supervisor, Comandante Macario Enrique Ramirez Zamora. Comandante Zamora will personally vouch for me. There is no justification for this treatment."

"You will remain here for the time being. I have all of your belongings. We searched you and your motorcycle when you were taken into custody. I have already called your station. They confirmed you work there but do not know where you are, where you went, or why you came to our jurisdiction. They simply expect you back in a few days. Why were you hiking where we found you?"

"No special reason. Just random. I often pull off the road, park, and hike when an area appears interesting. It's my way of being adventurous while at the same time staying in shape."

"I don't believe a word you are saying. Tell me the truth."

Jesus gingerly touched his right ear felt the crusted blood and asked, "Can I see a doctor?"

"Sleep on it. Tough it out. I have some work to do. We'll see how it looks in the morning."

Detective Zambrano abruptly walked out of the cell. The door was slammed shut and locked. The window in the door slid closed. A bright light in the ceiling turned on.

Jesus removed his shirt folded it lay down and covered his eyes with the shirt. He tried to sleep but couldn't. He kept admonishing himself for being so stupid.

Chapter Twenty

TRIPLE A DROVE SLOWLY PAST A single story metal industrial building with a large sign identifying it as the home of 'Huerta's Auto Body Shop.' It was in an industrial park across Highway 50 from Pueblo Memorial Airport. They entered the park from a street running parallel to the highway called Frontage Road. The Huerta's building was located at the end of a short cul-de-sac. They checked the address, 120 Industrial Avenue, Unit B. They looked at the front and both sides then went back to Frontage Road made a right, another right, and another right which brought them to a point on the next street where they could see the rear of the body shop. There were no windows. All the doors, roll-up doors front and rear, and an office entry door in the front were closed. Both roll-up doors were equipped with man doors, doors which allow entry without opening the bay door. It was freezing cold outside. They had awoken to an unexpected early-season snow storm. They had checked out of The Copper Mine Convention Center the previous morning and drove, in bright sun until darkness came, fourteen hours from Arizona through New Mexico to Pueblo, Colorado. They only stopped for food, gas, and bathroom breaks. On their trip they went out of their way to by-pass Albuquerque, New Mexico. They gave the site of the former Sun Port Airport a wide berth. Sun Port was one of the airports destroyed by nuclear explosion on September thirtieth. At ten twenty-five yesterday they had called it a night retiring to three rooms in the Pueblo Holiday Inn Express.

In the morning, when they looked out their windows, they learned early snow in Colorado's Front Range, as the area is called, is normal. In

Pueblo, located in the Arkansas River valley, not the mountains, snow is also not unexpected in October. After enjoying complimentary breakfast in the hotel lobby they set out to find the Huerta clan. That wasn't hard as Lauren, Ed Grass' office manager, did the research for them and said the Huertas all worked together at Huerta's Auto Body Shop. She had provided the address and directions.

After viewing the situation, Garcia devised a plan on the spot. He sent Cruz around the back to make sure no one bolted through the rear. Mendez was to prevent anyone from leaving through the front roll-up door. Because they were not really dressed in warm clothes designed for snow Garcia directed them to enter the man doors in two minutes securing those exits from inside. All three hung their shields around their necks outside their clothes. Al Garcia opened the office door and walked inside.

He quickly glanced around. He stood in a small dim waiting room surrounded by a couch, some chairs, and a few tables stacked with magazines. A short hall had a sign directing people to the restrooms. He moved to a counter with a sliding glass window, which provided a view of a big well-lit office. The office had two walls, consisting mostly of glass that allowed a full view of the body shop. A door led to an adjoining large room with a table and chairs, TV, refrigerator, microwave, sink and cabinets. No one was in that room. In the shop area Garcia could see twelve separate bays with vehicles in them. He counted seven workmen in identical blue uniforms attending to various tasks. Car doors, bumpers, fenders, and other components arranged on the floor and workbenches. Welding torches and paint sprayers functioned in different areas. All areas of the building were meticulously clean and organized. Electric space heaters operated in the office and waiting room. Reflector type ceiling units directed heat down onto the shop floor space. After a minute and a half Garcia tapped on the glass. A man and two women sitting at desks looked up at him. He pointed to his badge and held up his credentials wallet for them to see. All three dropped what they were doing and looked at each other. The man reacted first. He motioned with his hands for the women to remain where they were. He stood up and walked to the glass. He slid the window open.

Like the two women in the office the man wore blue pants and a white shirt. His name, Leon, sewn in above the right shirt pocket. A Huerta's Auto Body decal appeared on the left pocket. An American flag patch was on the left shoulder. All of the workers both in the office and on the shop floor had similar patches. The man facing Garcia smiled broadly. He was a handsome well-built young Latino man with fashionably styled pitch black short hair and bright black eyes. He asked, "How may I help you?"

Garcia responded, "My name is Al Garcia. I'm with the FBI. I have some questions for Consuela, Leon, Jose, Alphonso, Maria, Roberto, Filipe, Vincente, Manlio, and Diego Huerta. Are you Leon Huerta?"

Leon nodded and waved his hand in a broad circle saying, "Yes sir, I am Leon. Maria and Consuela are right here in the office. The others are all out in the garage area. Can I ask what this is about?"

"I'd rather go over this once with everyone present. Can you bring them all in here?"

Leon replied, "This is a terribly inconvenient time. As you can see everyone is working. We close at five, can you come back then?"

"No, now is a good time."

"Agent I am trying to cooperate. As you can see we are exceedingly busy doing tasks we cannot stop doing. I can speak with you now, so can Maria and Consuela but the others are in the middle of operations that once started cannot be halted until they are finished. The men in the shop wearing the air-supplied respirators are working with compressors, power jacks, and body fillers doing frame and metal straightening and dent removal. They are also busy filling and sanding on various vehicles out there. Others are working in paint spray booths. They are in the middle of applying base coats, clear coats, prime coats, and or top coats of vehicle paint jobs. So I have to insist now is not a good time. Come back at five."

Garcia asked, "Do the shop workers stop for lunch?"

"Yes at noon for forty-five minutes. We also close the office at noon for forty-five minutes. Our phones automatically inform callers we are closed for lunch and to leave a message or call back. Do you want to speak with everyone at lunchtime?"

"Noon will be good."

Leon turned his back to Garcia, took two steps, looked into the shop area and immediately returned to the window. He pointed toward the shop and said, "Are they with you?"

"If you mean the two agents by the two exit doors, yes they are with me."

"They can't stay in there. That is dangerous. Our insurance does not cover anyone but employees in the shop. Tell them to come in here."

"No they are going to stay by the exits. When all of the workers are in here they will come in also."

Leon whirled and told the women, "Connie get Sidney on the phone for me. Maria call Walter Goff. I'd like to speak with him."

Leon walked back and slid the window dividing the office and waiting room shut. He returned to his desk picked up his phone, pressed a button, spoke, then he pressed another button and had another brief conversation. He then grabbed a microphone pulled it to his face and spoke into it. His voice could be heard over a loudspeaker system. Garcia could hear Leon explain, the people standing inside the garage doors were FBI agents, everyone should ignore them. Keep working, stop work as usual for lunch. He advised everyone to speak to no one until they all spoke together in the break room.

The Huertas took a moment to look around, identify the agents, then they all went back to work. They did not appear to be upset or nervous at all.

Leon said something to Consuela and Maria. Maria stood, entered the break room, went into the fridge and cabinets, took things out and appeared to be preparing lunch.

About fifteen minutes before noon most of the mechanical noises stopped. Power tools were put on benches, compressors shut down, and paint equipment was disassembled and cleaned. Respirators, gloves, and safety glasses were removed. The workers went to semi-circular wash sinks, cleaned up, went to the restroom, and milled about whispering quietly amongst themselves.

At five before twelve a short, heavyset man in a grey suit, red tie, and brown topcoat came through the front door, walked past Garcia, and entered the office. He shook hands with Leon and Connie. They exchanged some quick words then he motioned them into the break room. Leon waved to the others who joined them.

Two minutes before noon the front entry door pushed open again. A tall, about six-one, burly, middle aged man in a blue uniform came in. He was followed by a younger but taller, heavier man also in a blue uniform. Both men approached Garcia. The older one said, "I'm Walter Goff, Pueblo's police chief. Who are you and what do you want here?"

Garcia pointed to his badge, displayed his credentials and said, "I'm FBI agent Al Garcia. I am here with agents Cruz and Mendez to ask the Huertas some questions."

"Why wasn't I informed about this, agent? You are in my jurisdiction here. The Denver office always informs my department when agents I don't know are working in Pueblo."

"I would say the Denver office didn't inform you sheriff because we don't work out of Denver. We work out of Washington and our superiors did not tell the Denver office about our investigation here either. This case does not involve you or them."

"What is this all about agent?"

Garcia decided to placate the sheriff and said, "We are not trying to exclude your department chief. If you want to listen in please join us."

Goff replied, "I intend to." He nodded to the other officer and said, "Bobby stay with the agent, I'm going inside."

Goff went through the office into the break room. He shook hands with Leon and the man in the suit. He gave Connie a peck on the cheek. They all huddled again, then the sheriff waved to Garcia and Bobby to come in. Garcia motioned for Cruz and Mendez to join them.

The break room table had twelve chairs around it. The Huertas sat around the man in the suit and tie. The man draped his topcoat over the empty chair. Around the table ten sets of piercing black eyes studied Garcia, their expressions apprehensive. All the men appeared much the same; wiry, muscular, average height, straight black hair, dark skin, and stoic. The two women were medium height and thin. Their tight white uniform tops revealing firm breasts accenting obvious hard bodies. Uncommonly attractive, their complexions a shade of mocha tan, like they spent their weekends in the sun or their nights in tanning booths.

Chief Goff, Bobby, Garcia, Mendez, and Cruz stood against the walls. The man in the grey suit addressed Garcia saying, "I'm Sidney Korash. I am an attorney. I represent the Huertas. Now what is this about?"

Garcia nodded at Korash, displayed his credentials and said, "Glad to meet you Mister Korash, I'm Al Garcia, this is Alexandra Mendez, and this is Alfred Cruz. We are FBI agents. We are on special assignment investigating a double murder which occurred in Arizona."

Korash asked, "What does a double murder in Arizona have to do with my clients?"

Garcia replied, "That is what we are trying to determine. In order to clear this up we need some answers. Please give us the location of each of your clients between midnight and eight on the morning of October eighth."

"Anything else?"

"Possibly, it depends on their whereabouts."

Korash said, "I need to speak with my clients alone."

Garcia motioned Cruz and Mendez to follow him into the shop. Before closing the door he said, "We'll wait out here."

The chief and Bobby went into the office and closed that door.

The Triple A team walked to the middle of the shop. Garcia told them the lawyer and the sheriff being there restricted what they could do and say. He reminded them they had to keep Emmett Thompson's name out of it. They couldn't even insinuate they had a witness, the bottles with fingerprints, nor the recording. Cruz asked, "How do you want to work it boss?"

Garcia responded, "I don't know. Let's play it by ear. Let's listen to what they have to say."

They looked back into the lunch room. After a flurry of hand waving and everyone talking at the same time Maria went to a file cabinet and brought a folder back. Leon pointed to some papers as Korash listened. Korash then waved everyone back into the break room. Once everyone settled in he announced, "All of the Huertas were in Las Cruces, New Mexico. They went there in mid-September. They took a bus back to Pueblo leaving Las Cruces late evening on the ninth of October arriving in Pueblo about mid-day on the tenth. Anything else?"

"Yes. Where did each of them stay while they spent all of that time in Las Cruces?"

"They tended to a family emergency. They split up and stayed with different family members. They all gathered together and stayed at a hotel the night of the eighth the night before they caught the bus." Korash showed the paperwork to Garcia saying, "I can provide you with copies of receipts for the hotel and the bus. Anything else?"

Perusing the receipts Garcia said, "I'll take those copies and yes there is something else. Where did each of them stay on all the other nights? In order to complete our investigation we need the names, addresses and phone numbers of the various family members they say they stayed with in Las Cruces. Let's make it easy, start with the night on the seventh. That is the night before they stayed in the hotel. That is the night which includes the timeframe, midnight to eight, on the morning of October eighth. And counselor, please provide accurate information. We already know a lot about their activities."

Leon Huerta leaned over and whispered in Korash's ear. The lawyer nodded and said, "The relatives they stayed with live incognito. Most are in the country illegally. They move around frequently and do not have fixed addresses or phone numbers. We can't help you there. If you already know about their activities then you know that."

Garcia decided to bluff. He slowly looked each Huerta in the eye, quietly and calmly saying, "Mister Korash your clients are lying. They crossed the Mexico border into Arizona with a major drug shipment. They were among a group of drug smugglers who brutally murdered two American citizens. We need to clarify whether or not they are murderers, co-conspirators, or witnesses. They need to level with us."

Chief Goff turned red-faced with anger. He blurted out, "I've known these people for years. I can personally attest to their character. They are pillars of this community. You come in here and accuse them of lying, of murder and drug smuggling. That is outrageous. They wouldn't have anything to do with drug smugglers. Don't you realize their history? Drug people killed their relatives. They themselves have threats against their lives. Not one of them has a criminal record. Nothing at all, no violence, no deceptive business practices, no alcohol or drug abuse. They told you they visited in Las Cruces with family. They have receipts. What have you got?"

Korash said, "The chief is right agent. I too can attest to the standing in the community of the Huertas. They're a close family, completely stable. This is disgusting racial profiling. Drug dealers, murderers—you are way off-base with your accusations. Show us what you have or this interview is over."

"All right, excuse us for one minute." With that Garcia, Cruz, and Mendez went into the shop closing the door behind them.

Garcia asked, "Alex do you have the recording of the Huertas when the Comforts seeing them was discussed."

"Yes. Do you want to play it?"

"Sure. They don't have to know how the recording was made or where we got it from. Set it up to start with Maria. We'll play it through them being told to get in the vans."

Alex set up the portion Garcia asked for and said, "Okay boss. It's all ready to go."

Returning into the room, Garcia smiled, placed his clasped hands solemnly in front of his body and lied, "You all are aware the United States is extremely concerned about security along our borders. What you may not know is, utilizing our latest spy-in-the-sky surveillance equipment, we have the capability to see and hear everything that occurs in areas we are concentrating on. One of those satellites hovered over southeast Arizona on the night in question. Agent Mendez please start the recording."

Alex placed the device on the table and pressed play. They all heard, "You can't leave them. They've seen us.—Be quiet Maria.—Don't tell her that.—You too Connie.—Who made you boss Leon?—It will be taken care of.—They can't be allowed to say they saw us.—Relax, we'll take care of it.—Come on, I don't like standing around here. Cops or border patrol could come by anytime.—Don't worry about that either. The cops are all sleeping or someplace else, and the border patrol are bought and paid for. There is no chance of us or you getting caught tonight.—Yeah the big border guy does what we tell him. He's got all his men twenty miles away.—What are you going to do about the couple you caught spying?—That's none of your business. I already told you it will be taken care of. Get in the vans and get out of here. An example will be made. You have nothing to fear from these people. Now take your group, get in the vans, and get out of here. You have a long trip." Alex pressed stop and returned the recorder to her pocket.

Garcia confidently continued, "We also have video of you all entering the two white vans. We already confirmed your registration records from the Postada Hotel and Greyhound. Do you still want to deny being there?"

A furious Korash exclaimed, "I need to speak privately with my clients again."

Chief Goff, obviously recognizing the voices of the Huertas on tape, was no longer red-faced. Instead, so irate at being played for a fool, he turned purple, sputtering, "I've heard enough. I'm going back to the stationhouse. Agents if you need me call me there." He handed Garcia his card and stormed out with Bobby trailing behind.

With the Triple A team conversing softly in the shop the Huertas and their attorney talked. Then Maria took a pot out of the microwave spooned the contents onto dishes and handed them out. Korash held up his hand indicating he didn't want any. As they ate they continued to talk several times looking through the glass wall to observe the agents. They laughed. Cruz remarked, "Look at those bastards. They aren't concerned at all. In fact they look relieved. They think this is funny."

The Huertas with the names Jose and Alphonso sewn on their shirts stood, gathered the dishes, utensils, and pot. They filled the sink, washed and dried everything, and placed it all into the cabinets. When they sat back down Korash waved the agents back inside. Korash sipped from a bottle of water. The Huertas each had a can of soda or a bottled water. The agents weren't offered anything.

Korash began, "My clients were in Mexico not Las Cruces for their family emergency. They drove down across the border and they did transfer title to their vehicles to other poorer family members. When time came to return home they found out a passport was required for even American citizens to cross the border back into the United States. They had no idea previously about this law. All of the Huertas are naturalized citizens. But none of them have ever applied for or obtained passports. They were confused. They did not want to get into any trouble. They were afraid. I explained to them they would have been admitted back even without passports. Driver's licenses and social security cards, which they all have, would have sufficed. Maybe the border patrol at the check station would have had to call me or Chief Goff but they would have been allowed back in. They will know next time. In fact they are all going to apply for passports. My office will handle that for them. At any rate, one of their family members knew a guy who knew a guy who agreed to guide them back across the border for three hundred dollars each. For an additional two hundred each he agreed to provide van transportation to Las Cruces. They paid five thousand in cash. They did not smuggle drugs. They did not carry or handle any drugs. They did not murder anybody. They don't know the names of anyone who crossed the border with them. No names were spoken. They are profoundly sorry if they caused you any trouble. They apologize."

Garcia asked, "Would they be able to identify any of the men they crossed with?"

Korash looked at Leon. Leon admitted, "I could probably identify the leaders. I spoke with two of them. I could possibly identify one or two more."

Garcia asked, "Anyone else? I know the women were also in contact with the leaders, weren't they?"

Maria said, "I think I could recognize a few of them."

Connie nodded, "Me too."

Garcia said, "We don't have any IDs yet on any of the smugglers. We are working on it. When we have suspects can we ask your clients to look at them in a lineup?"

Korash quickly replied, "Yes, no problem at all."

Garcia looked over at Cruz and Mendez asking, "Do either of you have any questions?"

Cruz shook his head. Mendez said, "I do." Pointing at Maria she asked, "What's the meal you served for lunch? It smelled delicious."

Maria laughed, "Chicken and rice. An old recipe of my grandmother's. I don't have a copy. It's in my head."

Smiling at the break in tension, Korash asked, "Anything else?"

Mendez said, "Yes, can I get the cell phone numbers for the Huertas in case we have any more questions? In case something else comes up."

Korash handed each of the agents his card saying, "The Huertas are represented by my office. If you have any further questions please feel free to contact me anytime. I have all of their contact information including their cell phone numbers. If they need to be contacted I'll do it."

Leon interrupted, "If there is nothing else we have to get back to work."

Garcia replied, "That is all. Thank you for your cooperation. We'll call your attorney if we have anything else." Garcia then handed Korash and each of the Huertas a business card. He instructed Cruz and Mendez to do the same. He explained, "In case anything else comes to mind. Our office and individual cell numbers are on there. Please feel free to call any one of us."

The team bade everyone goodbye and stepped outside into driving windblown snow. As they moved toward their car Cruz mumbled to himself, "Fucking cold, go to sunny Arizona and wind up freezing our asses off in the snow in Colorado. What bullshit. Those people are hiding something. This sucks."

Mendez told Cruz, "What are you babbling about Al? Garcia bluffed them, they fell for it, and they agreed to identify the Comforts' killers. We'll be on a plane back to D.C. by tonight. Stop bitchin'."

Cruz stared back, "Something's not feeling right. I know it all fits with everything Emmett told us, but something's fishy. Shit, they almost seemed relieved, they're happy, laughing. I don't know what exactly, there is something wrong."

Shaking her head Mendez said, "Yeah you think about it Cruz. When it comes to you let us know. Now shut up and get in the car. Let's get the heater going."

Garcia's phone began vibrating in his pocket. He answered, "Yes director, I was just going to call. We finished up here. Good news, it appears a few of the Huertas may be able to identify Hector Castaneda, Aliberto Castaneda, and Esteban Nunez. Hopefully they will be able to put them at the scene of the Comforts' murders...Yes sir, they were cooperative…No shit, we knew that fucker was slimy…Yes sir, I'll tell the others…We'll head right back tomorrow morning…Yes sir…Thank you sir…Goodbye."

Garcia turned to the others and said, "It's John Marrone. The phone taps paid off. We're going back to Arizona."

Chapter Twenty One

5:16 p.m. Mountain Time, October 24

JESUS WAS DOZING WHEN THEY CAME for him. Two guards entered Jesus' cell, different men from the ones before. They pushed a stretcher inside, told him to strip naked and to lie down on the stretcher. After he did as he was told, they tied him down on the wheeled stretcher with his arms at his sides, securely strapped with restraints across his chest and his upper arms, at his waist, across his forearms, across his thighs, and at his ankles. Naked, not a stitch of clothes, no shoes, no socks, the guards wheeled him out of his cell, into an elevator, where he was taken down to an even lower level. Rolled out of the elevator and into the middle of a dark room, a bare light bulb suspended two feet above his face glowed. The air was especially hot and humid.

"Are you comfy Jesus?"

Jesus recognized the voice. He said, "Detective Zambrano, where am I? What day is it? What time is it? I need a doctor. My ear hurts. I'm hungry. I'm a fuckin' cop. What is goin' on here?"

Zambrano responded, "Standard procedure. I bring all of my special prisoners down here for little talks. I like you. I just know we're going to get along. We're going to have a great time. You simply need to answer some questions first. Okay?"

Jesus said, "Arturo can I please have some water?"

Ignoring the request Zambrano said, "You had a cell phone in your pocket when I brought you in. I checked your cell phone records. You received a phone call from a United States area code at 9:17 a.m. on

October twentieth. That phone call lasted twelve minutes. Who called you? What did you talk about?"

Jesus swallowed hard. If they knew about the phone call they probably know he crossed the border and went to Hernando's Hideaway in Tubac. Thank God Alex walked him out and kissed him goodbye. He decided to lie. If they were watching it could fly. He responded, "A girl I know called me. We talked about old times. She asked me to join her for lunch. I did. I met her that afternoon."

"Why did she call you again at 9:35 if you already agreed to meet for lunch?"

"She called back to confirm what time she could make it. I then called Hernando's and made reservations."

The bottom of Jesus' right foot was slammed with a nightstick. He howled in pain. When he regained his composure he said, "I'm a cop. You took my clothes. You have my ID. Call my commanding officer please. He'll tell you I'm a cop. Please don't hurt me. We're all on the same side."

The cop laughed, "I already called your headquarters in Nogales. I spoke to one of my contacts there. I know who you are. And Jesus we are not all on the same side. You for instance are on the side of the Americanos. My allegiance is to Mexico and all things Mexican. You know what I think? I think you're lying to me now."

"No. No. Please I had lunch with a girlfriend."

The cop swung the nightstick into Jesus' left foot. Jesus howled in pain again. The cop said, "Stop lying, asshole. My man checked your desktop computer. You received a photo by e-mail at 9:28 the morning you say your girlfriend called you. That photo is of a friend of mine. Tell me about the picture. Why the interest in my friend? Who did you really speak on the phone with? Who did you really meet at Hernando's?"

"Just a girl. You have this all wrong. A picture did come through on e-mail but I think it was sent to me by mistake. I remember now there was no cover letter. I simply disregarded that picture."

Detective Zambrano unwrapped a cigar. He made a show of clipping one end off before lighting it. He sat in a chair next to the stretcher drawing on the cigar blowing out the smoke thinking. Apparently making up his mind he asked, "Ready to tell me everything, Jesus?"

"Of course I'll tell you whatever I know. Please believe me."

"Jesus, my contact checked, you signed out a file on Angel Figueroa after you spoke to your girlfriend. You signed the file back in thirty minutes later. Just enough time to copy the file don't you agree?"

Jesus responded, "No that's a mistake. I didn't sign out any files on El Jefe. I didn't make any copies. You have to believe me."

"You had a topographic map of El Jefe's ranch when we found you. Why did you have that map?"

"I always carry a map of where I hike."

"The last time we spoke you said you pulled over at random. Why did you have a map of the area if the location was random?"

"That's not entirely correct. I knew the general area I wanted to hike, I just didn't know exactly where, until I got there."

Zambrano laughed, "Cooperate with me Jesus. I like you. Tell me the truth."

"I am. I've been telling you the truth."

Zambrano sucked on his cigar, blew smoke into Jesus' face and said, "Sorry. I think you're lying."

Zambrano pressed the burning end of his cigar against Noriega's stomach. The stretcher rocked. Noriega screamed.

Detective Zambrano withdrew the cigar and calmly waited for Jesus to stop screeching and bouncing the stretcher cart around. When Jesus' breathing returned to near normal Zambrano wiped the tears from Jesus' eyes and said, "My contact found more, buddy. He found you e-mailed your girlfriend my pal Esteban Nunez' fingerprints at 3:17 p.m. on the afternoon of October twenty-second. Tell me about that Jesus. You also sent Angel Figueroa's address and property coordinates to her. Why did you do that Jesus?"

Jesus feebly replied, "Somebody else must have used my computer."

Zambrano sucked on his cigar to get it good and hot and ground it down into Jesus' chest. He then swung his nightstick as hard as he could into Jesus' shin bones. Jesus Noriega shrieked uncontrollably, a high pitched wail escaped his lips, then, thankfully for him, he passed out.

When Jesus regained consciousness Zambrano was sitting in the chair again. Zambrano had a friendly smile on his face. He asked, "Would you like me to kiss and make better?"

Jesus said, "No, I'd like some water. Please I'm so dry."

Zambrano replied, "Of course."

Zambrano walked to a sink in the corner of the room, ran the tap, and returned with a glass of water he sipped from. Jesus became alarmed.

He saw Zambrano's penis hanging out of his pants. *What is this sick fuck up to*, Jesus wondered

Zambrano stood over Jesus and said, "Open your mouth Jesus I'll pour it in."

Jesus did as he was told. Zambrano began pouring, Jesus swallowed. Then Zambrano started urinating simultaneously into Jesus' mouth. Jesus spit up and closed his mouth as Zambrano roared with laughter. He emptied his bladder onto Jesus' face then opened the door and instructed the guards in the hall to take Jesus back to his cell.

At 7:27 p.m. Eastern Time, October 25, Ed Grass leaned back in his desk chair, eyes closed, feet up on the desk, going over in his mind what had transpired.

Several days ago, when Triple A was still in Pueblo, they got a break. Lauren couldn't wait to tell him the keyword 'Angel' had come up on one of the tapped cell phones in Arizona. United States Border Patrol Deputy Chief John Marrone used his phone to call a woman, Lisa Strump, whom he informed about the detain and notify order the sheriff put out on Esteban Nunez, and Hector and Aliberto Castaneda. Marrone is overheard asking her to pass that information on to Angel and to tell Angel to keep them away from any contact with United States border patrol agents or any other law enforcement. She said she would do that, adding she looked forward to seeing him later in the month. Marrone replied he too looked forward to seeing her again.

That phone call started a lot of wheels in motion. Garcia was directed to head back down to Arizona, separate Marrone from his patrolmen, and use whatever means necessary to get to the bottom of his involvement with Angel. Lauren was tasked with following up on Lisa Strump.

The following day Lisa Strump was a known quantity. Twenty-seven years old, five foot six, one hundred fifteen pounds, blue eyes, red hair; a graduate of the University of San Diego, Lisa worked as a public relations representative for her own firm, Strump Focus. According to her most recent personal income tax return Lisa pulled down five hundred sixty-four thousand dollars per year in salary. She owned a two million dollar home in Carlsbad, California. Lisa's public relations firm appeared to have only one client, a company headquartered in Panama called the Alliance. The Alliance paid additional funds monthly to Strump Focus which covered all of that firm's overhead and expenses.

Corporate records from Panama indicated Angel Figueroa as the chief executive officer of the Alliance.

When Grass spoke with Garcia again to bring them up to date with what Lauren had found out about Lisa the team was on the road in New Mexico. When they asked, Grass gave his permission for them to find accommodations for the day. They all felt the effects and were worn out from the travel. The team elected to stop outside Ruidoso, New Mexico, at the Inn of the Mountain Gods. Grass didn't object. He had been to the resort himself and thought it would be a good place for the team to relax and unwind. He remembered the four diamond resort/casino located in the Mescalero Apache Reservation, spectacular mountain views, rooms overlooking a lake and a top rated restaurant, Wendell's.

That evening Lisa Strump called Marrone making definite plans to stop by his house with his package on the night of the thirtieth. Marrone could be heard wisecracking, "Cha-Ching!" Before hanging up Lisa accepted Marrone's dinner invitation and his proposal she spend the night. Grass called the team again, told them of the developments, and after discussion agreed there was no rush to speak with Marrone, they should spend another night at the Inn. They all agreed it would be best for the team to place Strump and Marrone under visual and audio surveillance the night of the thirtieth. There was no need to hurry to get to Arizona.

Later that same night Lisa again called Marrone. She told him Angel wanted him to set up for another movement on the next Angel's moon. She said Angel told her his same crew would come through the same place as last time on the night of the next full moon. He would set up several dozen illegals running on foot east of Douglas and also a couple of dozen through Lochiel starting at one in the morning. That should be enough to keep Marrone's guys busy.

They decided to sleep on that information. In the morning they agreed to put picking up Strump and Marrone on a back burner. That could wait until later. Intercepting the shipment would take priority. Where to stay was a problem. The Inn was getting old. The Mountain Gods looked more and more unfavorably upon Mendez, already down several hundred on slots, and Cruz, down two nights in a row playing blackjack. Garcia was getting bored because he didn't gamble. Where to go was a problem. They ruled out lodging around Bisbee and Sierra Vista. Everyone there thought they had wrapped up their investigation and left the area. They all thought it best to allow the locals to continue think they were gone. They didn't want to take a chance on being seen. They were also going to need to bring in more manpower and equipment to facilitate taking down the smuggling operation. They needed a place with more room and a lot of privacy.

After much discussion Grass and Garcia agreed to avoid requesting help from the sheriff's department, local Homeland Security, and any other border patrol units. They agreed on enlisting Emmett Thompson as a civilian guide and reassigning a dozen other Spanish speaking Special Operations agents from within Grass' command to assist the Triple A team with the capture of the drug smugglers. Spanish speaking agents would also come in handy if the team eventually went into Mexico. Grass would enlist Homeland Security Director Charlie Swanson's aid in getting the Phoenix FBI field office chief Phylis Driscoll to provide a small group of Phoenix agents if Garcia thought they would be necessary for the operation. But Grass reminded Garcia the Phoenix office was totally bogged down investigating September's Sky Harbor Airport bombing, not to count on a lot of help from that source.

Grass felt a gentle push on his shoulder, than another nudge. He heard Lauren telling him, "Director, sir, I have General Ehrich on the phone."

Grass took his feet off the desk and sat up. He shook the cobwebs out of his head remembering what this was about, "What line?" He heard, "Line three, sir."

He picked up the phone, pressed three saying, "General Ehrich, how are you sir?"

Ehrich responded, "I'm fine Director Grass, what can I do for you?"

Grass said, "General I have a group of about fifteen men and women who need immediate accommodations in a private area in southeast Arizona. I understand your base has several such facilities."

"We do sir. We have a lot of troops come through here who require anonymity for their training. How long will you need these accommodations?"

"Not sure. Possibly several weeks."

"That's fine. Will you need anything else from me Director?"

"I believe so. Some of my people will arrive by car but others will require helo transport from Tucson International. They may need the use of a couple transport trucks for a couple of nights. And we expect to take some prisoners who will require brig space."

"No problem with any of that sir. Any weapons or equipment?"

"General, one of my agents, Al Garcia, will have to let you know about those items. Can he contact you directly?"

"Of course Director, give him my direct line. Anything else?"

"Not for now General. Thank you very much for your cooperation. Garcia and two other agents will be arriving at your Sierra Vista gate in a day or two. The ones coming into Tucson airport I'll have to let you know on. I'm not sure myself yet."

"I'll leave word with the duty officer to notify me as soon as your people arrive at the gate. When that occurs I'll go to the gate myself and guide them to the billets I'll assign to them. I'll order the kitchen serving those accommodations manned immediately. Let me know on the others. Your people are in good hands Director. I'll tell Garcia to inform me about anything he needs when I meet him at the gate."

"Thank you General. I'll call Garcia right now and let him know."

"Goodbye Director."

Lauren, who had been standing there and overheard one side of the conversation said, "Director that general is certainly very nice."

"Yes he is." He continued, "Lauren you should call it a day. Before you leave make sure the overnight researchers find out everything there is to be known about this Lisa. Good night."

As soon as Lauren closed the office door Grass called Garcia and brought him up to speed. He added General Eric Ehrich was an old friend. Grass had investigated an incident in Afghanistan years before. He explained a unit under the command of the then Captain Ehrich had been involved in an action where accusations of brutality were made. Grass, then an officer attached to the Judge Advocate General Corps, looked into the incident thoroughly and determined there was no basis for any of the allegations. They were completely unfounded. Grass told Garcia he was confident General Ehrich would provide whatever Garcia requested. He told Garcia to call him after they settled in.

Chapter Twenty Two

7:12 a.m. Mountain Time, October 26

GUARDS CAME INTO HIS SOLITARY CONFINEMENT cell. He was still strapped onto the stretcher. One of them slapped his right ear. Jesus shrieked. The guards chuckled. They covered him with a blanket and wheeled him through the common cellblock and through another door outside into a back alley. There was no one around to see him but if there was, he simply looked like any other prisoner going to the hospital. Regretfully there was no hospital visit on the agenda for Jesus. The stretcher's frame folded underneath and Jesus was slid into the rear of a van marked 'Hermosillo Policia.' The guards slammed the doors shut. Arturo Zambrano was the only other person in the van. From the driver's seat he said, "Buenos Dias my friend. I hope you slept well. Still thirsty?"

Jesus cursed, "Fuck you, you sick pervert."

"Oh Jesus, my friend, by the time today has run its course I'm confident you will regret not being honest with me. I could have saved you. You'll see. You're going to be sorry."

Jesus closed his eyes tuning Zambrano out. His body racked with pain. Even if he somehow could free himself from being strapped down onto the stretcher, what could he do? Could he get to his feet? He didn't think so. They were killing him where he was hit with the nightstick. The same for his shins. Could he stand? Could he support himself? His right ear and his whole head ached. The cigar burns seemed minor in comparison. He felt sure, given the opportunity, he could get the better of Zambrano. But would that opportunity arise? He determined to feign severe discomfort. Maybe Zambrano would loosen his ties. He gasped,

"Arturo I can't breathe. I can't swallow. I'm choking. Please pull over. Let me stand up. Please."

A peal of laughter came from Zambrano. He taunted, "Man up, tough guy. Suck it up. We're nearly there."

"Please pull over Arturo. I'm going to die."

Zambrano snickered, "How right you are. Shortly Jesus. Nearly there."

"Where's there?"

"Amateur hour is over Jesus. You, my friend, wouldn't talk to me, now you are going to see Stewie the bone crusher. I pity you. Say your prayers. If your God answers them you will choke to death before Stewie gets his hands on you."

The van slowed then made a left turn proceeded a ways and stopped. Zambrano opened his window and said, "Detective Arturo Ramirez Zambrano of the Hermosillo Municipal Police. I have a delivery for Esteban Nunez. He's expecting me."

Whoever he spoke to responded, "Yes sir, you are on my list. He is expecting you. Do you know where to go?"

"No I haven't been onto the ranch before."

Jesus heard an electric motor running. The voice directed, "When the gate opens fully, pull inside past the gate and wait. A car will come and signal you to follow."

Zambrano replied, "Yes sir." The van moved forward and stopped again. The electric motor ran again. There was the sound of a gate shutting firmly then the motor turned off. After a few minutes, an eternity to Jesus, the van started moving again. Subsequently following several turns the van stopped, the engine turned off, Zambrano climbed out, and the back doors opened.

Jesus was pitiful to observe, the terror in his eyes, his body shaking, shivering with fear. Two men, guards from the guide vehicle, pulled the stretcher out lowered the wheels and began rolling Jesus into a large building through an open garage door. One of the guards smiled and said to the other, "This guy appears to be scared shitless. Obviously being a cop he knows what to expect."

His partner giggled, "Yeah I wouldn't want to be him. Poor fucker."

A man with dark penetrating scary eyes and a Pancho Villa moustache handed a roll of reinforced duct tape to each of the guards and directed, "Shut the fuck up. Bring him over here. Park him under my chain fall. Unstrap him. Roll him over. Face down. Tape his ankles together. Put his arms over his head. Straight up. Tape the wrists together. Use plenty of tape. We don't want any weak points."

The man had a control in his hand. He pressed a button and a chain with hooks attached lowered from the ceiling. He pointed and said, "Hook him up. The lower hook under the ankle tape. The upper hook under the tape around his wrists."

He pressed another button on the control and the chain started rising up. Noriega screamed in pain as his body was lifted off the stretcher. His frame forced into an arc, contorted and bent. His body a semi-circle, wrists and feet at the highpoints. The lowest skin, his privates, dangled at the low point. The stretcher was rolled out of the way. The chain fall hoist was a traversing type. Hand held electric controls allowed the operator to lift or lower a load. It was set up on an overhead trolley system to move the load east, west, north or south. Stewie pressed buttons steering Jesus up and over a large open vessel. Once centered over the tank Jesus' body was lowered. Jesus cried out for them to please stop. He yelled for help. He prayed aloud but his prayers went unanswered. His tormentors standing on the ground observing roared with laughter. The chain lowered slowly, link by link, until his lowest point, his penis and testicles, wound up positioned slightly above the surface of the liquid in the tank. At this point all motion ceased. He was left hanging in place, peering down. Esteban Nunez, Zambrano, and the two guards moved to the side. They sat in a row of comfortable overstuffed easy chairs. Nunez announced, "We have to wait for Angel."

After what appeared to Jesus to be an eternity, but in actuality only a few minutes transpired, a golf cart drove up. An extremely well built man about six feet tall with jet black hair slid off the driver's seat. He wore a white cotton guayabera shirt, white linen pleated pants, sandals, and dark sun glasses. The four men sitting in the lounge chairs jumped out of their seats, stood at attention, bowing in deference. Esteban Nunez said, "El Jefe, sir, everything is ready."

Angel Figueroa walked inside, removed his glasses, put them in his shirt pocket, gazed around, taking everything in, looked at Zambrano and asked, "What did he tell you Arturo?"

"Nothing El Jefe. He is abnormally strong-willed. He denies everything. Blames others for using his computer, says his reconnaissance of your property was a random hike. He's lying of course."

"Is there a record of his arrest?"

"No El Jefe, no report, no booking, no record of him at all."

The man turned his head upward gazing toward Jesus. Jesus silently stared back. He had taken control of himself. He tried to brace himself for what was coming. The man coldly asked, "Do you know who I am?"

Jesus nodded and answered, "Yes El Jefe. You are Angel Figueroa."

"What is your interest in me?"

Jesus replied quickly, "I have no interest in you El Jefe."

Figueroa turned to Nunez directing him to, "He's lying. Splash him a little."

Nunez carrying a metal ladle, stepped up on a platform next to the vat, dipped the ladle into what Jesus knew to be concentrated sulfuric acid, took a small amount of acid and raised the ladle. Jesus watched, his eyes getting wider and wider as Esteban slowly drew the ladle in front of Jesus' face. He couldn't control himself. He begged, "No. No. Please no."

But Esteban was enjoying himself. He smiled sadistically as he shook the handle of the ladle splashing acid onto Noriega's back. Jesus cried out in pain as the liquid dissolved his flesh.

Figueroa held up his hand. Nunez stopped. Figueroa asked, "Jesus you know what will happen if we dip you, if Esteban lowers the chain even one link?"

Jesus cried. He pleaded, "Please El Jefe. Please I'll tell you everything. Please stop!"

Figueroa signaled Nunez by raising his upturned thumb. The hoist was raised one link. Angel asked in a quiet voice, "Everything?"

Jesus nodded, "Si, El Jefe, the whole story. What's the point in hiding anything? You know everything anyway."

Figueroa told Nunez, "Bring him to me Esteban. I want to look into his eyes as we talk."

Stewie replied, "Si El Jefe." He manipulated the controls steering Jesus to a point where Jesus was hanging with his eyes about five and a half feet off the floor his face inches from Figueroa's.

Angel Figueroa smiling, his handsome features and pearly white teeth dominated by his piercing black eyes, asked, "Well?"

Thinking only of the pain and agony to come Jesus implored, "Please I'll tell you everything I know. Please don't hurt me anymore. Please don't put me into the acid."

Angel's face hardened, "Don't waste my time."

"Yes, El Jefe. The Americans called me. They knew me. I had worked with them before.

They are a special group of investigators known as the Triple A team. Their names are Al Garcia, Al Cruz, and a woman, Alex Mendez. They did not ask about you El Jefe. They are investigating some murders in Arizona. They sent a photo of Esteban Nunez. They wanted information on who Esteban is, where he worked and for who, where he lives, and his fingerprints. They only asked for information on you because he works for you and on your ranch because he lives here. They told me they did not have permission from their superiors to come to Mexico to arrest Esteban."

"Why did you snoop around my ranch?"

"They told me they may get orders to bring Esteban back to face murder charges. I took it upon myself to reconnoiter around your property. A big mistake on my part El Jefe. I'm so very sorry."

"Assuming I believe you, why didn't you tell all of this to Detective Zambrano?"

"I mistakenly thought I could bluff my way past Detective Zambrano. I have no respect for him. He is not a good policeman. I am truly sorry. I should have told him the truth. "

"He did work very hard for me. His loyalty is to me. I owe him for capturing you and for bringing you here."

Angel Figueroa asked Zambrano, "Arturo why does this man hate you so?"

"El Jefe he constantly lied to me. He made it awfully frustrating. I hit him, hurt him a little."

"What should I do with him? What would you recommend?"

"Dip him slowly. He has to go. Make it painful."

Figueroa said to Jesus, "You know the acid is a painful way to go. I've seen Esteban suspend people the way you are tied and dip them playfully, then hang them by their wrists wetting their toes, then hooking their ankles with the arms outstretched down until the fingertips are gone, then tying the arms to the sides and soaking the top of the head, then lowering so the acid gets the eyes. You can't imagine the misery, the pain, the screaming. And you did give up Esteban to your friends. What would you have me do with you Detective Noriega?"

"Please El Jefe I've told you everything. Please just shoot me. Kill me quickly." Jesus continued, "Please El Jefe let me apologize directly to Detective Zambrano."

Angel was quiet, his thoughts kept to himself. He looked from face to face, from person to person, then announced, "How is this? Esteban you are going to get Noriega for your acid eventually, either alive or shot dead. You don't get a vote. Arturo you are the aggrieved party here. So how about

we allow Jesus to plead his case directly to you. If you believe he is sincere you shoot him. If not Jesus gets the slow dip treatment. Arturo smiled widely. Angel noticed and said, "Arturo judging from your expression, I'll count your vote as a yes. That leaves you Jesus. What do you say?"

Jesus closed his eyes. In resignation he said, "El Jefe I need a fair chance. My mouth is dry. I begged Arturo for water and he pissed in my mouth. Can I have water? I need a moist mouth to have a chance at having my spoken words convince Arturo."

Angel nodded at Esteban who fetched a glass of water and a straw. He held it under Jesus' lips. Jesus emptied the glass. Angel asked, "Ready Jesus?"

Jesus nodded and whispered, "Please come close detective Zambrano."

Arturo gleefully pushed his face forward positioning himself so he was as close in as he could get. Now face to face Arturo yelled, "Beg me asshole. Beg me."

Angel, Esteban, and the two guards sat in the easy chairs and watched. One of the guards playfully asked, "Stewie do you have any popcorn?" They all laughed and snickered.

Angel asked, "How's he doing Arturo?"

Zambrano chortled in a squeaky voice, "Not good. On a scale of one to ten only a three so far, I can barely hear him. He has to try harder, a lot harder."

Angel warned Jesus. He told him, "Jesus I'm trying to help you out here, but you're trying my patience."

Jesus gasped, moved his head around, appearing to try to get closer to Arturo. He took a deep breath, then he lunged, clamping down as hard as he could with his teeth. Before anyone realized what had occurred Jesus had Zambrano's throat in his mouth. Jesus determinedly moved his head violently from side to side. Zambrano howled in agony. He tried to pull away but Jesus had a death grip with his teeth. Blood oozed from Jesus mouth. Arturo wailed, "Help me. Get him off me."

The two guards jumped up and started punching Jesus around the head and shoulders. Esteban pressed the control which lifted Jesus up. Arturo shrieked in pain as Jesus took him with him. Jesus' jaw was locked in a pit bull's vise-like grip. He shook his head his teeth tearing at Arturo's throat.

Total bedlam and panic ensued. Arturo reached into his shoulder holster pulled a 9mm Glock and started shooting round after round at

Jesus. But Jesus had accomplished what he had set out to do. Arturo's body, gushing blood from his torn carotid artery, fell away from Jesus. Jesus smiled as he spit out Arturo's blood. His body went limp. Jesus died with a smile on his face.

Angel was the first to realize what happened. He took off his fancy guayabera shirt, rolled it into a ball and directed one of the guards to hold it against Arturo's bleeding neck. He told the guards to get Arturo on the stretcher and into the police van.

He ordered Esteban to lower Jesus' dead body with its grinning face into the vat of acid.

A shot rang out as Angel ran out of the garage door to check on Arturo's condition. As he cautiously approached the van he was greeted by the two glum guards. One of the guards shook his head saying, "He's dead. He was in a lot of pain, bleeding out. He put an end to it. He put his gun into his mouth and blew his own head off. We're sorry El Jefe, it happened so fast, we couldn't stop him."

Angel recovered his composure first. He ordered the guards to bring Zambrano's body back into Esteban's shop. He told one of them to drive the police van back to the police station and the other to follow. He said he would call the comandante, they should leave the keys to the van at the front desk and leave. He cautioned them not to say a word of what happened to anyone. Angel instructed Nunez to place Arturo's remains into the acid vat also. When both detectives' bodies were dissolved in the acid, Esteban was to pulverize their bones, and to spread the remains over the ground in the horse pasture.

At 0714 Mountain Time, October 27, the military policeman signaled for them to stop the car at the Fort Huachuca main gate. Mendez drove, Garcia sat in the passenger seat, and Cruz rode in the back. As soon as team identified themselves the MP told Mendez to pull up in the parking area past the guard station and wait. The MP hollered to another MP in the guardhouse, "Call the general. They're here."

Mendez parked, opened all the windows, shut the engine, and waited. Cruz remarked how nice it was to be in Arizona, warm in the day, cool in the evening, much more pleasant than the shit weather, cold—snow—rain, in Colorado. Garcia relaxed, he was exhausted, his mind confused by all of the constant plan changing, phone updates, and conference calls.

Eleven minutes after they arrived a jeep pulled up alongside. The driver, asked, "You Grass' people?" Noting the affirmative nods he continued, "Follow me."

The jeep headed west into the direction the sun had recently set. They drove down Fort Huachuca Road, what appeared to be the main street. Streetlights lit every intersection. What appeared to be administration buildings and warehouses lined both sides. The traffic, already minimal, thinned considerably as density lessened, clusters of buildings became infrequent. At a four-way stop the jeep turned south. About two miles later they stopped at what appeared to be a tee intersection. The jeep continued straight across onto a lightly graveled dirt road. Brightly lit signs cautioned 'GUNNERY RANGE, Keep Out, Danger.' The jeep did not slow down.

Both sides of the road were lined with dark chaparral and cactus intermixed with magnificent Arizona oak and walnut trees. Periodically other signs appeared, 'Turn Around,' 'Do Not Proceed,' 'Authorized Passage Only.' After driving continuously on an uphill grade they followed the jeep over a crest and headed down a steep section of paved road. The road leveled off, the jeep turned right…a group of four two-story buildings appeared, two on either side of a single story structure. Lights were on in the single story portion, three vehicles parked in a front lot. The jeep pulled to a stop next to the vehicles. Triple A parked next in line. Headlights extinguished, the engines shut down, all of the occupants exited the vehicles. The driver of the jeep, a man appearing to be mid-forties, about six feet tall, two hundred pounds, close cropped gray hair, gray eyes, and a warm smile, offered his hand. Shaking each of their hands firmly he introduced himself, "I'm General Eric Ehrich. Welcome to Camp Vigilant. Follow me, I'll show you to your barracks."

Ehrich walked ahead, entered the closest door into the first building on the right. He flipped a light switch on, stood aside, holding the door, and motioned them inside. He said, "Each of the two story buildings has ten single rooms each. All have private baths. Six rooms are upstairs, four down. Downstairs also has a common room. The common room contains a large screen television, and computer terminals. There are enough comfortable chairs for twelve. Another dozen folding chairs are available in a closet for larger groups. I would suggest each of you grab a lower level room near this door. The single story building is a central mess hall, Building 3. There are several men on duty inside. They will provide whatever grub you desire prepared, within reason of course. When the rest of your party arrives please utilize the rest of this building, designated Building 2. If more space is required then use the next one to the right, Building 1. As of now you will be the only ones housed in this complex but that could change. Buildings 4 and 5 should remain vacant just in case. Any questions?"

Garcia replied, "Sir, thank you for your hospitality. I'm Al Garcia. This is Al Cruz and Alexandra Mendez. Director Grass has already briefed us and provided your direct number. I don't know how much the director has told you but we won't have a lot of questions until the rest of our group arrives. We will visit our area of operation, before we design our tactics. I'm sure I will call upon you after we devise a plan of action, once we better know our needs. We will be going off base tomorrow. What will be the process when we return?"

Ehrich handed each of them a card. The cards read 30-Day Special Pass; it was signed by General Eric Ehrich, and commenced today. He said, "You won't have any problems with these. Once on the base use the same route we used tonight. That will take you directly in and out. If you need to shop at the Post Exchange (PX) it is the first building to the north, on the right, after the gatehouse. Anything else?" When they shook their heads he continued, "All right then, let's go meet your mess sergeant."

Ehrich led the way to the mess hall. He introduced Sergeant Ralph Mulia. The sergeant, a good-looking tan-complexioned man, about five-eight, one hundred seventy pounds, had dark eyes, black eyes, and appeared to be in perpetual motion, his lean hard frame taking him quickly from one spot in the kitchen to another. Mulia paused long enough to firmly shake hands all around and in turn introduced Corporal John Kitnoya, and Privates Moosey Briggs and Jesse Charles. When Garcia explained the team had stopped on the road for a burger two hours previous Sergeant Mulia suggested fresh-baked apple pie and coffee for dessert. He said the pie and coffee would be ready in forty minutes. The team used the time to say goodbye to the general and to move their belongings into their rooms in Building 2.

At 8:45 p.m. the team sat down at a table by a window in the dining hall. Low mood music piped out of speakers around the room. Briggs and Charles served baked apple pie and freshly brewed hot coffee. Kitnoya brought cream dispensers, a sugar bowl, and a container of vanilla ice cream. With no indication none was wanted he placed a big scoop of ice cream on each pie plate. Kitnoya said, "Enjoy. If you want more pie or ice cream just call out. We'll leave you alone now." With that the mess crew left a full decanter of coffee and returned to the kitchen.

Mendez knew Cruz thought the same thing so she asked, "Boss what are we going to do off base tomorrow?"

Cruz nodded, "Yeah, I'm wondering the same thing."

Garcia replied, "We're going to find out where Marrone lives, whether or not he lives alone, and as soon as we are sure no one's home we are going to visit his house. Cruz I assume you have listening and recording devices in your kit. Hopefully you have some remote visual recorders too."

Cruz answered, "Of course Boss. I never leave home without that stuff. A toothbrush and bugs are both essentials for me."

Mendez inquired, "How are we going to get his address and his whereabouts tomorrow?"

"I'm going to call the director tonight. He asked that I call when we settled in. I'll bring him up to date and ask him to have his people in Washington get Marrone's address for us and to use Marrone's cell phone to determine his whereabouts. They can keep track of Marrone and if it appears he is headed home while we are still there they can give us a call. They should be able to tell us if anyone is at his house just from listening to the bug in his phone. I imagine if someone else is around he will speak to them. If not, we will be proceeding carefully. That Lisa broad is supposed to bring his package in three days. I want to see and hear everything that transpires in that house during their visit."

The team stopped by the kitchen on the way out, thanking everyone for the pie and coffee. They were advised the dining hall would be open at 6 a.m.

Chapter Twenty Three

0934 Mountain Time, October 28

NOBODY PAID ANY ATTENTION AS THE big man, shorter man, and pretty woman walked out of the base PX with their packages. There was a slight glitch earlier when the check-out clerk asked to see military ID but concern quickly waived when they produced their 30-Day Passes issued by General Ehrich. After that they had to resist the fawning. They declined the clerk's offer of help carrying their purchases and they refused directions they didn't want or need. They exited the PX, and returned to their car.

They deposited camouflage colored sun hats, backpacks, and lightweight utility jackets with lots of pockets. They also placed a case of bottled water, sunscreen, insect repellent, and a bird identification guide on the backseat next to Cruz' laptop. Those items would be needed in addition to binoculars and cameras, which each of them already had in the luggage they always carried.

Grass had called Garcia that morning before dawn. Marrone lived about fifteen miles north of Nogales. He lived alone. A housekeeper came in only when he called and only when he was home. Marrone's house was situated on a twenty acre parcel on top of a hill adjoining Lake Patagonia State Park. His gated driveway accessed off the park entrance road. No neighbors appeared close, the nearest other homes all came into view to the east and they sat at lower elevations. Grass had e-mailed maps of the area and other information about Marrone's neighborhood.

Over breakfast of bacon, eggs, bagels, orange juice, and coffee, served by Sergeant Mulia and his crew, the team reviewed the maps and other information. They found Lake Patagonia State Park was part of the

Patagonia-Sonoita Creek Preserve, one of southeastern Arizona's premier birding areas. They decided the best way to approach Marrone's house to plant their bugs was through the state park. They planned to blend right in, masquerading as ardent bird-watchers, spending a relaxing day in the preserve's woodlands.

With Mendez driving they, for the most part, backtracked the route they had taken the previous week after meeting Jesus Noriega. They took Highway 90 north to its intersection with Highway 82, made a left, heading west past the fledging vineyards of Elgin. Peering out the car windows, they observed the rolling Arizona grasslands, home to numerous horse ranches until they passed the town of Sonoita and Highway 82 veered south.

Mendez followed the sign to Patagonia, entering a long valley separating two mountain ranges rising abruptly from the valley floor. The natural beauty of the Patagonia-Sonoita Scenic Road was evident in the varied scenery as the road wound through rolling hills and surrounding Coronado National Forest. The gorgeous Santa Rita Mountains rose to the west, the Patagonia Mountains to the east. Beautiful fall foliage, autumn colors of red, muted yellow and browns, copper, and greens lined the road as far as the eye could see. Mendez slowed the car as the highway passed through the small town of Patagonia. South of town private drives led to homes perched on the hillsides or into narrow canyons which led further into the mountains. Seven miles south of town Mendez made a right onto Lake Park Road. She continued on a winding road, up and down small hills, around wide turns past mailboxes and driveways. Garcia read off addresses. Cruz said, "Marrone's place should be the next one on the right."

Mendez stopped in front of the next driveway. It had a gate across it. The number on the mailbox was the one they were looking for. The name of the resident did not appear anywhere. Garcia pointed to a hill left of straight ahead. He asked, "Al is that hilltop accessible by foot from the park? Is it parkland?"

Cruz followed to where Garcia pointed, checked the map on his computer, and responded, "Appears so."

Garcia told Mendez, "Keep moving."

Around the next curve they came to a booth in the middle of the road. Mendez pulled up and stopped. A park ranger leaned out a window inquiring, "Do you want a day pass?"

Mendez responded they did, paid the fee, and handed the brochures and park map the ranger gave her to Garcia. She drove on, over a hill into a parking lot overlooking a boat launching ramp and parked next to the riparian area along the bank of the lake. For a few minutes they observed fishermen in boats trying their luck, and birds, mainly pelicans, herons, and egrets flying over the water searching for a meal. After a brief review of the park map and the maps provided by Grass, Garcia said, "Alex, drop Al and me off up on that hill then take yourself back to the other side of the boat ramp, park the car, walk in to the hilltop we saw from the car on the way in and when you are in position call us. Once we know you're in position watching Marrone's gate Al and I will go in and set up the bugs. Call us if anything happens."

Fifteen minutes later Alex called Garcia informing him she was in place, had scanned a wide area with her binoculars, and saw no activity. The men who had taken a hold position and pointed at some imaginary birds nesting in trees on the park's property line, immediately stopped the charade and headed toward Marrone's house.

They walked slowly, in single file, Cruz in front, eyes down, scanning the ground and tree trunks for motion detectors. Two hundred feet from the house everything changed. They had hiked through dense stands of cottonwood, maple, oak, walnut, and willow trees, now there was nothing. All vegetation within two hundred feet of the house had been cleared. They stopped and Cruz used his binoculars to examine the house. The home, a newer contemporary design, utilized metal roofing wrapped around the fascias and soffits. The exterior was stucco, the doors all solid metal with metal frames. The designer windows were stacked, operable windows under fixed glass windows. The lowers had heavy drapes guaranteeing privacy. The uppers had no window coverings, obviously to allow natural lighting in. Cruz paid special attention to the windows and overhangs. When he convinced himself no one was peering out at them and there were no cameras or motion detectors mounted on the structure Cruz led the way forward pausing again when they came to the side of the house. They then circled the perimeter. Cruz carefully examined each window and door. Completing the circuit Cruz shook his head saying, "Boss this place is protected like Fort Knox." He pointed to a utility shed, "I'm going to bring a ladder over so I can look through the upper windows."

Garcia observed, "Those uppers are fixed. We can't get in that way."

Cruz returned with ladder, climbed up, looked in the window and confirmed, "Just what I thought." He came back down moved the ladder to another upper, examined the window, looked inside, and said, "Boss this is tough. I could pick the front door lock in thirty seconds but Marrone has installed one high tech alarm system. Once I open the door, I would need to punch in the code, disarm the system, automatically cancelling the silent alarm, and overriding the exterior sirens. I have no idea what the code is. He has a fire sprinkler system inside; the exterior is all fireproof construction. The vegetation is cleared two hundred feet back. He doesn't want anybody inside, no firemen, and no intruders. He spent a lot of money to ensure privacy and safety. We have to rethink our options. Why do we have to get inside again?"

"To bug the meeting between Marrone and Lisa."

"Boss, we already have both of their cell phones bugged. They'll have their phones with them. We'll hear."

"You're right Al, but I want to see too."

"Boss, I can mount fish-eye cameras to the upper windows. I can put them in the corners. They'll never see them and we can check him punching in the code when he comes through the door. So if we come back we'll know the code. It will be a piece of cake."

"I want more than that Al."

"Boss, it's a two bedroom, two bathroom home. The living room, dining room, and kitchen are one large open space. I can set three cameras and get everything going on in the main room and the bedrooms. I set one more concentrating on the alarm panel. Four cameras, we'll have everything but the bathrooms. I'll get everything real-time on my computer."

"Can you get a view of the outside too, Al?"

"Sure, a camera on the shed will take in the porches, parking area, and driveway. No problem."

Garcia thought for a few minutes then said, "Okay Al, set it up."

Once he returned the ladder to the side of the shed, Cruz checked the projection reception from the various cameras on his computer, then returned it into his backpack. They called Alex telling her they would meet her by the road. They set off back through the woods. On the return trip Garcia went over to a small grove of maple trees. The trees were at their peak color, bright red. Garcia paused while he took his backpack off. He laid it on the ground, extracted plastic baggies, and gloves. He started to fill the plastic bags with maple helicopter seed pods which had fallen to the ground. Cruz watching from a distance finally couldn't contain himself any longer. He asked, "Boss what the fuck are you doing?"

Garcia smiled and muttered, "You'll see in due time. Just an old recipe I learned a long time ago. I hardly ever get the opportunity to harvest helicopter seeds anymore."

After placing several full bags in to his pack, Garcia shouldered it and continued down the hill to meet Mendez.

On the way out the gate the ranger asked if they enjoyed their day. Remembering what she read in the bird-watching guide as she played lookout Mendez enthusiastically replied, "Oh yes, I saw my first Vermilion flycatcher and a yellowthroat today. Thank you so much."

All of them wore their camouflage colored sun hats, and lightweight utility jackets. They looked the part. Everyone smiled and waved.

On the return trip to Fort Huachuca Garcia called Grass informing him of the difficulty accessing Marrone's house and how they resolved the problem. Grass was put on speaker and informed them the company jet would fly the rest of the special operations agents into Tucson International the following afternoon and General Ehrich agreed to have a helo waiting to transport them to the barracks. Grass also told them the study of Lisa Strump's phone, expenses, and travel history was progressing. So far, numerous calls between Strump and Angel Figueroa had been documented. Many calls made by Lisa were confirmed to have been made to border patrol, immigration and customs agents based throughout the country. Strump traveled the southern border extensively. She rarely flew, mostly drove. She traveled to Kansas City a lot both by air and by car. Mendez asked, "Director, did Marrone call Strump on August seventeenth or eighteenth?"

Grass shuffled his notes, found what he was looking for, and answered,"Yes, on the seventeenth."

Mendez inquired, "Did Strump call Figueroa thereafter?"

"Yes right after. Does that mean something?"

"Yes sir. The seventeenth was the day County Attorney told Marrone about the upcoming meeting with the Rynnings. That sequence certainly points to Marrone being the one who set the Rynning boys up."

Grass said, "Good thinking Alex. Ask Marrone and Strump about that when you get the opportunity."

"Yes sir we will."

Chapter Twenty Four

0800 Mountain Time, October 30

EIGHTEEN PEOPLE GATHERED IN BUILDING 2'S common room. Everyone was seated, chatting. Al Garcia stood and thanked them all for coming. He pointed to a table holding coffee, donuts, bottled water, and said, "Anybody wanting refreshments please get them now." Apparently they all had what they wanted because no one moved.

Garcia continued, "Al Cruz, Alex Mendez, and I know everyone here and you all know us. But some of you don't know who all the others are. I would like each of you to stand as I introduce you then return to your seat."

"First up is General Eric Ehrich. The general is our host here. He also is a good friend of Director Grass. Next is Sergeant Ralph Mulia. Sergeant Mulia is the only person in this room who has not served either in the military or special operations with the director, but Sergeant Mulia comes highly recommended by General Ehrich. Sergeant Mulia is in charge of the mess hall here. Third is Emmett Thompson. Emmett along with the general served in combat with Director Grass. Emmett is a local and will act as our guide. All the remaining people are special operations agents currently serving under Director Grass. The gentlemen are Fabio Pineda, Cesar Catalino, Ernesto Sanchez, Antonio Preciado, Francisco Valdez, Edwardo Carvalho, Marco Mendes, Zacarias Vega, and Rey Oropeza. The young ladies are Stefania Chavez, Paola Calderon, and Maribell Robles."

Garcia said, "I'm here to brief you on an upcoming operation authorized by the United States Director of Special Operations." He continued, "We have information leading us to believe a large shipment of drugs will be smuggled across the Mexican border in several days. We believe this shipment is being made with the knowledge and protection of corrupt border officials. It is our assignment to capture the drugs. It is our intent to allow the drugs to be loaded onto a truck and allow that truck to proceed several miles before intercepting it. It is also our job to apprehend the armed force protecting the drug shipment. We will do that after they drop off the drugs and when they are on their way back to Mexico. It is believed some of these armed men viciously murdered American citizens, Sam and Ida Comfort, during a shipment last month. An effort will be made to capture them alive. Please focus your attention on the screen."

A screen set up in the front of the room came alive with an overhead photo. Garcia used a pointer to direct attention to the United States/Mexico border, "This is where they cross." Using the pointer he followed the trail from the border to the rock outcropping Emmett Thompson photographed them coming through. Garcia said, "At this choke point the bearers and guards have to pass in single file. They regroup and break in this clearing right after the choke point."

Garcia then pointed to the television screen, "This is last month's group coming in. As you can see the armed guards are exceedingly alert, awfully fierce looking."

Getting back to the overhead picture Garcia dragged the pointer all the way to the highway. He said, "The truck is loaded at this abandoned farm. After dropping their loads onto the truck the bearers immediately leave, retracing their steps across the border. Once the loaded truck leaves the farm the armed guards go back."

Garcia again directed everyone to the TV saying, "These are the armed guards on the way out. They look like a girl scout troop on a field trip or a picnic. Their weapons are shouldered. They're not paying any attention at all. We plan to hit them in the break area, right before the rock outcropping. Hopefully with the element of surprise on our side plus the fact their job is done will cause them to give up, enabling us to take them alive. However if they resist we are authorized to take whatever steps necessary to protect ourselves. Any questions?"

Emmett Thompson asked, "Can you be more specific. I have to put in for time off. "

"Yes of course Em. This is going to go down the night of November sixth. That is the next full moon. These guys like to move thru the desert in the brightness of the full moon."

Sergeant Mulia asked, "Sir, where exactly is this ambush point?"

"Approximately nine miles west of Douglas, about two miles south of Highway 80."

Mulia asked, "How are you and your men going to get there and what are you going to do with your prisoners? What are you using for transportation?"

Garcia addressed General Ehrich saying, "General, the sergeant brings up an excellent point. Of course we could rent a bunch of cars and pull them off the road someplace close to the ambush point but I'm hoping maybe you have some vehicles we can use."

Ehrich responded, "Agent Garcia, you only have to let me know what you need. A CH-47 Chinook Cargo Helicopter, a twin-turbine, tandem-rotor, heavy-lift transport helicopter with a useful load of up to twenty-five thousand pounds brought your group in here from the airport. You could use that. It will carry thirty-three men, all of you and a bunch of prisoners, but it is not stealthy or quiet. In order to not draw attention we would have to drop you six or seven miles away and you would have to hike in. On the way out noise wouldn't be a concern. Or I could give you say four deuce and a half cargo trucks. Four would be more than enough for your purposes, four would allow extras for breakdowns, and additional space actually needed for prisoners. Emmett could probably find a spot close by where you are going to park the trucks."

Emmett said, "Yeah of course my dad's friend Calvin Van Der Byl has an abandoned farm which would provide easy access to the ambush point. Great cover for the trucks there too. They could be parked where they would never be seen by passersby."

Ehrich asked, "Anybody have experience driving a deuce and a half? They aren't pickup trucks you know."

Sergeant Mulia and Oropeza raised their hands. Mulia said, "The three men in my kitchen crew all are qualified to drive the deuce and a half sir. We can drive, stay with the trucks during the operation. Rey can be a back-up driver if one is needed for some reason."

Ehrich said, "I can vouch for those men agent. They work these barracks. All of them have experience driving trucks loaded with meals prepared in the mess hall out into the field. All kinds of secret operations go on here. We don't place men who aren't competent or can't be trusted in positions like this."

Garcia said, "Okay, sounds like a plan. When can we get the trucks general?"

"Half an hour quick enough?"

"Yes I'd like to take a field trip to the site at 1000 hours. Can everyone come?"

Mulia said, "I'll have my men make sandwiches."

Everyone else agreed they could be ready.

Ehrich said, "I'll make a call to supply. I'll have them bring a selection of camouflage jackets and caps right over. If you're going to ride in army trucks you have to appear to onlookers to be soldiers."

The general continued, "As much as I don't normally do this stuff; go into the field, ride in the back of trucks, this is going to be damn interesting. I want to see what is happening. I want to be there. I want to make sure my friend Ed Grass' troops have everything I can possibly provide to help make this operation of his a success. That's okay isn't it agent?"

Garcia replied, "Sir, having you come along is fantastic. We, and I'm sure Director Grass, appreciate everything you've done. We look forward to having you and listening to any and all suggestions you may make during the planning stage."

"Is that a polite way of telling me I can't come on the mission agent?"

As diplomatically as possible Garcia said, "Sir, special operations missions such as ours are best left to special operations agents such as ourselves. I'm sure Director Grass would be happy to speak with you directly sir."

General Ehrich laughed and said, "Just kidding agent. I'm sure you and your men and women don't need me along on your actual operation. But, I do think I should go along on today's reconnoiter. I might have some useful thoughts and ideas about equipment I can provide."

"Agreed."

At 1042 hours, under the now bright sun, the four vehicle convoy pulled out of the Fort Huachuca main gate. Sergeant Ralph Mulia drove the lead truck. Emmett Thompson rode shotgun, giving directions. Trucks driven by Corporal John Kitnoya, Private Moosey Briggs and Private Jesse Charles followed. They were accompanied in their cabs by Stefania Chavez, Paola Calderon, and Maribell Robles, respectively. General Eric Ehrich sat in the back of the first truck along with Al Garcia. Al Cruz, Cesar Catalino, Ernesto Sanchez, Antonio Preciado traveled as passengers in vehicle two. Alex Mendez, Francisco Valdez, Edwardo Carvalho, Marco Mendes rode in vehicle three. Fabio Pineda, Zacarias Vega, and Rey Oropeza were in the truck bringing up the rear. Twenty-one people in all.

No other drivers or pedestrians appeared to take undue notice. After all, military trucks and troops were a common occurrence around the base. After leaving the front gate Sergeant Mulia made an immediate right south on Buffalo Soldier Trail. Doing so allowed the group of trucks to avoid Sierra Vista city traffic, staying adjacent to the base until they intersected Highway 92 where they rolled south at a steady fifty-five miles per hour. Emmett used his phone to call his dad's friend Calvin Van Der Byl who had relocated to Idaho several years previously. After exchanging pleasantries, Em explained he was leading a group of Cochise County Border Brigade members on an orientation of the area and needed a secure, private place to park some vehicles while they hiked. Could they use his abandoned farm? Van Der Byl readily agreed even telling Em where the farmhouse key was hidden in the event he wanted to turn on the water and use the facilities. Emmett thanked him, assured him the property would be left cleaner than they found it, agreed to pass best wishes to the rest of the family, and signed off. Em told Sergeant Mulia, "All set. When we get to the traffic circle at Lowell take the 80 east toward Douglas."

Everyone seated in the back of the vehicles sat on bench seats, the seats folded down for passengers, up for cargo. This morning all passengers sat as close to the tailgate as possible trying to avoid the intense heat under the soft camouflage material covering the truck beds. They smiled and waved to kids in the cars that passed. They looked the part of real soldiers. General Ehrich's supply people had outfitted Emmett and each of the special operations agents with Desert Camouflage Uniforms; shirts, pants, and wide-brimmed boonie hats, all in the three-color desert camouflage pattern of light tan, pale green, and brown. All of the troops wore dark glasses. Clearly a bored group of non-descript troops from the local base on a morning's detail.

Fifty minutes into the trip Emmett told Sergeant Mulia to slow down, to make the next turnoff on the right. Mulia followed directions, led the convoy a quarter mile down a gravel drive swung behind a boarded up farmhouse and parked under the shade of a copse of trees. The base camp had been reached. Privates Briggs and Kitnoya set up a folding card table and four comfortable folding chairs for the drivers.

Mulia and Jesse Charles handed out two sandwiches and two bottles of water to each of those who were going to walk into the desert. Garcia told them to put the food into pockets; they would eat once they reached the ambush site. They would carry out all garbage they generated. He told everyone they had at least a two mile walk each way in the sun and to take more water if they thought they would need it. Emmett reminded them all to pay particular attention to their route. He had everyone set their compass headings to the southeast. They set out with Emmett in the lead.

Twenty-five minutes later Emmett, Garcia, and General Ehrich stood on the path they expected the drug smugglers to take in and out. The special operations team spread out on the west rise. Emmett distributed topographic maps of the planned ambush site. He pointed to the choke point, the opening in the rocks where the smugglers would pass through in single file. He recounted where everyone was positioned the night last month when the Comforts were murdered. He steered everyone's attention to the depression he had laid in, where the Comforts had been, and how the smugglers and their guards were deployed. Al Garcia then took over.

Garcia said, "All right everybody, listen up. From what we know from Em's firsthand experience these guys are exceptionally alert on the way in. For that reason all of us will be on the other side of the rises to the east and west initially. Thirty minutes after they pass and are busy loading their drugs onto their truck we will reposition into ambush mode. All of the bearers will be allowed to go back unmolested. We are only interested in the armed guards. Before the first of the guards reaches the rock opening I will trigger an array of flashbang explosives to blind, numb, and momentarily disable them. While they are confused, disoriented, and distracted I will set off overhead flares. Your action will follow immediately. You will announce your presence, that you are police, in English and Spanish, and instruct them to lay face down hands over their heads. You will not need night vision equipment. In fact, hopefully they will be wearing theirs because anyone wearing night vision will be at a great disadvantage. I will count down into your earpieces so you know to cover your ears and eyes prior to detonation of the flashbangs. Any questions?"

Oropeza asked, "Al, how are we going to deploy to keep them surrounded but still keep from shooting each other?"

"We are going to concentrate on the east side of the gully. There is a lot of cover on the east, virtually none on the west. A fire group consisting of you and Zac will be to the north to prevent any of them from running back in that direction. Another team, Steffi and Paola, will cover the entrance of the rock passage preventing any of them from running south. I will set-up high on the east slope with Cesar and we will take down anyone who tries to flee up the west slope. The rest of you, Maribell Robles, Al Cruz, Alex, Cesar, Ernesto, Antonio, Francisco, Edwardo, Marco, and Fabio Pineda will all be strung out under cover on the east side on the path. Emmett is here purely as a guide. He will be with me and Cesar. Does that sound about right to everyone?"

When no one said anything Garcia added, "Okay everybody move into the position you've been assigned."

Six minutes later General Ehrich and Emmett Thompson walked back and forth along the trail. Ehrich pointed to and repositioned several team members. When he satisfied himself no one could be seen he called up to Garcia, "I don't see anyone anymore agent."

Garcia asked, "How about you, Emmett?"

"I don't see anybody either, but the ambush is going to be at night and the smugglers do have heat-detection goggles. If any of them are wearing those devices the bad guys could detect body heat."

Ehrich interrupted saying, "That is not the case. The battle dress uniform (BDU) you were each issued, and are all wearing is made from a special fabric containing an infrared protective coating. The BDUs and boonie caps automatically adapt to the temperature of the surrounding terrain. What you have to remember is your face and hands aren't protected. But, that is not a major concern because the exposed area is so small it will be taken for a small desert animal or rodent not a human. Do your best to stay hidden. You'll be fine."

Rey Oropeza asked, "Does taking these guys dead or alive make a difference? Should we shoot to maim not kill?"

Garcia responded, "If it is a life threatening situation shoot to kill. No hesitation whatsoever. That said we really want these guys alive, three of them anyway. Esteban Nunez, and Hector and Aliberto Castaneda. You will all be provided with pictures of the three. Try not to kill them."

Ehrich said, "I can help there agent. In addition to your regular weapons, I can provide each of you with 12-gauge shotguns that can accurately deliver non-lethal taser projectiles from a range of 300 feet. These are wireless long-range electro-shock projectiles that can be used immediately on any of the smuggler group who doesn't comply with your orders to drop their weapons and lie on the ground at once. We have a shooting range for your use at your facility. My trainers will qualify all of your agents as taser sharpshooters in no time."

When no one had further questions, Garcia told them to walk around and familiarize themselves with the terrain. He told them to go through the opening in the rock outcropping. He said they would head back to the trucks in ten minutes.

Garcia, Cruz, and Mendez went over the west ridge. Garcia went to a flat spot that looked suitable for what he wanted, close but out of direct sight of the ambush spot. He made a small pile of sand about a foot high and wide, packed it down, and told Cruz to lie down spread eagle not on top but alongside so he could figure where to put the tent pegs. With four pegs hammered into place they returned to the group. At 1320 hours the convoy was back on the road to Fort Huachuca.

Chapter Twenty-Five

1710 Mountain Time, October 30

"**Wow. What a hot looking babe.**" Al Cruz exclaimed. Sitting at a picnic table outside Building 2 at Camp Vigilant, he viewed the screen of his laptop. The screen displayed images from five cameras set up at John Marrone's home. Cruz concentrated on watching Marrone working in his kitchen. He had previously recorded then replayed numerous times the recording of Marrone disarming his alarm when he entered the home. The code is 4653. Cruz had watched as walked to a speaker box on the living room wall spoke with a visitor at the front gate and pressed a button, which allowed the closed gate to open. After a few minutes a silver Mercedes-Benz CL 600 coupe emerged at the top of the driveway and parked. Now Cruz was intent on staring at the yard view.

Lisa Strump had arrived. She was stunning, a beautiful redhead in her twenties. She wore a multi-colored long sleeve blouse with a floral design over tight jeans and sandals. John Marrone bounded out the front door smiling. He greeted Lisa warmly giving her a light hug. She pecked him on the cheek and asked, "How have you been John?"

Marrone replied, "I've been great Lisa. How was your trip?"

"It's been a tough drive John. I left San Diego yesterday, spent the night in Yuma, had breakfast with a contact there and they drove through to here this afternoon. As usual I'm always pleased to arrive here. You are always so hospitable."

"I'm happy you feel comfortable coming here Lisa. I'm always glad to see you. Got a new car I see."

"Yeah, Angel bought it for me. He was concerned I drive a secure, reliable, comfortable car on my route every month. I put a lot of miles on, San Diego to Brownsville with stops along the way, then some months up to Kansas City before going back. Angel says I deserve it."

"I agree. I didn't realize you went to Kansas City. That is a lot of driving."

"I drive because I deliver wads of cash to different people all over. I can't take the cash on a plane. But I don't drive to KC every month. Most times I fly in and somebody already there brings me the cash I need for the delivery. Angel wants me to do all the drops. He feels more secure that way. And John let's change the subject, Angel wouldn't appreciate me talking to even you about what exactly I do."

"Right forget I mentioned it. Let me help you with your things. Where is your bag?"

Lisa reached into the back seat and withdrew a bag, which she handed to Marrone. She said, "Here John put this on the bed in the spare room please. I'll be right in."

As Marrone went inside Lisa opened the trunk and extracted a brown paper bag. She closed the trunk lid, went inside, and handed the bag to Marrone. She said, "Here John, Angel sends his regards."

Marrone took the bag opened it, thumbed through the packets of hundred dollar bills, thanked Lisa and said, "I'll be right back."

Cruz glanced over to Garcia and said, "Look at this boss, Marrone has a wall safe in the master bedroom. He's opening it now."

Garcia looked up and said, "You're getting the combination aren't you Al?"

"Yes boss plain as day. The code is 4653, same as the front door."

Garcia replied, "Good, let me know if anything interesting happens." He went back to what he was doing.

Cruz who was monitoring the screen intently said, "Boss I think this is interesting."

"What?"

"The safe is full of stacks of cash."

"I expected that Al. Where else is Marrone going to keep his bribes. It was apparent he kept his money in the house when we saw how secure it is. You don't think he needed that alarm system to protect his dirty underwear do you?"

"No boss. I'll let you know if anything else interesting happens."

He watched as Marrone asked Lisa if she wanted her usual. She nodded yes and he prepared a martini for each of them. He used chilled glasses he took out of the freezer, olives that he previously placed on spears and took out of the refrigerator, a dash of vermouth, and a large portion of Beefeater Gin. He asked, "You want to have these outside, Lisa?"

Strump replied, "Of course John, you know I love watching the sun go down sitting on the rocking chairs on your patio. Let's go outside. When does the sun set anyway?"

Marrone handed one martini to Strump then took a tray of crackers with sliced cheese and olives off the counter. He said, "I know you like these too. I finished preparing them right before you drove up. Sunset is in a few minutes, about half past five this time of year. Let's enjoy it."

John and Lisa made small talk sitting on the patio seeming to enjoy each other's company. Lisa stood up walked to her car and returned with a lightweight hooded sweatshirt she put on, leaving the hood down her long red hair hanging over her shoulders. She remarked, "Getting chilly John."

"Yeah once the sun sets it goes down into the low to mid thirties this time of year. You want to go inside?"

"Oh no, I love it. With the sweatshirt I'm warm and snuggly, comfortable."

As Cruz watched and listened to Strump and Marrone he kept glancing over at Garcia who sat on the other end of the table. Garcia had a dust mask and rubber gloves on. He worked on top of a plastic tablecloth he had set out. Garcia rubbed two of the seed pods he had picked up in the woods together. Hair-like matter fell onto a sheet of paper he had placed on the tablecloth. Cruz asked, "Boss what the fuck are you doing?"

"I'm working Al. I'm making some special potion."

"You've been scraping pods together for a while now, boss."

Garcia nodded, "Yeah, I've been putting the scrapings into a sealable plastic baggie. I'll transfer the scrapings onto paper towels on the window sill in my room for a couple of days to make sure the slivers of pod are all dried out. Then I'll fold the dried slivers into the towels, place everything into the bags, and leave them there until I want to use them. Damp or fresh slivers don't do the job."

"What job, boss?"

"In due time Al. You'll see."

Garcia sealed the bag, removed the mask and gloves and carefully, not to allow anything to touch bare skin, rolled everything but the bag into a ball which he deposited in the trash. The bag of shavings he put in his pocket. He turned to Cruz and told him, "Done for now. Anything new going on at Marrone's place?"

"All the time. Come watch with me."

Garcia moved to Cruz' side of the table. Both of them spied on Marrone barbequing steaks, opening a bottle of red wine, and sitting down to eat dinner with Strump. Garcia rose up abruptly. He told Cruz, "I have things to do Al. You keep monitoring what transpires. It's being recorded; you can tell me later if anything interesting happens."

Cruz said, "Boss, before I forget again. You told me last week to tell Jesus to put his investigation of Angel's ranch on hold because we don't plan to go in after Nunez and the cousins anymore. I haven't been able to contact him. I've tried his cell phone a lot and never get an answer. I called the Sonora State Police yesterday inquiring about him and all I get from them is he's taking time off to go hiking. He's on vacation, they don't know his whereabouts. I'm worried boss."

Garcia replied, "He's hiking, he's on vacation Al. Keep trying to call him. He's a big boy. He knows how to take care of himself. He's okay."

The following morning over breakfast Garcia asked if anything else important happened at Marrone's house. Cruz reported, "Not really, Strump wore a skimpy nightgown to bed. She had coffee and a banana for breakfast, was on the road by six-thirty. Marrone locked up, set the house and gate alarms on the way to work at six-forty."

At 12:30 p.m. Pacific Time, November 1, the camp manager, who everyone knew as Ozzie, quietly crested the hill. The newer Ford F-150 four wheel drive pickup truck he drove idled noiselessly as it rolled out of the pines down toward the beautiful lush green meadow, slowly coming to a stop. He watched the Huertas play like children, flying kites, five foot round weather balloons, and small party balloons tied together. Ozzie shut the engine and quietly observed. He considered what they were doing strange but knew better than to comment. Under orders of the owners he had held open the back four cabins for them or some others like them for the last two years. He always knew they would come he just never knew when. Now that they finally arrived, he had no idea what they were trying to accomplish. But it was his job to help in any way possible. He was a gofer. None of them had left the property since they arrived in different new Ford vehicles at different times between noon and six on the twenty-seventh of October. He obtained the balloons, kites, and tanks of helium they used. He also brought them multiple lead weights normally used for fishing, both fresh water and heavier models used for deep sea lines. They paid for everything they sent him for in cash. They paid for everything else, food, lodging, utilities, cooks, and cleanup help in cash also.

They had been out here nearly all day for the past three days. They spent hours launching balloons and flying kites, all carrying different weights, in differing wind conditions, cheering whenever the balloon, balloons tied together, or kite they started on the west side of the clearing actually flew over the tree tops on the east side. When they crashed into the trees they booed. They had notepads and had kept meticulous records of their successes and mishaps. Ozzie never saw or even heard of this stupid game before and he was close to sixty now.

Ozviv Rozaki, better known these days as Ozzie, was an Iraqi refugee who with his family, a wife, and two children resettled into the United States years earlier. Originally placed in a group home in Detroit, Rozaki was approached shortly after he arrived by a traveling imam who remembered him from Iraq. The imam knew Rozaki spoke fluent English and worked for the Americans as an interpreter during the Second Gulf War. He also knew Rozaki was an active al-Qaeda spy when he worked as an interpreter. Convinced Rozaki's sympathies remained with al-Qaeda the imam offered him a position in California. A group secretly funded by al-Qaeda had purchased a non-denominational meditation retreat that served individuals, private and organized groups having need for solitude. The clientele consisted of both repeat customers and new visitors who heard of the place by word of mouth.

The Heavenly Sky Spiritual Camp located 43 miles east of Redding, off state Highway 44, seven miles south of Highway 44, up a dead end dirt road became Ozzie's baby. The facility could accommodate from one person up to groups of one hundred fifty people comfortably. Visitors could eat and sleep or pray, sing, dance, paint, take photos, read, hike, bike, bathe in hot springs which maintained ninety-four degree water, or use a row boat, fish, swim, or canoe in the secluded pond located on the west side of the camp's central building group. The main complex had facilities for one hundred thirty-four guests consisting of any number of groups. There was one huge dining hall that could accommodate everyone. Or, each building had a small dining area where meals could be served to smaller groups if that worked better. It all depended on individual needs.

The four guest cottages housing the Huertas each slept up to four guests. There was one kitchen and dining facility that could seat sixteen and there was a table and chairs for four in each cottage. The four cottages were a mile into the forest past the main complex. The road that led to it had a chain across it. 'PRIVATE, No Entry, Not a Part of Heavenly Sky Spiritual Camp' the sign hanging from the chain said.

None of the employees remained from the people who had worked there when Rozaki first took charge. Over the years they had all been replaced by new residents of the United States that Ozzie recruited at the Redding Refugee Resettlement Center. All of them had become naturalized American citizens. Only the most vetted, trusted employees stayed overnight at the camp. Ozzie had found five employees on each overnight shift provided ample manpower to handle any emergency and to start the kitchen up in the morning. A large passenger van shuttled two shifts of employees back and forth from their homes in the poorer area of Redding each day. The two nine hour shifts overlapped one hour to allow for smooth shift change. One shift worked five in the morning to two in the afternoon, the other one in the afternoon to ten at night. The employees originally came from predominantly Muslim countries. They were mostly Somali, Libyan, Iraqi, Afghan, and Bangladeshi. They were all devout Muslims.

Ozzie shut the engine, stepped out of his truck, and stood leaning against the hood. The leader of the Huertas, who he had been introduced to as Leon, came over. Leon said, "Good afternoon my friend. Another beautiful day isn't it?"

Ozzie nodded, "Hello Leon. Yes another day in California. I have come to appreciate even rainy and snowy days here. Even those days are nice. Anybody win your game yet?"

Leon responded, "Oh yes, we are all winners. The game couldn't be better."

"You sent for me. How can I help?"

Leon produced a catalog and a list, He asked, "Would you be so kind as to order these clothes in these sizes and these paints in these colors for me. I would certainly appreciate it. I've calculated everything to come to four hundred seventeen dollars including tax and shipping." Leon handed Ozzie five one hundred dollar bills saying, "If you would order on-line using your credit card I would be thankful."

"Sure. I'll order it all as soon as I return to the office. If any questions come up I'll be in touch right away."

Leon ended the conversation saying, "Thank you Ozzie." He turned and jogged back to join the others.

Ozzie started his truck, turned around, and left.

Chapter Twenty-Six

6:35 p.m. Eastern Time, November 4

Tom Eagan sat behind a desk in a darkened office in the FBI headquarters on Pennsylvania Avenue in Washington DC, the only light dimly glowing from a small desk lamp. His disgust more and more evident as he shuffled through the hundreds of field reports which appeared on his desk every day for slightly more than a month. Discouraged, not a thing had been discovered that could help pinpoint who was behind and of course who executed the attacks on September thirtieth. Everyone knew there had to be a connection between the obviously coordinated, simultaneous nuclear attacks on several cities in the southwestern United States. Yes, al-Qaeda had immediately released a video from somewhere in Pakistan claiming responsibility. That happened over a month ago. To date there were still no suspects, no leads, no headway made on the case at all. Because he was the FBI Special Agent in Charge of the Anti-Terrorism Task Force currently investigating the attack he received the heat. Eagan was harried every day by superiors who wanted answers, answers that simply weren't there.

Eagan sat with his head bowed. He knew he should have retired several years ago but he wouldn't bring himself to admit it. All of the other agents he had come up though the ranks with had put their papers in and now collected a pension, wrote books, worked for private security firms, or played golf and fished in Florida. He was about five ten, slightly built, about one hundred fifty pounds, wore glasses, and hardly smiled anymore. Eagan was sixty-one years old and definitely felt his age.

For the umpteenth million time he recounted the facts as he knew them. At 12:17 p.m. Eastern Time, on the thirtieth of September, all hell had broken loose. Across the southwestern United States bright flashes of light penetrated the morning sky. The flashes had been followed by large dark mushroom clouds rising from the ground. Then there had been the noise, wind, heat and vibrating ground. It all had happened at 9:17 a.m. Pacific Time in Los Angeles, 10:17 Mountain Time in Phoenix and Albuquerque and 11:17 Central Time in Houston.

Five separate nuclear devices detonated in four cities. Two in Los Angeles, one each in Phoenix, Albuquerque, and Houston. The epicenters of the blasts appeared to have been the parking facilities at Los Angeles International, John Wayne, Sky Harbor, Sun Port, and Hobby Airports. All of the devices appeared to have been suitcase size bombs. That is to say approximately an explosive charge of one kiloton. Each one had the explosive power of one thousand tons of TNT. The terrorist group al-Qaeda issued a statement claiming responsibility for the attacks. The al-Qaeda claim was considered reliable because they mentioned suitcase nukes left in cars in airport parking facilities.

FBI Evidence Response Teams (ERT) consisting of forty members divided into five teams immediately dispatched to the blast sites. They donned protective suits, took photos, and made sketches. There were no fingerprints or trace evidence recovered. Nothing of use had survived the blast. Everything had been incinerated. If surveillance tapes had recorded the blast sites, the perpetrators, or their vehicles, none could be recovered. The tapes, like all the other evidence, were radioactive dust. The photos and sketches gathered had been sent to the Terrorist Explosive Device Analytical Center but for the most part, they were determined to be totally useless, a waste of resources.

Satellite generated tapes and recordings made before, during, and after the blasts confirmed the streets of the targeted cities had been alive with people. The schools filled to overflowing with the daily droves of children. Business went on with the normal flow of humanity commerce brings. The roads crowded with vehicles. One second people were laughing, working, playing, going about their routines. In the next second thousands were caught in an enormous fireball. For up to a mile away from the blast center people caught outside, in the open, instantaneously incinerated, their clothes burned and melted. Cars, trucks and buses had been blown apart, rolled over, crashed and burned. Passengers who were lucky died quickly. In buildings flying debris killed many. The structures collapsed on top of their occupants crushing those not already dead. Broken gas lines had burst into flames igniting the remaining construction not already on fire. As seconds passed wide circles of destruction had spread out further. An onslaught of high temperature winds blew out for miles leaving death and destruction behind. Aboveground power lines were knocked down. Many concrete and steel reinforced commercial buildings and all wooden structures, houses, fell down and ignited. People who didn't die from the initial effects of the bomb become trapped by fallen debris blocking their way. Many who had been exposed to radiation suffered for days before succumbing. If they had been looking into the direct flash they were blinded. Outside the area of immediate devastation stunned survivors didn't know what to do. Many of them suffered lung or ear drum damage. Would-be rescuers waited for instructions that never came. No one in America had experienced anything like what happened. Other than the military no one was equipped or trained to deal with nuclear bomb attacks. Police and fire crews did their best. Volunteers had attempted to assist wherever they could. Hospitals had provided the care they could. People who could had evacuated as far away from the epicenters of the attacks as possible. In the aftermath families searched for lost loved ones. The injured were cared for, and the dead that were recoverable were buried.

Projections provided to Eagan estimated when all was said and done Los Angeles would have an approximate total of three hundred fifty-two thousand dead, and two hundred seventy-two thousand injured. Phoenix would have one hundred thirty-two thousand dead, one hundred two thousand injured. Albuquerque would have forty-four thousand killed, thirty-four thousand injured. Houston would have one hundred seventy-six thousand killed, one hundred twenty-six thousand injured.

The explosives had been well placed. Los Angeles, Phoenix, Albuquerque, and Houston had been the most populous cities in their respective states. LAX, Sky Harbor, and Sunport had been the largest and busiest airports in their states.

The dense residential neighborhoods of Inglewood, El Segundo, Culver City, Marina del Rey, and Venice Beach surrounded the Los Angeles International Airport. Loyola Marymount University with its five thousand students had also been within range of the blast.

Sky Harbor Airport had been located just east of Central Phoenix. Arizona State University's thirty-four thousand students had been in the bomb's immediate vicinity.

Sunport Airport located in South Albuquerque had a Veteran's Administration Center next to it and had been surrounded by University of New Mexico facilities and the University's twenty thousand students.

Hobby Airport was not the largest or busiest airport in Houston, but it had been the closest to Central Houston and the eight thousand students at Texas Southern and the eight thousand students attending the University of Houston.

John Wayne Airport had been in the middle of the communities of Santa Ana, Tustin, Newport Beach and Irvine. Twenty thousand students at the University of California Irvine campus had been within the perimeter of the blast.

A fiasco, an utter disaster, all of it dumped on Eagan and he had no idea how to proceed except to diligently follow-up on every lead.

At 6:50 p.m., he came across the Denver Regional Office memo containing Mary Pelton's field report dated October twenty-first. Apparently, on October twentieth, Mary Pelton, a certified trainer with the National Explosives Detection Canine Team was routinely inspecting auto parking garages in the Denver area. She and her dog Clancy, a specially trained animal who can sniff out trace radiation and other explosives, came across a 1997 black Chevrolet Astro cargo van, belonging to the American Charities for Madrassas, and registered to Imam Dr. Umar al Jamai, parked in the Valet Parking Garage on Blake Street in Denver. The van was impounded after Clancy alerted Pelton to trace radiation and directly after Mary's own testing equipment definitely detected the presence of gamma and neutron radiation. The van was towed to the Buckley Air National Guard Base where a subsequent examination by lab techs did not expand upon the original findings. On October twenty-first, Pelton notified the charity by mail their van was impounded, they should contact her for its return. She also filed the report he was now reading.

At 4:59 p.m. Mountain Time, Eagan called the Denver Regional Office. He was immediately put through to David Porter, the senior supervising duty officer. When he explained who he was Porter agreed to find Pelton and have her call him.

Less than a half hour later Eagan's desk phone rang. It was Mary Pelton. While waiting for her to call back Eagan had made arrangements to fly out to Denver first thing in the morning. Mary agreed to change her schedule, to pick him up when he arrived, to show him the van from the Valet Parking Garage, the parking garage, and to take him to the last known addresses for the American Charities for Madrassas, and Imam Dr. Umar al Jamai. She admitted to him she did not believe anyone else from Homeland Security or the FBI visited either place.

At 9:17 a.m., the following morning Eagan was pleasantly surprised when he emerged from his flight to see a beautiful woman, about thirty, and about as tall as him standing, smiling broadly. She held a sign with his name hand-printed on it with a magic marker. She was dressed in a blue Department of Homeland Security uniform with a National Explosives Detection Canine Team patch on the shoulder. He headed straight to her, held out his hand, and warmly greeted her, "Mary I presume. I'm Tom Eagan. Thank you for coming."

Pelton smiled and replied, "Any way I can help sir. My boss told me to stick with you until you don't need me any longer. So I'm at your service. I'm pleased all the walking in and out, up and down, in all of those parking garages may somehow help your investigation."

"Mary, please call me Tom. Did you bring Clancy?"

"No, did you want me to? If you do, that won't be a problem. His kennel is right near where the van is in storage. We can look at the van first and pick up Clancy at the same time. He's assigned to me. As long as that's the case, he's my dog, no one else but me takes him out."

"Yeah sure I want to meet Clancy. And I want to take him with us. You never know what he might turn up. I only have this carry-on. Can we get started?"

"Yes sir, my car is parked at the curb. Follow me."

In the car Pelton asked, "Where to first?"

"I want to see the van and pick up Clancy."

"That's easy. They are both at Buckley Air National Guard Base. Hold on tight, we'll be there in ten minutes."

The guard at the gate of Buckley recognized Pelton and her National Explosives Detection Canine Team car and waved them through. Pelton drove to the right around the airfield and pulled to a stop alongside a black van. She announced, "This is it, all out."

Eagan circled the van, looking inside through the windows. He tried to open the rear doors. The van was locked. Mary asked, "Want to get inside? I have the key. I had a copy made. I thought you might want to get in."

Following Eagan's nod she unlocked the rear doors, continuing around the vehicle, she opened all of the locks. Mary then stood back.

Eagan deeply attentive to detail, searched under the seats, in the glove box, in all the little cubby holes in the doors and floor. Finally he turned to Mary and asked, "Where was it last?"

"At Valet Parking Garage."

"Before that?"

"How would I know?"

"It has a GPS."

"So?"

"So the lab techs, they examined the van. Where did they say the GPS history told them the van had traveled to and from prior to the parking garage?"

"They didn't say. I don't think anybody looked at that. We were investigating for explosives not road trips. They confirmed my findings, Clancy's findings, and concluded the van wasn't a danger in the condition it was in."

Eagan snapped, "Mary it may be terribly important where this van traveled from and to. Let's do it right and get the techs out again to check the GPS."

Eagan called the Denver Regional Office. He connected with David Porter, the same agent who was working as duty officer the previous day. Porter recognized the urgency in Eagan's voice and agreed to have a tech go to the van, remove the GPS, return to the lab with it, download all of its history and call Eagan on his cell phone. Eagan agreed to leave the driver's side door unlocked.

After collecting Clancy, Pelton, Eagan, and the dog went to 1112 Jasper Avenue, the address listed on the van registration for the American Charities for Madrassas. They found the address in a rundown area of Denver, a storefront in the middle of a strip of commercial spaces on the ground level of a six-story building. The door was locked. There was no indication the American Charities for Madrassas, or anyone else for that matter, occupied the space. Eagan pounded on the door to no avail. Clancy acted up, barking, climbing on the door. Mary said, "Clancy detects something."

Eagan replied, "I'm going to find the manager."

He walked down the street until he found an occupied storefront, a realty firm. As luck would have it they employed the building's manager, Joe App. After Eagan showed his credentials App used his passkey to unlock the charity's door. They told Joe to go back to his office; they would let him know when he could lock up.

There was a pile of junk mail on the floor under a mail slot in the door. Clancy pulled Mary over the mail, past what appeared to be a receptionist's desk, into an empty room in the back. She left him alone there went to her car returned with her sensing equipment and nodded in the affirmative. She told Eagan, "It was here. But it's gone now."

Eagan who had searched the desk and one virtually empty file cabinet replied, "Okay let's get out of here. We should look at the apartment."

Eagan walked back to the manager's office and asked, "Joe, when was the last time you saw someone in the charity's office?"

App replied, "Nobody has been in there for about two months. Before that for three years a guy, Umar, used to come in every day. He worked by himself. I never once saw anyone but him. Always on time with the rent, paid six months at a time, in advance. I'd have to check but I think they're paid up for three or four more months now. There's no problem is there? Great tenant."

Eagan handed App a card and replied, "No, no problem. Why don't you lock up, Joe. We're going to leave. If Umar or anyone else comes in, call me please. Don't let on we were here."

"Is something wrong?"

"No, it's some minor paperwork issue which needs to be cleaned up. Thanks Joe, have a nice day."

Five minutes later they pulled in front of 17 Mohawk Drive, the home of Imam Dr. Umar al Jamai. According to the directory in the lobby al Jamai lived in apartment 3C. After repeatedly ringing the bell and getting no answer Eagan knocked on the door of the resident manager. He displayed his credentials and asked to be let into Umar's apartment. The manager, Dee Farley, said al Jamai had not been home for six weeks or more but his rent was paid for several more months. Eagan explained it was important he contact al Jamai. He explained something found in the apartment could provide an address or phone number. Farley opened the door and let Eagan in. He told her to go back to her apartment he would get her when he finished so she could lock up again.

Once he was sure Farley had gone Eagan called Mary on her cell phone and told her to bring Clancy in.

Clancy sniffed around the one bedroom apartment, found nothing, made himself comfortable on the kitchen floor, and napped. Eagan and Mary searched the nearly empty bedroom closet and dresser. They looked under the bed and in the bedding. The bathroom medicine cabinet was empty. The kitchen cabinets had a sparse amount of utensils, dishes, pots and pans, a couple of cups and glasses. There wasn't any food. The living room had a couch and a coffee table, a TV, and radio. There were no papers, mail, magazines, or books. The trash can was empty.

Sitting in the car outside al Jamai's apartment after they searched,

Mary said, "It appears the radioactive material that was in the van was also in the charity's office. There is no trace here in the apartment."

Eagan nodded in agreement, "Another damn dead end."

Eagan said, "It's getting late Mary. How about we bring Clancy home and stop for a bite to eat before I go back to Washington."

Mary replied, "We didn't hear back from the tech yet."

"Yeah which probably means the tech didn't find anything. Start back to Buckley, I'll call Porter."

Porter answered right away. He said he knew the tech went right out, he hadn't heard anything further. He would check to see if she was finished or had anything. He would call right back.

Porter didn't call right back. It was closer to a half hour. Mary was inside the kennel making sure Clancy was comfortable, had his dinner, and a bowl of milk. Eagan waited outside, leaning on the car, when his cell rang. Eagan answered, "Eagan here."

David Porter sounded excited. He asked, "Agent Eagan it's four o'clock. Can you be here in less than forty minutes? The tech wants to see you before she leaves for the day. She is the type who constantly complains about being overworked, underpaid, and not appreciated."

Eagan replied, "I don't know. I'm at Buckley Air National Guard Base. How far is that?"

"Fifteen minutes, even at this time of day. Don't waste time. She won't stay a second after five."

"I'll get my driver. We'll be right there. The Denver Regional Field Office, right?

"Yes, ask for me at the reception desk."

Eagan ran inside and told Pelton. They patted Clancy goodnight and hurried out to the car.

The lab at Denver Regional Headquarters was a busy place. David Porter, a tall solidly built middle aged guy with a black moustache, escorted them by a maze of cubicles, all occupied by people totally engrossed in what they were doing. No one looked up from the task at hand when they passed. Everyone ignored Eagan and Pelton until Porter led them into an office lined with computer equipment. A heavyset young black woman glanced their way, held up her right hand in a signal to stop, and said, "Far enough. David, close the door please."

Porter did as he was told and introduced her as Beulah Bilodeau to Eagan and Pelton.

Beulah stopped what she was doing and said, "Before we start I want to make perfectly clear I was not told to download this GPS on my first visit to the subject van."

Eagan said, "That's clear. Nobody is insinuating you did anything wrong. Please tell us what did you find if anything?"

"I didn't find much. This is a real cheap GPS unit. It has about thirty day's storage, tops. I recovered all of the readable vehicle travel history. This vehicle has gone back and forth between 17 Mohawk Drive and 1112 Jasper Avenue, both in Denver, constantly, every day."

Eagan said dejectedly, "Is that it? We've been to both of those addresses."

Bilodeau replied, "I'd like to finish if you don't mind." After a pause… she rotated her huge ass in her seat, licked her lips, and with eyes bulging pompously announced, "That routine occurred every day but the last day. On the last day, the thirteenth of September, the van made one trip outside of those parameters. The last day it was used, an address in Pueblo was typed into the GPS. That address is 120-B Industrial Avenue. The van made the one roundtrip to that address on the thirteenth, from 17 Mohawk Drive to 1112 Jasper Avenue then to Pueblo then back to 17 Mohawk Drive, then to 70 Blake Street in Denver then finally to Buckley Air National Guard Base in Aurora where it is now. Here's a copy of my report. Hope it helps."

Eagan, deciding to overlook her shitty attitude, responded, "Hopefully, maybe, thanks very much Beulah. Great job."

Eagan thanked David Porter on the way out. At the curb he asked Mary, "How far is it to Pueblo?"

"Not far, about a hundred and ten miles each way along Interstate 25. Do you want to go there tomorrow?"

"Yes I do and I need a place to stay tonight."

Mary dropped Eagan at a Holiday Inn Express right off Interstate 225 in Aurora. The motel was close to Buckley. She explained she would pick up Clancy first then get him about seven in the morning. Then Eagan asked, "How about joining me for a bite?"

Pelton replied, "It's too late now Tom. Dinner is out. I have to get home to prepare supper for my husband. I'll be here tomorrow early. Be ready."

You grumpy old fart, Eagan thought, *what made you think a pretty young woman like Mary would be interested in you?* He resigned himself to eating alone again tonight.

Chapter Twenty-Seven

8:58 a.m. Mountain Time, November 6

The Department of Homeland Security National Explosives Detection Canine Team car glided to a stop in front of Huerta's Auto Body at 120 Industrial Avenue, Unit B. Mary said, "This must be it."

Eagan, Pelton, and Clancy all exited the car. They were in an industrial park across Highway 50 from Pueblo Memorial Airport. They walked to the front door of the Huerta's building. Eagan tried the handle. It was locked. They walked around the building, checking all the doors they came across. Everything was locked up. There were no vehicles parked anywhere on the property.

Eagan told Mary to stay put and he went next door. He returned in a few minutes shaking his head. He told Mary, "The machine shop guy next door says they've been open, then closed, and then open, and then closed, several times over the past two months. He said that was highly unusual because as long as he's been here, for years, Huerta's has been open every business day. He says we should call the sheriff. The sheriff was out here a couple of weeks ago. Huerta's closed a few days after that and he hasn't seen any activity since. He gave me the sheriff department's phone number."

It was forty-six minutes past nine when the Speedy Locksmith van pulled up. Two minutes later a Pueblo police car came to a stop. Eagan had called both the locksmith and the sheriff. One man, older, about sixty, with sparse gray hair, and walking with a pronounced limp introduced himself as Speedy. Two policemen emerged from the police cruiser, both big, over six feet tall. One appeared to be in his thirties, the other over forty. The older one said, "I'm Walter Goff, Pueblo's police chief. Who are you and what do you want here?"

Mary Pelton was in uniform, holding Clancy by a leash and her clearly marked, red, white, and blue Homeland Security patrol car, complete with the department's red white and blue eagle and shield emblem was parked in front of the police car.

Tom Eagan displayed his credentials saying, "Good morning sheriff, I'm Tom Eagan, FBI special agent in charge of the 9/30 anti-terrorism task force based in Washington DC. This is Mary Pelton and this is Clancy, both with the National Explosives Detection Canine Team based in Denver. Clancy is a specially trained to detect trace radiation emitted by uranium, and/or plutonium. Mary is a certified dog trainer and explosives expert. I assume you know Speedy. I called you and Speedy because the premises here at Huerta's are locked. We need access to check for suspected terrorism. We want Speedy to open the door with you witnessing our actions."

Goff threw up his hands, looked at the other cop and said, "What's with you fucking FBI boys and girls. A couple of weeks ago you accused the Huertas of being murderers and drug smugglers, now they're terrorists."

Eagan interrupted, "What are you talking about sheriff? And sheriff, watch your potty mouth. That language is totally uncalled for."

"What, you FBI people don't talk to each other? I know we, the local police, don't count for you big time investigators, but amongst yourselves one hand doesn't know what the other is doing?"

"Chief, what you are talking about?"

"Three big shot FBI agents, Garcia, Cruz, and Mendez arrived here a couple of weeks ago. Rolled in unannounced, caused a big ruckus, proved to be about nothing, then they skedaddled. Now you two want to break in to Huerta's business with my okay. Fuck you. We are not going down that path. These are good people, the best."

Eagan clearly annoyed said, "Chief, I don't need your okay for anything. I'm conducting a Department of Homeland Security terrorism investigation. I don't need you or your okay. I have blanket search warrant powers. I called you strictly as a courtesy and to find out why you were here recently. Let me be blunt, if you don't drop the attitude I'm going to arrest you for obstruction. Now you stand there, shut your mouth, and wait. Clear?"

Without waiting for reply Eagan pointed at Speedy saying, "Unlock that door."

Speedy moved to the door, set to work with some picks, opened the lock, saying, "FBI orders and all you cops present are enough for me."

Eagan directed, "Mary take Clancy and check it out."

Eagan told everyone else to stay out of the building. Mary opened the door, moved into the waiting room, no reaction, entered the office, no reaction, went into the break room, Clancy lunged up on to the door leading to the workshop. She turned to Eagan and said, "Clancy's on to something."

Mary opened the door to the empty workshop. Clancy pulled her to five separate locations. Eagan, who was watching, instructed Mary to put Clancy in the car and to go back inside with the mechanical sensor to check Clancy's findings. After Mary confirmed the trace evidence residue Eagan told Speedy to change the lock and give him the new keys. When Speedy finished Eagan had the charges put onto his bureau credit card and dismissed him.

As soon as Speedy drove off Eagan turned his attention to Chief Goff. He asked Goff, "Do you know how many people work here?"

Goff didn't hesitate. By now he understood enough to realize whatever Eagan wanted it was important. He responded, "The Huerta family. They don't have any employees outside of family."

"Where are they?"

"I have no idea Agent Eagan. Normally they or at least most all of them would be here."

"How many Huertas are there?"

Goff paused, thought a little, bent fingers one at a time, then continued, "There are ten of them. Consuela, Leon, Jose, Alphonso, Maria, Roberto, Filipe, Vincente, Manlio, and Diego."

"Do you know where they live?"

"I'm not sure. But I can sure as hell find out."

"Okay, find out. Mary and Clancy have to inspect wherever these people live."

Goff nodded and instructed Bobby, "Find out where the Huertas live. They all drive, tell the office to drop everything and find addresses. Check first with motor vehicles. I know they are all real good about voting too. Check the board of elections registrar. If neither of those works come back to me. Leon is in the Sunrise Rotary they'll have his address and Maria she's in the Kiwanis. Roberto belongs to the Lions Club. The fact is all the Huertas have been associated with service clubs and the Chamber of Commerce for years. Someone will know where they live."

Eagan said, "Chief, while we're waiting get another car here to secure this building. Find out what each Huerta drives. Put an APB out on each of them. I need to question them now."

"Understood. Bobby you heard the man. Tell the front desk to do what he wants. Alert all of our cars to pick up the Huertas on sight. And hurry-up with those addresses. Tell them we will be staying with Agent Eagan."

Eagan used his phone to call David Porter at Denver Regional. He asked, "David this is Eagan. I'm in Pueblo with Pelton and her dog. We got a positive for radioactive residue at the location we went to this morning. This location needs to be photographed, searched, and inventoried. I'm sure I'm going to have more locations as the day progresses. I need some more agents down here. Can you help?"

After a pause Eagan said okay and hung up. Goff who huddled with Bobby said, "We have five addresses. Two locations where two people each live, one where four of them live, and two locations where one each live. If you follow us we'll go to the closest location first."

Before they could leave Eagan answered his phone. It was Porter who said, "Agent Eagan we have a FBI Resident Agency in Pueblo. I spoke to the supervisor in charge there. He agreed to bring his two resident agents to Huerta's. They are on their way. ETA seven minutes."

"Thank you David. We'll wait here for them. The sheriff came up with five more locations. Mary and I will check them out and get back to you if we determine more help is needed. Thanks again."

Chapter Twenty-Eight

1715 Mountain Time, November 6

As Team Intercept, the name General Ehrich gave the group, waited to board trucks that would take them to the Van Der Byl farm Garcia's phone vibrated. He was surprised to hear the voice of Tom Eagan. Triple A had worked with Eagan on the Fort Mason terror bombing earlier in the year in California. The perps there turned out to be Latino separatists. Garcia responded to Eagan by telling him, "Tom good to hear from you. Hope everything is well with you. I don't want to cut you short Tom but what's up. I'm leaving on an operation in ten minutes. Our departure can't be delayed. Our truck transport has to be in place with us unloaded before dark. We don't want to be seen driving off road with our headlights on."

"Let me get right to the point then Al. An investigation of mine has brought me to Huerta's Auto Body in Pueblo, Colorado. I understand you and your guys worked on something here recently. Could you tell me what that was about?"

"Okay Tom. Before I start be aware this is going to take more than ten minutes. Another thing is once I'm aboard the truck it's at least a forty-five minute ride. We can talk all that time so call me back if we get disconnected."

Al Garcia brought Tom Eagan up to speed on Triple A's assignment by President Burns to the drug smuggling and multiple murder investigation. Eagan listened continuously muttering uh huh. Garcia did not bring Emmett Thompson's name into it. He mentioned a hidden video caught images of the Huertas and the smugglers, fingerprints on trash, and a tape recorder in one victim's pocket. He recounted during the interview Triple A had with the Huertas they at first insisted they stayed with family members in Las Cruces. However when confronted with the tape recording of their voices they admitted coming in with the drug smugglers. The Huertas said they attended a family gathering in Mexico. They told us they gave their cars to needy relatives, and bought new ones as soon as they arrived back in Pueblo. Said they did not have passports so determined sneaking back into the United States was their best course of action. They agreed to identify the smugglers who escorted them if and when the smugglers are taken into custody."

"When was that Al, when they came in with the smugglers?"

"They came in early morning the eighth of October. They spent that night in a Las Cruces hotel, and took an overnight bus from Las Cruces to Pueblo leaving late on the ninth, arriving Pueblo late morning the tenth. They all bought new vehicles and reopened the business."

"What day did you interview them?"

"October twenty-fourth. We did it right after lunch. They wanted the police chief and their lawyer present. The chief is an asshole. He was vouching for them like crazy until we played the tape, then he abruptly left. Their lawyer, a guy named Sidney Korash was much better. He's their contact. You want to speak to them you go through him. He has their cell numbers."

"So you didn't take to Chief Goff? If it's any consolation he didn't think much of you and your guys either."

"Fuck Goff. Why are you there Tom?"

"A lead in a case I'm working has brought me here. I'm in charge of the investigation into the nuclear devices that detonated at the airports out west. A van left in a Denver parking garage was found to have radioactive residue in the cargo area. Its GPS shows Huerta's was one of the last stops the van made before the driver dropped it off at the Denver garage. Huerta's shop has trace residue on the floor."

"Wow, what do the Huertas say about that?"

"Nothing. The shop hasn't been open since you guys were there. Their houses are clean for residue but they are nowhere to be found. They skipped right after talking to you guys."

"You can't trace them through their phones or their cars?"

"I didn't know about the phones until now. I'll follow-up on the car angle too. After I set him straight Chief Goff has been extremely helpful to me. He put an APB out on all the Huertas this morning."

"Sounds like you have everything under control, Tom."

"I do. Al, if you get the opportunity to confirm their story with the smugglers please do. What they told the people who smuggled them in might be interesting."

"I will. Call if anything new comes up Tom. I have to go now. Bye."

The convoy arrived at Van Der Byl's farm in fading daylight. The special operations force left Sergeant Mulia with the other drivers and followed Emmett into the desert. They were in good spirits, confident the night would go well.

During the walk in, Garcia brought Cruz and Mendez up to speed on his phone call with Eagan. Cruz summed up all of their feelings saying, "Eagan is a good investigator. He'll figure it out. We have to concentrate on the task at hand."

General Ehrich, while not going along on the mission, made sure the Special Operations troops received everything they needed from him to be successful. He arranged night firing range work, both close range and long distance, with the M4 carbine and taser shotgun. Stealth night patrols were practiced where self-protection from the effects of exploding flashbang grenades along with prisoner submission, disarmament, and security had been emphasized. He made sure all the troops were issued body armor and 'Massif hot johns.' The hot johns were Nomex long underwear to wear under their BDUs and wool socks to keep the operatives comfortable, dry, and toasty as they lay on the cold ground exposed to the chilled desert air in wait for the ambush to occur.

At the planned ambush spot they all went to the locations where they would be at the start of the action. Once everyone was comfortable that they knew their place Garcia and Emmett walked by in the gully. Satisfied everyone was hidden well enough Garcia had everyone get up and carefully make their way up and over, reconvening on the far side of the east ridge. He told them all to try to get some shuteye. It was going to be a long night. Cruz set up two cameras, one focused on the opening in the rocks and the other on the area where the smugglers had taken a break the previous month. Garcia supervised twenty flashbang grenades being wired together, one every fifteen feet on the east side of the gulley path used by the smugglers. General Ehrich had recommended the three hundred foot length covered as twice what would be needed if the Mexicans maintained ten foot intervals.

Shortly after one in the morning Cruz waved his hands alerting everyone to be extra quiet. The smugglers had arrived. Twelve minutes later he whispered to Garcia, "They've all gone through boss. They didn't take a break."

Garcia hand signaled Emmett Thompson. Thompson nodded back and silently headed north toward the Hernandez ranch. Staying well to the east of the ridge separating him from the smugglers Emmett shadowed their progress. At the high point where he watched previously Em watched as the bearers loaded a tractor trailer with their packages. He took notes, writing down what he observed through his binoculars. As soon as he was satisfied he had what was needed he backtracked rapidly. Several minutes later Emmett stopped, dialed his cell phone and waited. He heard, "Phylis here."

Emmett said, "Dark blue tractor trailer, Mayflower Movers on side and rear, Arizona plate BZ582J, loading through a side door on the driver's side toward the front of the trailer."

Phylis repeated what Em said. Emmett confirmed, "That's right. Over." He hung up and dialed Garcia. He told him, "It's done. She got the message."

Emmett then returned to the east ridge where he reported to Garcia. Garcia motioned over the ridge and whispered, "I positioned everyone when you called. They're all ready."

Within minutes bearers started filing past on their return trip. The ambush force wasn't interested in them. They let them pass. At 0247 hours the first of the armed men appeared. None of the alertness displayed on the way in was in evidence. The soldiers carried their rifles slung over their shoulders. They moved at a quicker, noisier pace. Garcia watched as the camera spied on the men. He saw Hector Castaneda, Aliberto Castaneda, and Esteban "Stewie" Nunez. The three walked in the middle of the line, six soldiers in front of them and five bringing up the rear. All fourteen crowded together, no more than five feet from each other, about seventy feet in total. He whispered into his mike, "Everyone cover your ears and close your eyes, three, two, one. As he detonated the flashbang grenades he told Emmett, "Light em up Em."

Emmett fired off two flares and gave Garcia a thumbs up.

Two megaphones blared in English and Spanish, "*Somos policía.*" "We're police."

The smugglers were instructed to lie down on their face, arms stretched overhead. A few complied. The first two in line bolted for the opening in the rocks. Steffi Chavez and Paola Calderon tasered them with shotgun blasts. The two dropped in their tracks bellowing in pain. Zac Vega moved in fast from the rear of the column, Maribell Robles, Al Cruz, and Fabio Pineda covered by the others on the slope cautiously approached from the east. The armed smugglers did as they were told. They lay with their arms over their heads looking to the Castanedas for direction. Maribell Robles caught a lot of grief because she was a woman. The guards on the ground, all Mexican men, called her, "*Puta*—whore, bitch." "*Besame el culo*—kiss my ass."

Al Cruz stepped into the group on the ground telling them to knock it off. They replied, "*Chinga tu madre*—fuck your mother." "*Chinga usted*—fuck you."

Cruz smashed two of the loudest in the back of their heads with the butt of his shotgun.

Aliberto Castaneda hollered loudly, "*No mas*—no more. Stop. We are Mexican Army soldiers. We must be lost. Did we cross the border by mistake?"

By now all of the special operations agents were gathered around the Mexicans on the ground.

Amid the smell of explosives, the stink of sweat and fear, the odors, stench, foulness, and fumes they were breathing, Cruz yelled, "Pay attention to your chief or I'll crush all your skulls. Lie still, shut up, and do exactly what you are told."

The ambush site took on an eerie atmosphere as soon as the overhead flares burned out. The special operations agents moved about among the Mexicans lying on the ground. The Mexicans weren't saying anything anymore. Cruz bellowed, "Much fucking better. Stay quiet; do as your told, no more broken heads. Here's what is going to happen. First we are going to take all loose possessions. You are going to empty your pockets into bags, we will tag the bags by owner's name and an assigned number one through fourteen, knives go into separate bags labeled by owner's name and assigned number, we are going to take shoe impressions. The impressions will be bagged by owner's name and number. You are each going to be fingerprinted. The fingerprints will be labeled by name and number. You all comprende? Simply lay where you are. As you're told to do something by an agent do it."

Aliberto Castaneda raised his head and protested, "I am Captain Aliberto Castaneda of the Mexican army. These are my men. We are lost."

Cruz walked over to Castaneda kicked him in the head and said, "We know exactly who and what you are. Now shut the fuck up."

Rey started at the end closest to the rocks. He had a clipboard. Maribell put number one on the first man's forehead. Rey wrote number one and listed the name the man gave him. Alex followed unloading each man's weapon before having them sling the empty rifle over their shoulder again. Steffi and Paola collected, bagged, and labeled handguns. Edwardo and Cesar followed, bagging the man's possessions, tagging the bag. Ernesto and Antonio searched each man removing, tagging, and bagging any knives in their possession. Francisco and Marco made a big deal out of having each man stand on heavy paper sheets, one shoe on each sheet. They then labeled and bagged the sheets and instructed the man to lay down again with his arms over his head.

Emmett who watched from the slope with Garcia asked, "Why are you doing all this now? What are the footprints for?"

"Well Em, we don't want any of them to switch possessions, like their knives, with another. And, they don't know you, your father, and your brothers trampled the Comfort crime scene making it difficult to recover evidence. We learn a lot by screwing with people's minds. We'll tell them we have useable fingerprints and footprints from the scene even when we don't. We can use that as leverage to make them talk and to rat on each other. The knives will go to the FBI lab to see if there is any DNA trace evidence of blood and guts from the Comforts on them."

Soon after Nunez's possessions including his knife had been bagged and tagged, and his prints were taken, and his shoes impression made, Garcia, Cruz, and Mendez led Esteban Nunez over the western ridge to the area they previously prepared. Nunez didn't appear to notice the four pegs in the ground or the pile of dirt they had made. Garcia and Cruz each had a hand on an arm. They steered Nunez so he wound up standing between the two front pegs. Mendez got in his face. She told him, "Spread your legs, Stewie."

Nunez stared directly into Mendez' eyes. He was accustomed to people cowering at the air of menace he conveyed. His swarthy, piercing, closely set eyes positioned under ferocious heavy eyebrows combined with his thick Pancho Villa moustache normally made those he looked at cringe. He replied, "Fuck you *puta*."

Mendez immediately snapped her right wrist. In her hand she held a Peacemaker Expandable Baton which she had unholstered on the way up the hill. Out of a 6" X 1 1/4" handle in Mendez' hand popped a two foot long ¾" diameter machined steel baton with a larger broad flat end cap, which allowed the baton to be used for jabbing without impalement. Mendez slammed the baton into Nunez' left thigh. He cried out in pain and tried to reach for his leg with his restrained hands. Garcia and Cruz held his arms firmly. Mendez put the baton between Nunez' knees, tapped them, and calmly told him, "Stewie, spread your legs before I break them."

Nunez spread his legs. Mendez put the baton between Nunez' knees, tapped them, and calmly told him, "Wider."

Nunez opened his stance and Garcia and Cruz simultaneously tied his ankles to the pegs. When Nunez' arms were again firmly in the hands of Garcia and Cruz, Mendez told Nunez, "Drop your pants boy."

When Nunez hesitated Mendez raised the baton swiftly into his crotch. Nunez howling in pain, quickly unbuckled his belt, unfastened and unzipped his pants, allowing them to drop to his knees. Mendez tapped Nunez crotch again saying, "Underwear too Stewmaker."

Nunez tried to push his shorts down but they hung up on his spread hips. He looked at Mendez obviously afraid that wasn't far enough. He pleaded, "That's as far down as they will go."

Garcia let go of Nunez' right arm, quickly unsheathed a blackened Nightedge combat knife with a six inch blade, pulled Nunez' shorts away from his body and sliced the right leg hole from top to bottom allowing the remaining shorts to drop down onto Nunez' left knee. Just as quickly he sheathed the blade and secured Nunez' arm. Mendez said, "Very good, now the shirt and undershirt, Stewie boy."

Nunez wasted no time removing the rest of his clothes and dropping them on the ground. Typical of Mexican gangsters, his upper body was covered with tattoos, his chest, his arms, his back, and his neck. He took a deep breath and said, "What the fuck do you people think you're doing? I'm a Mexican army officer. If we crossed your border it was a mistake. There is no excuse for this treatment of a Mexican serviceman."

Mendez jabbed him in the stomach as hard with her baton as she could causing him to expel the air in his lungs. Nunez doubled over in pain and shock. Mendez brought a knee up into his chest, Garcia and Cruz threw him back onto the ground, raised his arms and secured his wrists to the other two pegs. A rope was run under his chin and tied to the upper pegs preventing him from raising his head off the ground. He could only look up. When Garcia, Cruz, and Mendez stood over an incapacitated Nunez, Garcia said, "You're not a Mexican soldier. We know exactly who you are Esteban Nunez."

Stewie's eyes shifted from one to the other and replied, "That makes us even. I know exactly who you three are also. My boss Angel knows who you are too and you can count on him retaliating if you don't stop hurting me now. What do they call you, the Triple A team? You think we don't know? We know. The Mexican cop you sent told us everything."

Cruz kicked Nunez in the ribs and stepped on his throat. He raged, "What happened to the Mexican cop? What did you do to Jesus?"

Garcia pushed Cruz off Nunez saying, "Al back off. Stewie will tell us everything we want to know. We'll learn everything, all in due time."

Nunez said, "Untie me. Let me up. Let me get dressed. I'll tell you what you want to know."

Garcia replied, "Nah. But let me ask, you feelin' anything crawling up your ass yet Stew?"

Nunez' eyes widened. He shifted his rump on the hill they had prepared. He tried to shake his head saying, "No I'm not but I'm warning you Angel won't like this at all. Let me up."

Garcia leaned over Nunez and said, "Stewie, let me tell you the predicament you're in. You're tied down spread eagle with your butt on top of a colony of fire ants. That dome-shaped mound about eighteen inches high and twenty-four inches in diameter you feel is their home. Red fire ants are excessively aggressive, readily attacking anything that disturbs them. You're disturbing them. Red fire ants have a painful sting, causing blistering. Most people notice blistering occurring after being bitten. I see you're sweating Stew, is that from the ants biting?"

Garcia took a sealed baggie out of his pocket and showed it to Nunez. He said, "This is sugar Stewie. Fire ants love sugar. I'm gonna sprinkle some of this on your stomach, your belly button, and your prick, up your chest to your nose. We'll watch and see where the ants go first."

As Garcia spread the potion he had made he said to Cruz and Mendez, "I'll put ten dollars on his nose. Ants like to tunnel the nasal passages."

Cruz said, "I'll put ten on his belly button."

Mendez said, "Leaves me with his prick. I've got ten on his prick. It's shriveled up so much I hope the ants can find it."

The Triple A team walked away, out of earshot of Nunez. Cruz asked, "What is that shit you put on him boss? What does it do?"

Garcia smiled and told them, "Its homemade itching powder. He's going to itch like crazy and think its fire ants crawling on him. But remember he's tortured a lot of people. Let's let him scream for a while. It will do him good."

When they came back Nunez was squirming. He pleaded, "Please take the ants off. I'll tell you whatever you want to know. Please."

They ignored him. Mendez said, "Look at that one he has to be a half inch long. Most of the others are little, only three eights of an inch."

Garcia said, "They're all soldier ants. See the copper colored heads and red bodies."

Not to be outdone Cruz continued the charade. Nunez was shaking uncontrollably as Cruz said, "Look at the stream of little ones heading down his prick. Oh-oh they're going inside, right down the pee hole. How's that feel, Stewie?"

Esteban screamed and screamed. He pleaded, "Please make it stop."

Mendez said, "Look, big tough Stewie is pissing himself."

The team laughed at him. Garcia said, "Oh that's bad Stew. What you did can be fatal. Usually you only get pain, swelling, vomiting, and shock. However, when you open the penile urethral sphincter to piss you allow fire ants into your bladder. Now that you stop pissing and the sphincter closes the rest of them are going to detour right into the scrotum sac. That's a lot of spongy soft tissue Stewie. Does it burn Stewie? That's why they call them fire ants, their bites burn like hell. You poor fuck."

Nunez screamed, screamed, and screamed in agony, his wide-open eyes darted right and left, he sputtered, shook in fear, he pleaded, "Please stop them. I'll tell you whatever it is you want to know."

Garcia told Nunez, "We'll stop the ants and give you a shot which will kill the ant venom and all the ants in your body if you tell us all about the Mexican policeman, and all about who killed the Rynning boys. And, after you triggered the Rynning explosion, who did you call on your cell phone? Who accompanied you when you killed the Comforts last month? Who carved their eyes out? You also have to agree to answer any other questions we might have after today. You agree?"

"Yes, please make it stop."

Garcia went to his backpack and retrieved a portable battery operated vacuum. He put on gloves and a face mask, gave masks to Mendez and Cruz, told them to back off a little bit. He put a mask on Nunez and cleaned up the maple leaf itching powder. Eventually Nunez calmed down. When his breathing returned to normal Garcia untied his wrists and told him to stand. He vacuumed Nunez some more and directed Mendez to set up and start the video equipment. "Head shots only" Garcia told Mendez.

Garcia said to Nunez, "Esteban Nunez, tell us about Jesus Noriega, the Rynning brothers, and Sam and Ida Comfort."

"Yes, yes, yes. Angel made me dip the Mexican cop into acid slowly, very slowly, until he told Angel everything. He told Angel all about you three. The cop, he was a tough man. He fought as best he could. He died. Then Angel told me to submerge the cop in the acid vat he keeps for that purpose. When his flesh and stuff dissolved, then Angel had me crush up the remaining bones and spread the fragments on his ranch. The cop is dead. Angel told me when, where, and how to kill the Rynning boys. I blew them up like he said. Angel has a contact, a big shot that works for the border patrol, who told him how to get the Rynnings. I don't know who Sam and Ida Comfort are."

"They are the two people murdered last month when you brought the drugs across."

"Last month, those two people, it was me and Hector and four of the others Antonio Rodriguez, Juan Quintero, Izzy, wait I mean Isidro Fuentes, and Fernando Santacruz who killed them. They are all here on this trip. Aliberto ordered us to do it. He said Angel told him to tell Hector 'cut their eyes out.' Hector did it. There I told you. Angel would kill me if he finds out what I've said. I've told you everything. I'll tell you anything I know anything about, just ask me. Please don't send me back to Mexico."

Garcia injected him with a sedative which immediately put Nunez to sleep. He crumbled. Garcia then took out a silenced pistol which he fired into the ground next to the body twice. The two soft pops resonated through the desert hills.

Garcia told Cruz and Mendez to untie his ankles, pick up Nunez, and put him on a litter he spread out. Garcia brought along one of the new absorbent body bags that didn't allow body fluids to leak out. Garcia zipped up the top cover, leaving Nunez' face exposed so he would be able to breathe. The sedative he had injected would lead anybody looking at the body in the bag to believe he was dead. The litter had four handles, one at each corner. When they were done they would let four of the Mexicans carry Nunez out.

Returning to the Mexicans gathered face down Cruz asked, "Who is Izzy?"

When no one responded Cruz said, "Isidro Fuentes?"

The fifth man in line appeared to shake convulsively. Cruz glanced at

Rey. Rey looked at his clipboard, nodded, and held up five fingers. Cruz walked over, kicked Izzy commanding, "Get the fuck up."

Izzy stood but he could not control his trembling. Cruz told him, "Calm down Izzy, you won't be alone. Antonio Rodriguez, Juan Quintero, and Fernando Santacruz get up and join Izzy."

With the four of them standing Cruz said, "Follow me."

He led them up the western slope. They walked past Nunez lying in the litter. They all glanced but refused to stare. Cruz had them kneel down in front of Garcia. Mendez had set up a camera which she turned on and trained on the four Mexicans.

Garcia said, "We already know what happened and who did what from other testimony, fingerprints and footprints recovered at the scene. But we need everything documented. Answer yes or no for the camera. Last month you four along with Esteban and Hector escorted an elderly American couple you captured observing your actions away from the spot where the drugs you smuggled into the United States were being loaded by the drug porters onto a truck? Answer yes or no."

They all nodded and said, "Si. Yes."

Garcia continued, "The man and woman were gutted and their eyes cut out by who, answer one at a time now as I call your name. Antonio you're first?"

"Hector did it."

"Juan?"

"It was Hector."

"Fernando?"

"Hector did it."

"Izzy?"

"Hector was the one. He did everything."

Garcia gave the hand across his throat signal to Mendez. She turned the camera off. He told Cruz, "Bring them back. Bring Hector up here."

Hector appeared confident coming over the top of the slope. Then his eyes saw Esteban. His demeanor changed instantly. Cruz stopped him in front of the camera, pushed down on his shoulder and ordered, "Kneel."

Before the camera was rolling Garcia said, "Hector you are a despicable piece of shit. I would like nothing better than to cut your prick off, gouge your eyes out, and throw you back over the fence. But you're lucky, you're in America, we don't do things like that. Let me qualify that. Most times we don't do things like that. I might make an exception for you. I want a confession and some answers, okay? I hear what I expect to hear you will live. Alex start the camera."

Garcia continued, "Hector why did you gut and cut the Comforts' eyes out?"

Hector responded, "I didn't. Stewie did it."

Garcia laughed, "Asshole, you think because Stewie is in a body bag you can blame him. He said you did it. Four other participants said you did it. Fingerprints and footprints say you did it. And Hector, the DNA evidence on your knife is going to confirm you did it. Let's not be stupid, you work with us, be truthful, and we'll speak to the prosecutor about not going for the death penalty. Now remembering what I said before, why did you gut them and cut their eyes out?"

Hector appeared to weigh things in his mind. He blurted, "I did my job, my duty. I'm a Mexican soldier. I obeyed orders. Captain Aliberto Castaneda of the Mexican army ordered me to execute them in the manner I did. I demand my rights."

Garcia told Mendez to shut the camera down. When she did he flicked his knife open, grabbed Hector by the hair, and pulled his head back. Hector squealed uncontrollably. Garcia held the point of his knife against Hector's right eyelid. Hector fainted. The team injected Hector with a sedative and placed him in a body bag litter on the ground next to Nunez, his face left uncovered.

Cruz went down the slope, stood over Aliberto, and said, "You're next. Let's go"

Aliberto followed Cruz up the hill, glanced at the body bags, stopped in front of Garcia, and said, "I am a Mexican army officer. My name is Aliberto Castaneda. My rank is captain. My serial number is RA126061. I demand my Geneva Convention rights."

In one motion Alex Mendez snapped her wrist and stabbed the blunt end of her baton into Aliberto's stomach. He expelled all the air in his lungs and dropped to his knees. She bent over and softly said, "Speak only when spoken to."

Aliberto closed his eyes in pain. He gasped for breath. When it appeared he was again breathing properly Garcia had the camera turned on and said, "Berto my boy, tell us why did you order the Comforts murdered in such a brutal way?"

Aliberto answered, "My name is Aliberto Castaneda. My rank is captain. My serial number is RA126061."

"We know Berto. You told us already. Now tell us, you did order the Comforts murdered didn't you?"

"My name is Aliberto Castaneda. My rank is captain. My serial number is RA125061."

Mendez turned off the camera. Cruz tied Aliberto's elbows together behind his back. Garcia reached down unbuckled, unzipped, and pulled Aliberto's pants down. He placed his knife blade in front of Aliberto's eyes where he could see it. He then took Ali's penis in his grasp, put the blade against the skin, and said, "Berto, if you do not answer the questions I'm asking you I will cut your prick off, jam it in your mouth and watch you bleed to death. Do you understand?"

Mendez interrupted, "Wait boss, let me do it. Ever since I spoke to the families of the Rynning boys I've been waiting for an opportunity like this. Please, let me do it."

Cruz laughed, "Alex, I distinctly remember you saying you wanted to cut Nunez' balls off. Now you want to do this guy instead? You are one sadistic bitch."

"Yeah that's what I said but this asshole will do. In my mind they are all guilty. This one is fine with me."

Garcia put an end to the bickering. He said, "Okay Alex, if it makes you happy, it doesn't matter to me who does the cutting." He handed the knife to Mendez.

As she stepped in front of Aliberto Castaneda and he saw the gleam in her eyes, Aliberto paled. He was terrified. *The hell with Angel. They can't touch him. I'm here. He's protected in Mexico* thought Aliberto. All bravado gone, he excitedly blurted, "Get this crazy lady away from me. I'll talk. I'll tell you everything you want to know. Take that knife away from her, please."

Garcia asked, "Everything, no more bullshit?"

Aliberto nodded and said, "Yes. Yes I'll tell everything."

Garcia took the knife back from Mendez and directed her to focus the camera to a close-up of Aliberto's face. With the camera ready, Garcia asked, "Berto, you did order the Comforts murdered didn't you?"

"Yes."

"Why?"

"Angel said to."

"Angel who?"

"Angel, Angel Figueroa, El Jefe."

"Did he tell you to mutilate them?"

"Yes, to set an example, so people know, don't spy on the Alliance."

"What is the Alliance?"

"Angel runs it. The Alliance controls the drugs."

"Who is Angel's contact in the border patrol?"

Aliberto cringed, "Please, I don't know his name. Angel doesn't tell me that."

"Berto you brought in ten people last month, why did they come with you, what did they carry in their backpacks?"

"They came with us because Angel said to bring them. You have to ask Angel why. They brought their own stuff in their backpacks. I don't know what they carried."

"Okay Berto, I believe you."

With the camera turned off Cruz untied Castaneda's elbows. He told him, "Pull your pants up."

Team Intercept was all business. The ambush and after action interrogations successfully completed they headed back to the Van Der Byl farm. Emmett Thompson led the way. The two body bags were carried by eight Mexican smugglers, one man on each handle of each litter. The remaining four smugglers walked immediately behind in the event one of the eight needed to be replaced. Special operations agents flanked both sides. The Triple A team brought up the rear. Alex Mendez remarked, "Did you guys notice Emmett's facial expressions? He seems truly pissed off."

Cruz responded, "I didn't see his face but he wasn't talking to anybody. Everybody else is real happy. Things went well. It appeared to me something is bothering him."

Garcia said, "I didn't look at him specifically. I was busy organizing everybody for the walk out. I'll go up and see if he's okay."

Al Garcia moved off at a pace slightly faster than the rest. As he passed different members of the team he made a point of telling them what a good job they did. Eventually he reached Emmett, pacing himself so they were moving side by side. Garcia remarked, "You did great out there tonight Em. I know now why Ed Grass speaks so highly of you. When I give him my report he'll probably try to recruit you to come to work for him."

Emmett glanced over at Garcia scrunched his face in distaste practically spitting the words out, "That will never happen."

Garcia asked, "Something wrong, something bothering you Em, you want to say something?"

"You're damn right something is bothering me. You and your fucking buddies are no better than the animals who carved up the Comforts and blew up the Rynnings. You tortured and murdered two people tonight. I'm sorry I ever asked Ed for help. You make me sick."

Garcia laughed good-naturedly. He smiled at Emmett saying, "We fooled you too, huh. Emmett, I told you earlier we learn a lot by screwing with people's minds. We didn't torture or murder anybody."

Emmett shook his head, "Yeah, what are you going to say, those two guys in the body bags died in a knife fight? I'm here, I know what happened. You took them up over the hill where the rest of us couldn't see. We heard the screams, the drill, and the gunshots. For Christ's sake the bodies are being carried out in bags. I sure hope you got the answers you were looking for before they died."

"Em, I know it may be hard to believe, but nobody is dead. I injected them with sedatives. They will both come around before we get back to base."

"Al, I heard the sounds. You can't fake that."

"You think that Emmett, but reality paints a decidedly different picture. That's why everything took place over the hill. Neither you nor anyone else could see what indeed happened. You could only imagine. Everything was designed to induce fear. There is a saying in our business, 'Fear perceived is fear achieved.' After we took the first guy, Esteban, over the hill the rest of the smugglers listening to the noises scared themselves shitless. When it came to their turn, they reacted like putty, soft and pliable. At one point their leader, that Aliberto character, nearly shit himself. Cruz and Mendez had him convinced Alex was going to go psycho on him. His tough guy façade evaporated."

"Al, the end does not always justify the means. What I heard will forever haunt me."

"Emmett let me explain. The first guy confessed to triggering the explosives that blew up the Rynnings. He fingered who ordered that hit. He, along with the four guys who we questioned second, all rolled on Hector, the second guy in a bag. Hector confessed to gutting and cutting the eyes out of the Comforts. Everything is on tape and we know who the kingpin is. And the best part is this all came as a result of mind games. The first guy who did all the yelling, his bare ass was tied down over a mound of dirt. We sprinkled some itching powder, simply ground maple seed pods, the helicopter ones, on him and convinced him he felt fire ants crawling into his orifices. When he said he would confess I used a battery vacuum to clean the itching powder off him. That was the drill you thought you heard. Yeah I fired a couple of silenced rounds into the ground, but that was to convince the others we were ruthless. It worked, even on you."

"There are no fucking fire ants in the desert. They need water. All ants nest in moist areas, lake or river banks, and in watered landscaped areas. Everybody knows that."

Garcia smiled, "Apparently not. Stewie, he didn't know that."

Emmett was still skeptical. He halted the column, walked back to the liters and felt the necks of both men being carried. Satisfied both had strong pulses he returned to the front, signaling the group to resume marching. He said to Garcia, "All right Al, I guess I had it all wrong. Congratulations if everything you say is true, you and your team did a fantastic job. My apologies for doubting you."

"Apology accepted. Giving credit where credit is due, we would not be at this point without you and your family's courageous actions. You guys deserve the praise. We on the other hand are doing our jobs. Thanks.

Chapter Twenty-Nine

4:14 a.m. Mountain Time, November 7

OSCAR, THE FORTY-THREE YEAR OLD DRIVER for Mayflower Movers, lay on the paving with his hands trussed behind his back and his feet tied together. This was not supposed to be happening. He had driven this route once a month for the past two years and this border patrol truck check station had never once been open. As usual he had driven down from central Arizona, met the Mexican mules at the abandoned farm like always, loaded up, and started back. Then it all changed. The truck inspection station on the west side of 80 that had always been closed abruptly lit up. The electronic signs that tell truckers to pull in for inspection, the ones that are always turned off, fired up. A car following him at a distance for the last several miles pulled closer and an emergency light started flashing. Headlights appeared in both lanes in front of him, both the eastbound and the westbound lanes. Shit, what was a car doing facing him in the westbound lane?

To avoid a head-on collision he had no choice but to follow the lit up directional arrows into the truck inspection lane. Quickly he dialed the emergency number they had provided for circumstances like this. He informed them he was being pulled over and gave them the location. A guy wearing an FBI vest, holding a shotgun, stood in the lane. When the truck stopped, another FBI agent, also with a shotgun, stood in the road next to his window and made a hand signal for him to turn the key off. He did. When he rolled down the window and asked is there a problem, a broad came forward and told him to get out, lie on the ground, and put his hands behind his back. He did as he was told. She cuffed him. Even though he was face down in the road grime, grease, and oil he knew they had cut the padlock, opened the side door, and climbed inside. He didn't know what they were doing in there, but one thing for sure, if they were FBI he was going to jail, if they were hijackers he was dead.

Racing down the road, out of the west, the border patrol car with lights flashing and siren blasting could be seen and heard long before it arrived. When it did the driver made a screeching u-turn pulling to a stop. The headlights shone over Oscar, the open side door, and several people dressed as FBI. The car's engine shut down, both driver and passenger doors swung open, two people in border patrol uniforms emerged. One, the driver, stood quietly next to his door. The other, the passenger, bellowed, "Who the fuck do you people think you are? I'm in charge of this inspection station. You have no authority here. What do you think you're doing? This is a border patrol facility. I'm in charge here. I want some answers. Now!"

The woman who had cuffed Oscar came to the tractor trailer door. Tall, thin, attractive, about forty, she jumped to the ground, walked to face the man, offered her hand, and said, "I'm Phylis Driscoll, Special Agent in Charge of the Arizona District, Phoenix Regional Office. The FBI, under my authority, is undertaking a drug interdiction here. May I ask who you are?"

The loud man hollered, "I'm United States Border Patrol Deputy Chief John Marrone. I run this facility. You have no business here. This station is closed tonight. Now get your people off this truck."

Driscoll, now smiling, said, "Sir, I just got off the phone with the people in charge of Team Intercept. They are en route as we speak. They should be here in minutes. If you have a problem with jurisdiction please be patient for a few minutes, then you can take it up with them."

Marrone turned to the other border patrol officer commanding, "Mel, call headquarters. Tell them to get some of our people out here now."

Mel sat down in the car and got on the radio. Shortly he came back and said, "Chief, headquarters says everyone on duty is in the boonies chasing illegals at Lochiel and east of Douglas. It will be awhile but they'll have some patrolmen here as soon as they can."

Despite the roadway lights that directed passing trucks to go into the inspection area being turned off and only a few other lights still being on, a convoy of United States Army trucks entered into the inspection station. They came to a stop on the road behind the Mayflower Movers truck. The engines shut down, headlights extinguished, and several soldiers in uniform got out of the back of the last truck in line. They came forward.

Driscoll said to Marrone, "Oh good, Team Intercept is here. Speak to them Deputy Chief."

As Garcia, Cruz, and Mendez walked closer, Marrone recognized who they were. He roared, "What the fuck is going on here. Aren't you agents supposed to be investigating murders?"

Garcia responded, "We have our murderers, Chief. They are in the trucks under arrest. As for what is going on here, take a walk with us. It's not everybody's business."

Garcia put his arm around Marrone's shoulders and guided him away from the congestion. The group stopped close to the highway. Garcia, without loosening his grip on Marrone's shoulder spoke into his ear, "Chief we have you talking to Lisa. We know you're Angel's buttboy. We know you're dirty. You can come quietly with us or I'll be happy to stomp you into submission here and now."

On the other side of the lot, the convoy drivers and other members of Team Intercept climbed out of the trucks and were milling around the vehicles. Marrone's eyes flashed all around, his mind plotting what to do next. Then he saw Emmett Thompson and blurted, "I know who he is. What's he doing here?"

A crooked grin then crossed Marrone's face as he looked straight into Garcia's eyes and told him, "I see the problem right now. That's the Bisbee Brigade kid, Emmett. You fuck with me and my first conference with my lawyer will be to get a message to Angel. He'll be told who the rat bastard troublemakers are. That whole fucking Thompson family, the father, sons, wives, and kids will die. Their blood will be on you asshole. Now get your hands off me."

"Please John you don't need to do that. We know you told Strump about the Rynning boys and she told Figueroa. We saw what happened to them. We don't want that to happen to the Thompsons. You did tell her, right?"

Marrone grinned, nodded, and said, "Damn right asshole. Now back off or your friends are dead."

Garcia let him go. He pleaded, "Hold on a second John, calm down. We can work this out. I just have to okay everything with my team. Give me a few will you please?"

Marrone smiled as Garcia conferred with Cruz and Mendez. He saw a lot of heads nodding then they broke apart. Mendez appeared annoyed. She walked toward the border patrol car. Cruz shook his head and backed up a ways. Garcia returned to Marrone. He offered his hand slapped him on the back saying, "You win John. They don't like it. I don't like it. But we can't have the Thompson's blood on our hands."

Mendez sat on the border patrol car fender chatting with Mel. Mel paid rapt attention to every word. Driscoll and her agents talked among themselves. The men and women around the convoy trucks split into small groups and talked. Cruz was behind Marrone looking at the entire scene. He continuously nodded his head up and down like he thoughtlessly kept time to music.

No one paid any attention to Garcia and Marrone. Marrone seemed pleased with the way things were going until Garcia, standing between Marrone and everyone else, grabbed his collar with his right fist and grasped his right shoulder with his left hand. Garcia was a big powerful man. Garcia saw Marrone was uncomfortable. He leaned in and said, "Gold John, G-O-L-D."

Marrone's eyes opened wide. He breathed deep and said, "How do you know? No, you can't. You don't know."

Garcia while looking intently at Cruz said softly, "Yes John, I know. I'm going for all of it. I want you to know that before you die."

The paving on which they stood vibrated, there was a rumbling sound, and a push of air as Garcia flung his right hand straight out and pushed hard with his left, hurling Marrone onto the highway. Garcia called out loud enough for everyone to hear, "Look out John."

Everyone heard the warning yell and looked in time to see John Marrone stumble in front of the passing Mexicana Tours bus going by at full speed. The sound of the impact was sickening, Marrone flew in the air for sixty feet, the body coming to rest in the road only to be run over by the front tires of the bus. The bus driver had immediately slammed on his brakes but the rear wheels also went over the body. As everyone ran to see if they could help Cruz went the other way toward the convoy stopping Team Intercept members, directing them back to guard the prisoners. Cruz told them, "There's nothing you can do for him. What a shame, poor guy merely out here trying to do his job."

At 6:10 a.m., Cochise County Sheriff Edwardo "Big Ed" Mata-Villa arrived to find his local deputy, who he knew had been roused out of bed as soon as the call came in, being assisted by at least a dozen border patrolmen. They worked together directing early morning rush hour traffic around a body lying on the side of the road. A Mexicana Tours bus was stopped on the road in front of the body. Passengers from the bus sat on the ground in the early morning sunshine. They were back from the accident site, in the border patrol's truck inspection area. For the most part the bus passengers sat leaning against the several border patrol cars parked there. Several other passengers consoled the bus driver. Mata-Villa conferred with the deputy and learned about a huge drug bust the previous night. Border Patrol Deputy Chief John Marrone had been on the scene supervising. He accidently stepped in front of the Mexicana bus, was run over, and killed. FBI agent Albert Garcia was the only one who literally witnessed the accident. His signed statement agreed with that of the bus driver's. Marrone accidently walked in front of the oncoming bus. The bus driver was not at fault. It was unavoidable.

At about the same time as Mata-Villa arrived at the border patrol inspection station, Team Intercept's four truck convoy passed through the main gate of Fort Huachuca. Two official FBI cars and a Mayflower Movers tractor trailer being driven by a Phoenix FBI agent licensed to operate a big rig followed the convoy. The procession drove directly to the brig, where General Ehrich met them.

The general had handshakes, backslaps, and attaboys for everyone. He met Phylis Driscoll and her agents for the first time. Phylis proudly explained to Ehrich the Director of Homeland Security had called her personally with the assignment to work with Triple A and Team Intercept on a major drug bust. She jumped at the opportunity, drove down from Phoenix the previous day with four agents from her office, met with and walked the ambush site, the Hernandez farm, and the border patrol inspection facility with Garcia and Emmett. She gushed about Emmett's whispered phone call and the subsequent intercept of the drug laden tractor trailer. She was sincerely remorseful about the deputy chief who lost his life in such a tragic accident. The poor man was so upset we used one of his facilities without his permission. She guessed he wasn't told or he never received the message. Driscoll declined the general's offer for Phylis and her agents to come back to Camp Vigilant for breakfast. She thanked him profusely but explained, as soon as her agent who drove the big rig parked the truck and left it under guard in the impound area of the motor pool, they would all be leaving. She was also waiting for mug shots, fingerprints, DNA samples, and names for AFIS files and the federal criminal database. She told him all the confiscated knives taken from the suspects were turned over to her under chain of custody rules. She needed to take them back to the Phoenix Regional Office so the lab could examine them. She confided Triple A felt at least one of those knives would definitely have the blood and guts of the Comforts on it. They wanted answers as soon as possible. The ever helpful Ehrich had an army big rig driver relieve the FBI driver and ordered expedited booking, fingerprints, mug shots, and DNA samples of the apprehended trucker and fourteen smugglers. Within thirty minutes Driscoll and her agents were in their cars on the road back to Phoenix.

At 9:23 a.m. Eastern Time, November 7, Ed Grass gazed out his office window at the gloomy rainy morning in Washington. He could not hide his foul mood. Although he knew from the brief hurried report he received earlier from Garcia, the previous night's ambush went well, he wanted the details. Not only that, as much as he realized Triple A had a lot of after action activities to tend to in addition to reporting to him, he had news to pass on. Finally, Grass decided the information he had recently received was too important to wait any longer. He dialed Al Garcia. Garcia looked at caller ID and cheerfully answered, "Good morning Director. I was just going to call you. The operation is over, a great success like I mentioned when I called earlier. Sorry I didn't get back sooner but I just finished having breakfast with Cruz and Mendez. If you have time I'll put you on speaker and we can all fill you in."

Grass testily replied, "Do that Al, put me on speaker. I'm sorry if I interrupted anybody's second cup of coffee but we have a job to do here."

Sensing the director's annoyance the team responded in unison, "Yes sir."

Grass continued, "Before you report on last night I'd like to update you all on those Huerta people you interviewed a couple of weeks ago. It seems they are not quite who they appear to be."

Garcia asked, "What do you mean Director?"

"I didn't want to worry you while you were in ambush mode, but if you remember we obtained their DNA from the water bottles Emmett brought in. Well, Lauren sent those samples to a lab which does studies from DNA that will confirm blood relatives. The Huertas are not related, no brothers, sisters, and cousins like their asylum applications say. In fact this lab threw in a bonus DNA check Lauren didn't ask for. Turns out the Huertas are not Latino. They are not of South American heritage. Their DNA proves they all come from the Middle East. They are not related in the least. However, their bloodlines are all Middle Eastern. They are Arab, Persian, or some such heritage. To make matters worse I went to the director of CIA. The director had his resident agent in Montevideo check out the story about drug dealers having a hit out on the Huerta family. There is no basis to the story. The CIA agent believes the file contains a false statement from Montevideo police chief about that. It turns out the chief may have been bribed to come up with that story to deceive the consular unit of the United States Embassy in Montevideo, Uruguay so they would confirm the plight of the Huertas before they our government granted them permanent asylum. It appears the Huertas are a fraud."

Cruz said, "Fuck. I knew there was something wrong. They said they prepared chicken and rice for lunch the day we interviewed them. We all thought they referred to eating Spanish chicken and rice. What bullshit. They were eating stuffed grape leaves. They had chicken with rice all right. Spices, flat bread and long grains of basmati rice in a chicken biryani. A creamy, spicy blend of onion, garlic, ginger, turmeric, cumin, tomatoes, ginger, saffron, curry, eggplant. That's Arab shit. I remember that aroma now clear as a bell. Arab chicken and rice with all their seasonings. It stunk all over the Middle East from that crap when I was stationed there. I should have realized earlier. I screwed up."

Mendez said, "It's not your fault Al. We were all there. At least you realized something was wrong. You said it didn't feel right. We thought you were imagining things."

Garcia added, "Director, I received a call from Tom Eagan before we left to do the ambush last night. You remember him, the FBI investigator at the Fort Mason bombing earlier this year. He's investigating the nuclear bombings that took place in Los Angeles, Phoenix, Albuquerque, and Houston. He told me a van left in a Denver parking garage had radioactive residue inside. Its GPS led him to Huerta's shop. He found trace residue on the shop floor."

"What did the Huertas say about that?"

"Nothing, they weren't there."

"What do you think we should do Al?"

"We have a lot on our plate with this case. I'll pass this new information on. I'll let Eagan know about it sir. He'll keep me informed. I'll keep you informed."

"Better informed than you've kept me on this ambush I hope."

"Yes sir, I'm sorry for the delay. We had a lot to finish up here. I meant to call you just as you called. It won't happen again sir."

"All right let's not dwell. What happened last night? Where are we? Where do we go from here?"

"The operation went as planned. The drug truck was seized by Driscoll and her agents who came down from Phoenix. They did a wonderful job. Please thank whoever was responsible for assigning her. We, your other special operations agents, and Emmett Thompson took the drug smugglers armed force without a hitch. Your friend, General Ehrich, should be thanked personally for all his help and guidance. One tractor trailer loaded with drugs is under around the clock guard in the impound area in the general's motor pool. Fourteen smugglers and one truck driver are currently housed in separate cells in Fort Huachuca's confinement facility. An excellent, secure, truly modern jail entirely housed in one building incorporated into Huachuca's intelligence training complex facility. All of the detainees had complete physicals and photos records taken of their bodies. Any accusations of abuse later can be proved wrong by no evidence at all of bruising, blistering, or maltreatment. We have notified Sheriff Mata-Villa we have apprehended the Rynning and Comfort killers, and we have confessions. They are being held in military detention cells because they claim to be lost Mexican soldiers. The killers confessed and implicated Angel Figueroa. They say they killed the border watchers on the orders of Figueroa, who they call El Jefe—the boss. He had them brutally murdered to make an example. They gutted the Comforts; gouged their eyes out, on the orders of Angel, the Comandante en Jefe, their commander-in-chief. The Rynnings were blown up on the direct orders of Angel. The information on when and where they could be gotten was provided by their connection in our border patrol. Unfortunately Deputy Chief John Marrone was run over by a bus and died. I think he committed suicide after I told him we had the goods on him and he would spend the rest of his life in jail. I knew that bus was coming, in my opinion he certainly did too. The chain of custody on the murder knife or knives is intact. Driscoll and four agents from the Phoenix office signed for them and are transporting them to the FBI lab. She is also going to deposit all of the suspects' names, DNA, and booking records into the FBI's files."

"All right Al. That was very complete, thank you. What is the plan now?"

"Well sir, first we have to toss Marrone's place before anybody else gets there. Then we have to speak with Lisa. Not only was she paying Marrone, she has a regular route of payoffs. We need to interrogate her, find out who she pays along the border, and in Kansas City, and what they get paid for. We, or better yet the other members of Team Intercept after they get a couple of days off, will need to pick all those people up. And we will have to see if Lisa knows anything else."

"Okay it sounds like you have everything under control. Keep me informed."

"Yes sir. Goodbye sir."

After clearing with General Ehrich that staying a few more days at Camp Vigilant would be all right and informing the other special operations agents, they had the next few days off the Triple A team headed out of Fort Huachuca in their rental car. Mendez drove.

On the way, Garcia called Tom Eagan to inform him the Huertas no longer appeared to be Latinos or even relatives. DNA tests show them to be Middle Eastern and not related by blood. The CIA in Uruguay could not confirm any of their claims that they were running from drug dealers or drug dealers killed the rest of their family. In fact, the story appeared to be a hoax perpetrated upon the cultural attaché so they could gain legal status in the United States. He told him the drug smugglers had no insight on the Huertas. They brought them across the border because their boss told them to.

Eagan laughed, telling Garcia, "Yeah, I figured out the relative thing was all bullshit as soon as I went through the houses. The supposed brothers, sisters, cousins, whatever didn't hold up. I found two situations where Chief Goff told me brothers and sisters lived together. Well guess what, I found only one big bed in each of those houses. Either they weren't related or there was a lot of incestuous behavior going on. Bringing you guys up to date, the Huertas are in the wind. Your visit spooked them. The homes, two single bedrooms with one guy each, one four bedroom house with four in single bedrooms, and the two incest situations are all empty. We searched. No radioactivity, no clues so far. Everything is sealed off and will be gone through with a fine tooth comb. All-points bulletins are out on both the people and their vehicles. Nothing else so far. I'll keep in touch."

The pretense of bird watching no longer necessary Mendez pulled up to Marrone's security gate. She asked, "What's the code?"

Cruz answered, "Try 4653."

Mendez dialed the code, the gate swung open; she pulled through, stopped and pressed another button mounted on a stanchion easily reached by a vehicle's driver. That activated the gate closing procedure. She continued to the front of Marrone's house, parked, and popped the trunk. She retrieved a zippered duffle before following Garcia and Cruz to the front door. Garcia told Cruz, "Pick the lock, Al."

In less than a minute the door was open. Cruz entered and immediately entered the 4653 code into the alarm controller. All three went directly into the master bedroom. Cruz went to the wall safe and pressed 4653.

The safe door open, Garcia instructed, "Al, take the cash out, put it on the bed. Alex you count it and put it all in the duffle."

Mendez made twenty-six stacks of one hundred thousand each, then counted another eighty-five thousand dollars, all in hundreds. She said, "Two million six hundred eighty-five thousand, boss."

Garcia ordered, "Put five thousand back in the safe and relock it. Put the rest in the duffle bag and lock it in the trunk."

Leaving through the front entry, Cruz reset the alarm and relocked the door. He told the others, "No one will ever know we were here."

Garcia said, "Al, go get the ladder and retrieve your cameras. The sooner they are back in your bag of tricks and we're out of here the better."

On the highway traveling back to Fort Huachuca Cruz said, "That went well boss."

Garcia replied, "Yeah, so far."

Cruz then asked, "Boss, I've been meaning to ask you, before Marrone stumbled in front of the bus last night you said gold to him. That seemed to freak him out. Why? What am I missing?"

Garcia replied, "G-O-L-D is his combination. Think about it Al, on any phone faceplate 4653 also represents the letters g-o-l-d on the buttons. Before he died I wanted him to know we knew his code and were going to get his cash. He died broke."

Mendez said, "It's fitting neither he nor his heirs, whoever they may be, should benefit from his crimes. The scummy prick will be remembered as a hero, a real border protector."

Garcia opined, "I guess it all depends on whether or not Lisa and Angel go to trial. Either one of them could blow the whistle on Marrone. But there is no longer any money trail now is there."

Mendez laughed, "I guess you can't have everything."

Chapter Thirty

1:17 a.m. Pacific Time, November 8

THE SOUNDS OF WAVE AFTER WAVE rolling in to shore soothed the minds of those who listened. Lisa Strump chose to live high on a secluded bluff overlooking the Pacific Ocean because she enjoyed the noise of waves breaking on the beach, the distinctive breeze, and the delightful tangy smell of the sea lacing the fresh air. Whether it was a quiet whisper, a thudding murmur, or a roaring thunderous crashing of waves she had slept peacefully every night since moving to her home, a single story ranch style house, in Carlsbad, a small California beach city. She found the tranquil environment calmed her conscience. Tonight was no different, until it was too late.

Strump heard earlier on CNN about the major drug bust in Arizona, the arrest of over a dozen smugglers, and the tragic accident that took the life of a heroic border patrol agent. Her first thought was she was safe. With John Marrone dead the authorities would not be able to tie her to anything.

Angel Figueroa had called that afternoon. He raged on. Not at her, but at John. He said it was a good thing Marrone was killed by a bus, things would have gone far worse for him if he was still alive. Marrone's incompetence had cost a lot of money and caused a lot of problems. Angel confided in Lisa he had received calls from the other Mexican cartel leaders questioning his leadership of the Alliance. He was concerned they could make a move on him. They knew his position was weak. Some of his most able protectors are in jail in the United States. It was a good thing only he knew the particulars of her and Abe Silverman's contacts. Angel told her to call him immediately if any of the other cartels approached her. She said of course she would, but she was not certain how she would react if contacted by any of the other cartels. Those people are scary.

Lisa bolted awake. A strong hand over her mouth kept her from crying out. Hands on her arms held her down. She felt more than afraid, a feeling more akin to overpowering fright. Slowly she opened her eyes. She saw three of them. All dressed in black. Black hoods over their heads covering their faces. No one spoke to her. Lisa slowly started breathing normally. *Who are these people*, she asked herself, *what do they want?* Then her heart stopped beating as something flashed before her eyes. It was a straight razor being intentionally waved back and forth slowly. Terrified, Lisa shook violently, uncontrolled. One leaned close to her face and whispered, "If I take my hand off your mouth will you be quiet?"

Lisa nodded her head. The voice said, "One sound and I'll cut your face. Understand?"

Lisa nodded again. The hand was removed. The voice now so low it was barely audible said, "Get out of bed. Move to the bench in front of the make-up table and sit."

The hands on her left shoulder released, Lisa was guided out the right side of her bed to her dressing table bench. She sat down in front of the mirror. One person stood behind her holding her down by her arms. A small flashlight was turned on. It was placed on the table facing up, illuminating Lisa's face. The voice said, "Remember, one sound and I slice your face."

Lisa nodded. She understood. She watched as they opened several of her lipstick tubes. One of the intruders selected a dark deep red. A handful of Lisa's red hair was grabbed, her head pulled back sharply, and lipstick was applied. Bright red lines were drawn on her earlobes, her nostrils, and from the corners of her mouth back toward her ears imitating a gross, wider than normal smiling face. The outside edges of her eyes to her temples were marked. Her hair was released. The voice said, "That's very good Lisa. Don't make a sound. I'll let you know when to talk."

Lisa acquiesced, inclining her head. The voice, pausing often for shock value, spoke, "In Africa when women know something and won't reveal it they are sometimes disfigured. Marks like the ones on your face would be opened up with a blade until they spoke. Someone takes a pair of scissors, a straight razor, or garden snips and cuts each nostril so it flaps—then they cut the mouth from the sides all the way to the ears. The victim watches— so can you—watch and taste the blood. Then they cut the ears off—a little at a time. They take scissors or pliers and jab them under the finger or toe nails and rip them off—cut your nipples off with a blade—and using the blade cut the flesh to the armpits—I think you get the picture."

The voice provoked the desired reaction. Lisa, eyes wide in fear, nodded.

"There are times when women don't speak quickly enough. In those instances they do eventually talk but not fast enough to prevent being cut up. In your case if you are the least bit reluctant to tell us what we want to know we could cut your eyelids off, maybe we'd be nice and do your ears first. They could still covered by a hairdo. Do you understand?"

Lisa looked in the mirror at her beautiful face grotesquely marred with lipstick. She nodded vigorously. She wanted them to know she would talk. The voice said, "Good."

A recorder was set on the dressing table. It was turned on. Lisa could see tiny lights blinking. She made up her mind. *Fuck Angel, these people are savages. He's not here to protect me. I have to tell them what they want to know.* The voice asked, "You're Angel's bag woman with the border patrol?"

"Yes."

"You have been doing this for how long?"

"Five years give or take. I'd have to check my records for the exact dates."

"That's okay. We simply want to make sure you are the right person. Do you have a record of the people Angel has had you pay?"

"Yes I have the records."

"Where?"

"In my computer in my office here at home. I have back-up discs in my safe deposit box at my bank."

"Can you print a copy for us?"

"Yes."

"Okay that's good. Stand up, go to your computer and make the copies."

Lisa stood up and asked, "Can I get dressed, put some clothes on?"

Lisa got slapped hard. She fell back on to the floor. The voice said, "No you can't get dressed. We're not done with you. Make the fucking copies and speak only when spoken to. You're lucky you aren't getting cut bitch."

Lisa sniffled. She wanted to cry but was afraid to. The voice told her, "Get up, and go to the computer. Printout the copies. Make a disc too. You can make a disc can't you?"

"Yes."

When Strump finished the copies the voice asked, "What else can you tell us?"

"Nothing, I work the American field people, the border patrol and customs. The politicians and the like are done by others. Your bosses were at the Tortuguero meeting. They know the Mexican contacts are taken care of by Diego Perez. And, the American politicians are taken care of by Abe Silverman. I don't have those answers, the others do."

After writing down her password and telling Strump to sit still the hooded people stepped out of the office. The voice asked, "Do either of you have any idea what she's talking about? Has anybody heard Tortuguero, Perez, or Silverman mentioned on any of our tapes?"

When both others shook their heads the voice said, "Okay, change in plan. We need to try the good guy approach. Mendez you need to talk to her woman to woman."

"Right boss."

Alex Mendez went into the office. She took her hood off and said, "Come on, let's get you cleaned up and dressed."

Alex led Strump back to her bedroom. She instructed, "Take some cold cream to that lipstick then take a shower and get your clothes on."

Lisa sat on the bench and applied some cold cream. She rubbed and rubbed, wiped the excess and started crying softly. She murmured softly, "It all won't come off."

Alex said, "Try some baby oil, you have some, right? Petroleum jelly will work too."

"That stuff is in the medicine cabinet. Can I go into the bathroom?"

Alex smiled, "Of course."

Alex followed Lisa into her bathroom. Some baby oil applied to a washcloth removed the remaining lipstick. Alex said, "That's good Lisa. Take a shower now, I'll wait in the bedroom."

"Thank you. Please don't hurt me. Don't let them hurt me. I've told you everything I can. I don't know anything else."

Alex soothed, "I won't let anyone hurt you. Now take a shower, get cleaned up, then we'll talk some more."

When Strump finished showering, toweling, and was dressed, Lisa said, "You look nice."

Lisa grinned, "I feel much better. Thanks for being so nice."

Mendez told her, "Lisa, our boss didn't mention the Tortuguero meeting or anybody named Perez, or Silverman. Tell me please."

"Oh shit I'm dead. You're going to kill me. If you don't Angel will kill me just for talking to you."

"No Lisa, I told you I won't let anything happen to you. Trust me, work with me. Start with Tortuguero. What is that?"

"You know, where the Alliance met in Costa Rica last month."

"No I didn't know. Now who is Diego Perez?"

"He's Angel's bagman for the Mexican Government. He says he pays out ten million dollars each month."

"Wow, that's a lot of money. Where do we find him?"

"I don't know. Someplace in Mexico I guess."

"Who's Abe Silverman?"

"Abe pays American politicians for Angel."

"How much does Silverman pay out?"

"I didn't really pay much attention to how much he paid each person. He did say he paid members of Congress, four of them, monthly. Then he said he paid other congressmen, governors, mayors, and some agency big shots on occasion. I remember him saying he paid out about ten million last year in Washington."

"Where does he live?"

"Virginia, someplace. I don't know exactly where. I do have his e-mail though."

"How much money do you pay out?"

"The amounts and the method of payment vary. Most are done by wire transfer, a few I deposit cash into a designated account, and some of my clients I hand cash to. It's all in the records from my computer."

"Off the top of your head, how much Lisa?"

"John Marrone got one hundred thousand each month. Three more border patrol big shots get one hundred thousand a month each. Fourteen supervisors at high-volume border crossing stations get eighty thousand each. Ten supervisors at low-volume crossings get fifty thousand each. Eighty-four border officers, the ones who handle the commercial trucking lanes get thirty thousand each per month, and twenty-four more officers who handle pedestrian entrants get twenty thousand each. I also pay some customs guys too. One of them gets fifty thousand each month; five get twenty, and forty get ten thousand each. By my count, I pay out five million five hundred seventy thousand a month. That comes to sixty-six million eight hundred forty thousand dollars each year. That's all in the records I gave you."

"Okay, who else was at the meeting in Costa Rica?"

"Don't you know anything? All the members of the Alliance were there. A whole bunch of people, mostly foreigners, from all over the world."

"Who else knows who Angel's contacts are, who you and the others have been paying?"

"Nobody. As far as I know, that's only me, Abe, Diego, and Angel. Angel has his records on his computer at his ranch. Angel would not allow that info to be shared. He flat out refused to let any other Alliance member have access to that information. At the meeting in Costa Rica they asked and he wouldn't tell any of them anything."

"How did you get involved in all this drug dealing and payoffs?"

"I started as Angel's girlfriend during the early years. I met him at a club where I worked, we clicked. We dated and spent a lot of time together both here and on his ranch. We took vacations together. Then we evolved into business associates and our social contact slowed then stopped. We haven't slept together in years."

"All right, get me Silverman's e-mail address."

"It's on my computer."

When Mendez and Lisa came out of the bedroom Garcia and Cruz had their hoods off. Strump stopped in her tracks. Mendez asked, "What? Is there a problem Lisa?"

Strump broke down crying. She moaned, "You're going to kill me. I've seen your faces. You're going to kill me."

Mendez put are arm around Strump and told her, "No Lisa, we're federal agents. We're not going to kill you. We are going to protect you. You are our prize witness."

"You're not federal agents. You were going to cut me up. Government agents wouldn't be allowed to do that. You're lying. Who are you really?"

Mendez showed Lisa her ID. She explained, "We've had your phone tapped for some time now. We know you were John Marrone's contact with Angel Figueroa. You passed information which cost people their lives. You paid Alliance bribe money to Marrone and others. You facilitated drug snuggling. You are an accessory to numerous murders. You are a criminal. You could go to jail for the rest of your life. Or, you can be a cooperating witness, testify against all the others, and we will protect you. You will be placed in witness protection. You can start over."

"Start over? What happens to my house, car, clothes, and furniture I've spent years accumulating? What about my savings?"

"You'll keep it all. Witness protection people will sell your house and car, pack up and move your possessions, and open new bank accounts with your money under a new identity they will obtain for you. Just keep cooperating. You're off to a great start."

"Federal agents can break in and threaten to cut me up?"

"Lisa that was all subterfuge. We listened to the call Angel made to you. We realized you had to believe another cartel may come a callin'. We decided to take advantage of that fear. After all if we came here and told you we're police you would have lawyered up. Everything worked out better for all concerned this way."

Strump paused, thought momentarily, and said, "Okay, let me get you Abe Silverman's e-mail address."

Mendez explained to Garcia and Cruz that Lisa had decided to cooperate in exchange for witness protection. Garcia asked Strump, "Did you pass on a message from Marrone to Angel about a meeting the Cochise County Attorney had planned with three brothers, the Rynning brothers?"

"Yes, I remember that. Was it important?"

"Everything could be important. We speculated that is what happened. It's something my supervisor wanted me to clear up, okay. My boss wanted me to confirm. For witnesses in your position it is definitely important you answer every question truthfully."

After setting up their videotaping equipment and having Lisa retell her story, Triple A confiscated Strump's desktop computer and her laptop. Later they went to her bank with her and retrieved all the computer discs in her safe deposit box. Then they dropped Lisa at the United States Federal Witness Protection Program's office in San Diego.

From there, they then wasted no time boarding the Special Operations jet that was waiting for them at Lindbergh Field.

Once in flight Cruz plugged Lisa's disc into his computer and sent the information to Ed Grass. Garcia called Grass, provided Abe Silverman's name, his reported ties to Washington politicians, and his e-mail address. They agreed the team would get some sleep on the flight to DC and Grass would have Lauren track down Silverman. Grass also agreed to have all one hundred thirty-two border patrol employees and the forty-six customs employees named by Lisa thoroughly investigated; their location of employment, residence, cars, other personal possessions, bank accounts, spending habits, and so on needed to be confirmed. They agreed no moves would be made on any of them until after Silverman was interviewed.

The cabin steward had finished making up three beds. The window shades were drawn. The cabin lights dimmed.

Garcia jumped as his phone rang. It was Phylis Driscoll calling. She said, "I wanted you to know as soon as possible the techs found trace evidence of both Sam and Ida Comfort's DNA on Hector Castaneda's knife."

Garcia thanked her, hung up, told the others, and fell fast asleep.

Chapter Thirty-One

10:31 p.m. Eastern Time, November 8

ABE SILVERMAN DROVE HIS NEW SILVER Porsche Cayman S slowly down the brightly lit street in Arlington, Virginia. He gazed around carefully, seeing nothing out of the ordinary and most important to him, no one near the entrance to his building's parking garage. He reached up, activated the electronic roll-up security gate, immediately drove in, and pressed the button closing the gate. He watched the gate drop into place before proceeding to his reserved parking space. Silverman summoned the buildings elevator with a remote control he kept in his pocket. When it arrived he quickly stepped out, locked his car, trotted to the elevator, and once inside pressed the close door control. As the door shut he pressed the button labeled nineteen. The elevator rose quickly to the top floor. Silverman lived in one of the building's six penthouse condos. Exiting the elevator, the door closed behind him.

Silverman walked down the hall smiling, thinking about his most recent visit to his mom and dad. Man, thirty-seven years old, still have to go for dinner with the parents at their home in Baltimore. It's the same every week. Mom, Edith, gushing over her successful boy, he makes her so proud, so much money he has. Dad, Marv, complaining, yeah so much money and the prick never paid back what it cost us to send him to college and law school at Towson University. The campus less than three miles from the house but he couldn't live home and commute, no he had to live in a dorm, a coed residence hall, eat at the cafeteria. Always complaining, never ever offered to pay back one cent.

His father worried about nickels and dimes. He had to worry about the crazy spics he worked for. Angel Figueroa called him complaining about losing a shipment and babbling on about those other jealous Mexican cartel leaders who want his job. They all want to be El Jefe. Why can't they simply eat a minor set-back and move on?

Abe unlocked the door and walked into his condo. It was dark, he reached for the light switch, was hit hard in stomach. He felt tape stretched over his mouth; a bag pulled over his head, his hands bound behind back. *Fuck, I knew this was going to happen. He figured out I was skimming. No. No, maybe it's the other cartels; they want to know who I pay. They asked down in Pachira Lodge. Either way I'm dead.* Powerful hands roughly pulled him across the living room. The sliding doors to the spacious outdoor terrace slid open. He was pushed outside, dragged over to the balcony rail. *Oh fuck. It's Angel. He knows. He's going to throw me off.* His body was bent at the waist. He was half over the side. Someone grabbed his ankles and lifted. He couldn't scream. His heart stopped beating. It was raining freezing cold water. His clothes were getting soaked, chilling his body. He was so cold, so scared. *Why did he ever get involved with these crazy animals?*

He heard a voice. The voice said, "Wait, maybe we should ask him first."

Yeah ask me. Ask me cause believe me if I know I'll tell you. Don't throw me over. Come on ask, Abe thought, *please ask. Please.*

After an eternity, slowly his feet were lowered. He was stood up, backed up away from the edge. His heart beat again, he breathed through his nose. Then he was hit in the stomach again, harder than the last time. Strong hands on each arm held him up. They dragged him inside again. Threw him on the floor, he was kicked repeatedly.

The hood was removed from his head. He blinked. His eyes slowly adjusted to the light. A bright lamp had been lit. He could make out two Hispanic men and one Hispanic woman standing over him. They stood staring at him for a long time. Finally the woman said, "So ask him."

One of the men, the bigger one, inquired, "Do you want to talk to us?"

Abe nodded his head vigorously. The man asked, "If I remove the tape will you remain calm, quiet, and only answer the questions I ask?"

Abe nodded. The bigger man told the other two, "Lift him up. Sit him in a kitchen chair."

Once Abe was placed in a chair in the middle of the living room floor the big man opened the door to the terrace. He said, "I'm going to take the tape off your mouth. If you scream or refuse to answer a question I'm going to throw you over the side. Understand?"

Abe nodded. The tape was ripped from his mouth. The big man asked, "You're Abe Silverman?"

Abe answered, "Yes."

"You answer to Angel Figueroa?"

"Yes."

"You understand you represent the entire Alliance here in Washington don't you?"

"Yes."

"Do you have a record of each and every payment made by you on the Alliance's behalf?"

"Yes."

"You realize the Alliance is more than Angel, don't you?"

"Yes."

"Where are the records?"

"They're here, in my file cabinet and in my computer."

Garcia decided to play a card Lisa Strump had provided. He asked, "Do your records reveal the names Angel would not allow you to reveal at the Pachira Lodge meeting?"

"My computer records and the hard copies have code names of the individuals."

"You understand we want the names, not the code names, which go with each of the payments? We want to know who, when, where, and how these people you paid were paid."

"Yes, I have everything. You can have it all."

"Start talking. Give us the names. Start at the top."

"The top people are Senator Harvey Dwight of Idaho, Senator John Babcock of Delaware, Representative Ezra Higgins of Newark, and Representative Vito LaCrocca of Richmond. Richmond that's Staten Island in New York, you know that right?"

"Give us some details."

"Yes, sure, first there's Barney. That's his code name. In the United States Senate I have the chairman of the Homeland Security and Governmental Affairs Committee Senator Harvey Dwight of Idaho in my pocket. Harvey is in the closet, a gay Republican, and I have several videos of him in action with other men. In addition to the movie shoots featuring Senator Dwight he has been accepting eighty thousand dollars each month in off-the-books payments for his efforts on your behalf. Mister Figueroa came in for the first meeting with Senator Dwight. We had the meeting here. I have video of the whole thing. First we showed him the movies of him with other guys, then Angel told him his secret would be safe as long as he did as he was told."

"Can you prove what you're saying?"

"You remember that phony Arab sheik sting the FBI did in 1980 where they filmed all those crooked congressmen taking money? I have them all on tape. My whole place here is wired. Just like ABSCAM. This boy's momma didn't raise any fool. All the congressmen wanted to come here. They felt safe here. They believed lawyer/client privilege applied to anything said or done here."

"And you know it doesn't right? You are going to tell us everything right?"

"Yes. Yes."

"You mentioned Senator Babcock. What do you have on him?"

"He's the previous committee chairman. I call him Porky. He's a Democrat. He still serves on the committee. He's the ranking minority member now. Senator John Babcock, he represents Delaware. He also receives eighty thousand dollars per month, a continuation from when I first recruited him five years ago. I have video of that meeting. Babcock is not gay. If he was that wouldn't help anyway since he is a Democrat and gay members of the Democrat Party are regularly reelected. The fact is we have no dirty little secret on John. He is simply driven by greed. He is in this for the money."

"What about Higgins?"

"Representative Ezra Higgins, House Homeland Security Committee chairman, is a Democrat representing a district in Newark, New Jersey. Another eighty thousand dollars goes to him monthly. Representative Higgins is a pedophile. He has a sexual preference for young girls. Angel filmed Higgins engaging in sex acts with a twelve year old girl while he was traveling on a congressional junket to the Philippines. The age of consent in the Philippines is twelve years of age. But when we provided Higgins with a copy of the film and copies of still pictures he agreed to do all he could to help the Alliance. I have copies of all that stuff in my file cabinet. That pervert is so horny he bought a vacation home in Haiti so he can have easy sex with young girls. He told me he rents them for practically nothing down there. His code name is Chester."

"La Crocca?"

"He too gets eighty thousand dollars a month. He's the ranking minority" member on the house committee. He's a Republican from Richmond County, New York. Before Vito La Crocca was first elected to the House of Representatives he ran a construction union. In that position he took numerous bribes from employers. Angel was here when La Crocca came in the first time. Angel went through all the particulars, how much, when, where, for what reason the gratuities had been paid. Angel told me he had obtained the facts from acquaintances who actually ran the mobbed-up firms that paid the bribes. Representative La Crocca, he laughed, said those incidents could never be proven, but he was enthusiastic about helping anyway. Angel told him bullshit. Angel had all the details about several retirees from La Crocca's union who never worked a day in their lives. Mob guys, no-shows Angel called them. Vito denied that, saying it didn't matter those guys are all retired now getting three grand a month. They're not going to roll on the congressman and have their pensions revoked. But it doesn't matter, Vito does whatever I say. Vito loves his eighty thousand dollar gratuity each month. He says thank you so much every payment. His code name is Riddle."

"Anyone else?"

"Not on the monthly pad. A lot of congressmen have come through here on one time basis. Most of those times I don't give them cash in an envelope. It is more a campaign contribution. In return they agree to vote a certain way or make an amendment to a bill, something simple like that. I've made a lot of contributions on your behalf to different groups who exert influence on certain issues that delay even the consideration of building the fence. Issues like endangered bugs and animals, endangered plants, that kind of thing. I distribute money, campaign contributions, to many state politicians, governors, mayors, city councils, sheriffs, who for one reason or another fight the building of the border fence. It doesn't matter what their cause is—just that they are opposed, are vocal, and fight. I have records of all those expenditures."

"What is your computer password?"

"Ezmoney."

"Do you have a laptop?"

"Yes. It's on my desk."

Garcia nodded his head and said, "Okay we have everything for now. Al, wrap up your video equipment. Alex pack up his files. Abe, you carry your computer down to our car. I'll take your laptop."

Silverman asked, "Where are you taking my stuff? How am I going to work?"

Garcia responded, "Abe we're federal law enforcement officers. You're under arrest for bribery of federal officials."

"You were going to kill me. You threatened me. This will never hold up in court. I'm a lawyer. You can't do this."

Cruz said, "Mister Silverman I recorded everything you said after you sat in that chair and gave us your name. Now, you realize when you are charged that tape will be released to the press don't you? Do you think Mister Figueroa is going to give a shit whether or not we legally obtained it? How long do you think you will continue to live when you get out on bail?"

"Wait, can't we work something out? I can verify all my records. I can testify against all these dirt bags. I can make your case. You can use me. Put me in witness protection, please. I know more."

"What more do you know?"

"I can give you the Alliance's bagman in Mexico. He can give you all the Mexican politicians."

"You mean Diego? We have him."

"I can give you the American bagman. It's a woman, but she pays all the dirty border people."

"We know all about Lisa. Try again."

"All the members of the Alliance. I can tell you where to get the names of all the representatives of all the individual member organizations in the Alliance. All the big shots."

Garcia said, "All right Abe, give us the names and I'll get you into witness protection."

"Wait, I said I can tell you where to get the names. I don't have all the names myself."

"Tell us what you have Abe."

"Jose, the head of security at Pachira Lodge in Tortuguero National Park in Costa Rica has all the names."

"How do you know he knows?"

"I went to an Alliance meeting there last month. Jose picked me up from the small airstrip serving the place. He addressed me by name, Abe Silverman. He told me he was in charge of accounting for each guest as they arrived. He said I was the last arrival. But he knew my name. Cabins were assigned by name. All the names would be in the Lodge's records. Jose will know."

"Okay Abe, if it all checks out, that was something we didn't know. Now pick up the computer and let's go."

Chapter Thirty-Two

8:22 a.m. Eastern Time, November 9

DRIVING WINDSWEPT RAIN POURED FROM DARK skies severely limiting visibility as the black Lincoln Town Car pulled to a stop under the portico at the Pennsylvania Avenue driveway gate. A uniformed secret service guard dressed in raingear struggled to keep a large umbrella from blowing away as he meticulously checked the identification of both the driver and front seat passenger. Satisfied he instructed them to proceed to the west entrance. Al Garcia drove slowly until waved to a stop beneath the green canopy which protected White House visitors from the elements. Garcia got out and followed Ed Grass into the West Wing entrance as an attendant parked the car.

They walked unescorted to the President's Conference Room. A secret service agent dressed in a suit and tie opened the door for them. As they entered Grass nodded to several others already present. They were gathered around a crackling fireplace built into the wall at the south end of the room. Overlooking the Rose Garden the large formal room was tastefully decorated with portraits of past presidents. A large oval mahogany table surrounded by twenty leather chairs dominated the room. Grass who had been here previously for meetings was familiar with the pecking order. He guided Al Garcia to the west side of the table, away from the windows. That's where they stood a few minutes later when President James Burns, a five eleven, slender man with wavy salt and pepper hair and dark eyebrows entered the room. Burns was followed by a short, heavy-set man, Parvis Khademi his Chief of Staff. National Security Advisor Roger Williams brought up the rear. Williams a lean, middle-aged, intense looking, ex-

CIA operative closed the door behind him signaling everyone scheduled to attend the meeting was present.

Burns headed straight for the only high backed chair in the room and sat down. Traditionally the president occupies the taller chair at the center of the east side of the table. That space has a call button available to summon a White House steward. Secretary of State Evelyn Colosimo took the chair immediately to the president's right. Secretary of Defense Leroy Adams sat next to Colosimo. Khademi took the chair to the president's left. Williams sat next to him. Vice President William Pitts made himself comfortable in the chair opposite the president. Attorney General Roberto Zapata took the chair to the vice president's left. Homeland Security Director Charles Swanson sat next to Zapata, and the Chairman of the Joint Chiefs of Staff Robert Coyle settled in alongside Swanson. When they were all in place Director of Special Operations Edward Grass sat down to the vice president's right. He directed Al Garcia to sit next to him.

A steward walked around the table taking orders for coffee, tea, pastries, and water. They made small talk, mostly about the Redskins horrible performance so far this season. The Skins had lost consecutive home games to the Giants, Cowboys, and the Eagles. Rumors of another head coaching change were rampant.

Once the refreshments had been served, President Burns said, "Okay everyone, let's get started. Evelyn, you have a question?"

Colosimo, a thin, slightly built brunette, who usually had a warm smile frowned and said, "Yes I do sir. The Mexican ambassador has been raging for two days now about a missing squad of Mexican soldiers. He claims they accidentally crossed the border into Arizona the other night and they haven't been heard from since. He fears we may have apprehended them as illegal border crossers. Does anyone know anything about this?"

Ed Grass replied, "Yes, I do. Those men are not lost soldiers. They were taken into custody by my people, charged with committing crimes on our side of the border. They are all drug smugglers. In addition, some are charged with murder. Some are accessories to murder. A few of them are witnesses to murder. These so-called soldiers are one of the reasons I requested President Burns call this meeting."

Colosimo addressed Burns asking, "So sir, what do I tell the Mexican ambassador?"

Burns said, "For now tell him we are investigating and will get back to him as soon as we know something for sure. In the meantime let's move on. Last month, on the seventeenth of October, I asked Ed to have his people look into allegations Mexican drug smugglers had murdered American citizens and had bribed what they referred to as 'a border patrol guy.' I asked all of you here so we can hear the report of that investigation. Ed, please proceed."

"You all know about Sam and Ida Comfort, the people who were found gutted, with their eyes gouged out, next to an Arizona highway last month. What you don't know is Sam Comfort had a recording device on him which recorded the hours before they died. The recording implicated Hector and Aliberto Castaneda, the Mexican nationals who had to be released by the United States Attorney's office after Larry, Jimmy, and Craig Rynning, the only witnesses willing to testify against them for the August murder in Sierra Vista of Juan Puga, were themselves murdered later in August in Bisbee. That recording also contained the allegation a border patrol guy had been bribed. After receiving President Burns' instruction, I informed Homeland Security Director Charles Swanson that I had assigned the Triple A team to the investigation. I believe you all know Al Garcia, the leader of Triple A."

Grass gestured at Garcia sitting to his right, "Al is here to give his report and answer any questions first hand. Al, please proceed."

Garcia began, "We went to Arizona and interviewed all of the players involved. We reexamined the crime scenes and we tapped some phones. We caught a break in the case when my colleague Alex Mendez noticed an image from a reflection on surveillance tapes at the Rynning murder scene which had been overlooked. In the initial investigation we contacted a Mexican police official, Jesus Noriega, who identified the image as a Mexican national. His name is Esteban Nunez. He works as an enforcer and executioner for Angel Figueroa. Figueroa heads the Alliance, the world's major drug trafficking group, with world-wide connections, headquartered in Mexico. Nunez lives on Figueroa's ranch in Mexico. We received a second break when one of the phone taps we placed captured John Marrone, a border patrol deputy chief, tipping off Figueroa's bag lady, Lisa Strump, that the sheriff out there had issued a detain and notify order on Nunez as well as Hector and Aliberto Castaneda, the cousins who beat Juan Puga to death in Sierra Vista. A short time later Marrone's phone tap provided the breakthrough we needed. Strump informed Marrone that Figueroa was sending a load of drugs across the border. Marrone was told to assign the border patrolmen on duty to the opposite side of their area of operation so they would not interfere with the shipment. Marrone did as directed by Figueroa but my team, with the help of FBI agents from the

Phoenix office, additional special operations officers, a civilian guide, and several soldiers from Fort Huachuca confiscated two hundred bundles, twelve thousand pounds of marijuana. We impounded a tractor trailer, arrested the truck driver and fourteen armed guards, the so-called lost soldiers, who were protecting the shipment. The shipment I just referenced has a wholesale value of five hundred dollars per pound—six million dollars total. Does anybody have any questions at this point?"

Attorney General Zapata a short, thin man, about one hundred sixty pounds, with clear black eyes, and a narrow moustache interrupted, "Am I correct in assuming the border patrol guy responsible for clearing the smuggling route of border patrolmen is John Marrone? And, he's the deputy chief who was hit by a bus and killed at the scene of the drug bust?"

Garcia answered, "Yes, but I don't believe it was an accident."

"Not an accident?"

"No sir. When I informed Marrone he was going to be taken into custody, that we had taped his conversations, that's when he ran in front of the bus. It was suicide."

"It's all over CNN that John Marrone was a hero, killed in a horrible accident."

"Marrone was a highly decorated officer. His office walls are covered from floor to ceiling with official awards and pictures of him with dignitaries. As of right now the fact he was dirty is pretty much contained. The smugglers didn't know who the dirty border patrol guy was. Angel Figueroa and Lisa Strump, the Triple A team, a couple of special operations office personnel and all of you now know. What is done with that information is above my pay grade."

Ed Grass said, "Move on Al, Marrone's status can be decided later. Show them the tapes. Use the equipment on the north wall."

Garcia responded, "Yes sir." He stood, walked to the video player, turned it on, put in the disc, and said, "I know some of you have seen these tapes and some have not. Let's review them together. We recorded the first group in the field in Arizona. This is Esteban Nunez."

When Nunez' taped confession concluded Al Garcia asked, "Any questions?"

President Burns quickly inquired, "Al, the Mexican cop who helped you identify Nunez was murdered? How did that happen?"

"Sir, Jesus Noriega was a good cop, one of the few honest ones in Mexico. According to Nunez, while undergoing questioning under torture

Noriega said he was trying to impress us, Triple A, by snooping around Figueroa's ranch. They caught him."

Garcia resumed, "Now the four guards Nunez named."

No one had any questions about the guards' statements so Garcia went on, "This is Hector Castaneda."

When Garcia asked for questions Evelyn Colosimo wanted to know, "These guards, these killers, claim to be soldiers?"

"Yes ma'am they all claim to be Mexican soldiers. They're not. They are criminals and should be treated as such."

With no more questions Garcia said, "Now we have Aliberto Castaneda."

Garcia told everyone, "That wraps up the interviews in the field. Are there any questions?"

President Burns asked, "Al, what is this talk about ten people being brought in last month? What is the significance of those ten people?"

Those ten are the Huerta family sir. There will be more on them later. Can we wait until then?"

"Yes of course Al. I can wait. But what's the story on Angel Figueroa and this Alliance, Al?"

"The next two interviews pretty much answer your question, sir."

Burns nodded stoically and said, "Go ahead."

Al Garcia resumed, "This next one is a little confusing without some explanation. We intercepted an earlier call from Figueroa to Lisa Strump where he told her he feared the other Mexican cartels may try to move on him and may attempt to get information about his contacts from her. At the beginning of the interview she assumed we were from the other cartels. We did not correct her assumption until after we spoke to her on camera. Alex Mendez questioned the woman. I'll play the interview."

When Alex finished her questions Garcia said, "That's it for Strump. When we told her we were federal agents she was relieved. She thought the cartel people were going to kill her. She agreed she would testify to everything. She would back up all of her records and finger all of the customs and border patrol agents she paid in court. We promised her witness protection in exchange."

President Burns asked, "Al, do we know who these American politicians are?"

"Yes sir. The Alliance's lobbyist is next. I questioned him. It worked so well with Strump I let him think I was from Figueroa's rival cartels."

Garcia started the tape.

At the conclusion of Abe Silverman's interview Garcia shut the video down, retrieved the disc, and said, "After the session that was taped and Silverman knew we were government agents he asked for witness protection in return for testifying. When I didn't agree right away he told me a fellow named Jose, the head of security at Pachira Lodge in Tortuguero National Park in Costa Rica, has all the names of the Alliance members who attended their meeting there. He said only Alliance members were present. Cabins were assigned by name. All the names would be in the Lodge's records."

Vice President Pitts, a tanned, compact, middle-aged man ran his fingers through his curly dark brown hair. He laughed mirthlessly, bitterly saying, "What a fucked up mess."

Charles Swanson, tall, thin, dressed in brown corduroy pants and a blue sweater over a beige flannel shirt added, "I agree. Some office staff and I worked on verifying information since it has come in. We've worked on this non-stop since we got Strump's notes and it's bad. We confirmed most of the payments, bank transfers, direct deposits, cash deposits made to the officers that coincide with Strump's records. We uncovered guys spending cash way beyond their means. It is probable every Mexican port of entry and the World Freight terminal are corrupted. The Alliance has bribed enough customs and border protection agents to accomplish that. On the Mexican border they have bribed supervisors who assign corrupt agents to allow certain commercial tractor trailers through without inspection. They utilize lanes dedicated for the supposedly pre-screened express truck crossing program, the Free and Secure Trade Lane (FAST) for that. For smaller loads the Alliance has enticed drivers who have been approved under our Secure Electronic Network for Travelers Rapid Inspection (SENTRI) program. Those drivers are people who have gone through criminal, law enforcement, customs, immigration, and terrorist investigations and interviews before approval. After they get certified they are approached by the Alliance who offers a death or money choice. Easy decision. Those drivers of course then have their vehicles loaded with drugs by the cartels. After which they cross the border using their SENTRI passes we issued. The vehicles driven by people who we processed and validated. It goes like this. The vehicles have transponders attached to them. The computer in the SENTRI lane reads the transponder and the vehicle is approved to enter the United States. It is similar to how an easy pass works at a toll booth on an American highway or bridge. If secondary inspection is randomly determined by the computer, which does happen on rare occasion, bribed agents working the SENTRI lane wave them through. The Alliance owns World Express Air Freight. They run their own terminal in Kansas City. World flies drugs in every day. All forty-six of the customs inspectors stationed at World's Kansas City facility are controlled by the Alliance. One chief gets fifty thousand each month, five supervisors get twenty thousand dollars each month, and forty inspection officers each get ten thousand dollars per month. Every shift is covered."

Burns said, "Charlie, catch as many dirty agents in the act at World and at the border ports of entry as you can. But arrest them all, even if they are not caught in the act. We have more than enough on them as it is. Arrest them at home if you have to. And shut World Express Air Freight down. Revoke the company's import license. Do it as soon as possible."

"Yes sir. I'll take care of it."

Burns asked the Attorney General, "Roberto, what do we do about the senators and congressmen?"

Zapata replied, "Lawyers from my office have gone through all of Silverman's tapes. We concluded even with the tapes and Silverman's testimony this will be a tough case. Senator Harvey Dwight of Idaho may be gay. He may have had gay sex with another man, but it appears to be consensual. The Supreme Court has ruled that is not against the law, that gay men 'are entitled to respect for their private lives.' Senator John Babcock of Delaware isn't accused of having something in his closet. Representative Ezra Higgins of Newark will deny the girl was underage. He'll insist she was eighteen. He'll deny paying her. In the Philippines twelve is the age of consent unless money changes hands. There is no evidence of that happening. There is no proof of anything illegal happening in Haiti. Representative Vito LaCrocca of Richmond will deny any wrongdoing whatsoever regarding all these unnamed mob connections. There is no exchange of cash seen on any tapes. Manila envelopes are exchanged. Lawyers for the defense will simply say the envelopes contained paperwork pertaining to legislation. No cash is ever tracked. If cash was exchanged it disappeared. I'm sure it's hidden in a safe place but no judge will issue a search warrant based on this evidence. There is no physical evidence of money being paid to influence action. This is simply a 'he said he said' case. It is profoundly weak. If we arrest them, lawyers for all four will immediately obtain release without bail citing the debate clause, Article One, Section Six, of the United States Constitution. Their lawyers will make the case the framers of the constitution recognized the fundamental necessity of protecting members of congress from arbitrary arrest. That clause provides members 'shall in all cases, except treason, felony and breach of the peace, be privileged from arrest during their attendance at the session of their respective houses and in going to and returning from the same.' The purpose of that clause is to prevent the executive branch from intimidating members of the legislative branch, either or both houses of congress, by arresting them or even detaining them. They will argue they are within their rights, doing their duty as elected officials, holding hearings on every aspect of the border fence. They will contend these are trumped up charges brought by an administration which cannot control the border. They will argue these charges do not involve treason, felony, or breach of the peace, and should therefore be dismissed. They will cite separation of powers. It is my fear a judge, an independent member of the judiciary branch, will be completely understanding."

Burns asked Garcia, "Al, is that true, there is no exchange of cash shown on Silverman's tapes of his meetings with the congressmen?"

Garcia replied, "Yes sir, but that only proves the congressmen are cagier than the customs and border agents. And, before it is brought up by someone else, I admit special operations have not been able to trace any of the cash payments to the congressmen either."

Burns said, "Okay here's what I want done. As soon as Charlie has arrested of all border patrolmen and customs agents implicated I want the congressmen arrested. Roberto, very publically arrest the congressmen. Even if they may get released quickly by a sympathetic judge that's okay, embarrass them. I want their constituents to know their trust has been betrayed. Who knows, maybe party leaders will remove them from the committees they have been manipulating."

Zapata replied, "Your call Mister President. Charlie, call me when you have all your scumbags locked up. We will then round up ours."

Garcia said, "Sir, one more thing. We believe the drug smugglers and the terrorist nuclear bomb explosions last month may be linked."

A bright flash lit the room followed by the crash of thunder. The windows shook bringing back the horrible memories of September thirtieth. They were still vibrating when the president, visibly upset, demanded, "What. How?"

"Sir, the night the Comforts were murdered there were ten people apparently crossing the border under the protection of the smugglers. You asked about them earlier. We traced those ten individuals to Pueblo, Colorado and questioned them. They claimed to be ignorant, naturalized citizens without passports, who went to Mexico on family business. To avoid problems they crossed the border with coyotes on their return, an innocent mistake they said. They agreed to testify against the smugglers and had character references from the local sheriff and others. Since we spoke to them DNA tests confirm they are actually Middle Easterners not South Americans as they claimed. After we questioned them, they disappeared. We know that because Tom Eagan's investigation into the bombings independently brought him to Pueblo eventually to the same people, the Huertas. Eagan found trace radioactivity residue at the Huerta's place of business. The Huertas may have a connection to the nuclear explosions which occurred September thirtieth. The smugglers told us Angel Figueroa instructed them to bring the Huertas with them. They didn't know any more."

Secretary of Defense Adams raised his hand. President Burns nodded. Adams, a gray bearded ex-paratrooper who walked with a limp, the result of a leg shattered on a practice jump, pointed to Chairman of the Joint Chiefs Coyle, a tall, lanky man with a hawk-like nose dressed in a military uniform and said, "Why are we here?"

Burns smiled mischievously and said, "Strump can be replaced. So can Silverman and this Perez fella. The corrupt customs and border people and politicians can be replaced. We need to take down the top cartel members and get Angel's records and computer. Roy I want you and Bobby to get together with Ed and Charlie. I want to know within forty-eight hours what it will take to go into Mexico and take out these cartels. We can put a missile up a terrorist's ass half way around the world. We sure as hell can go a couple hundred miles south and take out the cartel leaders. All but Figueroa, Triple A goes for Angel Figueroa and his computer. And I'd like Mister Figueroa alive if possible Al. Roger, I want you to get together with the CIA. Get the Alliance member list of attendees at Pachira Lodge. Try a black bag job, if that doesn't do it then persuade Jose. Al, you and your team met face to face with and have unique knowledge of these Huertas. I want your team to go to Colorado and work with Eagan for a couple of days."

Evelyn Colosimo asked, "Mister President, what do I tell the Mexican government?"

"Not a damn thing Evelyn. The Mexican bureaucrats are all crooks anyway. You tell them we're going in, they'll tell the cartels."

Chapter Thirty-Three

2:36 p.m. Mountain Time, November 9

TWENTY-EIGHT THOUSAND FEET IN THE AIR, high above the sparse cloud cover, Garcia peered out the window next to his padded leather seat thinking to himself. *Who the hell are the Huertas? Where have they gone?* As the monotonous tracts of crops swept in and out of view simply to be replaced by another group of the unending fields of the mid-west Garcia sensed the plane beginning to slow down. They would be steadily descending now as they approached Denver.

Since they had left Washington, Mendez and Cruz reported to Al Garcia that while he and Director Grass met with the president they had taken care of their end. They had gone to Virginia, met with John Quincy, the attorney/financial consultant they all had agreed upon. They authorized his office to set up several annuity accounts. They had handed over two million six hundred eighty thousand dollars in cash to Quincy to be used to fund the annuities. Quincy agreed to launder the cash and complete the legal paperwork while Cruz, Mendez, and Garcia concluded their current assignment. Quincy made clear to them cash bank deposits totaling ten thousand dollars or more made to one account during a single business day had to be reported to the federal government. He explained he controlled several hundred separate annuity accounts so he could make many deposits over the course of numerous days then simply transfer the funds to avoid making the deposit reports. Understanding the administrative expense, Cruz and Mendez paid Quincy a twenty-six thousand seven hundred fifty dollar retainer. They reported to Garcia they agreed to a total three percent fee for laundering the cash, payable when the cash was safely deposited in the annuity accounts Quincy set up for them. Plus they agreed Quincy would receive an annual fee of three percent per year for managing the accounts. Travel, if incurred, would be extra. Those costs would be itemized as they occurred. Because the smaller the paper trail the better for everyone concerned, statements would be prepared only upon formal request. Garcia commended Cruz and Mendez, telling them the terms negotiated were extremely fair.

Garcia had then called Fort Huachuca, and spoke with both General Ehrich and all of the special operations troops he had left there. He had informed them they had to start training for a nighttime helicopter insertion into a Mexican ranch approximately nine thousand acres in size. He gave them the address and coordinates Jesus Noriega had provided. He told them they should anticipate securing the property and the exterior of a ranch house, which Triple A would enter to take into custody one narco-terrorist. They would then exfiltrate by helicopter. They should start training with rifles outfitted with night scopes and silencers, and silenced pistols. A hostile force of about thirty or more armed guards could be expected. Preparations should focus on nighttime maneuvers carried out on farm and ranch type terrain. He informed them Triple A would join them in a day or two.

Garcia also had spoken at length with Tom Eagan. Extensive searches of the Huertas' residences, place of business, and known haunts had turned up nothing. The all-points bulletin Chief Goff had issued had led to several false sightings, nothing of any consequence. It was like they had fallen off the face of the earth.

As they landed and approached the private jet terminal he saw Tom Eagan accompanied by another taller man waiting. They looked glum.

A rolling staircase was placed against the jet. Garcia opened the door waved and told Eagan and his companion, "Come aboard."

Both men climbed the stairs and entered. Denver Regional FBI supervising agent David Porter was introduced, they all sat around a conference table. Porter was middle aged, much younger than Eagan. Porter had a black moustache with one of those little tufts of facial hair below the middle of his lower lip. Tom Eagan was visually haggard, his face flushed. He appeared every bit of his sixty-one years. Garcia inquired, "How is the investigation going Tom? How are you doing?"

"We're at a dead end Al. I'm tired. I sure am glad you guys could come. We need some fresh ideas. It's like the Huertas fell off the earth."

"Bring us up to date, Tom. How about their phones? Any news with them?"

Porter interrupted, "My office handled tracing the phones. We presented a subpoena to Sidney Korash, the Huerta's attorney. He immediately complied providing ten cell phone numbers one for each of the Huertas. It was fruitless. Either they removed the batteries or destroyed the phones. The phones were no help."

Cruz asked, "Can I have a copy of the names and corresponding numbers please?"

Porter opened his briefcase, extracted a sheet of paper, saying, "Here's an extra copy. My office already has an alert on each of the numbers. We will be notified instantly if any of them are activated."

Cruz nodded his thanks as he went to the plane's on-board business center and sent the information to Lauren with instructions to obtain each number's history of usage, come up with acquaintances, maybe places they had visited.

Garcia asked, "Have you been able to locate any of their cars, Tom?"

"No. Harvey Taitz, the owner of Belmont Ford, the dealership who leased the vehicles to the Huertas, activated hidden LoJack radio transceivers which had been factory installed in the cars. We traced all ten of them to the same location way up in the mountains. I went up there yesterday with David and another thirty local agents. We surrounded a hunting cabin; about a hundred and sixty miles west of Pueblo, up by Blue Mesa Lake. It was utterly secluded, at the end of a single lane dirt road with no other houses for the last eight miles. We hoofed it in, surrounded the place in daylight, then we swarmed in at three this morning. There was no one there. We found the ten LoJack gadgets in a box. These people run an auto repair shop. Of course they knew where the transmitters were and how to remove them. We only arrived back a couple of hours ago. Two fuckin' days wasted."

Mendez asked, "Did you find anything in the cabin that may provide an indication of where they may have been or might be headed?"

Porter said, "Not yet. We're still searching the property with a fine tooth comb. Neighbors are being questioned, but everyone up there stays to themselves. Ownership records show the property was purchased by American Charities for Madrassas six years ago. The taxes are all paid up to date."

Eagan said, "That's the same charity that the radioactive van we found in Denver belongs to. That's the van that led us to Pueblo and the Huertas."

Mendez asked, "So nothing on the cars?"

Porter responded, "Not yet. They probably switched plates so even if the police find a car with the plate numbers we're looking for it won't be them. They could even be driving completely different cars. We have no idea where they are. They could be anyplace."

Garcia asked, "How about bank accounts, credit cards?"

Porter shrugged, "Dave Attig, the president of Pueblo Community National Bank, another friend of the Huertas, complied with a subpoena obtained by my office. Leon Huerta closed the company account right after you guys left town. He withdrew two hundred twenty-seven thousand dollars in cash, big bills, mostly hundreds. The Huertas all had personal accounts with the bank that were also closed. They were all paid off in cash. They all have active credit cards. None have been used since they left town. With that much cash at their disposal we don't expect them to use the cards either. We're right on top of things. We have all the routing notices out. My office will be alerted by the companies instantaneously if the cards are used."

Cruz asked, "Can I have the account numbers and the credit card information please?"

Porter handed over the requested information. Cruz asked for and received the home addresses of each of the Huertas. Cruz sent it all on to Lauren with instructions to get the account histories, all deposits, withdrawals, and check transactions. He asked if she could determine how did they get over two hundred thousand dollars in their business account.

Mendez asked, "Any follow-up on the original cars, the ones they supposedly gave to relatives?"

Porter replied, "No those cars are a waste of time. We need to find the new ones they took the LoJack radio transceivers out of. They wouldn't have gone to all that trouble simply to abandon them."

Garcia sensing an investigation going nowhere under agent Porter asked, "Tom you don't mind if we follow-up on those old cars do you?"

Eagan replied, "No, not at all. You're here. Let's not leave any stone unturned."

Porter said, "You'll have to contact Colorado Motor Vehicle about the old cars. I don't have any of those records."

Garcia said, "That's okay Agent Porter, we'll follow on that aspect and we'll touch base again tomorrow. Tom, good seeing you again."

Eagan replied, "Sounds like a plan, Al. Good seeing you guys too."

Porter stood up to leave, and handed out business cards. As they exited the plane he said, "Good meeting you all. It's great to have you working with us. Call if you need anything."

Eagan said, "Al, call when you get done with the motor vehicle office. David thinks we should continue tracing acquaintances and the old haunts of the Huertas in Pueblo. So we will be doing that until I hear from you."

As soon as the door closed, Garcia was on the phone with Chief Goff. After they exchanged pleasantries Garcia asked, "Walter, would you please run a check on the ten old cars the Huertas say they gave away. I need the year, make, model, each vehicle's identification number, plate number, owner's name, and date of registration. Just e-mail the info." He gave the chief Al Cruz' number and said good bye.

Triple A took a flight crew's shuttle to the main terminal, rented a Lincoln Town Car. Alex Mendez drove to Lakewood, immediately west of Denver, where they registered into three adjoining rooms on the fifth floor at the Marriott at Federal Center. They had an early dinner at the Union Restaurant. The restaurant was a short walk from the hotel. It was recommended by the girl working the front desk. While they were eating Chief Goff e-mailed the information on the Huerta's cars.

Chapter Thirty-Four

8:01 a.m. Mountain Time, November 10

THE TRIPLE A TEAM MEMBERS WERE there when the doors opened. They walked up to a circular kiosk, displayed their FBI credentials, and asked for help confirming current ownership of a list of ten vehicles. They were directed to a counter at the far end of a long curved corridor the exterior wall of which was glass. Predominantly fixed glass windows with an occasional glass door leading to a private courtyard orientated around raised gardens, weaving paths, and benches dominated one side of the hall. Their footsteps loudly echoed as they strode along the marble floor. The pretty young clerk with blond pigtails, blue eyes, and freckles behind the waist-high ledge they were headed toward answered a ringing phone, looked their way, hung up, and smiled. She had a name plate that read Susan. She said, "The information desk called to tell me FBI agents were coming my way. I guess you all are them."

They nodded. She asked, "How can I help you?"

Al Cruz spread a sheet of paper on the granite countertop he said, "Susan, can you please tell us who the current owners of these vehicles are? We've been told they were gifted to others recently. Your bureau would have a record of any transactions like that, correct?"

"Yes sir, we should. Let me check our files." The clerk took Cruz' list, sat at a desk, and started typing.

Cruz, Mendez, and Garcia were admiring the outdoor setting when the clerk startled them by saying, "Enjoying our view? The employees love the beautiful plantings, the relaxing atmosphere. Many believe it's magical, they wander through the trees and meditate all the time."

Cruz agreed, "It's a wonder any work gets done around here."

Susan placed ten pieces of paper out and said, "I hope this is what you need. Let me explain, these five titles are unchanged. Consuela, Jose, Maria, Filipe, and Manlio Huerta still own their vehicles. The other five are now owned by Jorge Campos, a Mexican auto dealer located in Hermosillo, Mexico. Mister Campos purchased them in early October. He submitted the proper paperwork transferring ownership to him and we issued new titles a month ago."

Garcia asked, "Do you have the prices?"

"Yes sir, right here. We require the sales price be reported in the event the vehicle is registered in Colorado. If it is we collect sales tax on that amount. It's noted in our records the reported sale price for each of the five vehicles was about sixty percent of book value. The figure for each vehicle is included in the information I'm providing you with. Is there anything else I can help you with?"

Cruz asked, "Is that the Marriott I see beyond the gardens?"

"Yes. If you are staying there you can walk directly back. You can never tell. Maybe something good will happen to you along the way."

Garcia placed the papers in his briefcase and responded, "Susan, thank you very much for everything. You have a nice day now."

They exited the closest door, headed back to the hotel by way of the winding walkways. In the middle of the gardens Cruz received an ominous phone call from Lauren. She said, "I e-mailed some of the data you asked for. Director Grass wants you to review everything then call him directly."

They quickly returned to the hotel where Cruz used the business center to make three copies of Lauren's report. Meeting in Garcia's room they each read the information themselves. Garcia asked, "Everyone ready?"

When they nodded in the affirmative he called Grass who said, "Let's discuss the cell phone usage first. Lauren, please lead us through your findings."

Lauren began, "Here goes. Although they are not in use now, the numbers of each Huerta has remained the same since they were first issued in 2007, and the accounts have not been cancelled. It's possible they may plan to power the phones up and use them at a later date."

Grass said, "I've instructed staff to be prepared for this eventuality. The phone carriers have agreed to inform us right away if any of these numbers are activated."

Lauren continued, "Since 2008 there have been frequent phone calls made and received by all of the Huertas from the Blue Mesa Lake/ Gunnison/Montrose area."

Garcia interrupted, "There is an answer for that. Eagan told us the American Charities for Madrassas own a cabin in that area. The Huertas had been known to use it. When the LoJack transceivers from the Huertas' cars were activated the signals emanated from the cabin area. Local FBI agents and Tom Eagan raided the cabin yesterday. There were no vehicles and there were no Huertas found. All the agents discovered were the transceivers stored in a box in a closet."

Lauren continued, "For years all other calls were local, basically Pueblo."

Garcia added, "That fits with what we learned. The Huertas pretty much stayed in Pueblo."

Lauren went on, "Until September of this year. On September twelfth, Leon Huerta received a call from the American Charities for Madrassas."

Garcia said, "That would be Imam Dr. Umar al Jamai. He runs the charity. Eagan's people found his van in long-term parking garage in Denver on October twentieth. It had radioactive residue in it. He traced the van to the Huertas' shop in Pueblo. The van had been parked at the garage on September thirteenth. The van had been to the Huertas earlier that day. Radioactive trace was recovered at the Huertas' shop. The Huertas closed the shop and left Pueblo on the night of September thirteenth. According to Eagan, Imam Dr. Umar al Jamai left the van at six forty-two in the late afternoon. The shuttle bus took him to Denver International Terminal 3. He said he'd be back on the first of October, he would call to be picked up. Tom checked, al Jamai took the red eye flight to Mazatlan, Mexico. Once there he took a limo to Aslama Mosque in Sinaloa."

Lauren said, "On September twenty-third, there was a flurry of calls between several of the Huertas. The numbers calling and receiving were located in Phoenix, Albuquerque, Houston, and several in Los Angeles."

Grass said, "Nuclear explosions occurred in those cities on September thirtieth."

"September twenty-fourth, Consuela called four other Huertas from San Diego. Jose was in San Diego. Maria in Nogales. Filipe in El Paso. Manlio in Laredo. She also called Imam Dr. Umar al Jamai's cell phone number. His phone was in Mazatlan, Mexico."

Grass said, "All the Huertas' calls were from border cities where entry into Mexico can be made."

"At ten-seventeen a.m. Mountain Time, on September thirtieth, several calls were made from phones belonging to Huertas from Mazatlan, Mexico. Consuela called a number. We traced the number she called to a disposable throwaway phone. The phone she called was located in Los Angeles. Jose called the same type phone in Orange County. Maria called a similar phone in Phoenix. Filipe called a disposable phone in Albuquerque. Manlio called an equivalent phone in Houston. The connections were made, then nothing. The nuclear explosions on that day took place in those locations at that time."

Grass pronounced, "Wow, if ever there was a smoking gun for the terror attacks in those cities that's it."

"There was a minimum of calls back and forth among the Huertas in Mexico between September thirtieth and October sixth. The calls centered in and around the cities of Mazatlan and Hermosillo. On October eighth Leon Huerta, from Las Cruces, New Mexico called Imam Dr. Umar al Jamai's cell phone which was in Hermosillo. That is a city in Sonora, Mexico. The Huertas resumed local calls in and around Pueblo from October tenth up to October twenty-fifth. On October twenty-fourth Leon called Imam Dr. Umar al Jamai's cell phone which was in Hermosillo not Mazatlan. The Huertas phones have been dead since then."

Garcia said, "Eagan told us the Huertas' cell phones are not traceable anymore, that in all likelihood the batteries have been removed. Obviously the call to the imam was to report our visit. They were instructed to split. Let's move on to the charge cards."

Grass responded, "Okay. Lauren go over what you turned up regarding the Huertas charge card histories."

"Prior to September thirteenth all of the Huertas used their credit cards freely, mostly in the Pueblo area. From September thirteenth through September twenty-second all ten used credit cards for gasoline, motel, and food purchases. Consuela, Leon, Jose, and Alphonso between Pueblo and Los Angeles. Maria and Roberto between Pueblo and Phoenix. Filipe and Vincente between Pueblo and Albuquerque. Manlio and Diego between Pueblo and Houston."

Garcia said, "Sounds like the imam called, then visited, then he flew out to Mexico and the Huertas left Pueblo en route to their target cities."

"From September twenty-third through October sixth the pattern of charges changed, only Leon, Alphonso, Roberto, Vincente, and Diego charged gasoline. Those purchases were all made in Mexico. Leon and Alphonso also charged the fare to ferry their cars across the Sea of Cortez from La Paz to Mazatlan on September twenty-fifth."

Grass said, "So ten Huertas but only five cars crossed the border. Five cars were left behind. They made their way to Mazatlan and triggered the nuclear devices from there. The Huertas stayed in Mexico until they thought the coast was clear to come back."

Garcia told Grass, "We just left the Colorado Motor Vehicle offices. We learned five cars belonging to the Huertas were sold to a Mexican used car dealer. Cruz e-mailed the owner's name, vehicle year, make, model, color, and plate numbers to you."

"So?"

"Would you have the Homeland Security people review the tapes of the vehicles leaving the United States on September twenty-second and September twenty-third? If they find the car we are looking for and they have a photo of the vehicle from the front we should be able to identify who was in the cars. Let's see if we can confirm Leon and Consuela crossed from San Diego into Tijuana in Leon's car. Alphonso and Jose should also have crossed from San Diego into Tijuana in Alphonso's car. Roberto and Maria would have used the Nogales, Arizona crossing into Nogales, Mexico in Roberto's car. Vincente in his car would have crossed into Ciudad Juarez from El Paso with Filipe. Lastly Diego would have driven his car from Laredo into Nuevo Laredo with Manilo as his passenger.

"Okay I'll do that."

Lauren continued, "From October eighth on, all credit card charges were made in the USA. The charges all include gas again after they all get new cars October tenth. All credit card charges stop on October twenty-sixth, when they closed bank accounts and left town."

Garcia said, "At first they thought they were home free. They thought the coast was clear, but us showing up in Pueblo spooked them. The bank accounts are next."

Lauren said, "I found the following about the bank accounts. In 2007, the Huertas obtained a tax ID number and incorporated Huerta's Auto Body Shop in Colorado. The business bank account and all ten Huerta private bank accounts were opened in 2007. All of the accounts maintained exemplary records, no overdrafts. The business was successful, generating enough income to pay all of its bills on time and meet its weekly payroll. The business account averaged less than twenty thousand dollars as a running balance. A quarter million dollars was wired into the account on October ninth at nine a.m. The payee was the American Charities for Madrassas. That money enabled the Huertas to lease ten new Ford vehicles. The two hundred twenty-seven thousand dollar cash withdrawal represented the remaining funds from that transfer."

Grass interjected, "Sounds like when Leon reported they had successfully re-entered the United States the imam financed their next project."

Lauren continued, "From the phone call records, the motel, gasoline, and food credit card charges, the record of sold vehicles, and the bank transactions it appears Consuela left her car at the Los Angeles International Airport parking lot and was picked up by Leon. They crossed the border into Tijuana from San Diego, drove down Baja California to La Paz where they took the ferry to Mazatlan. Jose parked his car in the parking facility at John Wayne Airport and was picked up by Alphonso. They also crossed into Tijuana drove to La Paz and took the Ferry across the Sea of Cortez to the pier in Mazatlan. Maria left her car at Sky Harbor Airport in Phoenix. Roberto picked her up. They crossed the border into Mexico at Nogales and drove down the Mexican coast to Mazatlan. Filipe left his car at the Albuquerque Sunport. Vincente picked him up. They crossed at Ciudad Juarez. They drove the main roads through Chihuahua and Durango eventually arriving at Mazatlan. Manlio left his car at the parking area at Hobby Airport in Houston. Diego picked him up. They drove across the border from Laredo into Nuevo Laredo. Then they drove through Monterrey on their way to Mazatlan."

Garcia said, "Yes we agree."

Grass said, "In Mazatlan the Huertas met up with the imam. Five Huertas detonated the nuclear bombs using phone activated instruments. After seeing no pursuit the Huertas felt they were home free. Their handlers sent them back in to resume their lives as naturalized Americans."

Garcia said, "Again we agree. Moreover, our showing up shocked and disrupted them. Because they are so well financed they abandoned their cover and went underground. They have to be found."

Grass said, "It needs to be determined why they came back. There has to be another target, or worse, targets. We need to find out what and stop them."

Garcia asked, "How do you want us to proceed, sir?"

Grass replied, "I'll inform the president and you brief Eagan on everything we have. For the time being, pursuing the Huertas has to be left up to others. You people have to move on, regroup in Fort Huachuca, and prepare for getting Angel Figueroa."

"Yes sir. The plane is still here. We'll check out of the hotel, brief

Eagan, and be on our way. And thank you Lauren. Without your work none of this would have come to light. David Porter the lead FBI guy out here blew off the phone, charge card, and bank records. Director, please let everyone know our very own Lauren Shein broke this case not the FBI."

Garcia arranged for a noon departure with the pilot and notified Eagan to be on the plane by 11:15 a.m. to be briefed on developments. Eagan arrived on time with David Porter in tow. Garcia sat them down, brought them up to date on what they and Lauren had found out. While they conversed, border photo records were found confirming the five border crossings at the border cities they identified did in fact occur. Two passengers matching the photos of the Huertas they suspected were confirmed in each car.

Garcia said, "The pictures confirm what we thought, these are the ones."

"Damn it Al, I feel so close. We haven't been this close before. We're gonna get these fuckers."

"Tom, me and my guys have something else to do. You are going to find out what they are up to and stop it."

"I understand and appreciate all your help. On our end David's agents searching the property found a makeshift shooting range. Thousands of shell casings of every imaginable type were discovered. They are definitely well armed."

Staring directly at Porter, Garcia said, "It's too bad that girl with the dog didn't find the van sooner. Or, considering she did a magnificent job, it's inexcusable her information wasn't sent on in a timely manner. The follow-up was poorly managed. Forwarding the report to you took so long and it wasn't even labeled urgent. Two weeks were lost from when the report was filed by Mary Pelton until you read it. Because of that delay you missed them by days. That is indefensible."

Porter interrupted, "Hey agent, don't you dare play the blame game here. You can't dump this on my people. Don't even try. You hotshots were the ones who had them and let them go. Not us."

Garcia grabbed Porter by the neck and pushed him out the door of the aircraft. He turned to Eagan and said, "Tom I'm going to include everything this asshole did and didn't do in my report. I expect you to do the same. I know my team and I spoke to the Huertas, but we had no inkling they were possible terrorists. Shit, we thought at worst they were smuggling drugs. That asshole, not his people, sat on Pelton's report because he didn't understand what she found. He snail mailed it to you.

Paul C. Gardner

He didn't understand the importance of the Huertas' phone and financial records, and now wants to make believe he acted responsibly. Tom, mainly because of him you face one tough task. It appears the Huertas have a two week head start on you. If he had sent word to you right away, you would have been here the next day, like you were when you did get the report."

"Yeah, it's frustrating. I have some catching up to do. I'll start digging but it's a deep hole. Don't you agree? They could be driving anything. The leased vehicles without the LoJacks or they could have abandoned them and bought other vehicles. To make matters worse, because there are no secure ID laws enforced in the states, we have to assume they are using easily obtainable false ID. They won't be using credit cards. They are spending cash. I've told Washington it won't be easy. They could be anywhere."

Garcia shook his head and said, "Yeah Tom, I agree with everything you say. It won't be easy but it's important. It's scary when you think about it. Remember they, the Huertas, were home free. You have to wonder, why did they return? They didn't have to come back." Then he laughed, "Well times up. Good luck to you buddy. Now get off our plane. We have things to do, places to go, and people to see."

Chapter Thirty-Five

6:46 a.m. Eastern Time, November 11

THIS MORNING THE PRESIDENT'S CONFERENCE ROOM located in the White House was again used for the president's update. The fireplace crackled at the south end of the room. The window draperies were drawn back exposing the Rose Garden. President Burns was sitting comfortably in the taller chair at the center of the east side of the table. He was flanked on his left by Chief of Staff Khademi, National Security Advisor Roger Williams, and CIA Director Randall Beck. On his right sat Secretary of State Colosimo and Secretary of Defense Adams. Chairman of the Joint Chiefs of Staff Coyle settled in alongside Adams. Vice President Pitts sat in the chair opposite the president. Homeland Security Director Swanson took the chair to the vice president's left. Director of Special Operations Grass sat down next to Swanson. Emily Rogers Secretary of the Treasury took a chair on the vice president's right.

Burns asked, "Who wants to go first?"

CIA Director Beck, a rotund black man with well groomed kinky gray hair, said, "I will sir."

Burns motioned his hand and said, "Go ahead. Randall."

"Sir I was informed by Roger you wanted a list of attendees to the Alliance meeting held at Pachira Lodge in Costa Rica. I assigned four operatives, two couples who normally operate in Costa Rica, to the task. They obtained reservations for last night and tonight easily. There were vacancies. While one couple stood watch the other couple entered to resort office copied the event file and sent it to me straightaway." Sliding papers across the desk Beck went on, "Here is your copy sir. I have additional copies for anyone else who needs one."

"Thank you Randall. This is excellent work, just what we wanted. Be sure to tell your agents I'm impressed. Evelyn, make sure you get a copy. We are going to have to figure out what to do with these countries that are producing this poison and sending it over here. Next?"

Secretary of Defense Adams raised his hand. President Burns nodded. Adams reported, "Per your instructions sir we have devised a plan to take out the leaders of Mexican drug cartels much like we would take out targeted terrorists. The DEA provided us with information on the whereabouts of each cartel's center of operations. We have been rotating MQ-9 Reapers, unmanned aerial vehicles, over each group's headquarters. The location of each base turns out to be the homes of the leaders of each of the four Mexican drug cartels. The drones have reported on the comings and goings of the drug lords. They are equipped with thermal cameras. The cameras are so good we can see them during the day, at night, and during inclement weather. We have been watching all four, including Angel Figueroa, the head of the Alliance and also the Cortez Cartel. He's not on our list because you want him alive, but we are providing all the info we gather on him to Ed Grass. We understand Triple A will be tasked with apprehending Figueroa. As we advised Ed, the Cortez Cartel controls all imports through the Pacific side of the Mexican mainland. Figueroa operates out of a huge ranch and farm about one hundred fifty miles south of the border near the city of Hermosillo. The Reapers tracking him fly from Libby Army Airfield at Fort Huachuca. That's about thirty miles north of border, a total flight of one hundred eighty miles each way. Figueroa pretty much stays in the house, is rarely seen outside, and appears to have increased security since we have been observing."

Ed Grass interrupted, "If I may. We believe Figueroa has increased his security because he is afraid the other cartel leaders may try a coup. When Roy is finished I'll go over our plan. We have accounted for the added guards."

Adams went on, "Continuing with the three that are my people's responsibility, Carlos Martinez leads the Gulf Group. He lives on a ranch located about one hundred forty miles south of the border in Monterrey. It is in an extremely wealthy area surrounded by the Sierra Madre mountain range. His group controls all of the drugs imported through the Gulf of Mexico. He swims every morning for exercise. He uses his private heated pool. We are watching him utilizing drones based at Kelly Field. This is the

Air Force base by San Antonio. Total flight distance is about two hundred ninety miles each way.

"Miguel Vargas heads the Central Syndicate. He lives on a cattle ranch west of Ciudad Juarez off Highway 2, right on the Rio Grande River. We can see his ranch from our side of the border. The drones watching him use Fort Bliss near El Paso as a base. Because he is so close, flight time and distance are negligible. His cartel runs all the drugs transported through central Mexico by land. Vargas says the city of Juarez is much too violent for his family. However, apparently it is not too dangerous for him. He spends his nights clubbing in town and always stays at his girlfriend's house for a while. He returns home early every morning.

"Ruben Miranda is in charge of the Baja Boys. He's located south of Tijuana in a winery in the Guadalupe Valley near Ensenada. The Baja Boys control all drugs coming through the Baja Peninsula. Miranda breakfasts every morning on his patio. He's located about eighty-five miles total south of Rockwell Field on North Island Naval Station, San Diego."

Burns asked, "What's the plan for taking Martinez, Vargas, and Miranda down Roy?"

"We can modify for any change, but currently the plan is the morning after we hear from Ed that Figueroa is in custody we do our three. The time zones work for us. Martinez swims at 0900 Central Time, Vargas is on the road going home from his girlfriend at the same time, and Miranda has breakfast at 0700 Pacific Time. Adjusting for the time variances we hit them all at the same minute with Hellfire missiles fired from the Reaper that is watching each of them. Each Reaper carries up to fourteen Hellfire missiles. Each missile locks on before or after launch and can be reprogrammed in flight if need be. We have had huge success against terrorists with these missiles. This operation should be no problem sir."

Burns said, "Okay, Ed you're up."

"Yes sir. Triple A joined the other special operations agents practicing maneuvers for taking Figueroa yesterday. They are rehearsing using mock-ups of Figueroa's ranch layout provided by guards from the drug shipment we captured the other night. The guards revealed the placement and schedules of ranch guards. Apparently none of the guards are allowed in the house so they couldn't help there. I contacted Lisa Strump and she provided a drawing and briefed Triple A on the ranch house interior layout, the living quarters and bedroom. Strump used to be a regular overnight guest. She was exceedingly helpful. General Ehrich has provided all the equipment that will be needed. His troops are playing the role of ranch guards during the practices."

"When will your people be ready to go?"

"Another day or two, I'll let you know, sir."

"Fine." Burns fiddled with buttons on his control panel, pointed to an array of TV screens, and said, "Let's check out this morning's news."

Parvis Khademi rose out of his seat, handed everyone some pages saying, "These are the press releases, the data they are reporting."

Burns turned up the sound on CNN. The perky female anchor was reporting, "It was a busy day for law enforcement on the Mexican border yesterday."

Everyone in the room followed along as she read from the press releases they had all been given. Video coverage of the numerous arrests made along the border was shown on a split screen. The press releases also rolled, scrolling across the screen as the newscaster described the video. Around the world people were made aware. She said, "In Kansas City, Missouri there was a huge drug bust." The scrolling press release read:

CBP Headquarters

Office of Public Affairs

1300 Pennsylvania Ave., N.W.

Room 3.4A

Washington, DC 20229

Massive Domestic Drug Crackdown

(November 11)

Washington, DC –The World Express Air Freight terminal, Kansas City, Missouri was the scene of a massive drug raid on November 11. 190 pounds of heroin with a wholesale value of $90,000 per pound, a total of $17,100,000 was seized. The heroin in four separate boxes labeled fabric samples. Also 4,090 pounds of cocaine with a wholesale value of $9,000 per pound, a total of $36,810,000 was seized. The cocaine was concealed inside 36 separate boxes containing music speakers and 66 boxes containing world globes. The estimated combined wholesale value of the drugs seized is more than $53.8 million dollars officials announced today.

A banner flowed across the bottom of the screen:

FORTY-SIX CUSTOMS AGENTS WERE ARRESTED IN CONNECTION WITH THE RAID

The news anchor continued, "Authorities announced that all along the southern border significant drug interceptions were made. Please follow the scrolling press release."

A split screen began showing video of the various drug busts as the scrolling narrative continued:

U.S. Customs and Border Protection
CBP Headquarters
Office of Public Affairs
1300 Pennsylvania Ave., N.W.
Room 3.4A
Washington, DC 20229
Mexico Ports of Entry Intercept Significant Narcotic Loads
(November 11)

Washington, DC – U.S. Customs and Border Protection officers conducting border security operations at various Mexico ports of entry seized 3,871 pounds of cocaine with a wholesale value of $9,000 per pound, a total of $34,839,000. They also confiscated 1,496 pounds of methamphetamine with a wholesale value of $17,000 per pound, a total of $25,432,000, and 59,762 pounds of marijuana with a wholesale value of $500 per pound, a total of $29,881,000. The drugs were taken in numerous separate drug seizures yesterday, November 11. The estimated combined wholesale value of the drugs seized is more than $90 million dollars officials announced today. Forty drivers were arrested and vehicles valued at over $1.5 million were impounded.

Another banner flowed across the bottom of the screen:
ONE HUNDRED THIRTY-FIVE BORDER PROTECTION OFFICERS WERE ARRESTED

As 'NOGALES REGION' flashed repeatedly on and off at the top of the screen the newscaster read from the press release, the same information scrolled down the screen in written form.

Just after 5 p.m. at the Nogales Mariposa port of entry in Arizona two tractor trailers were diverted for secondary inspection. One was found to have 6,668 pounds of marijuana hidden behind oriental rugs. The other truck had 7,745 pounds of marijuana in boxes marked men's shirts made in China. Two 2009 Izuzu trucks were impounded.

At the Naco port of entry, 128 pounds of cocaine were discovered hidden in a metal tool box in the bed of a 2005 GMC pickup.

At the San Luis port of entry a white 2009 Dodge was diverted to the vehicle secondary examination area for further inspection. Officials discovered 13 pounds of methamphetamine in 5 wrapped packages located in the cars center console.

Lukeville port of entry officers discovered 49 pounds of

methamphetamine hidden in a non-factory compartment in the wheel well area of the trunk of a 2008 Dodge. Customs and Border Protection agents seized the 22 packages of methamphetamine and the vehicle.

The Douglas port of entry reported 28 packages with a combined weight of close to 28 pounds of methamphetamine were found hidden within the walls of a 2010 Ford.

During routine inspection at the Nogales, Deconcini port of entry, a 2006 Chevrolet Blazer was searched. Officers found a total of eight metal collars attached to the four wheels of the vehicle. The collars contained a total of 99 pounds of methamphetamine.

At the Nogales, Morley Gate port of entry, close to 60 pounds of methamphetamine were discovered by officers. 22 packages were found hidden in a 2009 Ford F-150 in a compartment behind the engine.

The flashing 'NOGALES REGION' headline was replaced with one reading 'OTAY MESA REGION'—the droning newsreader and the scrolling continued:

The largest individual seizure occurred at about 3:45 p.m., at the Otay Mesa Commercial port of entry. When officers escorted a 2006 Kenworth tractor supposedly hauling a refrigerated trailer loaded with frozen seafood discovered 7,800 pounds of marijuana hidden behind a row of lobsters.

In California at the Tecate port of entry at 3:17 p.m. a 2009 International truck with a refrigerated trailer filled with frozen broccoli was deemed suspicious. Officers conducted an intensive examination of the tractor trailer at the cargo dock and discovered bundles of drugs intermixed with the broccoli shipment. CBP officers discovered 157 bundles containing 2,153 pounds of marijuana and three bundles containing 49 pounds of cocaine.

At the Andrade port of entry, 253 pounds of cocaine was found hidden in two metal tool boxes in the rear of a 1997 Ford Aerostar van.

At the San Ysidro port of entry, Agents found 55 bundles of cocaine weighing 227 pounds which were stuffed inside four backpacks lying in the rear compartment of a 2008 Ford Bronco.

At the Calexico, East port of entry, officers subjected a 2009 Chevrolet truck to intensive examination of the rear seats and discovered 30 packages containing 32 pounds of methamphetamine.

At the Calexico, West port of entry, officers subjected a 2007 Pontiac to intensive examination of the rear seats and discovered 20 packages containing 22 pounds of methamphetamine.

Otay Mesa port of entry reported 118 pounds of methamphetamine were located, hidden in a 2004 Chevrolet pickup.

'OTAY MESA REGION' was interchanged with 'LAREDO REGION'—the reading and rolling print went on:

In Texas at 6:42 p.m., at the Laredo World Trade Bridge port of entry officers directed a 2004 Freightliner tractor hauling a trailer laden with a shipment of raw onions to a cargo inspection area. After they conducted an extensive examination the officers uncovered 5,876 pounds of marijuana commingled with the shipment.

Officers at 5:12 p.m. at the Pharr port of entry in Texas searched a 2008 Mack truck and trailer and found 6,710 pounds of marijuana packed behind a load of tombstones.

At the Veterans International port of entry in Brownsville, Texas a 2008 Freightliner truck and trailer was sent to an inspection dock after officers were alerted by a drug sniffing canine. 7,340 pounds of marijuana was discovered behind cases of canned pickled jalapeno peppers.

Officers at the Del Rio port of entry noticed a discrepancy in the bed of a 2009 Dodge pick-up. Further inspection revealed there was a secret compartment built into the bed of the Dodge that contained more than 500 pounds of cocaine.

During secondary inspection at the Eagle Pass II port of entry officers discovered a 2008 Chevrolet Impala had over 360 pounds of cocaine sitting in the trunk.

Officers at the Progreso port of entry, while inspecting a 2010 Dodge Ram hauling a trailer, discovered 50 packages of cocaine hidden within the wall of the trailer with a total weight of 995 pounds

While undergoing secondary inspection at Roma port of entry, a Ford F-250 pickup truck was found to have a secret compartment under the truck's bed holding 38 packages of cocaine weighing 259 pounds

In the course of routine inspection at the Rio Grande City port of entry of a 2009 Chevrolet, 63 pounds of methamphetamine in 26 wrapped packages were discovered concealed in the vehicles quarter panels.

At the Hildago port of entry a white 2010 Nissan was discovered to have packages concealed within the walls of the vehicle. An intensive inspection of the Nissan by CBP officers revealed discrepancies and a non-factory compartment hidden within the walls of the car. CBP officers' intensified examination revealed five packages with a combined weight of more than 12.5 pounds of methamphetamine.

During routine inspection at the Brownsville, Los Indios port of entry, a grey 2007 Chevrolet Equinox, was found to have 22 wrapped packages of methamphetamine concealed inside the dashboard area. The packages weighed a total of 54 pounds.

Officers at the Brownsville, Gateway port of entry, searching a 2008 Ford found eight wrapped packages of methamphetamine concealed within the bumper. The total weight of the packages was 9 pounds.

At the Eagle Pass I port of entry, CBP officers became suspicious of a 2002 Ford F-150 carrying a complete living room set of furniture. Officers searched the vehicle and discovered packages concealed in the upholstery of the furniture. CBP officers seized more than 300 pounds of methamphetamine.

Officers at the Laredo, Bridge I port of entry reported a 2005 Ford Focus was searched and impounded. Officers discovered a non factory compartment in the undercarriage located above the vehicle's exhaust pipe. The non factory compartment contained five packages containing a total of 11 pounds of methamphetamine.

At the Laredo, Columbia Solidarity port of entry a CBP officer referred a 2008 Mercedes bus to secondary inspection after a routine non-intrusive imaging system scan indicated anomalies in the floor area. CBP officers conducted an intensive examination of the floor area and discovered 51 packages containing a total of 134 pounds of methamphetamine.

Officers at the Laredo, Bridge II port of entry stopped a unique attempt at smuggling narcotics into the country yesterday when they found "liquid" methamphetamines in the washer fluid reservoir of a 2009 GMC pickup. A narcotics canine alerted agents to the odor of narcotics coming from the vehicle. CBP officers searching the vehicle discovered the washer fluid reservoir contained what turned out to be a liquid form of methamphetamines. The narcotics, more than 13 pounds, were seized along with the vehicle.

During secondary inspection at Rio Grande City port of entry officers found 76 pounds of methamphetamine hidden in a 2005 Winnebago Minnie motor home.

'LAREDO REGION' was taken down—'EL PASO REGION' began flashing repeatedly on and off at the top of the screen, the newscaster read from a press release, and the new information scrolled down the screen in written form:

Also in Texas at 5:37 p.m., at the El Paso Ysleta port of entry, officials found 7,780 pounds of marijuana packed in boxes marked plumbing fixtures. Officers sent a 2005 International tractor and trailer to secondary inspection where the cargo was inspected and the contraband discovered.

Officers stationed at the Columbus port of entry in New Mexico intercepted 7,690 pounds of marijuana in a 2009 Freightliner truck hidden in a shipment of electrical control boxes. Columbus is approximately 30 miles south of Deming and 65 miles west of the Santa Teresa Port of Entry.

The Fort Hancock port of entry reported a 2007 Chevrolet Suburban had nearly 600 pounds of cocaine concealed in secret compartments built into the floor as well as the gas tank.

In the course of routine inspection at the Stanton port of entry a 2008 Ford 250 pick-up was detained. Agents discovered several false compartments in the truck, including in the bed. Inside the compartments, they found approximately 500 pounds of cocaine.

Agents at the Santa Teresa port of entry found 82 pounds of methamphetamine in 35 wrapped packages concealed in a specially built compartment under a 2008 Volkswagen Jetta.

At the Presidio port of entry a large wrapped package from a truck's intake manifold field-tested positive for methamphetamine. It weighed 20.5 pounds and was discovered hidden in a 2005 Dodge Ram pick-up truck.

At the El Paso, Bridge of the Americas port of entry, a 2009 Chevrolet pick-up had over 245 pounds of methamphetamine hidden in it. Officers found 150 pounds of methamphetamine concealed in the gas tank, 30 pounds of methamphetamine concealed in a backseat, 36 pounds of methamphetamine concealed in rocker panels, and 29 pounds of methamphetamine concealed in the tailgate of the pick-up truck.

Officers at the El Paso, Paso Del Norte port of entry, discovered a hidden compartment built underneath a 2008 Jeep Patriot's dashboard in the firewall, and removed 14 packages containing a total of 13 pounds of methamphetamine.

Agents at the Fabena port of entry sent a 2004 Nissan Titan to secondary inspection. Officers conducted an intensive examination of the firewall area and discovered packages containing 42 pounds of methamphetamine.

Mercifully the scrolling, flashing, and reading ended. But not for long. The CNN anchorwoman reported they were going live to a hastily called news conference at the White House press room. Myrna Stein, the president's press secretary appeared on the screen standing behind a podium.

Stein announced, "Homeland Security Director Charles Swanson informed President Burns this morning major drug arrests and confiscations had been made all along the Mexican border. Swanson said the past twenty-four hours of drug interdictions were typical of the daily cross-border shipments successfully brought into the United States from Mexico each and every day for years. Director Swanson assured the president he and the dedicated public servants working for Homeland Security will take the appropriate steps to ensure this free-flow of illegal drugs never happens again."

A reporter shouted, "Each and every day? Could you explain that statement?"

"You heard correctly. The amount of drugs intercepted over the past day is the quantity required on a daily basis to satisfy the cravings of addicts in the United States. The pipeline is plugged and will remain plugged. There are going to be a lot of junkies going cold turkey."

Stein continued, "Beginning today, President Burns ordered the SENTRI system for frequent border crossers discontinued. The president also ordered the express truck crossing program FAST, Free and Secure Trade Lane, cancelled until further notice."

In response to reporters' shouted questions Stein confirmed, "Yes, the drug cartels were indeed using the SENTRI lanes and the FAST lanes to import drugs."

Responding to another question Stein said, "Authorities acted on anonymous tips."

Stein put up her hands and waited for quiet. She then went on, "Officers of the United States Customs and Border Protection Agency, the largest of the United States law enforcement agencies, announced members of their Internal Affairs Division arrested one hundred eighty-one customs and border protection officers. The IAD emphasized the total charged represent only a minuscule number, less than one percent, of sworn officers. Those arrested have been charged with accepting bribes. Forty-six agents were arrested at World Express Air Freight in Kansas City. An additional one hundred thirty-five agents were taken into custody at ports of entry all along the Mexican border. The arrests come as the result of a long and arduous internal investigation conducted by the Customs and Border Protection Agency. President Burns wants all Americans to know how proud he is and how much he appreciates the over twenty thousand customs and border protection officers who risk their lives on a daily basis protecting the nation's twenty-one hundred mile southern border."

Stein thanked the reporters and walked back out of the press room.

The CNN anchorwoman continued, "In other breaking news CNN has learned two members of the United States Senate and two members of the House of Representatives were taken into custody by agents of the Federal Bureau of Investigation. They were charged with soliciting and accepting bribes intended to influence potential legislation. House and Senate leaders of both parties have protested the FBI action as an unacceptable executive branch attempt at intimidation of legislative branch members. In separate arraignment hearings yesterday afternoon, attorneys for Senator Harvey Dwight of Idaho, Senator John Babcock of Delaware, Representative Ezra Higgins of Newark, and Representative Vito LaCrocca of Staten Island all pleaded not guilty, argued separation of powers and had their clients released on their own recognizance. It was further ordered future court dates would be set after the current legislative session recesses. The lawyers for the defendants issued statements that under the United States Constitution the legislative branch writes and enacts laws and if the executive branch does not agree the president can veto the legislation. The offices of Senator Babcock and Representative Higgins said they were back at work in Washington. Senator Dwight and Representative LaCrocca were said to have traveled back to their home districts and would have no comment. CNN investigative reporters are looking deeper into the bribery aspect of the charges and have promised more later. Stay tuned to CNN for all the latest breaking news on this story. Now a word from our sponsors."

President Burns muted the volume and waved his hand, "Enough of this crap. Let's get back to business."

Ed Grass said, "Sir I want to clarify the anonymous tips acted on were verily information obtained by Triple A's investigation and hard work."

Homeland Security Director Swanson broke in, "Yes sir, these arrests were made possible using information uncovered by Triple A's investigation. Once waved through, cleared by a suspect agent, the vehicles which were identified from Lisa Strump's notes were stopped and sent to secondary screening. When drugs were found, the vehicles were impounded, the drivers arrested, and the border agents she bribed were taken into custody. Those intercepts of the vehicles identified by Strump's notes will continue on a daily basis until the attempts at bringing them across the border stops. In fact every vehicle is being looked at more closely. It has been made absolutely clear to our agents security is the goal not expedience. Also sir, there have been new developments in the investigation into the September thirtieth nuclear explosions at LAX and at John Wayne Airport in Los Angeles, at Phoenix's Sky Harbor Airport, at the Albuquerque Sunport, and at Hobby Airport in Houston. With the help of Ed's special operations group, Triple A again, Tom Eagan has identified ten suspects. Photos, descriptions, fingerprints, aliases, last know location, and last known vehicle of each of them are in a report sent to your office. At this time I recommend these ten suspects be placed at the top of the FBI's ten most wanted fugitives list, and Homeland Security's ten most wanted terrorists list. As you will find detailed in the report sir we believe these people were out of the country, home free in Mexico. Then they returned, smuggled across the border along with a shipment of drugs by Angel Figueroa's drug smugglers. Eagan missed apprehending them in Pueblo, Colorado, by at most two weeks. Tom feels adding these suspects to the most wanted lists may help in apprehending them."

Burns replied, "I want these bastards on all the lists. Interpol too. Let's do it. And Charlie, put as many people on this as necessary. I want them brought in."

"Yes sir."

Burns then turned to Grass saying, "Ed it sounds like we have another reason to bring this Figueroa character in. He must know something about these terrorists."

Grass nodded, "I agree sir. Triple A is well aware of the connection. I'm sure Al Garcia will get to the bottom of this as soon as possible."

The president then focused on Emily Rogers, the Secretary of the Treasury. He said, "Emily I want everything in this country, all of the money on deposit, stock and bond holdings, and real estate and other investments owned by the Alliance, the Mexican drug cartels, and the named principals of those organizations tied up as soon as possible. Can you do that?"

"Yes sir. I'll get right on it."

Evelyn Colosimo asked, "Mister President, you've authorized American personnel to go into Mexico to murder and apprehend Mexican citizens. What do I tell the Mexican government?"

Burns irritably replied, "I told you last time. Not a damn thing Evelyn. The Mexican bureaucrats are all crooks. You tell them we're going in, they'll tell the cartels. You tell them anything, they'll tell the cartels. What you need to do is take that list of Alliance members Randall passed around. After Mexico is dealt with I want your suggestion on how to deal with the drug producing countries of Bolivia, Brazil, Columbia, Ecuador, Paraguay, Peru, Venezuela,

Afghanistan, Burma, China, India, Laos, Nigeria, Pakistan, and Vietnam. Understand?"

"Yes sir."

Burns grimly pointed to Rogers saying, "Emily you too. You figure out what needs to be done to tie up all the funds and holdings in the United States belonging to any of the front groups and principals of the drug trade profiteers in the Alliance. We just experienced the perfect lesson. It does not take much corruption of our personnel for the Alliance to render our border crossing facilities useless. According to Lisa Strump's records they had everything well covered. All they needed was money. I want to ensure they don't have those funds in the future."

Burns, still glowering, turned to Leroy Adams and said, "Roy I want it clearly understood. I want fighter cover in the air, at the ready to take out whatever could be thrown at our guys, in the event Mexican armed forces try to intervene with the takedowns of these criminals."

"Yes sir. Understood, sir."

"Thank you everyone. If there is nothing else we're adjourned."

Chapter Thirty-Six

7:26 a.m. Mountain Time, November 11

ANGEL FIGUEROA PACED BACK AND FORTH in his office. The television was tuned to KECY-TV, Fox in the Morning, from Yuma. Angel cursed, swearing at the announcers. He had had no sleep in the last twenty-four hours, hardly any sleep in days. The Alliance had lost tens of millions of dollars in product and vehicles. American security people he had been paying for years were in jail. His trusted lieutenants, his enforcers, were in jail. He was being pressured by retailers in the states who wanted to know where their drugs were. He tried to cancel shipments whenever he could. Nothing was getting through. Figueroa picked up the phone and made some calls. People owed him. He was a powerful man. Ruthless drug dealers in Washington took his call. Vicious career criminals in Sacramento were happy to do his bidding. Angel raged, his mind on fire;

His partners were scheming against him.

He wasn't safe. He knew they would try to kill him.

Fucking American politicians took care of themselves, they wouldn't take his calls.

Lisa Strump and Abe Silverman had disappeared.

That fuckin' cunt, she had to have given all his inside contacts up. That's the only way they could know. Now she took off.

Bitch.

That scumbag fuck, Silverman, took his money for years, now he had turned the politicians in.

No one else could have done it.

No one else knew.

Now that cocksucker won't take his calls, won't call back.

They'll be sorry, the whole fucking bunch of them will regret this day.

The only one still loyal is Diego.

Diego Perez has called back.

Diego says the Mexican government officials are all in his corner.

He has spoken to them, they have his back.

Didn't believe that for a minute, money was all they were interested in.

They didn't care who paid them as long as they got paid.

If the money came from one of the others, not Angel, they would stab him in the back.

Fuck them all. He had increased security, he was taking precautions.

He would survive.

At 10:17 p.m. Eastern Time, November 11, Vito LaCrocca closed the front door to his mini-mansion on Amboy Road. When he was home on Staten Island it was his job to walk Duke, the family dog. Duke, a ten year old female cocker spaniel, would urinate in the house if not walked in the evening. Duke had a cheerful, sweet disposition. She was black, white, and tan about sixteen inches high, twenty pounds, uncommonly friendly, abnormally quiet, and rarely barked. Duke pulled at her leash. Vito followed. As usual they turned down Jefferson Avenue. It was secluded with many vacant lots where Duke could do her duty. Duke didn't go far before stopping. She sniffed around before deciding this was as good a place as any. Vito turned his back, looking into the street to give Duke her privacy. Vito was distracted, thinking about the mess he was in because of Angel Figueroa when he heard a low pop. As he spun around to see if Duke was all right he saw two short stocky men, dark complexioned, wearing baggy dungarees, plaid work shirts, and ball caps standing right there. At first he assumed they were day laborers who were sleeping in the brush and were disturbed, but looking closer he saw one was pointing a gun equipped with a silencer at him. Duke was lying on the ground. The one with the gun said, "Hey Vito, remember me?"

LaCrocca studied his face in the dark, leaned closer for a better look and was struck in the side of the neck by the other man. Vito felt a sting, then a fit a weakness and nausea. He fell to his knees. He placed them, remembered who they were, as he passed out.

Enzo and Louis Tommasso, muscle for the Testa family.

Less than an hour later, the Tommasso brothers entered New Dorp Beach Italian American Social Club on Staten Island. They reported to capo Peter Testa who sat eating pasta at a table in the rear of the club.

Enzo said, "He won't be tellin' any stories out of school boss. Your cousins' pensions are safe now."

Testa, who'd been bowling at the Colonial Lanes on Hylan Boulevard an hour earlier, replied, "Good job, boys. Some of the guys were worried Vito could try to make a deal and cause them problems. Did anybody see you?"

Enzo replied, "Yeah, people saw us walkin' the neighborhood before and after. Nobody got a look at our faces, only the general appearance. It went great. Just like you said it would."

At 6:42 a.m. Eastern Time, November 12, a huge traffic jam had built up on southbound 295, the Baltimore Washington Parkway, from its intersection with Route 193, Greenbelt Road, north to Powder Mill Road. The massive two mile long back-up of traffic was caused by drivers slowing to look at a scene unfamiliar in the United States. Two severed human heads were hanging from the Route 193 overpass where it crossed 295. Cars that normally maintained a slow but steady speed in this area were at a virtual standstill—being reduced to one lane as they passed by the grisly scene. Crime scene investigators climbed boom ladders extended from fire trucks in order to photograph and retrieve the heads.

WJLA-TV's traffic helicopter hovered overhead, the pilot describing the hectic spectacle for the morning's news show. The pretty blonde broadcaster in the studio interrupted the pilot to say that further south where commuter traffic crossed the Anacostia River vehicles had slowed again as they passed the National Arboretum. She reported that propped up against the perimeter fence under a group of magnificent, spectacular evergreen magnolia trees, normally a quiet, restful scene, were two headless bodies. She said people on their way to work had called the station to describe the grotesque scene. Station employees monitoring police radio communications learned the headless bodies carried identification belonging to Marvin and Edith Silverman, residents of Baltimore. A police spokesperson confirmed authorities believed the severed heads at the Route 193 overpass belonged to the Silvermans. Police were attempting to contact Abe Silverman, the only known surviving family member, to positively identify the remains.

At 7:14 a.m. Pacific Time, November 12, Officer James Lutrell of the Stockton Police Department drove his patrol cruiser south on Pacific Avenue. He hurried back to headquarters as it was near the end of his midnight to eight shift. As he crossed the Calaveras River overpass he observed a large group of young people gathered in the visitor's parking lot of the University of the Pacific. They were pointing up in the air in the direction of the Burns Tower. Lutrell glanced up and reached for his radio. He turned, made a right on Knoles Way into the campus. He told headquarters he was on the college campus, he thought there was a naked female hanging by her feet from one of the spires on the Burns Tower. From the distance the subject appeared to be dead, but of course, it could be a student prank. Lutrell parked his cruiser in front of the building, ignored the students assembled together in the lot, and ran to the tower building entrance doors. As he moved closer he saw a pool of blood on the sidewalk directly under where the body hung suspended from the spire. He could see her hands were tied at the wrists, her arms extended down. He also saw a hole smashed in the glass entry door. Lutrell stopped in his tracks, turned around, went back to his car, called headquarters again. He told them upon closer inspection he thought this was a homicide. He would secure the scene while he waited for a supervisor and crime scene investigators. He instructed them to contact campus security. They needed to send someone over too.

Two hours later Officer Lutrell watched as Julie Diaz, the University of the Pacific Campus Police Information Spokesperson, presented herself to the local press. She told them Lori Strump, an engineering student, a junior, had been murdered. Her assailants had broken into the Burns Tower, a landmark structure visible from anywhere on the college grounds. Tours for perspective students and their families started from the tower. The assailants forced Strump to the roof where she had been stripped, her throat slashed open, and her tongue pushed through the opening. A rope had been placed around her ankles, tied to a spire, and her naked body thrown from the building.

In a pile of her clothing police found a university issued passkey, the type used by hotels. The key was coded to open a dorm room. Campus Police determined the passkey belonged to Lori Strump, a twenty year old junior. University fingerprint records positively identified the body—five-six, one hundred twenty-five pounds, red hair, green eyes, and such a beautiful face—Lori Strump. The university had not yet been able to contact Lori's sister. Lisa Strump, her next-of-kin listed in their records. The sister did not answer her phone and Carlsbad, California police who visited Lisa's home said they could not raise a response at the residence. Diaz refused to take questions.

KOVR, Channel 13, CBS based in Stockton had a news crew at the university. Acting as the station's noontime feature correspondent, reporter

Randi Dotingo said she questioned professors and other students who all spoke highly of Lori Strump. No one claimed to be a friend or even close to her. Some described Strump as a loner. No one interviewed had ever met anyone in her family. The university financial office confirmed Lori Strump was not a scholarship student, had no loans or financial aid. They said her tuition, books, and room and board were all paid in advance each semester by her sister Lisa. Dotingo ominously stated anonymous law enforcement sources opined they did not expect any witnesses. The unidentified sources revealed the murder method chosen by the killer or killers definitely sent the message, don't talk.

At 1:06 p.m. Eastern Time, November 12, the afternoon edition of the Staten Island Advance reported Congressman Vito La Crocca was executed the previous night while walking his dog outside his Staten Island home. His dog Duke had also been shot. Police suspected a silenced weapon was used as no report had been heard by any nearby residents. Police also revealed LaCrocca's mouth had been duct taped shut. They believed that was a warning to others to keep quiet about anything they may have seen or heard. Neighbors who refused to be identified told police they had observed two short stocky men with dark complexions, baggy dungarees, plaid work shirts, and ball caps walking the streets. Apparently Hispanic day laborers had been seen in the area both before and after the time police believe LaCrocca was killed. According to the autopsy report, the medical examiner determined a hypodermic needle with a diameter of one point five millimeter had been used to inject a large dose of Demerol into the neck of LaCrocca. The drug incapacitated the congressman while an ice pick was shoved into his brain through his right ear. The police said they had no information linking LaCrocca's vicious execution style murder to Mexican drug cartels or his arrest by the FBI in connection with alleged influence peddling and bribery.

At 1710 Mountain Time, November 12, Sergeant Ralph Mulia, Corporal John Kitnoya, Private Moosey Briggs, and Private Jesse Charles greeted the Triple A team and the other special operations agents as they entered Building 3, the central mess hall at Camp Vigilant, in the secluded backcountry of Fort Huachuca. The somber soldiers all been previously informed by General Ehrich that tonight was the big night they had trained for.

A large wall-hung television screen was tuned to CNN. The anchors, a man and a woman, were reporting several incidents of uniformed security personnel being fired upon by assailants hidden on the Mexican side of the border. Three border patrolmen were in critical condition, two dead. The reporters recapped the stories of the day, the brutal murder of the Staten Island congressman charged with working with drug cartels, and the discovery of the heads and headless bodies of an elderly couple with no apparent connection to the drug trade in Washington DC. Citizens everywhere were upset. Many politicians reported receiving angry phone calls and e-mails from constituents.

Tonight the normally separated tables had been pushed together. The entire special operations group sat together. Al Garcia sat at one end with Al Cruz and Alex Mendez on either side of him. Garcia led the group in a prayer before Mulia's men began serving dinner. Mulia had prepared his specialty; baked clams as an appetizer, French onion soup, a surf and turf main course, broiled Alaskan king crab legs and prime rib. For dessert Mulia had prepared New York cheesecake.

Over coffee after the meal Garcia had shared with the other agents the young woman murdered in Stockton, California was also a victim of the drug cartels. He recounted the phone conversation he had earlier with President Burns. Garcia described the president as outraged with the attacks on American citizens. He said the president sent his regards to them all and wished them all a safe mission. Garcia told everyone to be outside Building 2, ready to go, at midnight.

Chapter Thirty-Seven

0100 Mountain Time, November 13

TEAM RETRIEVAL, THE NAME GENERAL EHRICH had assigned to the group, loaded up onto three MH-60 Ghost helicopters. Four Ghosts had landed at the Camp Vigilant shooting range. One was equipped as a field medical unit. Just in case, General Ehrich insisted. No one else expected resistance that would cause Team Retrieval problems. The MH-60 Ghosts were the latest version of direct penetration stealth attack helicopters available for use by the United States military. Each craft carried a crew of three and up to eleven passengers. Each was armed with six hellfire missiles, an under-mount M230 chain gun that fired six hundred twenty-five 30mm rounds per minute, eight Hydra rockets, and an Aero M134D electrically powered, six barreled, Gatling gun capable of firing four thousand 7.62 cartridges per minute. The Ghost was silent, invisible, and deadly. On this mission the four Ghosts would be joined by two MQ-9 Reaper Hunter/Killer unmanned aerial vehicles (UAV's) which were already on station over Angel Figueroa's ranch. The Reapers each carried fourteen Hellfire missiles.

For the flight to Hermosillo, the Triple A team split up. Garcia flew with Fabio Pineda, Cesar Catalino, Ernesto Sanchez, and Stefania Chavez. Cruz accompanied Antonio Preciado, Francisco Valdez, Edwardo Carvalho, and Paola Calderon. Mendez, Maribell Robles, Marco Mendes, Zacarias Vega, and Rey Oropeza were in the third helo. The fourth carried a standard crew plus two medics. All fifteen Team Retrieval members were standing on the side of the shooting range when the four Ghosts came in practically unnoticed. The Ghosts were painted black, blended into the dark night, and hardly made a sound. Team Retrieval had gone over the plan one more time before boarding the helos. Everyone was relaxed and confident. They knew their jobs. They were ready.

The Figueroa property consisted of about nine thousand acres, more than fourteen square miles, located twenty-six miles north of the Mexican city of Hermosillo. The ranch fronted on Highway 15 for more than four miles. There was only one road in and out of the grounds. The entry road had a guard post manned by two guards twenty-four hours a day. The guard detail shift commander's headquarters was also inside the gate guardhouse. The outside dimensions of Angel's ranch were three and two tenths miles east to west, by four and four tenths miles north to south. The boundary lines were secured by an electrified fence. A perimeter road paralleled the property lines right inside the energized barrier. Two jeeps containing two guards each patrolled the perimeter road twenty-four hours a day. Two roads dissected the ranch into approximate thirds. The southern sector contained Angel's living quarters. The middle third consisted of the guards' bunkhouse, the horse stables, horse pasture, and an exercise track. Cultivated farmland, a stocked fish pond, blacksmith's shed, vehicle repair garage, and several small cottages for help who lived on the property were all in the north section. Four more armed guards were stationed outside the main house, one at each corner. Each guard had a handheld radio and used it to check in regularly with the commander. There were eleven members of Figueroa's staff on guard duty at any one time. At least forty-four more guards were housed in the ranch bunkhouse at all times.

At 0116 the four MH-60 Ghosts crossed the border into Mexico. The pilots flew in loose formation thirteen hundred feet above the ground one mile west of Nogales. They passed outside the towns of Santa Ana and Querobabi. The pilots, wearing headsets, were in constant contact with each other. Because visibility was poor, slightly more than half moon, they relied on their instruments. They made good time. The helicopters cruised at about one hundred seventy-five miles per hour. There wasn't any noticeable turbulence, a smooth flight. If it hadn't been for the cabin noise generated by the wind the occupants of the Ghosts could have been in a luxury car. The new electric stealth engines and propulsion blades were nearly soundless.

At 0208 the formation slowed and descended. The pilots landed immediately south of the fish pond. The helos came to rest roughly in a half circle one hundred feet apart. With the water to their backs, the four Gatling guns were immediately manned by crewmembers, creating a perimeter protected by overwhelming firepower. The engines shut down.

Team Retrieval dismounted and regrouped on the road between the farm and the ranch. They were outfitted much differently than they were for Team Intercept. Dressed in desert camouflage BDUs of light tan, pale green, and brown, the boonie hats were gone. The soft hat was replaced with desert camouflage lightweight ballistic helmets equipped with tactical communications headsets, and flip-up night vision goggles. Exposed skin, face and hands, were painted with camouflage patterns blending with the BDUs. Everyone wore body armor, Nomex long underwear, and brown wool socks. Black clothing had been discussed at length but rejected. The team decided if something went wrong and anyone was forced to walk the nearly two hundred miles back to the United States, the camo BDUs would help them blend with the terrain. Al Cruz was the only person carrying a taser shotgun, and that was slung over his back, a second weapon only to be used on Angel Figueroa if necessary. They were free to kill everybody else. One medic, Harry Albers, joined the team. The other medic stayed with the medical helo, Ghost Four.

Each agent carried a M4A1 carbine especially modified for special operations. They had three trigger settings, S-1-F (safe, single, and fully-automatic). Each carbine had a sound suppressor, a laser/infrared designator, standard rear sight, and a night vision sight. Each member of Team Retrieval drilled endlessly with the fully automatic operation setting normally used during close quarters combat operations. They trained with single shot nighttime sniper action up to one hundred sixty yards. All the team members tested expert on the range.

Mari Robles and Zac Vega were the first to leave the group. Following the route they had rehearsed at Fort Huachuca they headed southeast across the horse pasture. Mari and Zac were to make their way to the intersection of the entrance road and the perimeter road. They were to wait under cover for one of the patrol jeeps to pass. When the lights were out of sight they were to cross the road, get within one hundred yards of the gatehouse, and position themselves to be able to pick off the two gate guards and the shift commander if the need arose. When they were in position they were instructed to break radio silence and report in.

Pineda, Catalino, Oropeza, and Mendes walked out just south of the road until they reached a point approximately three hundred yards east of the middle group.

Preciado, Valdez, Carvalho, Calderon, Chavez, and Sanchez went three hundred yards west.

Garcia, Cruz, Mendez, and Harry Albers stayed in the middle.

When everyone called in they were in position Garcia gave the order to move out. In unison the three groups slowly crossed the middle portion of Figueroa's ranch in single file. They maintained five yard separation. The lead person walking point halted every five paces to scan the area through the helmet mounted night vision goggles. When each group reached the east-west road before the ranch house section they stopped and checked in. Garcia's group stopped at the intersection of the east-west road and the driveway into the ranch house.

Fabio and Cesar set up a remote control horizontal acting mine three hundred yards east of the intersection. From here they could stop any vehicle trying to approach the ranch house from the perimeter road on that side. From their position on the south side of the road they could also fire upon any guards attempting to approach the ranch house on foot.

Fran Valdez and Paola Calderon arranged a remote control horizontal acting mine and a defensive position about three hundred yards west of the ranch house driveway. They were also on the south side of the road.

The guard's bunkhouse was positioned on the north side of the east west road fronting on the road. It was about one hundred yards further west of Fran and Paola's mine ambush and firing position. Ernie Sanchez and Steffi Chavez set themselves into firing positions on the south side of the road. Ernie had a firing field that included the front door and the west side. Steffi covered the east side and the front door. The bunkhouse also had a back door. Tony Preciado and Eddie Carvalho set themselves up about one hundred yards straight back from the rear door. The fashion in which the agents had aligned themselves protected them from being errantly shot by one of their own. That's the way it worked in theory anyway.

With everyone else in position Rey Oropeza and Marc Mendes joined Garcia, Cruz, Mendez, and Harry Albers in the push on Angel's ranch house. Oropeza and Mendes continued south in a line three hundred yards east of the ranch until they were one hundred yards past the back side of the building. They then turned west. As they cautiously approached the ranch house Rey spotted a sentry on the southeast corner. He was sitting on the ground, his back against a tree, an AK-47 cradled across his lap. Rey sank to the ground and got into a comfortable firing position. Mendes delicately picked his way to where he could observe the southwest corner of the house. The guard on that corner was lying down, his head resting on his crossed arms, his weapon on the ground. Marc settled into the prone firing position and sighted in.

Approximately one hundred feet in, the driveway followed a circular pattern around a large lawn. A five car garage was accessed off the right side of the drive before it continued under a portico then passed a covered guest parking area to where it went around completing the circle. Garcia and Cruz had gone around the circle to the left. They stopped when they were in range of the guard sitting in a lawn chair under the carport. Cruz went down on one knee and took aim.

Alex Mendez and Harry Albers approached on the west side of the circular driveway. After taking cover behind a clump of trees Mendez motioned Albers to sit behind a large oak. She leaned against another tree and utilized her night vision scope to zero in on the guard leaning against the front of the garage. The laser sight used by all of the snipers tonight pushed a beam of amplified light forward, the light unseen to the naked eye bounced off the precise aim point and appeared to the shooter's eye as a dot of red on the target through the sight.

Garcia used radio communications to let everyone know they were going to take down the four guards at the ranch house. Getting an all clear response from everybody he asked, "Rey you ready?"

Rey responded, "Red dot."

"Marc?"

"Red dot."

"Alex?"

"Lit up, boss."

"Al?"

"I'm a go."

Garcia said, "Okay then, on three. One, two, three."

Simultaneously four barely audible pops ensued. Garcia asked, "Done?"

Cruz nodded, Mendez said, "Mine's down." Rey and Marc both said, "Done."

Garcia then commanded, "Each of you put two more rounds into your target. Let's not take any chances."

After a slight pause Oropeza, Mendes, Mendez, and Cruz all responded, "Done."

Garcia told them, "Good job. Mark, Alex, Rey meet us under the portico."

Garcia positioned Oropeza and Mendes in defensive positions telling them, "Watch our backs. We are going to go in to fetch Figueroa out of his bed." He told Albers, "Take cover out of the way. If this scumbag resists and needs treatment I'll call you."

Triple A moved to the front door. Garcia was to one side, Mendez the other. Cruz stooped down, picked the lock, and exchanged his carbine with the taser shotgun. The M4A1 carbine slung over his back, shotgun in his hands, Cruz whispered into his mike, "The door is unlocked. Ready to go in."

Garcia lowered his night vision goggles and instructed, "Step aside Al. I'll go in first and go right. Alex you second. Go left. Use your goggles. It will be dark in there. We'll make a quick sweep of the ground floor then go up to the bedroom and get our guy. Al you follow us."

Garcia turned the handle pushed the door open and went in fast and low toward the right. Mendez quickly followed him in. She went to the left. Cruz stepped inside, went left, and stood with his back to the wall. The three of them were in a large circular entry foyer. A circular staircase led up to the second floor. It was quiet. Garcia and Mendez started to move into the living room. To the right was a huge dining room that led into the kitchen. On the left there was a hall with a study and a bathroom. It all appeared like Lisa Strump said it would be. Cruz moved to the bottom of the staircase anxious to get upstairs and get this over with. Garcia was in the dining room, Alex stepped toward the hall.

Without warning bright lights glared, gunfire erupted, Mendez screamed and went down. Garcia tore off his goggles, his vision blurred. He saw movement at the kitchen door, he fired. The figure dropped to the floor. Cruz already had lifted his goggles. He saw Mendez fall and ran to her. On his way he saw a gunman jump out of the hall leveling a gun at him. Cruz dove on top of Mendez' body, firing the taser as he fell. The gunman got off a burst of bullets in the direction of Cruz and Mendez. Garcia fired a long burst into the second guard. Cruz rolled off Mendez who was face down. He saw blood puddle on the floor. Cruz yelled, "Alex is hit! Medic! Medic!"

Garcia checked both gunmen, pumping two more rounds into each of them. He turned rapidly at noise at the door, holding fire when he saw it was Albers carrying his bag. Garcia pointed to Cruz and Mendez telling Albers, "Take care of them."

Oropeza and Mendes appeared at the open front door. Garcia shouted to them, "Check the rooms in the back of the first floor. There is a kitchen, study, and bathroom. I'm going upstairs. When everything is cleared on this floor follow me up."

Garcia yelled into his mike, "Everyone, maintain your positions. We have this under control. Take care of your assignments. Kill anybody that moves out there."

Garcia ran up the stairs two at a time. Figueroa's bedroom door was locked. Garcia stepped back and blew the door handle and locking apparatus apart. He kicked the door open and ran inside. No one was in the bed, but it was unmade. He touched it. The sheets were warm. Figueroa couldn't be far. The only window was closed and locked from the inside. The bathroom was empty. Garcia looked under the bed. Empty. Rey Oropeza shouted from the hall, "Coming in."

Garcia pointed to the closet door. Rey went to one side. Garcia kicked the door open. It was empty. Garcia howled, "Fuck. Fuck. Where is that cocksucker?"

Garcia turned to tell Oropeza to search the rest of the second floor when he sensed movement out of his peripheral vision. A wall in the closet slid to one side and out popped Angel Figueroa. With a furious roar a raging Figueroa jumped on top of Garcia before he could react. A long bladed knife rose and fell, Garcia stumbled to his knees. A horrified Oropeza unable to shoot for fear of hitting Garcia slammed the butt of his carbine into Figueroa's head again and again. Oropeza stopped when Figueroa dropped his knife and fell to the floor unconscious.

Oropeza went out of the bedroom, leaned over the rail, and saw Albers, Cruz, and Marc Mendes standing over Alex Mendez. He yelled for help. Cruz and Albers came running. Garcia struggled to his feet, blood running down his body armor. Albers went right to Garcia who waved him off asking, "How's Mendez?"

Albers ignored Garcia's gesture, looked and felt at Garcia's neck and upper body, replying, "She is unconscious, but luckily for her the body armor saved her life. Three slugs were in her vest another bounced off her helmet knocking her out. One went through her arm. One went through her leg. I've stopped the bleeding. It appears to be much the same for you. The body armor prevented the knife from passing through. You do have a nasty slice on your neck however."

Albers taped blood clotting battle field gauze to Garcia's neck as he spoke. He said, "I have the bleeding stopped. You can keep going now. Mendez will need to be carried. I need to look at this other guy."

Garcia said, "Harry I want you to give Figueroa a shot. Give him something to knock him out for a couple of hours."

Albers reached into his kit and replied, "Consider it done."

Garcia looked at Cruz asking, "You okay?"

"Yeah boss only some bruises where slugs hit my vest. Remind me next time. Never bring a taser to a gunfight."

Garcia said, "Tie this fuck up. Gather his computers, and all his discs. Have Rey help you."

Several minutes of constant gunfire that could be heard in the distance unexpectedly erupted into a loud explosion. Garcia remarked, "Sounds like World War Three out there. This was supposed to be a simple snatch and grab." He then hollered into his mike, "Mari, Zac report."

Mari replied, "We're fine Al. The gate house trio are down, believed dead. We're watching the road. We'll let you know if anybody shows up. Out."

Garcia asked, "Fabio, Cesar, how are you doing?"

Cesar replied, "Fine boss. That was our roadside bomb you just heard. That jeep and its occupants are no more."

Another explosion could be heard.

Garcia asked, "Valdez, Calderon was that you?"

Paola Calderon reported, "Yes sir. One more jeep gone and the people inside it are dust."

Garcia asked, "Ernie, Steffi how are you guys doing?"

Ernie Sanchez spoke. He said, "We have them pinned down Al, but they keep trying to come out. Eventually we may not be able to hold 'em."

"Tony, Eddie how about the back door?"

Eddie Carvalho replied, "We have them boxed in right now, boss, but if we try to move back to evacuate they are gonna be on us. Do we have anything to bring the house down on them?"

Garcia replied, "You have a point Ed. Let me think on it for a minute. I'll get back to you."

With Garcia in a lull Cruz interrupted his train of thought saying, "Boss we're ready to go. Figueroa is unconscious and tied up. We have all of the computer stuff. Alex is bad. She hasn't woken up. Harry says it is probably a concussion, but we need to medi-vac her ASAP. Just a suggestion boss but why not bring Ghost Four up here to pick up Mendez. They can land on the front lawn."

Garcia smiled and said, "Thanks Al, I wasn't thinking it through. You're absolutely right."

Garcia called Captain Barbara Elliot, the pilot of Ghost One and the commander of the air crews. With everyone listening in Garcia said, "Barbara would you bring Ghost One, Two, and Four up to the lawn in front of the ranch house. We need a medical evacuation here."

Elliot replied, "We can do that but why do you need Ghost One and Two, and why is Ghost Three staying here?"

Garcia said, "On the way here I'd like Ghost One to take out the guard's bunkhouse. If we try to back off them they will break out and come after us. Take them out where they are and we don't have to worry about them. Once Ghost One, Two, and Four pick us up, Mari and Zac can leave the entry road, high tail it back to Ghost Three, and we can all leave."

Elliot told Garcia, "We'll be right there. Al one more thing you need to know is I received a call from Fort Huachuca. Satellite images show a truck loaded with armed men has departed police headquarters in Hermosillo. Another vehicle carrying armed Mexican soldiers from the Arizpe Military Base east of Santa Ana is also on the road. They are racing south on Highway 15. Neither truck is that far away. We should take them out on their way here. Command suggests that with your permission they can dispatch the Reapers that have been circling the ranch."

"No. Have the Reapers continue circling. We are on our way out of here any second. Call me again if the police or soldiers become an immediate threat. They are just peasants. There may be no need to take them out."

"I'll tell them. Be there in a minute."

Garcia said into the mike, "Does everyone understand the plan?"

Mari, Cesar, Paola, Ernie, and Tony replied with a chorus of positive responses. Garcia instructed everyone in the house to go out to the lawn. Harry Albers spread out a foldable litter, which Al Cruz and Albers placed Mendez into before lifting. Rey carried the computer and discs. Marc Mendes hoisted an unconscious Angel Figueroa over his shoulder. Ghost Four had landed. As soon as Cruz, Albers, and Mendez were aboard they lifted off. To the northwest of where they were a series of explosions erupted as Captain Elliot unloaded on the bunkhouse. Ghost Two landed, loaded ten team members, and lifted off to hover as Ghost One retrieved Garcia, Figueroa, Mendes, and the remaining agents comprising Team Retrieval. Garcia leaned to talk to Captain Elliot. She laughed, rotated Ghost One and fired missiles into Angel's ranch house. It ignited into flame.

Everyone but Angel, who was out cold, cheered hysterically as they headed north. Ghost Three, Mari, and Zac joined the formation, which slowed long enough for Ghost Two to take out the blacksmith's shed and the vehicle repair garage. The horse stables and small cottages were left untouched.

Chapter Thirty-Eight

0517 Mountain Time, November 13

An ambulance from Fort Huachuca's Raymond W. Bliss Army Health Center waited at Libby Army Airfield when Ghost Four landed. Alex Mendez was gently moved to the ambulance. Al Cruz and Harry Albers rode with her to the Fort Huachuca base hospital. Mendez had awakened during the trip back on Ghost Four. Albers checked her out. Her eyes were clear. Pupils appeared fine. She was alert. She repeatedly told him she was fine. All she wanted to know was how it went, was everyone okay, did we get Angel Figueroa and his computer? No she insisted, she was not sick, not nauseous, her head felt fine, she wasn't sleepy, her chest hurt, her arm hurt, her leg hurt. Satisfied there was nothing more he could do, Albers let her talk to Cruz who told her everyone was on the way home. Figueroa had been taken alive. They had secured his computer and files. No, they didn't know who those guys were who were in the house. They weren't supposed to be there. They would definitely find out when they questioned Figueroa. Albers touched Cruz' arm, signaling him to let Mendez rest. Cruz put his finger on Alex's lips telling her, "Rest Alex. We'll talk later."

As soon as they arrived at the hospital Mendez was taken for a CAT scan of her head and X-rays of her chest. The photos revealed three broken ribs. Her bullet wounds were cleaned and bandaged. The bullets had gone right through flesh areas missing bones and arteries. The CAT scan indicated no internal bleeding. She had no pressure on the brain, no cracks or fissures in the skull. She would be kept under observation for several days. She was put into a private room and told to rest.

Al Cruz had X-rays taken of his chest. The rounds that had hit his body armor only bruised him. Al Garcia came in. He refused to get stitches until he was assured by Cruz that Mendez was all checked out and resting. Cruz explained the gunshot wounds were through shots, there was no damage there. She had some cracked ribs that would heal on their own, and there was no indication of any brain damage or head trauma. Only after Garcia confirmed everything Cruz had told him with the physician attending Mendez did he allow hospital personnel to clean and stitch up his neck wound.

After they were satisfied Mendez was okay, and they themselves had gotten the treatment they needed, Garcia and Cruz signed themselves out of the hospital and walked the short distance to the Fort Huachuca brig. This is where Garcia had brought Figueroa after the MH-60 Ghost helicopters carrying Team Retrieval had landed at the Camp Vigilant shooting range. Angel Figueroa had been locked-up in some unquestionably uncomfortable accommodations. The U.S. forces that were responsible for incarcerating captured terrorists all over the world used Fort Huachuca brig as a training center. The upper three levels were where the guided tours took place, the portion where the public and the politicians were taken. Not many people saw the basement cells, all high security isolation units. Dark, cold, damp, built and furnished to be uncomfortable. Truly stressful conditions for those held there. Angel was the only inmate currently in residence in the basement.

Upon entering the brig building Garcia and Cruz were escorted to the basement by way of an elevator hidden inside of a first level solitary confinement cell. General Ehrich was waiting for them in the basement control room. He told them, "He's awake. Do you want to watch? We have cameras in his cell. Not much to see, his wrists and ankles are tied to his bunk."

Garcia replied, "No sir we want to talk to him."

"Okay."

"Who else is on this level sir?"

"Nobody, we're alone."

"He hasn't had contact with anyone?"

"No."

"So he has no idea where he is?"

"No, I understand he was unconscious when you brought him here. I was watching when he woke up. That was about ten minutes ago."

Garcia inquired, "Sir, can the cameras be turned off?"

"Yes."

"Is there an audio recording of what's happening in his cell?"

"Yes, audio and visual recordings. Normally we record everything. We use the recordings of interrogations for training. That's what we do here, train interrogators to be effective. You fellows have a fantastic reputation. Your methods would be an asset to our library."

"General, would you turn them off please?"

"You don't trust me?"

"It's not you sir, not at all. Please understand, over the years we have had numerous investigations into our behavior. All of them unfounded, and we don't intend for this session to be any different. It's just audio and video records can be taken out of context by the politically correct crowd. We would rather not be recorded."

Ehrich flipped two switches and announced, "I understand. The audio and camera are off."

"You may want to wait upstairs sir. We'll call you when we're finished."

"Okay. Don't leave any marks please."

"Sir, he is already pretty marked up from when he was subdued. He'll be fine with us."

Ehrich pointed to a phone saying, "All right call me when you're finished. Dial O. When it's answered ask for me."

"Yes sir, thank you sir."

When the general entered the elevator Garcia and Cruz went to Figueroa's cell, opened the door and entered.

Figueroa asked, "Who are you?"

Responding in Spanish Garcia said, "I am Fuerzas Especiales Capitan Mauro González, and this is Capitan Enrique Lopez, also Mexican Special Forces."

"Do you know who I am?"

"Of course we know who you are."

"Where am I?"

"A safe place."

"How did I get here?"

"We brought you by helicopter."

"Why am I here?"

"We work for El Presidente de México Pedro Quiñones. He wants us to get answers to some questions from you."

"Of course, whatever Presidente Quiñones wants to know."

"El presidente wants to know why you are so stupid."

"I don't understand. My associates and I have been partners with Presidente Quiñones for years. We have always had a profitable relationship. Did one of my associates or I do something to offend el presidente? Just tell me. I will make them pay."

"We already made them pay. We got 'em all. They are all dead. Carlos Martinez of the Gulf Group blown up while swimming in his pool at his ranch in Monterrey this morning. The Central Syndicate's Miguel Vargas met an unfortunate accident on Highway 2 outside of Ciudad Juarez. He's dead. Ruben Miranda the big boy in charge of the Baja Boys had a tough morning too. He blew up on his patio near Ensenada. They and a lot of their soldiers are finished. The whole crew at your ranch are dead also. Your house is gone."

"Why, I don't understand?"

"When we were briefed before we moved on you and your compadres we were told you kicked the hornet's nest. The Americans are coming down hard on Presidente Quiñones for allowing your drug cartels to function so openly."

"But we pay much money."

"El presidente is right, you are stupid. I don't know why we're bothering."

"But I pay a lot of money, every month."

"There is no proof of that. The only contact, the only proof you had, Diego Perez, is dead too. A terrible fire in his office, Perez and his files were burned to a crisp."

"I have records."

"No Angel, we have your records. Any claim on your part you were paying Presidente Quiñones or his party will be explained as money you skimmed, that you stole from your partners. Now shut the fuck up or tell us what we want to know."

"What. What do you mean? What do you want from me? How do I make this right?"

"Angel, el presidente wanted us to speak with you. He knows you are the mastermind. He knows he needs someone to run the drug trade and keep his money coming in. But he needs to throw a bone to the Americans. El presidente wants an explanation, why did you help Islamic terrorists get into the United States?"

"I haven't."

"Enrique tape his eyelids open."

Figueroa pleaded, "No, please no. I am cooperating. I will tell you everything. But Islamic terrorists I have no idea what you are referring to."

Capitan Lopez took a roll of tape from his pocket. Figueroa shut his eyes tightly. Capitan González stood at the top end of the bed. He grasped Figueroa's head firmly with both hands. He forced Figueroa's eyelids open with his thumbs. Lopez taped them from lash to forehead. González released Figueroa who violently shook his head trying to loosen the tape. González grabbed Figueroa's head again, held it motionless, while Lopez taped it to the bed frame. Figueroa couldn't close his eyes or move his head.

González snarled, "Angel no one knows you are alive. Everyone thinks your body is one of the many dead at your ranch. We are extremely well equipped here. We can dip you in acid. We can burn you alive in our crematory. No one will know. No one will care. We can do with you as we want and place your charred bones in the wreckage of your home, to be discovered in the ashes. We can take your eyes. Leave you to live as a homeless bum on the streets in the slums of Mexico City. Or you can live, be the head of the Alliance once again. Your choice. Now, tell us about the terrorists you smuggled into the United States."

"Please understand guiding certain people across the border has been a part of what we do for years. I have no knowledge who might be a terrorist. Whoever has the money or the connections can come across with us. But nobody has ever been presented to me as a terrorist."

González turned to Capitan Lopez telling him, "Enough of this bullshit, get some acid. We'll burn out one eye at a time. This asshole will tell us the truth."

Figueroa screamed, "No, please don't, I'll tell you."

"Of course you will. Now last month ten people with backpacks came across with your big weed movement. Who were they? What were they carrying?"

"Oh them. They were bringing their own stuff, I don't know what. I was asked to bring them in. They were Islamic terrorists? I didn't know."

"How much did they pay you?"

"Twenty thousand dollars, two thousand dollars each. Normally I get three thousand each, but it was a favor. I gave a discount."

"A favor to whom?"

"A favor to Bashir Matyarzai."

"Who the fuck is that?"

"He represents Afghani interests in the Alliance. He approached me at the Alliance annual meeting in Tortuguero. He said I might get a call from a local holy man. I did. A Dr. Umar al Jamai living in Hermosillo, at the Madrassas Centro Cultural Islámico de Mexico, contacted me. This al Jamai said he had ten Americans staying at the Islamic conference center guest accommodations there who needed to be brought across the border safely. He told me it was some paperwork mix-up. As a favor I had my people pick them up at the cultural center, drive them to the border, bring them across, and had transportation take them to a hotel in Las Cruces. That was it, nothing more."

"Angel why were there guards in the house? We were told you didn't allow that. Those guards surprised our troops. One soldier, a favorite of mine was hurt by your guards."

"Should I be sorry? I changed my policy after all the drug busts at the border. I brought guards inside as a last wall to protect against other cartel hit teams. It wasn't enough against the whole Mexican army though. I can't say your attack was unexpected. I just never expected the government to be the ones to come after me. El presidente should be told your raid was well planned, brilliantly executed. Your troops were very brave. If only you people worked for me."

González spit in Angel's face. He laughed, "Stop the crap. It won't do you any good to butter us up. We're going to go now. We will tell Presidente Quiñones what you said. What happens to you after is up to him." Almost as an afterthought He instructed, "Enrique pull the tape off his eyes and head."

Figueroa screamed when the tape was ripped off. Garcia and Cruz locked the cell door and went to the observation room. General Ehrich returned after they called him. He asked, "How did it go?"

Garcia told him, "Fine sir. Turn the video and audio back on. You'll see he's fine. There is one more thing general, he thinks he is in a Mexican jail and we're Mexican Special Forces soldiers. So if he needs to be tended by anyone make sure they keep up the ruse."

"How long will you be keeping this farce up?"

"We intend to come back tonight, sedate him, and take him away."

"Okay no problem. One of my instructors can play a Mexican. He is also absolutely discreet. I'll have him bring the prisoner some bread and water later."

Chapter Thirty-Nine

1:10 a.m. Mountain Time, November 14

COCHISE COUNTY SHERIFF EDWARDO "BIG ED" Mata-Villa unfolded his ample gut and six foot four inch frame out of his cream colored police cruiser. He shut the engine off but left the headlights on. Assistant Sheriff Rich Farrell, slightly taller and much thinner than the sheriff, slid out the other side and joined him. It was drizzling, chilly, and dark. Farrell played the beam of his Pelican police issue hand-held flashlight around the area. Mata-Villa yelled, "Over there Rich, on the ground, next to the sign."

Farrell pointed the light toward the base of the sign and walked in that direction. He said, "I don't see anything, Ed."

Mata-Villa came up alongside Farrell. Farrell said, "This is it. The caller said Highway 80, by the federal 'TRAVEL CAUTION' sign. Well here's the sign. Where the fuck is he?"

The sheriff nodded his head, "Over there Rich, in the depression. That's the same area where we found the Comforts."

Farrell's light illuminated the gully. "There. Something is in the ditch." He placed the flashlight, which had an eight sided octangular shape which prevented it from rolling, on the hood of the patrol car. He aimed the light at the gully and exclaimed as he rushed forward, "It's a body, all trussed up, face down. Should I turn him over?"

Mata-Villa told him, "Feel for a pulse. See if he's alive. If he's dead it's a crime scene and you shouldn't disturb it."

Farrell touched the body's neck. He said, "The pulse is strong Ed. Help me pull him out."

Garcia and Cruz watched from behind some brush in the adjacent field.

They had returned to the Fort Huachuca brig earlier, sedated Figueroa, carried him out to their car, and drove him out here. After they tied him up and threw him into the drainage ditch by the sign, they hid their car at the Hernandez ranch and called General Ehrich telling him they were ready. Ehrich made an anonymous call to Sheriff Mata-Villa informing him Angel Figueroa, the Mexican drug kingpin, was waiting to be brought into custody in the same place where the dead bodies of Sam and Ida Comfort were found. The general used an off base pay phone. The sheriff was told Figueroa was sedated but would come around by about two o'clock. When the tail lights of the sheriff's car disappeared to the west Garcia and Cruz returned to Camp Vigilant and went to bed for some well deserved rest.

At 10:15 a.m. Mountain Time, November 15, on the steps of the County Building in Bisbee, Cochise County Attorney Felix Burgos presided over a hastily called press conference. With Joanna Castro, the Deputy County Attorney, at his side he announced, "Ladies and gentlemen I am pleased to inform you the perpetrators of the brutal murder of Juan Puga, who died on August fifth, from a savage beating, which happened the previous night in Sierra Vista, are in custody. Also the murderer of Larry Rynning, Jimmy Rynning, Craig Rynning, three brothers, witnesses to the Puga beating, whose murders occurred right down the street from here on August twentieth, has been arrested. The murderers of Ida Comfort and Sam Comfort whose bodies were found early on the morning of October ninth, outside of Douglas have been apprehended. This office has reinstated murder charges against Hector Castaneda and Aliberto Castaneda in the Puga case. Esteban Nunez has been charged with the murders of all three Rynning brothers. Hector Castaneda is charged with the murders of the Comforts. Angel Figueroa head of the Cortez Cartel has been charged with ordering all five murders. Four other members of the Cortez Cartel, Antonio Rodriguez, Juan Quintero, Isidro Fuentes, and Fernando Santacruz, have been charged as accessories in the Comforts' cases. I can take a few questions."

A female reporter in the front of the group asked, "The Mexican government has been extremely vocal recently in accusations concerning the arrest of Mexican soldiers who wandered across the border. Under what circumstances did the arrests of the men you are holding occur? Are the suspects you are holding Mexican soldiers?"

"Hector Castaneda, Aliberto Castaneda, Esteban Nunez, Antonio Rodriguez, Juan Quintero, Isidro Fuentes, and Fernando Santacruz were all turned over to the Cochise County sheriff after they were intercepted smuggling drugs into the United States. Whether or not they are members of the Mexican military is immaterial. Video statements from these men taken by federal authorities were turned over to the sheriff. After the suspects were read their rights by the sheriff they voluntarily provided written statements. Those statements implicate themselves and Angel Figueroa in the murders they have been charged with. They all admit to knowingly being illegally in the United States when they were detained. Mister Figueroa was arrested by Sheriff Mata-Villa and Assistant Sheriff Rich Farrell at the site of the Comfort murders. Mister Figueroa was read his rights by the sheriff and has signed a statement claiming he was arrested by Mexican authorities under the orders of Mexican President Pedro Quiñones. Figueroa has asserted Mexican soldiers deposited him on this side of the border where American police placed him into custody."

"Will these men be charged with drug smuggling?"

"I assume the federal authorities will pursue those charges when my office is done with them. But we have first dibs. Thank you all for coming."

At 2:35 p.m. Eastern Time, November 15, in the Oval Office, President Burns hosted a small get together. Chief of Staff Khademi, National Security Advisor Williams, Secretary of State Colosimo, Secretary of Defense Adams, Homeland Security Director Swanson, Director of Special Operations Grass, and Emily Rogers Secretary of the Treasury were all present.

Burns said, "I understand all is going well."

Charles Swanson raised his hand saying, "It's so funny, sir. News media are reporting when Angel Figueroa awoke he couldn't wait to tell the local sheriff he knew for a fact Mexican Special Forces working for Mexican President Quiñones took out the cartels. He told them Mexican soldiers destroyed his ranch, killed his guards, brought him across border, and left him for the American authorities. CNN News picked the story up and is publicizing that version. Quiñones is getting worldwide credit for decisively cracking down on the drug cartels."

Evelyn Colosimo smiled and said, "The sheriff told reporters Figueroa maintains Quiñones had denied responsibility and had tried to blame the Americans only because he was afraid there are still remnants of the cartels who would go after him. Figueroa admitted what we have long known. Quiñones has been getting regular payments to allow the Alliance to operate. The Mexican president denies taking a dime. But he has stopped blaming us for attacking the cartels. He is now basking in the limelight, taking credit for moving forcefully against the cartels. Apparently he enjoys being thought of as a national hero."

Burns pointed to Secretary of the Treasury Rogers, a petite, forty-two year old, red haired, green eyed, friend and past college roommate of the first lady, and asked, "Emily did you tie up the money?"

Rogers replied, "Oh yes sir. I've taken steps to tie up all investments, stocks, bank accounts, and real estate owned by anyone and everyone suspected of having ties to the Alliance or the individual cartels in the United States. They can't touch a nickel. While we can't take it either, the funds will be tied up in legal wrangling for years to come. That is what you wanted, correct sir?"

"I love it. Thank you, Emily."

At 10:55 a.m. Mountain Time, November 18, a well-dressed man pushed Alex Mendez out the front door of Fort Huachuca's Raymond W. Bliss Army Health Center in a wheelchair. He rolled her up to the passenger side door of a rented Ford pickup truck. After locking the wheels in place he helped Mendez into the seat, buckled her safety belt, closed the door, folded the wheelchair, and lifted it into the truck bed. He walked around, got in, started the engine, and inquired, "Where to Alex?"

She gave him an address in Sierra Vista. He typed it into the GPS and remarked, "It's not far."

Following a seven minute drive he pulled to the curb in front of a well kept suburban ranch house about five years old and said, "This is it."

Mendez nodded. He noticed she was crying. He asked, "Something wrong?"

"No, it's just I'm so happy we can do this."

"I know what you mean."

Back in the wheelchair he asked her to hold his briefcase on her lap while he pushed her to the front door. As he reached for the bell the front door opened. A pretty little girl said, "Hi. I'm Lori. I'm five. I saw you coming. Mommy and Aunt Jenny are waiting." She held the door open as he maneuvered the wheelchair inside.

Lori led them into the living room announcing, "They're here."

Three more little children played on the floor. Two women sat on the couch. They stood up. Alex said, "Hi everybody. I'd like you to meet John Quincy. John is an attorney. He's also a financial consultant. He has some news for you." Alex turned to Quincy saying, "John you've already met Lori. These two beautiful girls on the floor are four year old Kimmie and two year old Jill. The girls are all sisters. This is their mom Suzi Rynning,

Larry's widow. This little boy is Jimmy Rynning Junior. This is his mother Jenny, Jimmy's widow."

John Quincy smiled saying, "I'm very pleased to meet you all. Suzi you look like you're due soon."

"Yes the doctor says little Larry should be born about January twentieth."

Quincy continued, "I don't know how much Alex told you about why we are here."

Suzi and Jenny responded, "Nothing."

"Well this will be a surprise then. I represent some immensely wealthy people. These people who are anonymous and wish to stay that way have tasked me with setting up annuities for your children. The donors take care of crime victim's families. The donors realize how heroic your husbands and their brother Craig were. They do not want you to suffer financially because your husbands, the children's fathers, acted responsibly."

Quincy opened his briefcase and removed some papers. He handed one to Suzi and one to Jenny. He said, "Suzi this is the free and clear deed to this house. Jenny I've given you the free and clear deed to your house. The first thing the donors wanted was to ensure you would continue to have a good home to raise the children in. Any questions yet?"

Jenny said, "The mortgage on my house is a quarter of a million dollars. We could pay it when Jimmy was alive but it has been tough. Does this mean the mortgage is paid off?"

"Yes. Yours too, Suzi. The donors realize you have to stay home to raise the children so a job isn't feasible. By not having a mortgage payment you can each use the several thousand dollars per month widows and children's Social Security Benefits, that each family is entitled to, for everyday living expenses. Have I been clear? Are there any questions yet?"

Suzi asked, "Alex who is this guy? Is this true?"

Alex wiped tears from her eyes and said, "All true."

Quincy went on, "That's not all. There are also five trust funds of $250,000 each set up. One for each child, payable at age 21 or sooner as follows. Each child can take $50.000 per year at any age for college tuition and expenses. Any funds remaining at age twenty-one is theirs to use as they please. Also there will be a yearly payment of $10,000 for each family for each of the next twenty-one years. A little spending money, mad money if you will. Take the kids on vacation, or something." Quincy handed Suzi and Jenny each checks for ten thousand dollars saying, "Starting now."

Jenny exclaimed, "Oh my God, I don't know what to say. It has been so hard, especially for the kids. Thank you so much."

Suzi asked, "Can't we please meet the donors? We have so much to thank them for."

Quincy shook his head, "No, this is all anonymous. That's the way it has to be."

Jenny asked, "What if we remarry? We are both awfully young."

"No effect on our commitment. But check with a Social Security attorney about Social Security benefits. If you remarry you may lose some widow benefits. The children's benefits should not be affected but check. Publicity would be the only scenario that could affect the donor's payments to you and the children. It would be in your best interests to keep all the arrangements quiet. Tell no one. Understand?"

"Yes."

"Okay then, I'll give you each my card. If you need anything, have any questions, please contact me."

They all hugged goodbye. Alex, Suzi, and Jenny were crying as John and Alex waved and drove off. John Quincy returned Alex back to Bliss Army Health Center. She had only been allowed to leave for a brief two hour time period to attend personal business. General Ehrich had interceded with the staff on her behalf. Mendez, while not in intensive care, was still being monitored closely.

Chapter Forty

12:15 p.m. Pacific Time, November 22

IT WAS SHOWDOWN DAY. TEN SCHOOLS, all members of the Pacific-10 Conference, were playing this Saturday. They were scheduled for a full conference competition. It was finally game day. The hype was over. Five sellouts. Enthusiastic college football fans were filing into stadiums up and down the coast. No more bye weeks. No more filler games against non-conference patsies. Today all the games were meaningful.

Students, alumni, families, and friends all dressed in their favorite teams colors strutted through parking areas to get to the stadium entrances nearest their seats. Fans of the Oregon State University Beavers traveled from Corvallis all decked out in orange and black. They were playing their interstate rivals, the University of Oregon Ducks, at the Ducks' home field, Autzen Stadium. Many had arrived early, had tailgated, threw the Frisbee around, and exchanged barbs with rival fans who were all dressed in jerseys, hats, and jackets both green and yellow. Many fans from both teams sported faces artistically smeared with face paints matching the colors of their favorite team. Many waved banners and homemade signs. One couple with painted faces all decked out in green and yellow sat in lawn chairs tailgating. They had a group of green balloons tied together, filled from a helium party tank in the bed of their newer green Ford pickup. The balloons were tied to the cab of the truck. They handed helium filled balloons to children as they walked by. Everyone said thanks. Everybody was enthusiastically hollering, "Go Ducks."

The festive scene was repeated in the state of Washington. There the Washington State University Cougars traveled from Pullman in the eastern portion of the state all the way to the University of Washington Husky Stadium. Some fans parked across Lake Washington and boated over to the stadium. Those fans made their way through the parking lot, which was also full of tailgaters. Cougar fans stood out because they wore red and white attire and face paint. Husky faithful were dressed in purple and white. Here too a couple of fans, both male, had inflated purple balloons with helium. They fastened a large group of balloons to their white Ford pickup truck and were handing others to young fans as they walked by. Everyone was smiling and happy. Despite rooting for different teams they all agreed, a slightly cool breeze blowing from the west, sunny skies, a great day for a football game.

The PAC-10 rivalries were alive and well in California also. University of California Berkley, the California Bears, traveled across San Francisco Bay to play the Stanford University Cardinal. Outside Stanford Stadium, Bears fans decked out in blue and gold walked past crowds of Cardinal fans in their red regalia. A couple of guys with their faces painted red, tailgating out of the bed of a new red Ford pickup truck, were inflating red balloons. They had a bundle of balloons tied to their truck but were also passing out inflated red balloons tied to string to passing Stanford Cardinal fans.

In Los Angeles, the University of Southern California Trojans hosted the Arizona State University's Sundevils. They would be playing at the Los Angeles Memorial Coliseum. The Coliseum was located in a more urban area. Parking for sold out games such as today's game was at a premium. Fans dressed in combinations of gold and red paraded though streets adjoining the stadium. Many commercial buildings with parking lots charged game attendees to park in their lots. On the west side in one such lot across the street from the stadium two fans, their faces streaked with red and gold paint, sat next to a red Ford pickup. They used a helium tank to blow up gold balloons they handed to passing Trojan fans. They had a large group of balloons tied to their vehicle. Being a friendly good-natured pair they also gave gold balloons to Sundevils fans who wore maroon and gold. The gold color was representative of both teams.

The last PAC-10 game of the day was the University of Arizona Wildcats at the University of California Los Angeles Bruins. Their schedule brought them to the Rose Bowl in Pasadena. The Rose Bowl was a seven to eight hour drive from Tucson. But that didn't stop the Wildcat fans in their red and blue hats and shirts from making the trip. The Rose Bowl was situated in an upscale residential area off Interstate 10. Parking was scarce. Many fans were directed to a golf course where they parked in long parallel lines a close distance from the stadium. One guy and girl, UCLA fans, had come early. They sat in lawn chairs drinking soft drinks and eating sandwiches they had brought in a cooler. They had a bundle of powder blue balloons tied to the cab of their light blue Ford pickup truck. In the bed of their truck they had a small party tank of helium. They inflated and handed out light blue balloons to the many Bruins fans coming by. Around 11:30 a.m. in the morning a group of about ten Pasadena firemen had walked through the golf course. They carried portable fire extinguishers which they used to put out charcoal grills. They also made people turn off gas grills. A lot of people, mainly UA fans, complained. They were told the grills were fire hazards and could not be used. UCLA fans knew the drill. They had coolers with sandwiches, cold chicken, and the like. Many of the Bruins fans shared food with Wildcat fans. The most vocal of the UCLA fans apologized and explained the Pasadena firemen acted like assholes every game under orders of superiors. The rumor was the fire chief had the food franchise for the concessions in the Rose Bowl and wanted hungry fans. The couple inflating balloons appeared happy. They were thankful the firefighters didn't complain about their helium tank. But then they had no reason to. Stadium security had stopped by earlier and checked. The cylinder was clearly labeled low pressure and helium was non-flammable. The chief of security said as long as they were giving the balloons away and not charging for them security didn't mind. No vendor permit was required. Security and firefighters all had told them, "You have a nice day now."

Closer to game time the only people still in the parking area was the balloon couple. They put their folding chairs away when they heard the roar of the crowd indicating the kickoff occurred. The man started fielding phone calls. They were all abnormally short. He then climbed aboard the truck, untied the balloons from the cab, and let the bundle of balloons weighed down by a small package float away. A slight breeze coming from west to east directed the rising balloons up and over the high outside walls of the Rose Bowl. Soon after it cleared the top the woman dialed her cell phone. Within seconds a low pop was heard. The package blew apart and the balloons separated. People in the crowd who heard the small explosive sound or saw the division of the balloons applauded. Minutes later the balloons carried by the slight wind blew away. No one noticed the fallout from the package. A light white powder started drifting in the air. The wind spread the powder as it fell. By the time the powder reached the ground it had settled over the whole stadium. Watching the action, none of the ninety-one thousand fans in the stadium realized they were inhaling anthrax spores. They wouldn't know for days.

Leon and Consuela broke down their phones then used baby wipes and damp face cloths to remove the paint from their faces before driving out of the parking area. Within minutes they were on the 10 headed west away from the Rose Bowl and into the prevailing winds. They didn't want there to be any chance they might get caught in any anthrax droppings. As soon as they could they turned north back toward the Heavenly Sky Spiritual Camp. Leon and Consuela couldn't wait to get back and review the day with the others. They were confident that all of the test weights, varying breezes, random tree heights, and differing distances they practiced for weeks in the field prepared all of them for successful balloon flights that cleared the stadium walls.

After releasing their bundle of balloons and popping the package over the Coliseum, Alphonso and Jose drove west then north. Everything appeared to go well to them. They silently prayed to Allah the over ninety-three thousand fans at the game and the thousands more people downwind would all become infected and die.

Roberto and Maria drove to the west then turned south away from Eugene, Oregon after they departed the Autzen Stadium parking area. Just like they practiced, their cluster of about forty green balloons were released, picked up by the breeze, and blew into the stadium rising several hundred feet above the field. After they dialed the cell phone and the connection was made there was a small pop in the basket hanging from the cluster. The basket burst open. The balloons continued floating, rising to the east. The Oregon State University Beavers, the University of Oregon Ducks, and all of their fifty-four thousand fans in attendance loved the show.

Driving away from the University of Washington Husky Stadium, known as one of the loudest in college football, and where the wave supposedly was originated, Vincente and Filipe could still hear the more than seventy-two thousand fans cheering. They high fived each other confident in the knowledge their balloon launch and anthrax drop went as planned. They were smiling widely as they drove south away from Seattle.

Outside Stanford Stadium Diego and Manilo wrapped up their things and loaded their shiny red Ford pickup truck. Shortly after the opening kickoff the helium tank they had used was put away, as were their folding table and chairs. A cluster of balloons in the home teams colors, about fifty of them, were released. At the base, where they were tied together, a small packet hung. The cluster was picked up by the light breeze. Immediately after they had successfully released their grouping of red balloons and detonated their package over the stadium they left. Content they had accomplished their assignment they drove west and turned north onto the 280, the Junipero Sierra Freeway. The route they took when they left was drummed into them repeatedly over the past weeks. Even though all of the Huertas had received vaccination before leaving Hermosillo, to be doubly safe, they had to protect themselves from being exposed to the anthrax fallout they had unleashed upon on the fifty thousand stadium fans and the thousands more downwind victims. They were told in a light breeze the fallout would be concentrated on stadium fans but spores would carry about a mile to the east infecting those unlucky enough to be there. Better safe than sorry.

The Huertas were all thoroughly briefed. They knew the anthrax would take a while to act. Nothing would show up very soon. No one would die today. Some victims would develop symptoms within two days. For others it could be six to eight weeks. Those infected would suffer general chest discomfort, have trouble breathing normally, have headaches, upset stomachs, soreness of muscles, fever, and other aches and pains. Symptoms would probably show up big time on Thanksgiving Day.

Then the mortality rate among those who have not had proper antibiotics administered before symptoms developed would be extremely high, as much as ninety percent. Early treatment is vital.

At 7:05 a.m. Eastern Time, November 27, the Oval Office was again the site of a hastily called meeting. President Burns paced the room. He was extremely agitated. "How the fuck did this happen?" He asked.

Parvis Khademi, Roger Williams, Leroy Adams, and Homeland Security Director Swanson were present.

Charles Swanson was standing also. He replied, "Sir, from what I've been told at first we didn't know what to make of the phone activity. The Huertas' cell phones had gone off line when they disappeared from Pueblo, Colorado. Tom Eagan told us the Huertas' cell phones weren't traceable anymore, in all likelihood the batteries were removed. Nothing had turned up on them until November twenty-second sometime after noon on the west coast. At that time both Ed Grass' office and David Porter, the senior duty officer at the FBI's Denver Regional Office were notified by the Huertas' phone service carrier that phone activity had resumed on some and then within minutes all of the Huertas' phones. As quickly as the phones were turned on, after brief usage, they were turned back off. The carriers had gotten a fix on the locations of the phones and relayed that information to Grass and Porter. Both Ed and Porter notified Eagan who had FBI agents sent to the locations from field offices in Los Angeles, San Francisco, Eugene, and Seattle. Agents were sent out right away however they found nothing but parking lots full of vehicles. The vehicles belonged to college football fans attending PAC-10 games. Whoever used those phones was nowhere to be found. Security personnel in charge of the game surroundings were alerted but nothing unusual was reported. We thought we got a break when they turned the cell phones on but as it turns out they were playing with us. They must have installed the batteries, used the phones, then removed them again. Nothing further occurred, no incidents, no violence, and no leads whatsoever. Then yesterday came. Tens of thousands of people, men, women, and children flooded hospital emergency rooms. The common thread was the patients attended one of five football games or lived or had been in the vicinity of one of the five stadiums. The FBI re-canvassed as many security personnel and other witnesses from the vicinity of the stadiums and learned of an occurrence that was unique but then again common had happened at each stadium at the time the Huertas' phones were being used. Bundles of balloons were launched from the parking lots and those bundles popped or for a better term exploded over the stadiums. Given what we know now we believe anthrax was released into the air by the Huertas. We believe they carried that anthrax in the backpacks they wore into the United States when they were smuggled in with Angel Figueroa's drugs. Although no one has provided a positive identification, it appears the people who released the balloons, who wore face paint to hide appearance, were indeed the Huertas."

Burns hung his head and asked, "How many? How many are infected?"

Swanson said, "We don't know, sir. Health and Human Services says it is imperative anyone who possibly could have been infected must come in without delay. They have informed me nearly half of those who indeed inhale anthrax die despite antibiotics being administered before symptoms show. Cipro, the principal antibiotic used to treat anthrax infection, is in plentiful supply. The problem, sir, is identifying, locating, and treating everyone who attended the games or who inhaled anthrax spores that continued to travel downwind of the release points. Tests of the anthrax spores used in the attacks have been tested. We have found the anthrax to contain bentonite. Bentonite is a chemical additive that was used by

Iraq under Saddam Hussein in their production of biochemical weapons. Bentonite keeps the anthrax spores separated as the spores float in the air. The separated particles are much more effective when used on crowds. Many more individuals will inhale the separated spores. On the positive side, since 2001 when there was a series of anthrax attacks, mainly using anthrax hidden in letters sent by mail, most of the nation's military, health, police, and other first responders have been administered shots of anthrax vaccine, called Bio Thrax. It stands to reason some of the attendees and many of the security people will have been treated with vaccine already."

National Security Advisor Roger Williams asked, "Is it over? Has the danger of infection passed?"

Swanson shook his head, "Hell no. Emergency response teams who have received biothax shots have initiated treatment of all surfaces in all of the affected stadiums, the surrounding grounds, neighborhoods, and the vehicles that were present which we have been able to identify. There is a fear however the stadiums and the areas to the east may not be cleared for use again for years. Back in 2001 numerous buildings were contaminated with anthrax as a result of the anthrax sent by mail. One postal facility was not cleared for use until 2005. Unlike closed buildings the stadiums are open air facilities. They cannot be sealed and fumigated. We fear all surfaces of the stadiums which were attacked will have to be hand-washed with chlorine several times. Medical providers are going door to door evacuating people, administering antibiotics, but it may be too late for many."

President Burns sat behind his desk and said, "When is it going to end? Just like 9/11, just like the Huertas' suitcase nuke attacks, this bioterrorism was unexpected, well-planned, flawlessly, some might say brilliantly executed. I pray for our country."

DON'T MISS PAUL C. GARDNER'S

2014

On the thirteenth anniversary of the 9/11 terror attack on the World Trade Center and Pentagon, America is violently assaulted again. Muslim terrorists appear responsible for a deadly blast in San Francisco. After state police uncover weapons and explosives stored in mosques they gather up Muslims throughout California, Arizona, New Mexico, and Texas. Those detainees are eventually expelled into other states and mosques left behind are burned and demolished.

Muslims riot and attack police and civilians in Newark, Detroit, Toledo, New York City, and Washington, D.C. Faced with the realization that Muslim facilities nationwide are being used as the focus points of terrorism, the President of the United States orders the military, Homeland Security, and local police to seize the remaining mosques and to incarcerate or deport all Muslims who are not citizens.

When tourist destinations, sporting venues and shopping malls are savagely struck by murderous revolutionaries and Latino separatists seize control of the southwest United States President, James Burns orders the nation on Code Red terror alert. The round up of Muslims is expanded to include illegal immigrants, and gangsters with foreign connections. As the country slowly returns to normal another destructive development, the most diabolical, unfolds.